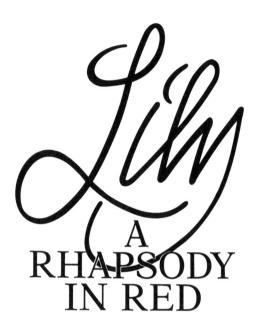

Lily

A RHAPSODY IN RED

HEATHER ROBERTSON

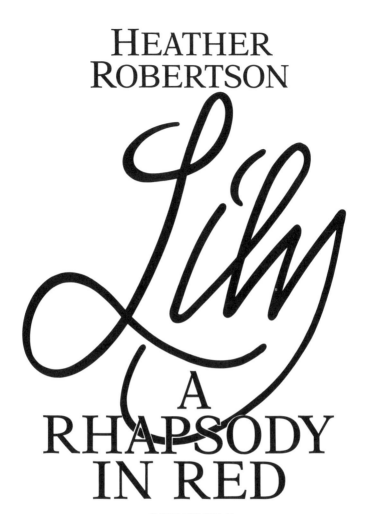

Lily

A RHAPSODY IN RED

VOLUME 2
THE KING YEARS

James Lorimer & Company, Publishers
Toronto 1986

ISBN 0-88862-954-0

Design: Don Fernley
Author photo: Arnaud Maggs

Canadian Cataloguing in Publication Data
Robertson, Heather, 1942-
  Lily: a rhapsody in red

ISBN 0-88862-954-0

1. King, William Lyon Mackenzie, 1874-1950 — Fiction.
2. Canada — History — 1914-1945 — Fiction.
I. Title.

PS8585.03215L5 1986   C813′.54   C86-094281-3
PR9199.3.R6285L54 1986

James Lorimer & Company, Publishers
Egerton Ryerson Memorial Building
35 Britain Street
Toronto, Ontario M5A 1R7

Printed and bound in Canada
5 4 3 2 1   86 87 88 89 90

"From the point of view of the absolute value of the human personality, revolution must be 'condemned' as well as war — as must also the entire history of mankind taken in the large. Yet the very idea of personality has been developed only as a result of revolutions, a process that is still far from complete. In order that the idea of personality may become a reality and the half-contemptuous idea of the 'masses' may cease to be the antithesis of the philosophically privileged idea of 'personality,' the masses must lift themselves to a new historical rung by the revolutionary crane, or, to be more exact, by a series of revolutions. Whether this method is good or bad ... I do not know ... but I do know that this is the only way that humanity has found thus far."

— Leon Trotsky, *My Life*

Acknowledgements

As in *Willie: A Romance*, the volume preceding this one, the portrait of William Lyon Mackenzie King is drawn from his personal diaries in the Public Archives of Canada. Willie King's accounts of his dreams, political intrigues and encounters with famous people are essentially his own. In some cases the diary has been quoted verbatim, although in condensed form; in other cases it has been paraphrased. However, King's references to the Coolicans are entirely fictional, as are they.

Excerpts from King's letters to Dr. W.L. McDougald are taken from the McDougald papers in the Public Archives of Canada.

Portraits of Vivian Macmillan, Mr. and Mrs. John Brownlee, Cora and Oren McPherson and Neil MacLean are based primarily on articles and transcripts of trials in the Edmonton *Bulletin.* I am also indebted to a PHD thesis on John Brownlee by Frank Foster at Queen's University, and to independent research by writer Alan Hustak. The dialogue and characterizations are, however, my own.

While *Lily: A Rhapsody in Red* is based on real people and events, it is a work of fiction.

My thanks to my editor, Roy MacSkimming, who helped me return King to chaos, and to everyone who, by liking *Willie: A Romance*, made this sequel possible.

H.R.
Toronto, April 1986

PART I

WAY UP NORTH

1

The post office is just a tarpaper shack. It's like all the other tarpaper shacks in Kirkland Lake except, out of respect for the Royal Mail, it lacks the skin of flattened biscuit-tins, dynamite boxes and Salada tea chests that keep the wind out of the other shacks. This means the place is damn cold, even now in June, when the wind blows from the west and the waves pound up to the back door. Lily keeps the stove going all day and wears a sweater. Her hair smells of wood smoke. She hasn't washed for a week. She feels terrific.

"Miss L. Coolican — Postmistress," the sign on the counter says. The word has a lovely, tragic ring to it, like posthumous, or postpartum, a whiff of sex and unrequited love, tears and scandal, and it sure describes the current state of her love life. "I am a post-mistress," she says to herself. It's a lot more exciting than being a hoor, or a friendless woman, and the little joke makes the hurt seem less. It's been two years since she was Talbot's "mistress" — such a silly word — and a year-and-a-half since he was killed at Passchendaele, but only yesterday, glimpsing the green flash of an Export tobacco tin in the weeds by the road, she bawled her eyes out. Kirkland Lake is full of sudden, deep, black holes. That's why she likes it.

Across the street, the shacks are still asleep in the morning sun. In front of Rolston's Pharmacy and Poolroom a man in a red plaid shirt is sprawled face down in the mud. He lies very still. Drunk? Dead? Time will tell. He will get up and walk away, or he won't. It doesn't matter. It's only a movie, after all. Why else would Kirkland Lake, Ontario, be built to look like Santa Fe, New Mexico? All the little shacks with their flimsy false fronts and wooden sidewalks are waiting for high noon when the Cisco Kid will ride into town and hitch his horse to the hydro pole at the corner of Government Road and Prospect Avenue.

She will offer him a cocktail. Cowboys don't normally drink cocktails, but the swill that passes for whiskey up here would blind the Kid for life without at least an ice-cube and a shot of soda. Lily makes the best cocktails in Kirkland Lake. Hers don't come with bits of straw and manure in the crushed ice. She has a refrigerator. It's the only refrigerator in town, a funny-looking metal box on legs: pretty dumb, when you think of all the time she spends keeping warm, but it was free, a gift from the T. Eaton Co. for increasing the mail-order business at the post office by more than one thousand per cent.

Lily doesn't give a damn about Eaton's, but before she took over last January the post office was in Foster's General Store, and when the Eaton's catalogues came out every year, Bill Foster hid them all in his shed, so there was no mail-order business at all. Bill Foster went broke anyway, and disappeared last fall with the $5,000 he'd persuaded the girls at 5 Main to leave with him for safekeeping. The girls love the Eaton's catalogue. They should have gotten the fridge, but it's Lily's only piece of furniture apart from four empty nail kegs, two packing crates, an air mattress, her trunk that she hasn't opened yet, and her chinchilla coat, which she uses as a bedspread.

The coat is a souvenir of her position as the richest woman in Kirkland Lake and sister of the richest man, Jack Coolican, who is owner — with the second-richest man, Harry Oakes — of the Rainbow and Lakeshore gold mines. That was before the gold ran out last March. The vein disappeared, *poof,* just like that. They dug and dug, four thousand feet, five thousand, front, back, sideways, zero. None of the mines in town could find a nugget. Money ran out. Shares fell from sixty cents to thirty cents, then to twenty-five. Harry went a little nuts. He got the idea that the vein ran under the lake, and it would turn up again to the west, at the Lakeshore Mine. That was okay with Jack. He and Harry were partners, fifty-fifty. The Rainbow Mine shut down. Harry persuaded a banker from Buffalo to sink the shaft at Lakeshore.

Harry struck the motherlode at eight thousand feet. When Jack arrived at the Lakeshore Mine shaft the next morning, to see the good news for himself, he found the shaft head fenced off with barbed wire and guarded by four Pinkerton men with guns.

"This is my mine," Harry said through the barbed wire.

When Jack went to Charlie Chow's café to find the deal they'd signed, fifty-fifty, Charlie's strongbox was empty. Charlie shrugged.

Harry told the banker from Buffalo that Jack was a crook and the Rainbow Mine was a fraud. By the end of the week, the news was all over New York. Harry hired a lawyer and charged Jack with stealing $40,000 from the Rainbow accounts. Rainbow shares fell to two cents. Lakeshore shares rose to sixty-five.

Jack says he will kill Harry Oakes. He will. Harry has built himself a big, log blockhouse with a lookout on top. People say the windows have bulletproof glass. Harry calls it a "*château*." Everybody else calls it the Alamo. It has a copper roof. Harry has a man pee on it every hour to turn it green. Harry never leaves the Alamo. It doesn't matter. He doesn't get any mail.

Lily props the front door open with a rock. The sun tints the granite cliff on Prospect Avenue a pale peach: in the shadows, indigo. It makes her laugh when her friends in Ottawa write to ask how she manages living in the bush. There isn't a tree for miles around Kirkland Lake. The rocks are bald as billiard balls. The bush was cut down years ago. Now the mine shafts stick up, rude and dirty, out of the stubble of stumps, scrub, scrap iron, oil drums and piles of rusting tin cans which covers Kirkland Lake with a strange, brown scum. The air smells of gasoline and new lumber, the ground thumps with the steady *thucka-thucka* of the rock crushers, washing flutters in the wind, and every day another little shack perches on the rocks like a newly-hatched bird. God, it's ugly! But it's fun, crude, unpredictable. A fresh start, as Willie would say.

Where is he today? At Kingsmere, taking toast and tea, scheming how to be the next leader of the Liberal Party and prime minister of Canada? It seems incredible. In Ottawa nobody thought for a minute that Willie King could be prime minister, except Willie and his mother, yet last week Lily saw his name mentioned in the Toronto *Star* as a leading contender. The *Star* says Willie is a "new man." Lily has always thought of him as being very old, although now that she's nearly twenty-six, forty-four doesn't seem quite so bad. Can it be he's going to drive the country crazy, as he did her?

Their marriage was a mistake, a casualty of the war, a hate match, instantly regretted. Lily had wanted to die, and Willie was very keen on

death, especially other peoples'. He had probably planned the flowers
for her funeral, and the little book he would publish in her memory,
with her pictures of him in it, and the marble bust he would place by the
rock garden at Kingsmere, but it was Willie's mother who died. Lily
didn't. Willie never forgave her.

She ran away. It seemed far enough at the time, eight hundred miles,
two days by train, four miles by sleigh. But every time Lily sees Willie's
name, or hears it mentioned, she feels her past pursuing her, *tick, tick,
tick,* like the alligator in *Peter Pan.* (Willie liked to think of himself as
Peter, but to Lily he was Smee, the oddly genial pirate who stabbed, so
to speak, without offence, and was the only Nonconformist in the crew.)
When she first arrived last Christmas, Kirkland Lake was Unorganized
Territory. She liked that. It sounded romantic, like Indian Country, but
almost as soon as she got there it organized itself into Teck Township
and now she has to pay taxes, chain her dog and burn her garbage, *tick,
tick, tick,* although nobody in town actually does these things, and it's
still okay to dump more or less everything into the ditch in the hope that
someone will find a use for it, and take it away.

She's put a sign in the window, although anyone who doesn't know
where the damn post ofice is in a place like this doesn't need it, and she's
hung framed portraits of the King and Queen on the partition that
separates the Royal Mail from her own half of the shack. The Queen,
Mary of Teck, is the patron saint of this particular piece of wilderness
and is treated by the miners as a combination of Santa Claus and T.
Eaton. A beaming face will appear in the door, a gnarled hand will
extract some cherished coins from an oilskin pouch, Lily will address
the envelope in block letters to Riga or Rimini, and, sure enough, weeks
or months later, a dogeared letter will arrive from Riga or Rimini — or a
parcel, or a wife.

At first Lily was shocked at the amount of mail. More than twenty
bags were hauled in from the dray, each one almost more than the driver
could carry. "Sort this," he said, handing her the smallest bag. "The rest
is for Dr. Rolston across the street. He'll send someone by for it." Dr.
Rolston came by himself. He had dark pouches under his eyes and his
breath smelled of peppermint. "Lime rickey," he said, nodding at the
sacks. "If you'd care to be my guest?" Hanging around a soda fountain
wasn't Lily's idea of a good time, but she went over later to be polite. It
was a posh place, cut glass and polished silver, but the counter was lined
with rough-looking men, each one holding a tall, fizzy drink. God, had

a foot soldier from the Sally Ann hit town?

"What'll it be?" said Dr. Rolston, hovering over the taps. "A rickey, chocolate syrup or cherry cordial?"

"I'll try the rickey, thanks."

A dead silence fell as Dr. Rolston pulled the handle. How could she drink being stared at? Lily took a deep breath and a big swallow. Holy cow! The top of her head nearly came off. Her eyes watered. She put the glass down gently.

"It's a special recipe," said Dr. Rolston wiping the counter. "I import it. From a friend. In Saskatchewan. I hope it's not an inconvenience?"

Lily put her hands on the counter. It stopped swaying and the room came back into focus. A pleasant buzz began at the back of her neck.

"I think I'll try the chocolate syrup," she said.

So he's running a blind pig. Well, the Queen enjoys her gin, it says so on the bottle, and it's not illegal, exactly. The bottles come in on the train, each crate clearly marked "Property of the Bienfait Export Co., Bienfait, Saskatchewan. FOR EXPORT ONLY." Trouble is, there's no address. What to do? The Temiskaming & Northern Ontario Railroad has never heard of the Bienfait Export Co. in Bienfait, Saskatchewan, and no one has ever turned up to claim the shipment, even though it arrives every Friday morning. It's a case for the Teck policeman, Chief Johnson, but he was fired for public drunkenness. Last month, Constable Dempster of the Intelligence Division of the Mounted Police was sent up from Ottawa to investigate. He arrived at the station wearing a cloth cap and a disreputable pair of overalls, not at all the dashing figure Lily remembered from Rideau Hall skating parties. "Constable Dempster!" she cried out. "Are you travelling in disguise?" Now he wears a scarlet tunic and claims to be hunting for Reds. He has never been invited to sample Dr. Rolston's famous 5 Star cherry cordial.

Half the people in Kirkland Lake don't want any mail, and the other half can't read or write. So things would be slow except for the Nob. Not every mining camp has an English peer, but David Freeman Mitford, Lord Redesdale, is the real thing. You can tell by his temper. He speaks through clenched teeth, and nobody can understand a word he says. Just as well. Lord Redesdale has a claim to the west, near Swastika, and lives there in a log cabin with four dogs and a Wedgewood dinner service for twelve. Lady Redesdale and her daughters, Dodo and Bobo, arived in April with a nanny, a lady's maid and sixteen calfskin trunks embossed with the Redesdale coat of arms. They lasted until the black flies came out. But the Nob stayed on, fishing, tramping about from lake to lake, up to his ass casting for bass or trolling at twilight for the giant trout that lurk in the reeds at the bottom, reeling in twenty, fifty, a hundred fish a day, his prospector's gear rusting and forgotten under a tarp. The Nob keeps the whole town in fish, even the dogs. God bless the Empire. Now the flattened biscuit tins on Mrs. Dzuba's shack are from Fortnum & Mason, the magazines in the barber shop are *Country Life,* Lily's packing crates are Mumm's, and there's hardly a shack without a scrap of board stamped "By Appointment to His Majesty," with the royal crest.

More parcels come every day, and letters from England in pale blue envelopes, just like the war. It's spooky. The letters remind her painfully of Talbot. So does Lord Redesdale. He dresses impeccably in khaki and polished riding boots. He has a cavalry officer's straight back and strong neck. He has Talbot's close-cropped hair, Talbot's moustache and Talbot's brown, weathered skin. Lord Redesdale is a very attractive man. Is it possible that Talbot would ever have become so unpleasant?

The resemblance troubled her until a stormy day last May. She was walking across a field of severed stumps towards the mine when she stumbled into an overgrown trench. She lay at the bottom a moment, frightened, and then she heard a dull *boom* and the ground shook beneath her. She covered her face with her arm. A shower of pebbles rained down on her back. As she scrambled over the side, she saw Skull, the mine foreman with the steel plate in his head, running across the scarred, rain-swept landscape towards the shaft, his old khaki greatcoat flying in the wind. Between them was nothing but blackened earth and boulders and barbed wire.

"Passchendaele," she said aloud. So this was what the war had been like, exactly this. Not her war (a paper war of photographs and parcels), but a real world of earth and rain and sky, and perhaps Talbot had been as happy there, from time to time, as she was happy here. Now she knew.

"The war isn't over yet," she said, "and I am at the front! What do I do now?"

The dray arrives with the mail at exactly ten o'clock. "For you," the driver says, handing her a large brown envelope. The handwriting is unmistakable. *Tick, tick, tick.* Is there no escape?

She hasn't summoned the courage to open it when Big Peter tiptoes in and closes the door softly behind him. Big Peter is a Red and always behaves in a very conspiratorial manner. It makes things more exciting.

"Trotsky is here," Big Peter whispers.

"Oh, sure."

"True!" He waves wildly towards the street.

Sure enough. There he is outside, sitting on a trunk, on the far side of the road, short, thick-set, a mop of curly brown hair, tiny beard, glittering steel-rimmed spectacles, an air of self-satisfaction. He looks around expectantly.

"Shouldn't you introduce yourself?" Lily asks Big Peter.

"Ah."

Big Peter peers anxiously through the window. Speak to Trotsky! Impossible!

"Maybe it's not Trotsky," Lily says. "Maybe it's a Fuller Brush man."

"Ah!"

Big Peter crosses the road carefully, as if the man on the trunk might blow up at any moment, then bows so low his forehead nearly touches the ground. Trotsky smiles and pats the trunk beside him. Big Peter sits down.

Trotsky in Kirkland Lake? Well, if John D. Rockefeller Jr. can come to Kirkland Lake, why not Trotsky? It seems an unlikely place for a revolution, but then so is Winnipeg, and Winnipeg's been taken over by the workers. Vancouver will be next, they say, then Toronto. Well, if the Reds want to assassinate Harry Oakes, that's okay with Lily, and if it's revolution or Willie, she'll take revolution, thanks.

She opens Willie's brown envelope. It contains a large photograph on stiff paper. It's a group picture, men mostly, farmers by the look of them, all crowded on to a porch, ribbons in their buttonholes, Sir Wilfrid Laurier seated in the middle looking grumpy, and Willie standing, smiling, to his right. Obviously a political picnic. The photograph must have been taken a long time ago because Willie still had hair, and it was parted rather charmingly in the middle.

"My dear C," the letter begins. Lily ran away when her name disappeared. When she and Willie first met, he called her "Miss Coolican," then it was her pet name, "Cookie," and later simply "C." Finally he stopped calling her by name at all. She fell into one of the great, white spaces in Willie's mind, where troublesome people and painful events simply vanish as if they had never existed. Their entire marriage disappeared into one of these deserts of the imagination; Willie behaves *as if it had not happened.* At the same time, he lives in constant dread that the real nature of their "friendship" will become public.

What can he want now?

"As you may know," she reads, "I have been approached by some friends with a view to allowing my name to be put forward as a candidate in the forthcoming Liberal leadership convention. I am personally indifferent to the leadership, lacking as I do the financial resources, should I give up my work for the Rockefeller Foundation, to take a leading part in public life...."

Money. Willie wants money.

"I have made it clear that I am prepared to consider such a sacrifice only because on three separate occasions before his death, Sir Wilfrid told me he wished me to succeed him as leader of the Liberal Party of Canada."

Oh, balls.

"Although Sir Wilfrid died without actually naming me his successor, or leaving any indication of his wishes in his will, it is well known that he regarded me in the nature of a son and heir and that my own unswerving loyalty to him was based on a personal affection as deep as my commitment to our shared ideals of Liberalism."

What a lie! Laurier couldn't stand Willie.

"The press has requested a photograph. I have been fortunate to locate one which illustrates, I believe, the unique nature of our relationship, the son on the right hand of the father, so to speak, and I am enclosing it in the hope that you might be able to enhance its significance by somewhat reducing the distractions in the background and eliminating unnecessary details, making it, in other words, a perfect 'silent witness' to Laurier's unfulfilled intentions...."

Lily glares at the picture. Willie's hand is resting on the back of Laurier's chair. It wouldn't be hard to crop the photo, paint out the rest of the crowd, and transform, with a few brush strokes, a public event into a private *tête-à-tête:* invent an intimacy that never existed, a liaison that Laurier never intended. No one would notice. Willie himself, with his infinite elasticity of mind, will be convinced within a week that the picture was taken in the solitude of Laurier's study. He will tell everyone so. They will believe.

Lily has the stove lid off before she notices the girl in the picture. She is standing next to Willie, to the left of Laurier's chair, a young woman, dark, skinny, not unlike herself, *circa* 1908. The girl is looking sideways at Willie with a simpering smirk on her face. Another match missed.

A silent witness. Lily smiles. She hasn't doctored a photo since she sold her studio in Ottawa.

Frank Krawchuk, of Krawchuk Photos DAY AND NITE, lends her ink and brushes and makes the new print in exchange for one hundred shares of Rainbow stock. She's pleased with the result. It looks phoney enough. Stiff. Shy. An engagement photo. Who's the girl? It will cause gossip.

She sends one copy to Willie, another to the Toronto *Star*. It's published ten days later on June 12, 1919, the day the Kirkland Lake miners go on strike. The story says Willie King is the man to bring labour peace to Canada. The girl isn't identified. The *Star* sends Lily $2. From Willie, she receives not a single word of thanks.

2

EIGHT WEEKS LATER:

The Trotsky caper had been a scream. Who'd have guessed that Trotsky would be a star up here? Lenin, the pig, gets all the foreign press. Kirkland Lake had felt like a ghost town when he was sitting there all alone in the middle of the street, but as soon as Big Peter came out of the post office to greet him, doors flew open everywhere. He'd been mobbed. Big Peter hugged his knees and wept all over his embroidered peasant blouse until the colours started to run (cheap shit, $1.25 at Swirski's on Spadina). To tell the truth, Trotsky wouldn't be caught dead in a *muzhik's* shirt. (Trotsky figures, like old Marx, that if one *muzhik* has the sense of a potato, then a whole lot of *muzhiks* together will be as revolutionary as a sack of potatoes. "But an army marches on its stomach," he'd reminded Lev Davidovitch. Useless. Trotsky is indifferent to food. He has an ulcer. He has a *muzhik* for a papa too — no, worse, a *kulak*. Lenin would never forgive Trotsky were Lenin himself not a *bourgeois*.) So once the sensation died down, "Trotsky" traded in the peasant blouse for a lumberjack shirt and a big white Stetson hat like the one William S. Hart wore in *The Desert Man*.

"My name is Esselwein," he told everyone. But he's known as the Russian Kid.

Esselwein organized the Kirkland Lake miners' strike in ten days. Dumb idea, he thought, since most of the mines except Lakeshore are going bust anyway, but if the Mine Workers Union wanted a strike, he'd give them one.

The day the men went out in Kirkland Lake, the general strike in Winnipeg collapsed. So now they're on their own. Nobody's paid much attention so far, only that Cossack, Dimwit Dempster, who follows the

Russian Kid around day and night, writing things in a little notebook. At the Lakeshore, Harry Oakes has trucked in scabs and a carload of Pinkerton men. His mill's still running, *thuckathuckathucka.* Otherwise, there's not much doing. The men play baseball. Marx missed that one. *Aphorisms of Esselwein: 1.* "Baseball is the opium of the masses." Revisionism. Better keep his mouth shut.

What is to be done? Esselwein has never organized a strike before. You just can't sit around. Something's got to happen. Already the guys are drifting away west for the harvest. If it just piddles away, he'll look like a total geek. How did he get talked into this anyway? Trotsky would know what to do. Trotsky always does. At least he does *something,* and convinces everyone it's the right thing. Where are you now, Lev Davidovitch? Somewhere in Russia, with the Red Army, but where? He can learn almost nothing from the papers except that Trotsky seems to be everywhere, fighting, winning, always winning, first at Kazin, on the Volga, then at Petrograd, next on the Siberian front. Not so very far away, after all. Siberia is a very big place. Here, on the other side of the North Pole, it is called Canada. The black flies are the same. True internationalists.

Ten years ago, when he had been living in exile at Novosibirsk, Esselwein had sometimes dreamed of escaping to the east, across the Bering Sea to Canada where the streets were paved with gold, and here he is, an exile among exiles — Finns, Ukrainians, Swedes, Latvians, Italians, Jews, people without passports — WOPS. The gold bars are piled up on the station platform at Swastika. Nobody lays a finger on them. There is no escape. He doesn't have a reindeer.

A hundred times Esselwein has told the men how he fled across Siberia in a sleigh pulled by reindeer, stopping neither for food nor sleep, the only sound the steady chuffing of the reindeers' breath and the drunken singing of the Zyrian driver. He's described how he hit the Zyrian across the face to keep him awake, and how, when the two lead deer went lame, they chased a herd, like cowboys, and lassoed two more. It's a good story. It's almost true. Only it was Trotsky in the sleigh, not Esselwein. His own escape was banal — a railway carriage, second-class, the stolen papers of a guard who'd died in camp the day before. The revolution may be all things to all men, but it must never be banal.

Esselwein flicks off the light and opens the front door of his shack. A night wind blows off the lake. To the west, beyond the Alamo, the sky is a pale, apple green, the light in the Alamo's lookout as bright as the evening star. Esselwein can see the shadow of the watchman in the lookout window. Harry Oakes has equipped the Alamo with heavy wooden shutters that he keeps closed day and night, but Esselwein can see everything that happens in the Lakeshore compound.

His shack is built on top of the biggest hump of rock in Kirkland Lake. From his front door, Esselwein can see the whole camp spread out at his feet. Every day he sits on a chair and watches Harry Oakes through binoculars. It drives Oakes nuts. Actually, he doesn't watch Oakes all the time. At ten o'clock, he watches the girls at 5 Main eat breakfast in their underwear, and at four o'clock the *shiksa* in the post office goes for a swim. What's that babe doing in a dump like this? She keeps to herself. Has he said something to offend? His English ain't so hot. He picked it up in New York and still has a Brooklyn accent. So, if it's a choice between Novosibirsk and New York, he'll take New York. He and Lev Davidovitch had made pretty good bucks playing villains for Griffiths Studios. Lev Davidovitch said it was only to understand the propaganda effect of motion picture films, but in truth they were both star struck. Lev Davidovitch saw himself in *My Official Wife* fifteen times. Neither of them had believed at first that the revolution was really happening *without them*. They grabbed the first ship home.

It was clear sailing until they docked at Halifax on April 3, 1917. They were dragged from the ship and taken to a concentration camp for prisoners of war. The camp contained eight hundred German sailors from captured U-boats. Trotsky immediately made a speech. He informed these *lumpenfisch* that the revolution would succeed and would immediately spread to Germany, where the Kaiser would be overthrown by the working masses and a Socialist republic would rise from the ashes of imperialism. By the following afternoon, Trotsky had organized the camp into ten discussion groups, dictated the Communist *Manifesto* from memory, in German, and copied it out ten times, sent telegrams of protest to the Prime Minister of Great Britain, Kerensky and the New York *Times,* and demanded a lawyer so he could bring charges of kidnapping and forceable confinement against the British army. At supper, he instigated a hunger strike, and afterwards lectured the officers for two-and-one-half hours about the policies of the Spartacus movement.

When the Russians were released a month later, the camp orchestra played the *Internationale* as an honour guard of cheering sailors carried Trotsky on their shoulders to the gate. Trotsky returned to Russia. Esselwein stayed. He does not dare write. How can he address a letter: "To Mr. L. Trotsky, Minister of War, the Kremlin, Moscow"? And he has no idea if anyone else in Moscow is dead or alive. Here, he has been able to locate only three Bolsheviks, besides himself, and because he missed the October Revolution, he's a little vague in his own mind about what, exactly, a Bolshevik is. Lenin is not a whole lot of help. Go to the masses! Well, okay, but what if there aren't any masses? What if there's hardly anybody at all?

Esselwein uncoils a length of copper wire from a spool on the side of the shack and attaches one end to the clothesline. His clothesline is connected to the twenty-foot lightning rod on top of his shack. Nobody has yet brought this to his attention, but then people don't hang around here in a thunderstorm. Neither does Esselwein, if he can help it, but he's beginning to feel like Doctor Frankenstein. He keeps the Monster in the closet, behind a curtain. It's a grotesque creature of coils and wire, tubes, batteries, knobs and dials, which is gradually expanding to the point where he will have to build it a lean-to. He put it together around a Sifto Salt box according to instructions he found in a *Popular Science* magazine. The Monster hums, crackles, sizzles, spits, bleeps, shoots sparks and blows its tubes, but it will not talk. *Oi.* When did an Italian invent something that works?

Esselwein carries the Monster, piece by piece, to the kitchen table. He hooks the pieces together, attaches the aerial, turns the switch, adjusts the earphones and leans over the microphone. His fingers gently work the dial. Outside, the sky is clear. Northern lights swoosh over the lake. Farther north, four, five thousand miles, on the shore of Lake Baikal perhaps, does another man sit on a rock and listen to the stars?

"Hello?" says Esselwein to the microphone. "CKL calling oh shit I don't mean that ' Здраствуйте? Здравствуйте? Скл! Скл! Канада, Канада?' "

Esselwein teases the Monster for nearly three hours. It does not talk. Then, suddenly it sings:

"Oh, everybody's doin' it, doin' it, doin' it,
Everybody's doin' it . . . ."

3

ONE WEEK LATER.
THE LUNATIC ASYLUM, QUEEN STREET, TORONTO:

"Houdini is coming."

"Hoo?"

"You remember, Granny. The famous magician."

"Why?"

"To test the straitjacket. He may want to see you."

"Pooh."

"Come, come, Houdini's very interested in the spirit world."

"Phooey."

"Now, look here Granny...."

"I am not your granny!" she shouts at the doctor. "My name is Christina Coolican and I'm only fifty-nine years old!"

Dear Lord, what is coming over her? She is behaving like a crazy woman. When the doctor leaves, Christina Coolican sits on her cot and takes a deep breath. Houdini. Why does he come here? What does he want? Why does he take his clothes off, and perform in his undershorts? Why does he throw himself on the floor and pretend to have fits when there are plenty of people having real fits? Why does he want to be bound and gagged and chained to a wall in a double-locked padded cell? Is he nuts?

Dr. Livingstone says Houdini is "practising." The first time, it took him more than an hour to get out of a straitjacket. He did it over and over until he got it down to ten minutes. That still wasn't as good as Bobby Williams in ward three, so Houdini took the jacket away with him and when he came back he could wriggle out in ninety seconds. He was very selfish and wouldn't let Bobby Williams try the magic coat.

"Beelzebub," said Christina Coolican when she saw him. She could tell right away from his double-jointed limbs and glittering eyes that he was a faerie, inhuman and malign. She stayed out of his way, but the fiend sought her out when he heard from the doctors that she could apparently cure hysteria and depression, even some forms of schizophrenia, by conjuring up the dead relatives of the demented.

"So, what's your *schtick?*" said Houdini, blocking the door to her cell.

"Stick?"

"Gimmick, you know. Trick."

What was he talking about? He stared at her insolently and picked his teeth.

"Lookit lady," he said. "I'm on to youse dames. Talking trumpets, tapping tables, magic lantern shows, ghosts made out of petticoats, all that crap. Knock, knock. Hello, God. You there? Yes, ma'am. At your service. Plenty of dough, eh? Lookit, cut me in. I'll make it worth your while." He made an ugly rubbing motion with his fingers.

"Wo bist du denn, mein kind?" said Christina Coolican. She sighed and wiped her eyes with the corner of her smock.

"Mama?" said Houdini.

"Ich liebe dich, Erich."

"Mama!" Houdini screamed and ran away down the corridor as fast as his little cloven feet would carry him.

What had she said? Christina Coolican had no idea what the words meant, or who had spoken them. They had come quite spontaneously, from a stranger, an old woman with sad eyes and a gentle face. It certainly wasn't the woman who has become Christina Coolican's constant companion during the past six weeks, a shrill, selfish, hectoring spirit with a halo of wild, white hair who repeats the same message over and over again, "Willie will win! Willie will win!" with an insistence that upsets the normal serenity of Christina Coolican's life in the asylum.

Who is she? Who is this Willie? There are three Williams and two Bills in the asylum, but their mothers are all living except one, and she had been a Cockney. Christina Coolican will have no rest until this message is safely delivered, but where, and to whom? She has prayed and fasted but the answer has not come.

"I must leave now," she says aloud, getting up.

She told the doctor three weeks ago that it was time for her to leave.

"But where is this Willie?" he asked. "The Lord will show the way," she replied. That did it. The asylum administrator was convinced that Christina Coolican was still much to crazy to be let loose on the streets of Toronto. She'd been committed six years ago, according to her chart, for "excessive religious enthusiasm." In a fit of Pentecostal pyromania she'd apparently killed her husband and set fire to their shack. She had no idea if she had or hadn't, but it seemed like a good idea, so she'd kept her mouth shut.

She's been happy here. It was a pleasant surprise to find the asylum built like a church, with a beautiful dome over the main entrance, otherwise severe and square, endless corridors of plain, monastic cells peopled by tormented souls speaking in tongues, a ready-made religious community, praise the Lord, more receptive to the Free Methodist gospel than the unregenerate sinners back home who spat at her and mocked the Word. Here the loonies listen with intent, if abstract, faces and express their need for the Lord's love by incessant masturbation. ("Do they masturbate because they're crazy," the doctors ponder, "or are they crazy because they masturbate?") They're not dangerous. The murderers, herself excepted, have all been hanged, and the others are mostly just old, and lonely and sad or scared out of their wits: not unreasonable responses, she thinks, to the human condition.

The Lord's love, despite Houdini's insinuations, is her only "*schtick.*" Christina Coolican has wrestled with each stricken soul to the limits of her strength, assisted only by the spirits, a visible army of angels, herself merely an instrument of God's grace, a celestial Victrola. She has brought many out of darkness to the light, but now she has been locked up, confined to her own wing and forbidden to use the grounds. The thick stone walls are cool in the heat, but she misses the soldiers. They are all being sent away. The end of the war has cured them. She only provided a mother's patience, a quality not much valued by her own two lost lambs, but urgently needed, apparently, by this mysterious Willie. She will leave now.

The corridor is quite deserted and the door into the main rotunda is open. Beelzebub must be up to his tricks in the ballroom. The function of the ballroom in the treatment of insanity remains obscure, but the purpose of the asylum's glorious dome was revealed one day shortly after Christina Coolican arrived. She had been reading aloud from Genesis in the women's dormitory on the top floor. She'd just started nicely on Noah, when rain began to fall from the ceiling, *plip, plip, plip plip, plipplipplipplipplip*. It rained harded and harder as she read. Pieces of plaster peeled off and crashed to the floor, then the whole ceiling split wide open, and a torrent of water poured down on their heads. This undetected leak in the asylum's water tank, explained away by the doctors on pseudoscientific grounds, established Christina Coolican's reputation for miraculous powers.

She walks as quickly as her shift and slippers will permit. Beneath the dome, she opens a small door leading to a wooden staircase that winds up and around the inside wall to the water tank. Christina Coolican climbs this whispering gallery of plumbing as often as she can, repeating, in her own perilous ascent, Christian's progress. It is here, the highest point in all Toronto, that she hears the voices most clearly. In a moment she reaches the top and emerges through a trapdoor into brilliant sunlight. Her shift flaps in the wind. She grabs the railing on the catwalk to keep from flying away.

"Willie will win," says the woman with the wild white hair. "Willie will win!"

Who, Willie? Win what? Where?

On the green lawn below, tiny figures come and go, or labour between the rows in the vegetable garden. The barns and stables form a square to the south, then long fields of ripening grain run down to the lake. To the east, railway tracks fan out towards the city, and on one of them, a miniature engine disappears slowly into the haze.

She will take the train.

In the ballroom, Houdini is writhing naked on the floor, the focus of all wild eyes. The doctors are in the front row. She finds the door to Dr. Livingstone's office unlocked, his keys, as always, in his desk drawer. She knows the key to his filing cabinet, and the key to the medicine chest, but which, if any, opens the door to the locker where her clothes are kept, and which are her clothes?

A pair of man's pants, neatly pressed, hangs on the back of Dr. Livingstone's chair; on top, a matching suitcoat. A white shirt is folded on the seat, a tie across it, a pair of black leather shoes underneath. The shoes are her size, four, a perfect fit, the suit soft, sky-blue silk with a small stripe. With her cropped, white hair sticking out from under Harry Houdini's new straw boater, and Harry Houdini's ebony cane under her soft, sky-blue arm, Christina Coolican bears a striking resemblance to John D. Rockefeller Sr. In fact, there's a fat wallet in her hip pocket, and a first-class train ticket to Ottawa. A copy of the Toronto *Star* in the side pocket advertises Houdini's show tonight at the Royal Alexandra theatre. Beside it, a fat man stares out at her with frightened eyes.

> ### "LIBERAL HOPEFUL
> The Hon. William Lyon Mackenzie King is among those who are seeking to succeed...."

Christina Coolican tucks the newspaper under her arm, twirls the walking stick twice, and saunters out the front door of the lunatic asylum.

AT THIS MOMENT IN OTTAWA,
THE LIBERAL HOPEFUL IS FIGURING THE ODDS:

This morning at daybreak I awoke dreaming vividly of Laurier. He was in bishop's robes, high in a pulpit, speaking as prime minister of the country. Tears of joy rushed to my eyes at beholding the very apocalypse of my aspirations!

If victory is mine tomorrow, it is God's doing. I have taken no part in the leadership campaign, spending the last weeks abroad and leaving the work to others. I am quite indifferent to the outcome. If another is chosen, there is still the work of the Rockefeller Foundation, and the offer to head the Carnegie Corporation. Both offer fine opportunities for service, a life of intellectual and social enjoyment, a comfortable house and library in New York, the chance to meet the best people in the world and to be in touch in a commanding way with the subjects I have most at heart, industrial peace and social well-being. There is also the opportunity to write Mr. Carnegie's life, and the sum of $100,000 for doing so, if I desired. It would be a life of study, rest and enjoyment, free from anxieties and harrassments of every kind. I could lay aside one or two hundred thousand dollars in a very short time and still be young enough to take an active part in politics.

Yet, even at this moment, when I am making $1,000 a week, I feel the call to public life with all its strain, misunderstanding, jealousies and bitterness. My soul is there. I can count on an income from investments which will protect me in case of misfortune. Why should I seek more money? An association with great wealth is an unnatural one for me.

Great purpose is my rightful environment. My nature will not allow me to be in any way dependent on Mr. Rockefeller Jr. or even under obligation to him. I cannot do it. He has been wonderfully considerate, but has revealed selfishness under the guise of charity. How we can deceive ourselves! Spiritual goodness, not material greatness, is what I must strive for above all else. To live and die honoured and respected here in my own country is closer to my heart than any other ambition. My desire is all for politics.

The one handicap is lack of independence. I have ample to live on alone, but I could not hope to have a home, and do what is expected of a leader, even with a leader's salary, and the leadership is not yet a certainty. It would be hell itself to lead a political party and be dependent on politics for a livelihood. The relationship with Mr. Rockefeller enables me to continue in politics and earn something as his advisor. That makes politics possible. I should be happier free of the Rockefeller connection altogether save for the funds it provides. I have never regarded the connection as other than a stepping stone, a means to lay aside enough to 'get into the fight.' I need action for my nature's highest expression. The primrose path does not make for greatness. It is freedom my nature craves, freedom to speak my mind anywhere and everywhere without restraint. The vindication of the right, of honour, truth and integrity is needed more than all else today if we are to have a national morality.

Above all, I recognize my limitations. I have a sort of moral courage, but have not been firm and true in much. I should have been watching every thought and word. I wonder sometimes if it's not too late. I shall not surrender to weakness but shall strive to rise above the past. Most of all I feel the need for someone to share my life, yet the fear of what is needed for politics, and married life, would terrify me out of both were I to stop to contemplate them.

What Mother would have wished I do not know. She feared the strain of politics. The Carnegie offer would have appealed to her, but she would have been prouder still of a self-sacrificing career. How much better a good name than all else in the world besides! To these words above all else I must be true — 'Well may I love the poor, greatly may I esteem the humble and the lowly, for poverty and adversity were my nurses and in youth were want and misery my familiar friends.' There lies my soul, not in ease and enjoyment, but in the service of those who toil.

4

The train trip was fine. Christina Coolican was shown to the club car and she rode the whole way in an armchair that swivelled in a semi-circle. The darky doctors treated her with a deference she had never known in her life, plying her with pillows and cigars, backing away in obsequious disappointment when she requested only a sandwich and a pot of tea, bowing to the floor when she paid with a $20 bill and waved away the change.

She slept most of the way, worn out from the long walk to the station. She'd been too nervous to take the streetcar, and Houdini's shoes began to pinch at Spadina Avenue. She spent the night sitting on a bench with a ragged assortment of men, who, like herself, seemed to have nowhere else to go. She found the station reassuringly similar in sound and smell to the asylum.

It is late afternoon as she passes under the arch of flags and bunting over the gate to Lansdowne Park. "Abandon hope, all ye who enter here," she mutters, wishing she'd remembered her Bible. The buildings in the park are familiar from her visits to the Ottawa Agricultural Exhibition years ago, before she was saved, and the mood is the same, balloons everywhere, and busy men with badges scurrying off in all directions. She follows the sound of band music towards the Cow Palace.

The doors are open. From the dark interior comes the faint, sweet smell of shit and an ominous mooing noise, the murmur of immemorial machination. The first national convention of the Liberal Party of Canada is choosing a leader. The results of the third ballot have just been announced. Mr. King is leading with 411 votes compared to 344 for the favourite, Mr. Fielding. The barn is abuzz. No one had expected Mr. King to run, much less win, yet he has led on every ballot. Not one of the eleven hundred Liberals in the Cow Palace will admit publicly to voting for him.

"I have a message for Willie," says Christina Coolican in a quiet voice. The men at the door pay no attention. They are busy putting on Fielding buttons for the final fight on the fourth ballot. It's not in the bag yet. To half the delegates at the convention, Willie King is a slacker, a socialist and a sanctimonious little snot. To the other half (one hundred of them are women), he is an aesthete, an intellectual, a man of peace and progress, a brave new face for a brave new world, exactly the sort of nice, Christian young man ("He's rather cute, don't you think?") mothers want their daughters to marry, a safe man for a world made safe.

Old Mr. Fielding, on the other hand, is a breath of stale air, a thorny reminder of the blight on Liberal fortunes, ghost of an *ancien régime* infamous for its venality. He supported conscription during the war and sits now as an Independent, anathema to French-Canadian Liberals, and almost all French-Canadians are Liberal. Mr. Fielding does not arouse sexual speculation. Mr. Fielding is not cute.

Christina Coolican peers into the barn, blinking in the gloom. The smoke stings her eyes. Through a fetid haze she can see two men seated alone on a platform at the far end. The delegates are swarming into the aisles for the vote. The din makes her head spin. She tries to push her way through, "Excuse me, excuse me," but she is mercilessly shoved and elbowed and stepped on until she is forced to take refuge on a chair.

"The asylum was never this bad," she says. Several people look curiously at this pale little man in the expensive silk suit.

"Willie will win," she says to no one in particular.

"What's that?" asks a gaunt old man beside her, proferring an ear trumpet. Sir Alan Aylesworth has been deaf for years, yet no man in the Liberal Party keeps his ear more closely to the ground, and no ear is more sensitively attuned to the first, faint tremblings of the popular mood. Sir Alan is wearing a King button. Personally, he thinks Willie King is a prick, but in his fifty years at the helm of the Liberal machine in Toronto Sir Alan has learned not to let personal prejudice interfere with political advantage. Being deaf, he has been spared Willie King's sententious bullshit, but Sir Alan has seen the message in Willie King's sharp blue eyes, and has read the signals in the busy fingers, the impatient licking of the lips. Never in all his fifty years has Sir Alan encountered a man so starved, so purely ravenous for political office that he will subordinate *all other* human considerations to this single goal. Moreover, King is a soft man, nervous, impressionable, an oyster easily opened, but concealing within those fleshy folds, Aylesworth prays, the pearl of power.

"Willie will win," Christina Coolican shouts into the trumpet. "Willie will win!"

"That so?"

Sir Alan gives the little man a hard look. A knot of people gathers around and a whisper runs through the crowd, *WilliewillwinWillie willwinWilliewillwinWilliewillwin.* Sir Alan looks anxiously towards the door. He is expecting the momentary arrival of Lady Laurier, who has not yet declared her preference. She is known to be fond of Fielding, and to dislike King, but King's emotional tribute to Laurier on Tuesday night (it is said he knelt before the portrait and kissed the painted hand) persuaded many that he is the chosen heir.

"Have you come from Laurier House?" Sir Alan asks the little man.

The stranger closes his eyes.

"The lady is pleased," he says. "She is smiling."

Williewillwin Williewillwin Williewillwin Williewillwin Williewillwin Willie willwinWilliewillwinWilliewillwinwinwin.

"Bless you," says Sir Alan. He elbows off into the throng to share the good news that Lady Laurier is backing King. The news hums through the crowd with the speed of electricity, reaching Willie himself in a matter of moments. He bends over, listens closely, then sits up straight, trying not to look too pleased or surprised. At this precise moment, a shaft of light from a window high in the rafters falls across the stage: Mr. King is in sun, Mr. Fielding in shadow.

Lady Laurier arrives as the ballots are being counted. Her blind, old face turns happily to the sound of cheers as she gropes her way to the seat of honour on the stage — Mr. Fielding, scowling, on her right, Mr. King, beaming, on her left. She sits expressionless as the convention chairman makes his way to the lectern, a slip of paper in his hand.

"Mr. Fielding," he cries, "four hundred and thirty-eight!"

A roar of applause.

"Mr. King, four hundred and *seventy-six!*"

Rising to acknowledge wave after wave of cheers, Willie grins, waves, shakes Mr. Fielding's hand and bows reverently over Lady Laurier's chair. He kisses her wrinkled cheek and whispers affectionately into her ear. Lady Laurier's face folds into a puzzled frown.

"Me?" she cries, looking around in alarm. "But I was for Fielding!"

LATER THAT NIGHT,
WILLIE KING GIVES PRAISE WHERE IT IS DUE:

How then came the victory? *Through God alone.* Being true, first of all, to principle, undergoing great sacrifice for truth, going abroad in July so the public could see I was disinterested. I decided to hit the snake on the head and make two main points: government by the people, and the end of machine influence in politics. My stand for labour won me the labour men. The farmers were with me due to my stand on freer trade. It was *the people* that won me the choice. I had the best hour to speak in the whole convention. Who will say this was chance? I did not disappoint my friends, I disconcerted my enemies, and I gave the shot that was needed to win the day.

When I heard the figures on the first ballot, with myself in the lead, I felt a momentary qualm, a feeling not of elation, but of depression at the thought I was likely to win, wondering if I could measure up to the task. Just before the result of the last ballot was announced, I sat quietly waiting on the platform. The sun came out very brightly and shone through the western window, making a flood of golden light about me. I turned to look at Sir Wilfrid's picture, which was beautifully illuminated, the eyes looking down straight upon me. I thought of his words that he wanted me to succeed him and I felt 'I shall win' or, 'I shall be chosen.' There was no thought of winning in my mind.

The majority was better than I anticipated. I was too heavy of heart and soul to appreciate the tumult of applause. My thoughts were of dear Mother and Father and little Bell, all of whom I felt very close to me. I thought 'It is right. I have sought nothing. It has come. It has come from God. The dear loved ones know and are about. It is to His work I am called, and to it I dedicate my life.' This dedication I made in my heart as I sat and heard the returns. Then I spoke more to my own satisfaction than on most occasions. The audience was wonderfully receptive. It was the most difficult of all moments.

There was a great rush to the platform. My right hand was bruised and swollen as a consequence of the handshaking. I had to turn my head towards the rafters to get breath, surrounded as I was on all sides by a pressing throng. I waited until the hall was cleared, then I took the North York men and a few ladies to dinner in the refreshment room on the grounds. As we were going in, Sir Alan Aylesworth drew my attention to a man who seemed to possess some foreknowledge of my victory and who had helped sway the vote in my favour at a crucial moment. He was seated on a bench outside the refreshment room surrounded by a considerable crowd. As I went over to express my thanks, I was forcefully struck by his resemblance to Mr. Rockefeller Sr., the same expression of saintly sweetness, a kind of radiance about his features, and I noticed that he was following Mr. Rockefeller's habit of handing out money to strangers, placing what appeared to be dollar bills in outstretched hands, although, in my experience, Mr. Rockefeller gave away only dimes.

I had never seen him before but he seemed to know who I was. I inquired how he had known I would be chosen, and he replied that it had come as a message from a spirit and he had gone to considerable pains to deliver it. I knew immediately that it must be dear Mother. Imagine my excitement when my questions elicited *incontrovertible evidence* that she had been guiding my steps from the Great Beyond! The messenger confessed that he had eaten nothing, through oversight, the entire day, so I invited him to join our little celebration, made so much more joyful in the knowledge that Mother was nearby. He appeared much fatigued by the intense heat and noise in the room, and when I asked his name, gazed out over the crowd in an abstracted way, admitting only, when I pressed him strongly, 'My name is Legion.' Learning that he had arrived in Ottawa only that afternoon, I secured Mr. Legion a room at the Château and spent a happy two hours in his company before coming home.

How God has revealed himself to me today I can never forget. This afternoon as I spoke, the word 'righteousness' came to me, put on my lips from the Great Beyond. It will be my guide. To make righteousness prevail in the country, that is my one great purpose now. Victory has been won over the corrupt machine in our own party. It seems to me now a straight road to victory in a general election. The people want clean and honest government, ideals in politics and a larger measure of social reform. I am unknown to the people yet, but soon they will know and recognize. The Liberal Party will yet rejoice in the confidence they have placed in me. They have chosen better than they know, though I say it myself. I say it in all sincerity.

Later that same night, Christina Coolican lies awake on the floor of her room. It's cooler and more comfortable than the bed, but still she cannot sleep. When Willie had offered her a room for the night, she had assumed it would be in his own home, and hadn't paid much attention to where they were going until she'd found herself trapped in the lobby of the infamous Shadow by a mob of drunken Grits. Phew. She'd thought the Cow Palace smelled bad!

"They've given you a warmer welcome than the great Houdini," the desk clerk said to Willie, pointing at a mountain of luggage. Christina Coolican felt a twinge of conscience, but the clerk did not say that the magician had arrived naked, or in a cotton shift, so he must have conjured up some clothes somewhere. She'd just as soon be rid of Houdini's suit, but what could she wear? Appearing naked would mean the asylum again. She misses the green lawns and the whispering gallery and her companions, but her room here is decent enough, with its own toilet and tub and a monkey who brings her tea whenever she wants. She'll be able to get by for several days on the chocolates and fruit Willie sent up.

Willie's mother is silent, at least for the moment. She'll be back. Oh, dear! Christina Coolican has already been introduced to Father, Grandfather (an irascible soul in a red wig), and Willie's departed sister Tinkerbell, no, Little Bell. On the whole they are rather dull company for a woman on intimate terms with Miss Nightingale and General Gordon of Khartoum (If only *they'd* gotten together!), but Willie is fond of them. She'll do her best. God knows he needs help.

Such a dark, desperate, wretched soul! What can she do? During her years in the asylum, Christina Coolican encountered some deeply deluded people, but she has never before encountered a politican. It's going to be a tough case.

THE NEXT DAY,
THE NEW LEADER OF THE LIBERAL PARTY HAS SECOND THOUGHTS:

I bought a pair of shoes today, $12. I couldn't afford a $20 pair. I looked up the salary of the leader of the Opposition and found it noted as a sessional allowance. That means by not being in the House this year I lose the indemnity *and* leader's salary this year. This, combined with a request from *Saturday Night* to buy up copies of an issue containing an article favourable to myself, has made me sick at heart. To pay McGregor's salary ($1,000 a year) and meet expenditures of other kinds on the party's account will leave me *nothing* to live on but the little principal I have saved. There can be no question of marriage at this time. Did I not believe God would provide, I would despair. Oh God, give me faith!

MEANWHILE, UP NORTH....

He did it! The Liberal Party must be really hard up. I sent Willie a wire anyway, and he wired back a bouquet of flowers this morning. I guess he didn't realize there's no florist in Swastika, not to mention Kirkland Lake, so Mr. Pratt, the station agent, picked me a terrific bunch of fireweed and sent them in on the dray. Perhaps Willie will come here himself to settle the strike. He's supposed to be very good at that, although I've never seen him actually *do* it. Willie has an effect on people a lot like infantile paralysis. Maybe he *is* what the country needs.

He'd have a hard time up here because everybody's speaking Russian, or some peculiar variation. Vee-ski. That's easy. To get the vee-ski you need zoh-loh-tuh. That's what the strike's about, more *zohlohtuh* for the Bolsheviki *robotski.* Russian's okay until you look at it. "Bread" is just *"klep,"* but it's spelled *"хлеб."* Jeez. It looks beautiful, but how do you figure it out? Constable Dempster's going crazy. Esselwein's put up posters in Russian on all the hydro poles, and Dempster can't figure out what they say. He doesn't even know the word for Red. (He'll never guess — he's just a dumb МИЛИЦИОНЕР.) When a bundle of Marx's *Manifestos* arrived in the mail, Dempster was all set to charge me with importing seditious literature until I convinced him they were religious tracts and Esselwein was actually a secret agent for the Free Methodists. Dempster took one away. Maybe he'll see the light. Every morning he hangs around while I sort the mail, keeping an eye peeled for contraband copies of *The Worker.*

Nobody comes in any more. I am the Class Enemy. The men stand around in the street all day, shuffling their feet in the dirt. Striking must be more boring than going to work. "Revolution is in the air," says Constable Dempster, sniffing. He thinks that revolution is something you catch, like the 'flu. You wake up one morning and all of a sudden your house is full of little dark men like Esselwein who throw you out into the street without any clothes and you have to scrounge through the garbage for food while the little dark men drink your whiskey and laugh at you out your bedroom window. All I smell is Big Peter's garlic. He chews it to keep away vampires. I'm sure it does.

I miss the Russian Kid in his crazy hat. I told him he'd seen too many movies. "Babe," he said, "I am *history!*" Sure, and I'm Lillian Gish. Now Esselwein is holed up in his shack. Big Peter says he has a Sifto Salt box that sings jazz, in English. The box only sings at night, so Esselwein stays up listening and sleeps all day.

My Sifto Salt box does not sing. Neither does my Quaker Oats box, the Robin Hood Flour or the Magic Baking Powder can. What's his got? I'm dying to find out. Will it sing for me? We could dance. Oh, everybody's doin' it, doin' it, doin' it....

5

The revolution in Kirkland Lake began on August 9, 1919. It was Saturday night. Just after dark, Lily saw a mob of men coming up Government Road, singing and carrying torches. They surrounded the post office, shouting "Death to the King! Down with Imperialism!" Someone banged very loudly on the door and called out "Come out wit' yer hands up!" Lily wondered what Lillian Gish would do under the circumstances. She adopted an expression she hoped was both brave and distraught and opened the door. Esselwein rushed in, waving a red flag, and claimed the post office in the name of the Kirkland Lake Soviet. Lily sat on a chair, pretending calm, as Esselwein broke open the cash box and smashed the pictures of the King and Queen on the floor. The men fell silent, shocked, and Lily felt a tremor of fear run through the room.

"So this is what it's like," Lily thought. When would she be shot? Then she noticed that the Russian Kid wasn't wearing his hat, and he wasn't carrying a gun. In fact, nobody was. Hey, that's not right. Should she point it out? How can she play a damsel in distress if the bad guys are just a bunch of drunken hunkies? She lit a cigarette.

Esselwein rattled the knob on the door to her room, then put his shoulder to it, but Big Peter, who brought Lily a fresh brown egg for her breakfast every morning, grabbed him with a massive arm.

"Lady," Big Peter scowled.

Esselwein glanced at her. Well, at least he's noticed. His eyes were deep-set and very black and his hair curled beautifully in front of his ears. Lily crossed her legs.

"The key is in the cash box."

But Esselwein gave the key to Big Peter and told him to guard her.

Then he stormed out and the mob rushed down the street to capture Constable Dempster. So much for free love. Lily stubbed out her cigarette on the floor. At least she won't have to sweep up in the morning.

Constable Dempster wasn't home. The mayor was asleep, simple enough, and at the Rainbow Mine they surprised the boss, Jack Coolican, making love to the new schoolteacher. "Buzz off," Jack said. "If you can make money out of this damned hole, you're welcome to it." Esselwein cut the telephone wires to Swastika and blew a crater fifteen feet deep in the road. By morning, his shack had been declared the Revolutionary Headquarters of the Kirkland Lake Soviet, and the Red Flag, cut from a pair of Big Peter's longjohns, was flying proudly from its roof.

"What do we do now?" asked Big Peter, presenting Lily with her fresh brown egg.

At first everything went on much as before. Charlie Chow's café became the People's Café, but Comrade Chow continued to cook and was paid, as usual, in mine shares, confiscated from his own hoard by the Commissar of Finance and distributed equally among the miners. "I get 'em all back," Charlie shrugged. "No good no how." The men went back to work in the mines, except the Lakeshore, where Constable Dempster and the Nob had taken refuge and fired at anyone who came within a hundred yards. The Nob was a crack shot. Comrade Esselwein, the Chief Commissar, had to cover the exposed side of his shack with corrugated iron, and the *ping* of the Nob's bullets so distracted the Soviet that meetings had to be moved out of range to the Union Hall.

Outside of Kirkland Lake, no one paid much attention to the revolution. Everyone was in a tizzy about the impending visit of the Prince of Wales. Besides, what could be done? The army was demobilized and the mounted police were mopping up Winnipeg. All that could be managed was a company of cadets from the University of Toronto. The cadets were dispatched on the Temiskaming & Northern Ontario Railroad with a Lewis gun mounted on the back of an armoured truck. At Swastika, the truck rolled off the station platform and sank out of sight in the muskeg. The cadets took cover on the third floor of Boisvert's Hotel and awaited developments.

Lily was released when she agreed to give up her cash, $42.65, her one thousand shares of Rainbow stock, and her chinchilla coat.

"Can you type?" asked Esselwein.

"Did you ask the girls at 5 Main that question?"

The Commissar blushed. He actually blushed!

"What *can* you do?"

"I can recite. Would you like to hear 'Cry of....,' "

"*Useful,* Comrade Coolican. Something socially relevant."

Lily was stumped. She was the most socially irrelevant person she knew. She smoked, she drank, she played bridge. She used to take photographs, but she gave that up. Now she isn't even a postmistress. Her ambition in life is to enjoy it. Not so easy, either. Willie considered her totally useless. That was the problem. She didn't write gracious letters, or arrange flowers, or invite people to tea, or all the other things the wife of a future prime minister is supposed to do. And now here she is, in Siberia, stuck again! She looked desperately around the table at the other members of the Soviet, silent and solemn in their faded check shirts, rough hair slicked back in honour of the occasion, faces weather-beaten, plain and patient — familiar faces, faces she'd known in the shanty on the Madawaska River watching Papa tend the kettles on the fire.

"I'd like to make bread," she said.

"Хорошо!" said Commissar Esselwein. Lily assumed from the smile on his face that it meant O.K.

Lily didn't have a clue how to make bread. It just seemed a pleasant thing to do, and she was hungry. She vaguely remembered Papa making it in huge iron pans buried in hot sand, but she had no iron pans, or hot sand. However, the big kitchen stove in the Rainbow bunkhouse did well enough, and she found a recipe book, and Bea, the schoolteacher, offered to help.

"Anyone who can read can cook," Bea said dubiously, peering at the book. "How many loaves do we need?"

"Oh, about two hundred."

The daily quota was only the first problem. Was the bread to be white or brown, whole wheat or rye, with caraway seeds or without? Was a big man to get a bigger loaf than a small man? Was the bread to be delivered or picked up from the kitchen? The Revolutionary Kirkland Lake Soviet debated the Bread Question day and night. No decision was reached, except that potatoes would be more economical, if they had any. The Nob's defection raised the Fish Question: should the fish be caught individualistically, on a line, or collectively, in a net? The Chicken Question posed a similar problem: should the chickens remain as they were, scattered in the streets and under various doorsteps, or should they be confined to a single coop? Then there was the question of Mrs. Dzuba's cow. It was the only cow in Kirkland Lake. Mrs. Dzuba refused to hand it over to the state. Mrs. Dzuba was denounced as a *kulak*. She killed the cow and dumped its carcass in front of the Union Hall. It made barely enough stew for one meal.

The more the Revolutionary Soviet debated these questions, the angrier everyone became. Shouting and screaming could be heard coming from the Union Hall, and from time to time the Commissar of Sanitation or the Commissar of Food would rush out cursing and shaking his fist. After a while there would be a reconciliation, with much embracing and kissing on both cheeks and tearful cries of *"Tovarich! Tovarich!"* but nothing was ever decided. It seemed that almost everyone had been given a job with a title, and an armband to wear, and no one showed the slightest hesitation in telling everyone else how to do his job, or the slightest inclination to accept the constructive criticism of his comrades.

"This is chaos," Lily told Esselwein. "I thought the state was supposed to wither away."

"That comes later," he said with a wave of his hand.

The first week, everyone had a terrific time being busy and feeling important. At night they danced in the streets and sang at the stars. Lily even got to see the singing Sifto box, although you'd never know what it was, it was so covered up with thingamajigs and doohickeys. It had made friends with another box in Toronto, CFCA, owned by the *Star,* so they were able to follow the progress of the Prince of Wales almost moment by moment. There wasn't a word on CFCA about the revolution. Esselwein was terribly disappointed. How he hated to be ignored!

The second week, food was rationed. A group of returned soldiers under Sergeant Plunkett organized a hunting party, but even the rabbits had long since fled the vicinity of Kirkland Lake. The Commissariat of Fish failed miserably to meet its quota. The third week, the taps at the People's Pharmacy and Poolroom ran dry. The fourth week, the machinery at the mines began to break down and fuel ran low. The mines went on half-days, then stopped. The men sat around playing cards and asking themselves: What is to be done?

They already had plenty of gold. Twenty-two bars were stacked in a corner of the union hall.

"We are rich," said Big Peter, scratching his head. "Why we not eat?"

What is to be done? Lily's friend Red Annie had smuggled in a copy of Lenin's pamphlet on the subject rolled up in a tobacco tin, but it was no help at all. Lenin was okay about how to *start* a revolution, but he didn't say what you do after the revolution has *happened.* From all the stories in the *Star* about famine and civil war in Russia, Lily had the sinking feeling that Lenin didn't know himself.

"Trotsky is right," said Esselwein. "We have to take over the *whole world!*"

On August 23, Big Peter did not bring Lily her fresh brown egg.

"Hen, she *kaput.*" He shrugged and made a wringing motion with his hands.

On August 25, Comrade Chow ran out of tinned food.

"No lice," he said on August 27. "One bag bean."

Lily emptied her last bag of flour on August 28.

"We're starving," she told Esselwein. He was busy drawing a map on a scrap of paper.

"See, once we've blown up the Alamo, here, that will open the road to Swastika along here, then we an grab the gun and surround the hotel, over here, then we'll occupy . . . ."

On August 29, at sunrise, Lily removes the red armband from her shirt, slips her pistol into her pocket and strikes off through the scrub in what she hopes is the general direction of Swastika. If she can make it to Ottawa, maybe Willie can think of something to do. Willie's grandfather had been a revolutionary, sort of.

She heads along the north side of the lake, keeping as far as possible from the road. She is afraid of the Finns. Three of them guard the crater, silent, unsmiling men with white hair and yellow eyes, and she figures they'd just as soon shoot anyone leaving as anyone coming. A lot of people have simply disappeared from Kirkland Lake and never been heard of again.

Lily comes out on the tracks unexpectedly. She stands very still, listening for a sudden silence, the warning chatter of a squirrel, watching for the glint of yellow eyes among the leaves.

"I say!"

A soldier is sitting on a boulder behind her. He scrambles down, impatiently brushing moss from his breeches, and runs towards her. His hair is the gold of the birch leaves, his eyes as blue as the sky, and he carries a sword. He smiles and waves as if he knows her. She certainly knows him. She has seen his face in photographs a thousand times. It is the most beautiful face in the world, the face that murdered a million men.

"Speak-um Eeng-gleesh?" asks the Prince of Wales.

Lily nods.

"Got-um smoke?" The Prince makes puffing motions with his mouth.

Lily offers her last pack. He takes one and puts the pack in his pocket. She offers her only box of matches. He lights the cigarette and puts the matches in his pocket. He doesn't speak again until the cigarette is drained, like a glass of water.

"You...live...here?" He points at her, then at the ground.

"Well, yes. Sort of. I mean, I've run away."

"Oh, jolly good! So have I!"

The royal train is back there somewhere, the prince says, gesturing vaguely towards Swastika, and on board is the worst stinking bunch of rotters and bounders and puking politicians he has ever met in his whole stinking life.

"It's horrible," he says. "I can't stand it." He turns towards her a face surprisingly pinched and sad. Lily notices there are dark smudges, like thumbprints, beneath the lovely, languid eyes.

"You wouldn't happen to live in a log cabin, would you?" asks the Prince of Wales.

"It's not log...."

"Aw."

"It's a shack."

"Oh, jolly good! Is it one of those cosy places, with the big stove you put your feet in, and moccasins and things hanging up to dry, and snow piled up...?"

"Well, it's summer now...."

"Do you think you could put me up for a while? I shan't stay long, only an hour or two. They'll find me, you know. They always do."

"There isn't much to eat. We're having a revolution."

"A plain chop would be splendid. Actually, I could use a drink."

"But, Sir...."

"Don't worry," says the Prince, taking her hand. "I shouldn't mind at all being assassinated."

Lily sighs.

"I've captured the Prince of Wales," she says to herself. "What do I do now?"

One hour later they come out on Government Road. Comrade McLeod is filling water pails from the communal pump. He stops in mid-stroke and snaps to attention.

"Infantry?" says the Prince of Wales.

"Forty-eighth Highlanders, Sir."

"Jolly good show."

"Water, Sir?" Comrade McLeod holds out an enamel cup. The Prince takes a cautious sip.

"Cigarette?" the Prince asks hopefully.

Comrade McLeod offers his last pack. The Prince lights one, then puts the pack in his pocket. At the door to Esselwein's shack, he flicks the butt into the brush. McLeod douses the blaze with both pails of water.

The dozen bleary, bearded faces of the Revolutionary Kirkland Lake Soviet stare up at at them from Esselwein's kitchen table, their expressions frozen into a tableau of The Last Supper. Esselwein, arms raised in an attitude of supplication, is in the centre.

"Don't let me interrupt," says the Prince, taking a chair. "Could I trouble anyone for a smoke?"

He chooses a crumpled Players from the small, white forest that suddenly materializes around the table and smokes it as if it is his last.

"Frightfully quiet," he says, looking disappointed. "I'd rather expected more in the way of shooting, and so on, you know."

"We go blow up Oakes, eh?" says Big Peter.

"The dynamite's in place, Sir," Plunkett salutes. "One thousand sticks."

"Just give the word, Sir," says Commissar of War Smith, formerly known as Big Boom Smith when he blew up the better part of a German division in France.

"Righto," says the Prince, pulling on his gloves. "Let's go blow up these oaks."

"Hold it!" Esselwein finds his voice at last. "I'm the boss here! This is *my* revolution!"

"Boss, hell," says Big Peter. "We all boss!"

"Three cheers for the working man!" says the Prince.

"All in favour of blowing up Harry Oakes?" cries Plunkett.

"Aye!"

"Who's Harry?" asks the Prince of Wales.

"It's okay," Lily says. "He's not one of us."

Outside, a crowd is gathered on the rocks and along Trotsky Prospect, formerly Prospect Avenue, but still just a dirt track. When the Prince emerges, a spontaneous cheer breaks out. He smiles and waves shyly. He shines so brightly in the light it's as if he carried within his own small sun, and Lily understands now why he dreams of Hollywood, and why he finds the single script he was born to play already intolerable.

"He really wants to live in a shack," she explains to Esselwein as the whole mob, the Prince in the lead, makes its way down the hill towards the Alamo.

"Who on earth *wants* to live in a shack?" asks Esselwein.

The Alamo has been completely surrounded by dynamite, the sticks tied together in bundles connected by a long fuse. The trick, Plunkett explains, is to knock out the enemy without destroying his supplies, especially Harry's cellar of vintage French wine.

"Ah!" says the Prince, wetting his lips.

"Look out, grenade!" screams Big Boom Smith, ducking behind a rock.

A bottle is flying towards them from the direction of the Alamo. It arches slowly, turning over and over, and shatters at the Prince's feet. He picks out a piece of blue paper folded into a tiny square, unfolds it and reads: "Never fear, Mitford here."

"Mad Mitford?" he says. "Here?"

A small Union Jack waves bravely from the window of the lookout. The Prince picks his way carefully around the dynamite, walks up the path and raps on the front door.

"I say, Mitford. Be a sport. Open up."

The Nob's suspicious, hatchet face peeps out.

"Good man. We're dying of thirst out here."

"There's no soda," Mitford mutters. "Oakes drank all the Scotch, the stinking sewer."

In the cellar, Harry Oakes and ⸺ ⸺ ⸺ in a litter of empty bottles. But Harry's canned goods are almost ⸺ and his wine cellar is barely touched.

Big Peter breaks the neck of a bottle of burgundy and pours the wine fountain-like down his throat. Lily drinks hers out of a tin cup. She eats two tins of peas and one of Klik. The wine is sour. It makes her mouth pucker. Her face feels numb. She can't stop smiling. The Prince of Wales is crying. He and Esselwein are leaning on each other's shoulders, toasting "the common man" and tossing Harry's crystal glasses, one by one, into Harry's granite fireplace. The glasses make a lovely tinkling sound. The common men are dancing a jig in the front parlor. Black Mary from 5 Main is undressing the Nob. The room revolves in a pleasant way. Lily falls down. The floor is slippery with the blood of the bourgeoisie. It's a terrific party.

Who invited the cops? There they are, one, two, three, four redcoats standing around the Prince of Wales. They have revolvers in their hands. The Prince is smiling at them in his most captivating way. What is that awful noise? Lily looks out the window. A monstrous goose-like thing is settling out of the sky on to the lake, two great wings of water rising on either side as it rushes towards the beach. There, in the very front seat, round and upright as an egg in a box, is Willie.

Six silver flying boats are lined up on the beach. They are the most beautiful things Lily has ever seen. If only she could climb in and fly away!

"Time to push off, I'm afraid," says the Prince of Wales, shaking her hand. "Pity there's no snow."

Esselwein, in handcuffs, is lifted into the seat behind him. The Prince stands and waves as the flying boat taxis out.

"The King's a shit!" he shouts.

"Was he speaking to me?" Willie asks anxiously.

Lily can't stop smiling.

"He might have said a word or two of thanks," Willie goes on. "It was entirely my idea to get the flying boats. No one had the slightest idea what was to be done. I had quite despaired of seeing His Royal Highness alive again and was trying to prepare what statement I should make to the press when Mr. Legion, my personal advisor — Where has he gone? He was here a moment ago — when Mr. Legion said to me: 'Willie

King, you must learn to *fly!*' Well, of course I immediately thought of aircraft, and I rang up the Minister of Defence who was entirely in sympathy and put me in touch with...."

Lily isn't listening. She is watching the flying boat churn through the waves and rise miraculously into the air. It circles towards the sun, its drone no louder than a dragonfly as it disappears in the western sky.

"Is it fun to fly?" she asks, interrupting. "What do things look like?"

"I don't know," Willie says, "I had my eyes shut the whole time."

It's dark by the time Lily is allowed to return to what is, once more, the Kirkland Lake post office. She picks the King and Queen up off the floor, removes the splinters of broken glass and hangs the pictures on the wall. Tomorrow she'll have to sweep up. She sighs.

"You're a shit," she says to the King.

In her little room, a lamp is burning and the kettle is singing on the stove. A small, slight figure in a rumpled blue silk suit is stretched out on her mattress, eyes closed. The face is older, more tired than Lily remembers, and the hair, which used to be pulled back in a knot, sticks up like porcupine quills, but the face is more familiar than her own.

"They've gone away, Mum," she says quietly. "You'll be safe here."

Oh, Esselwein, where are you? Have they killed you too?

6

It was almost a year to the day when the Russian Kid came back to Kirkland Lake. He hopped off the train one day, casual as you please, as if he'd only been down to Toronto for the weekend. The hat was gone, though, and the peasant blouse, and the red socks. Instead, he wore coveralls and a cloth cap. He was thin and pale as a ghost.

"I've gone undergound," he whispered.

Big Peter did not come back. Nor did any of the others who had been taken away in handcuffs on the day of the Riot, as it was now known. It was said they had all been deported. Nobody ever expected to see Esselwein again, but his shack remained empty and untouched, a silent reminder of the revolution. Nobody spoke of the revolution any more. Anyone who did was fired and blacklisted at the other mines. But nobody forgot. Instead, they talked about the day the Red Prince dropped out of the sky, and flew away again, and boy, had that put Kirkland Lake on the map!

All of a sudden, the place was swarming with reporters. (Remember that little snotnose from the *Star*, Sinclair, who asked everybody how much money he made?) When the stories about the Prince appeared, shares in all the mines shot up on the Toronto Mining Exchange. Fat men with black hats and big cigars arrived and started buying up property. One shack sold for $30,000! The mines started to hum again. The men went back to work. Government Road was paved. Streets were laid out, still bumpy and crooked, but real streets, with names, and real houses were built on them, all alike, with white siding and green roofs and running water and furnaces. The Imperial Bank moved in, and the T. Eaton Co. opened a store. Kirkland Lake acquired a fire engine and a dog catcher. Chief Johnson was rehired. Airmail whiskey flowed once more from Dr. Rolston's cut glass fountains. Kirkland Lake was having a boom.

When Esselwein returned, he hung out a sign on his shack: EVERY-THING PAINTED. DAY & NIGHT. ALL COLOURS. He began by painting his own tarpaper white. It started a trend. Lily was the only holdout. "Tar is black," she said. Everything Esselwein did, or said, was the object of intense regard. People followed him with their eyes, and conversation hushed when he passed. The Russian Kid was a legend in his own time. It *had* been his revolution. It had failed, but *it had happened,* and you had the feeling with Esselwein around that *it could happen again.*

"The problem is Marx," he said. "If you abolish capitalism, you abolish capital. You go back to barter, but that's why people invented money in the first place. Yet if you allow money, isn't capitalism inevitable? I wish the bugger hadn't croaked before he finished *Capital.*"

"I've always found it better to have money than not," Lily said. "If you could make everybody rich, instead of poor, you'd be a smash."

Why is she so chippy? Esselwein's back. She should be happy. What's eating her? Creeping civilization? A creep? He came in this morning, a manicured man in a dark suit and homburg, one of those men whose crisp, white shirt collar cuts into the flushed flesh of his neck, a close-shaven neck that smells of musk and money. Lily used to see Dr. McDougald in Ottawa, coming and going from the Rideau Club, a shark cruising the political shoals, showing a lot of teeth. The Doctor's teeth are large and yellow and even. If he is a medical doctor, which Lily doubts, she has him pegged as an abortionist.

Tell Willie I'm not pregnant, she was tempted to say, but it turned out the Doctor's business was with her brother Jack. Lily's heart sank. The only people who had business with Jack Coolican these days were lawyers and sheriffs and bailiffs armed with writs and summonses and bills. Harry Oakes had the Rainbow Mine so strangled with legal red tape Lily doubted it would ever open again. There they were, Jack holed up on the east side of town, Harry on the west. A stand-off. As Esselwein says, why be rich if you have to live in jail?

"I'm looking for a good mining man," says the Doctor, pulling a chair up to Jack's desk.

"You're lookin' in the wrong place. I'm bust."

"You've worked hard for this mine, Mr. Coolican. Perhaps too hard.

Take me, for instance. Would you believe that I am a partner in six mines, not to mention three railroads, a canal and a hydroelectric company? Look at my hands. Clean, are they not? All they touch is paper. After all, what is a mine, Mr. Coolican, but paper? Shares. Certificates. Paper that is worth exactly what someone is willing to pay for it. Have a cigar?"

"Sure. Well, my paper's worth exactly zero."

"At the moment. But who can say for certain what lies five thousand feet below us? Is it rock, or gold? You do not know yourself. No one knows."

"Ask Harry. He'll tell you I'm sittin' on a pile of crap. Harry oughta know, eh? He's a millionaire."

"Exactly, Mr. Coolican. Let's say you were to find a new partner, a prominent member of the financial world, someone with experience in the mining field — myself, for instance. And let's say an expert geologist were to confirm our own belief in the great potential of the Rainbow Mine, and let's suppose that we have on our board of directors an illustrious member of the Dominion government, a minister whole-heartedly devoted to developing the untapped riches of Canada's great northland...."

"Yeah. I get it. What if it's just rock?"

"A paper mine makes paper money, Mr. Coolican. I find it more negotiable than gold."

The Great Northern Ontario Mining and Exploration Co., GNOME, is incorporated the following week, with the Doctor as chairman of the board. The board contains several prominent lawyers, among them Sir Alan Aylesworth, and Peter Larkin, of Salada Tea. The Doctor had tried unsuccessfully to interest the leader of the Liberal Party, Mr. King.

"Mr. King, alas, is a poor man," the Doctor confides. "He told me he had not sufficient income to make even a small investment. Therefore, I have subscribed ten thousand shares in his name, as a personal gift."

GNOME's technical advisor is the famous prospector, sportsman and millionaire, the founding father of Kirkland Lake and personal friend of the Prince of Wales, John Rudolphus Coolican, Esq. The Prince himself is understood to be an investor. "I have every confidence that the future of northern Ontario will be a brilliant one," said the Prince from Buckingham Palace.

Stock in the Rainbow Mine rises from two cents a share to twenty, then to a dollar. Wild speculation on the Toronto mining exchange is fueled by a rumour that Jack Coolican is the bastard son of Canada's richest man, the Ottawa lumber king, J.R. Booth.

"You can't say that," Lily complains. "You're insulting Mum."

"Who cares? Mum doesn't exist."

It's true. Christina Coolican has disappeared. Mr. Legion has come to stay. At first it was a matter of convenience. Almost everybody in Kirkland Lake wears pants. Lily was puzzled, too, how to explain her mother's sudden presence, and fearful that if the theft of Houdini's clothes were discovered, Mum would be sent back to the bin. So Lily added a second storey to the shack for herself, and Mr. Legion settled into the back room.

He was quite delighted to be born again. He thought at first he had landed in a religious community, since everyone was speaking in tongues.

"They're just foreigners, Mum," Lily explained.

"Is that like Baptists?" Christina Coolican was a Methodist.

"No. Really, they're Reds."

They all looked pretty white to her, but then the black man on the train who brought Lily copies of *Vogue* was called Snow. What was happening to English? The war had blown the language up, sentences scattered every which way, grammar wiped out, whole vocabularies exterminated, words made short and sharp, like shrapnel. People fired them at each other *ratatattatratatattat* until they had to stop to reload.

Mr. Legion put Houdini's clothes away carefully, knowing Houdini would be back for them some day. Mr. Legion bought a very nice blue suit from Eaton's and opened a school. Christina Coolican had taught school, as a girl, in the Valley. She'd been fired when she got married. That wouldn't happen again. Mr. Legion's school was for adults, twenty during the day, forty at night. No one minded learning from the Bible except Esselwein, and his English could certainly stand improvement. Mr. Legion offered him a choice: the story of David and Goliath, or The Three Little Pigs. He capitulated. They became friends.

Mr. Legion is becoming famous. News of his amazing prediction at the Liberal convention has spread throughout spiritualist circles across Canada, and every week he receives requests for forecasts, dream interpretations, and messages from the Great Beyond. The letters enclose photographs, bits of hair and clothing, jewellery, tea leaves and

money, always money, with a stern request to forward the results by
return mail, if you please. Even the new governor-general, Lord Byng of
Vimy, is a firm believer in phrenology, and has sent a request, through
an aide, to have his head read.

Mr. Legion finds it all baffling. He is not a gypsy. He does not tilt
tables, blow trumpets or fly through the air. The spirits speak to him
unbidden and unpaid. He is horrified by persistent demands that he
"materialize" some poor, dead soul, when his only purpose is to spiritu-
alize the material.

"People get it all backwards," he complains. "It's that damn fool,
Freud."

Freud is certainly an unhealthy influence on Mr. Legion's most
frequent correspondent, Willie King, who has taken to writing out his
dreams at impossible length and mailing them up to Kirkland Lake for
interpretation, including, at even greater length, his own interpretation,
which is invariably wrong. Willie's dreams, as far as Mr. Legion can
make out, are utterly insignificant. He has told him so, but now Willie
stays stubbornly in bed for days on end, busily dreaming, and receives
important visitors in his pyjamas. Freud drives people nuts.

While Mr. Legion searches for Willie's soul, Willie entrusts his body
to the Doctor. A year ago, Doctor McDougald introduced himself to
Mr. King after a political meeting. He immediately diagnosed Mr. King
as the next prime minister and wrote a prescription for $50,000. Willie
perked right up. The Doctor takes care that Mr. King's delicate nerves
are not frazzled by financial worries, paying the most troublesome bills
himself, and sees to it that Mr. King gets enough rest by including him
on his frequent trips to the Adirondacks and Atlantic City, where the
whores are capable and discreet. He introduces Mr. King everywhere as
"Canada's next prime minister."

"Like yourself, Mr. King," the Doctor says with a wave of his cigar,
"I am interested only in doing good. I ask for nothing in return." At this
point, Willie King certainly has nothing to give, so when the Doctor
suggests that the ideal Liberal candidate for Temiskaming, in fact the
only acceptable candidate, is his friend and business partner, John
Rudolphus Coolican, Willie feels he has no choice but to agree,
although personally he considers Jack Coolican a thug. However, the
Doctor points out, touching on Mr. King's soft spot, Jack Coolican is
very popular with the working men — without actually being one,

another point in his favour. And while his personal habits may be considered a little rough by Ottawa standards, they are just the right thing in the north. Jack Coolican's personality, polished by the Doctor's money, will make Temiskaming a safe Liberal seat for years, and Willie King knows, after ten years in the political wilderness, that a seat of any kind is not to be sneezed at.

"Jeez, do I have to make a speech?" says Jack, appalled at the prospect of having to spend months in Ottawa with a bunch of bums and queers. He is assured that most members of parliament never speak in the House from one year's end to the next, and in fact some are so obscure, so completely invisible, that Mr. King has great difficulty remembering their names. As MP for Temiskaming, Jack's sole task will be to vote with the party, get re-elected and further the noble cause of Liberalism, starting with a $1,000 donation towards the personal expenses of the party leader. In return, should the Liberals form the government, he can expect a most enthusiastic interest in the development of the north and the prosperity of GNOME.

Jack buys a dark suit with a black homburg. He smokes cigars and walks in the slow, deliberate way that gives the Doctor such an air of authority. He gets his hair cut in Toronto (he stops short at cologne), and has his shoes shined every morning. He drinks his whiskey with ice, in a glass. He buys a big McLaughlin Buick and has it shipped in on the train, cruising solemnly up and down Government Road, which is only two miles long, from the Ashcan Hotel on the west, to the Pharmacy and Poolroom on the east, and buys drinks for everyone along the way.

Lily laughs at him, but Jack looks so pleased with himself she hasn't the heart to criticize. It's the first chance he's had to dress up and show off since he quit hockey. At least he doesn't come home covered with blood. (Willie can't stand the sight of blood.) Knocked-about now, beaten-up, Jack is handsomer than he was as a kid, a man with a past, and the brooding, black Irish melancholy that drives women wild. (Why doesn't it drive men wild? She'd like to know that. It scares the shit out of them.) Jack slips into the role of politician as gracefully as he had once stepped onto the ice, stickhandling with the audacity and good humour that had made him the star of the Silver Kings, cocky, rude, irresistible. Lily hangs his portrait up next to the picture of Himself which the Prince of Wales sent last Christmas. They are not unalike — men who exist only in the public eye, although Jack, she knows, is smarter than he seems, whereas the Prince, she suspects, is not. Does he too enjoy dressing up, and in what?

On June 10, 1921, John Rudolphus Coolican Esq. is nominated, unopposed, as the Liberal candidate for Temiskaming. An election is only a matter of time. Lily feels Willie's hot hand on her arm and his hot breath on her neck. He has her surrounded. Mum first, now Jack. It's only a matter of time. She begins to toy with the idea of being a prime minister's wife.

7

Just after midnight, Esselwein is standing outside a barn in Guelph. He can't believe it. He must have taken a wrong turn. Is the Communist Party of Canada going to be founded in a barn? A *barn*? Esselwein hates barns. He hates horses, and stinky straw, and shovelling shit. Did Marx hang out in barns? Lenin? Not on your life. Marx had the British Museum, Lenin the Finland Station and the Winter Palace, classy places, for crying out loud. But he, Esselwein, has Fred Farley's barn in Guelph, Ontario, Canada. *Oi.*

He's not supposed to know Fred Farley's name. It's a secret, like everything else about the Party, except the kid who'd driven him out in a wagon an hour ago had said: "This here's the Farley place. Fred'll be in bed, I bet. He expectin' you?" As if it wasn't suspicious enough skulking around the countryside in the middle of the night, every dog for miles around yapping its fool head off and lights going on in the houses. Might as well post a sign: Subversives Meeting. Straight Ahead, 500 Yards. Visitors Welcome.

Whose idea was this? Spector's probably. He reads too many books. Why do something easy, when you can make it hard? Two days ago, Esselwein had received word to check into a flophouse behind the railway station in Toronto. There, pinned to the pillow, he found his first instructions: buy a pair of overalls and a straw hat (he was already wearing overalls), wrap his clothes in a copy of the *Star*, and ask the ice-cream vendor on the south-east corner of Front Street and Spadina for a maple walnut cone. "Nuts to you," said Esselwein when the *babushka* handed him the cone. She told him to take the train to Kitchener (where was Kitchener?), wrap the clothes in the Kitchener

Record, and go to the farmers' market, where a boy with a dray would meet him behind the strawberries.

So here he is in a haystack. Big deal. What next? A crack of light appears in the side of the barn. A door opens. A thin, ascetic figure creeps cautiously towards the haystack.

"Nuts to you, numbskull!" Esselwein calls out.

"Shhhhh!" Spector grabs his arm fiercely and pulls him inside.

"Shazam!" cries Esselwein, sticking his head up into the loft where the others are seated around a single oil lantern. "Where's my trowel and apron?"

"This is not a time for levity," scowls Macdonald, the chairman. "We could all be arrested."

Levity is one of Esselwein's weaknesses. Marx never had much sense of humour (unless the whole thing is one huge joke). Esselwein also suffers from spontaneity. The Kirkland Lake revolution had been a spontaneous uprising. Lenin has criticized spontaneity as an "infantile disorder." Esselwein therefore is infantile and his Kirkland Lake action disorderly.

"But I proved *it can be done!*" says Esselwein.

"Do it right next time," says Macdonald.

"But I did it right! The trouble is, what do you do *after the revolution?* Look at Russia, it's a mess!"

Esselwein is always shooting his mouth off. He disrupts meetings with his infantile questions and insists on impossible explanations. The problem of Esselwein's spontaneity has been discussed with him by Macdonald. There is nothing wrong with his revolutionary spirit. The trouble is, he's a little *too* revolutionary. Rather than rushing to the barricades, Esselwein should content himself with quiet study, like Spector, the student at the University of Toronto, who reads aloud from *Capital* with the reverence of a Hebrew scholar consulting the Talmud and makes even the thorniest concept seem self-evident. Macdonald, for instance, had trouble getting his mind around the idea of democratic centralism until Spector explained that it simply meant democracy refined to its point of greatest efficiency, the power of the masses concentrated in the hands of those most able to wield it, the party leaders. Macdonald senses something vaguely amiss with this explanation but he can't quite put his finger on it.

"Sit down, please, comrade," Macdonald says. "We are discussing the peasant question."

"Is that why we're meeting in this stinking barn?"

Levity again. *Oi.* Will he never learn? Esselwein sits down contritely next to Popowich, the Ukrainian delegate from Winnipeg. Most of the sixteen faces around the lantern are familiar to him. He recruited the two Finns himself. The others he's seen at various meetings. A mixed bag, Scots, Jews, Slavs, a critical, sharp-tempered bunch, odd-men-out, displaced persons like himself, honest and good-hearted for the most part, but not the kind of guys to set the world on fire. That's where he comes in.

For all his faults, Esselwein is here because in the last two years the story of the Kirkland Lake Soviet has spread through every mining camp from coast to coast, embellished a little with each telling, so that now, with miners everywhere caged like wild beasts, his little revolution shines like a star in the night sky — a triumph, not a farce — and the Russian Kid himself is as famous as the Prince of Wales. (In some versions of the story he *is* the Prince of Wales, and is carried off into the sunset by a giant goose/pelican/albatross, depending on the story-teller's fancy.) From Glace Bay to the Crow's Nest Pass, hundreds of miners have flocked into the union and joined one of a dozen socialist sects. "Where's the Party?" they ask. And that's why the Party is here, in this stinking, stifling barn. Esselwein dips a cup in a pail of water by the door, takes a sip, and pours the rest over his head.

"Where are the peasants?" he says. "Let's hear from them."

"There aren't any," says Macdonald. "I mean, not here."

"Exactly what I say!" cries Popowich. "No peasant, only *kulak.* Thief! Robbing!"

"I believe you mean *'petit bourgeois,'* comrade," says Spector. "If you'll look here on page forty-seven, it says that anyone who owns property . . . ."

"But what if they don't really own their property?" asks Comrade Custance. "What if their debts are more than the land is worth? Then they're working for the creditor. That makes them proletarians."

"Or peasants," says Esselwein. "The question is, are they, or are they not, potatoes?"

"They can't be that dumb," says Macdonald. "The United Farmers have just elected a farmers' government in Alberta. One hundred per cent farmers. Class dictatorship. Trouble is, now the farmers say they don't like government at all. They want to give it back to the Liberals."

"Anarchism," says Spector.

"Fascism!" says Popowich.

"Idiocy," says Esselwein.

The peasant question debate rages the rest of the night. Since Canada has six million farmers, and only two million proletarians, Esselwein argues that he'd rather have the farmers with him than against him. Yet, in Russia, where the discrepancy in numbers is much greater, Lenin and Trotsky have declared war on the *kulaks* and peasant armies of the Ukraine. Down below, Fred Farley, the farmer, runs back and forth to the well, hoisting up pail after pail of cold water and bushel baskets of sandwiches. Comrade Bruce takes so many swigs from a pocket flask he becomes incoherent. This raises the Drink Question. Comrade Custance disapproves of drink. Esselwein argues, given prohibition, that drinking is a political act designed to undermine the moral and economic fibre of the state. It certainly seems to be working. It's hard to imagine a state more incoherent than Canada.

"Smash the system!" cries Esselwein, taking a big swig from Bruce's flask. "Give me a hundred flying boats and the country'll be ours!" He leans his head against Popowich's shoulder and falls fast asleep.

The meeting goes on all the next day and into the night. Agit-prop. Education. Membership. Finances. Constitution. "We sound like the Ladies' Aid at St. Peter's Anglican Church," says Esselwein. His remark does not improve Macdonald's temper. Macdonald is a lapsed Presbyterian with a secret conviction that communism is just the kirk without God. Then there's the question of the violent overthrow of the state. Isn't that a little extreme? This, after all, is Canada. "But it says right here, in the *Manifesto*, on page six . . . ." screams Spector. Okay. Violence it will be, then. What about the clandestine question? Will the Communist Party be above ground, or under? Legal or illegal? Spector, needless to say, argues for secrecy. "I went to a lot of trouble to find this barn," he says huffily. "We could have met at the corner of Bloor and Yonge."

"Good idea," says Esselwein. "We'd have made the *Star.*"

"We all be deported," says Popowich.

"But how can we bring people into the party if nobody knows who we are?"

"We don't want the masses to actually *join,*" says Spector. "That's much too unwieldy. We simply want to direct them."

"We can't behave like criminals," says Macdonald.

"But we *are* criminals!" cries Spector jubilantly.

Macdonald feels a little frightened. Why all these complications? Isn't communism simple common sense? It's as plain as the nose on your face. Spread the word and the revolution will be inevitable. Why sneak about? Why worry people with talk of war and bloodshed before they know which side they're on? Macdonald feels he's been caught up in a revolving door and flung out into an unexpected, unpleasant place.

"Do you know what's wrong with you Jews?" he shouts. "You cause too much trouble!"

Spector is shocked into silence. Esselwein is asleep. He is dreaming about the Sex Question. What would Marx have made of a long-legged *shiksa*....Oh, how Lily hates that word! "Babe" didn't go down too good either. What do you call a lady these days? Lady? Let me call you sweetheart. He'll try that when he gets home.

Two days later, Superintendent Roland Smythe of the Intelligence Division, Royal Canadian Mounted Police, receives on his desk a neatly typed report freshly translated from code:

Sir:

I have the honour to report that on June 12 to June 14, 1921, I attended the founding meeting of the Communist Party of Canada in a barn belonging to Fred Farley, farmer, R.R.I, Guelph, Ontario, as a delegate representing the northern Ontario mining camps.

Present were the following: Bill Moriarty, English labourer; Maurice Spector, Jew student; Jack Macdonald, Scot pattern maker; Florence Custance, English teacher; Tom Bell, Irish (criminal record); Trevor McGuire, Canadian veteran; Mike Buhay, Polish tailor; Alex Gauld, Montreal steamfitter; Jack Margolese, Jew tailor; John Boychuk, Ukrainian tailor; Malcolm Bruce, Canadian, builder; John Ahlgvist, Finn tailor; John Latva, Finn carpenter; Mathew Popowich, Ukrainian; John Navis, Ukrainian printer (both Winnipeg); Jacob Penner, Winnipeg baker; myself.

A draft constitution was agreed to and adopted unanimously. The Party will seek affiliation with the Third International of the Communist Party and will publish a newspaper, *The Communist,* when sufficient money is found.

The Communist Party is a secret organization. It will be organized as a series of cells, none of which will know of the existence of the others. The majority of supporters are foreigners. Support is particularly strong among the miners and garment workers, the Finnish, Ukrainian and Jewish national societies. The leaders, except for Spector, are British immigrants. The Party is designed on the Russian Soviet model and dedicated to the following principles:

1. The violent overthrow of the government of Canada.
2. The dictatorship of the proletariat.

The Party's program is as follows:

1. The forcible seizure of the government.
2. The complete destruction of all capitalist institutions and the substitution of Workers,' Peasants' and Soldiers' councils as governing authority.
3. Abolition of the Canadian army, disarming of police and army officers, arming of the workers and the establishment of a Red Guard.
4. Abolition of all law courts in favour of revolutionary tribunals.
5. The confiscation of all private property without compensation, including factories, mines, mills, railroads, and real estate, all property to be turned over to the working class.
6. The confiscation of all bank accounts (excluding workers') and the nationalization of banks.
7. Handing over farm land to poor farmers and farm workers.

General remarks:

The party leaders are dedicated Reds. Their devotion to secrecy indicates criminal intent. They have broad support among the Jews and foreign classes and have made inroads among the returned soldiers. There are some Party men among the radical farmers and many in the labour unions.

Party H.Q. will be Bill Moriarty's house, 155 Beverly St. (corner Grange Road), Toronto. Copies of minutes, directives etc. to follow.

I have the honour to be, Sir,
Your obedient servant,
John Leopold, Cpl.

8

SIX MONTHS LATER:

So many people are packed into Esselwein's shack that the walls are literally bulging. Lily can barely breathe. If they all inhale together they'll explode outwards like a firecracker. Esselwein's shack is Liberal Party headquartes for Temiskaming. Tonight's the night. The smell of victory mingles with wet wool, wood smoke and cheap booze.

Lily was astonished when Esselwein volunteered to run Jack's election campagin. It must have been the Liberal Party colour, red. As far as Esselwein was concerned, the more red ribbons and red bunting flying around Temiskaming, the better. Besides, Willie had made an impression during his brief visit to Kirkland Lake. The sight of Willie King standing precariously in the bow of a flying boat, leather helmet on his head and goggles around his neck, evoked an image of John the Baptist on the shores of the Dead Sea. "Beware of Baptists," Mr. Legion had muttered, but Willie made quite a passionate little speech, and promised the wholehearted support of the Liberal Party to the noble cause of the working man.

The working man has not forgotten. Just after eleven p.m. John Rudolphus Coolican is declared elected Member of Parliament for Temiskaming by a majority of more than one thousand votes over the Conservative candidate, Colonel Bullitt of Haileybury, who was followed everywhere during the campaign by flying squads of off-shift miners crying "Bullshit! Bullshit!" One question remains: will the new Liberal MP for Temiskaming be in the government, or out? Esselwein will be the first to know.

He hunches over the Monster, gently twiddling knobs. The Monster is twice as big as it used to be, and glows in the dark. Esselwein's shack is

so festooned with aerials it looks like a birdcage. He has even managed
to connect an aerial secretly to the Alamo's copper roof, and now the
Monster talks in several different voices, although only in English.
Mostly it plays dance music, but on Sundays it preaches and from time
to time it reads the news, new news, not the warmed-over stuff you get in
the newspapers, but news that even the station agent in Swastika doesn't
know yet. Everyone has heard the Monster speak, or sing, but no one
can quite figure out how it works. People have hidden under the table
while it sang, but found no one there. The shack and the scrub outside
have been searched in vain for gramophones, telephones and micro-
phones. Esselwein himself has been locked up in jail while the box was
speaking. Still it spoke. He has taken it apart and put it together again,
explaining how it works by electricity, voices travelling through the air,
like lightning.

"Yah, but lightning don't say 'Good evening,'" complained Mrs.
Dzuba.

Although the Bible has not prepared him for saxophones, Mr. Legion
is convinced the voices come from Heaven.

"No," says Esselwein, "mostly Pittsburgh."

Tonight Esselwein is frantically trying to get CFCA, the Toronto *Star*
station, but no matter how he twiddles and coaxes, the Monster only
makes rude noises.,

"Willie will win," Mr. Legion says confidently, having tuned in some
time ago to Willie's exuberant Mother. And sure enough, just after one
a.m. when the returns from British Columbia come in, Willie does,
more or less.

I HAVE WONWONWONWONWONWONWONWONWONWONWONWON-
WONWON! OH LUCKY ME! ME ME ME ME MEMEMEMEME!

I must get a grip on myself.

The truth is, while we have twice as many seats as any other one party,
we are still two short of a clear majority. Oh, those wretched Progs! Not
a seat in Saskatchewan! Alberta a wasteland, horrid farmers everywhere, narrow, selfish men who care only for their class, no sense at all
of the larger vision, spoiling it for everyone. At least in my own seat of
North York I trounced the Progressive candidate by some two thousand
votes, showing that ignorant sectarianism is no match for true Liberal-

ism. They will see when I'm prime minister... ah, prime minister!
... that they cannot hold me up to ransom demanding this and that in
return for their votes. Where would that lead us? Chaos!

No, if there's an injustice in the tariff, or in some other area of federal
jurisdiction, I shall endeavour to right it, but if the grievance is against
the CPR, or the Massey-Harris machinery company, or the banks, then I
shall make it plain that they will have to deal directly with these
companies, that the government represents the interests of the manufac-
turers as well as the farmers and will not be used as a scapegoat for
problems they have largely brought down on their own heads by wilful
ignorance, mismanagement and lack of effort. If the Bank of Commerce is gouging the farmers, let them deal with the Bank of Commerce!
I shall show it no quarter. It has been no friend to me, or to the Liberal
Party, a hotbed of Toryism through and through, the Bank of Montreal
no better. The Royal Bank is quite another story, a pillar of strength, a
truly Liberal bank with the people's interests at heart, Mr. Neil, the
president, as kind and gentle a man as one would wish to meet, the very
soul of generosity. His support in this campaign has made the difference
between success and failure in a number of constituencies.

How blessed I am with friends! Only two years ago I was wandering
alone, the untried leader of a defeated party, a young man of modest
means living in rented rooms, a pariah, and here I am today... Prime
Minister... occupying the post of highest honour and influence in the
Dominion of Canada, advisor to the King, confidant of the Governor-
General, consultant to the Rockefeller Foundation and personal friend
of Mr. John D. Rockefeller Jr., heir to Sir Wilfrid Laurier's splendid
house, a guest in the nation's most beautiful homes, sought after by the
nation's most successful men. Surely the hand of God can be seen at
work here! I have fought the good fight, kept the faith, remained true to
my ideal — the cause of the common man — and by my example have
drawn others to follow me, to choose the hard path of sacrifice.

I have promised nothing, other than the assurance that our friends in
this campaign will be remembered. All are unselfish in their devotion to
the common cause, modest and unassuming in their personal demands.
Nevertheless, as soon as I am called upon to form a government... ah,
Prime Minister!... I intend to see to it that their contribution receives
the recognition it deserves. Peter Larkin will get London. There is not a
man in the country who can bring greater dignity to the post of High

Commissioner. To the good Doctor I shall offer the Senate. It is an honour, and a small financial recompense, yet I am half afraid he may shrink from the burden. Had he not already lifted the weight of so many social and financial obligations from my shoulders, I am sure I should have quite broken down during the campaign.

I must guard against making mistakes through carelessness or negligence. One can never be too careful in public life. Subtle as the serpent and meek as the dove, that's the ticket. One false step, one unguarded moment, a slip of the tongue . . . . Dr. Freud has been a great help in this regard, although he is a Jew and too much a materialist to be of genuine value in the long run. One must choose the spiritual.

I must take myself in hand, make a fresh start, not allow my passions to get the better of me. I get alarmed at times at my ignorance of *everything*. I wish I understood more about finance. I am not as well read as I ought to be on international questions. I have wasted precious hours in sloth and indifference, indulging myself in selfish pleasures, allowing my mind to become morbid and introspective when I should have been preparing myself for the great task ahead. The secret is to get sufficient rest, keep in good physical trim and keep my conscience free of offence towards God. There is a need for *constant watchfulness.* If only I were happily married! My life would be a song.

By coincidence, the very first telegram tonight came from Temiskaming. It was from C reporting her brother's victory and predicting a Liberal government *a full hour* before we had confirmation ourselves by wire. She had the number of Liberal seats, 117, exactly right, and she said the news had come by electrical currents! This confirms *exactly* my own experience of Mother's presence, a sort of tingling and crackling in the air and a very bright, white light. I had left on my table Gladstone's *Life*, by Morley, with mother's picture in the chapter on the Prime Minister. It is where the book lies open on her lap in the Forster portrait. This was her secret and mine. Surely this message about my victory was her way of telling me she was nearby! It is almost miraculous!

I can see that this election is a great political earthquake that has toppled the Tory citadel to the ground. It will be mine to link Liberals, farmers and labour to form a truly progressive party in Canadian affairs. It will be mine. Mine mine *mine*! And Mother's. Dear, dear Mother.

At four a.m., after everyone has gone home, Lily and Esselwein make love beneath her chinchilla coat. It is nice and warm. So's Esselwein. Soft, too. (What is it about fat men?) When they wake up the next afternoon, a blizzard is blowing. They stay in bed for two days. From time to time Lily gets hungry, and thinks she should get up, but she can't bear not to touch him, so she stays. On the third day the sky is blue and the rocks of Kirkland Lake are as round and white as Esselwein's ass. Lily borrows the lid to his wash boiler and slides down Prospect Avenue all the way home.

9

Three weeks later, Lily received her invitation to attend the opening of Parliament in March as the guest of the Prime Minister. (God, he really *is* Prime Minister!) The following day, the Monster announced the appointment of J. Rudolphus Coolican, MP for Temiskaming, as Minister of the Interior, Mines and Indians.

"I know mining, and Indians are okay," said the Hon. Mr. Coolican. "But where the fuck's the Interior?"

Lily remembered that the Interior used to be way out west, but it had been turned into Alberta and Saskatchewan a long time ago. Inquiries by the Doctor revealed that the Interior was now the Exterior, a vast, Arctic wasteland inhabited, as far as anyone knew, by Eskimos, Mounted Police and the crazy explorer, Vilhjalmur Stefansson.

"If he stays up there, he can't make trouble," said the Hon. Mr. Coolican.

The Indians wouldn't be any trouble either. Mr. Coolican was assured by his Deputy Minister of Indian Affairs, the famous nature poet Duncan Campbell Scott, that within forty years there wouldn't be an Indian left in Canada.

"But they breed like rabbits!" said the Hon. Mr. Coolican.

"And die like flies," shrugged Mr. Scott.

Jack's little joke, that if the Indians disappeared, the poets would be out of work, sent Mr. Scott to complain in person to the Prime Minister. But Mr. King simply looked puzzled, and said that in forty years Mr. Scott would be well past the pensionable age, and comfortably provided for, and something else could surely be found for the poets, and if Mr. Coolican were somewhat uncouth, well, so was the Interior, not to mention the Indians, and Mr. King had been hard pressed, in fact fairly distraught, to find an Irish member for his cabinet who was not under the thumb of Rome, and could not Mr. Scott appreciate the grave difficulties the Prime Minister faced in trying to reconcile all the regions and factions in the country?

"A poet is better than nothing," said Jack. "Everybody else's been sacked."

Within a month of taking office, Willie King, who couldn't bear to throw out as much as a Christmas card, had dumped clerks, typists, deputy ministers, janitors and elevator operators out in the snow on Wellington Street, replacing them, in his own words, "with the most efficient, dedicated and impartially-selected public service in our nation's history."

Miss Coutu, the helpless, harelip companion of Lady Laurier's inherited by the Prime Minister, to his surprise, with Laurier House, was appointed Special Assistant to the Minister of the Interior, Mines and Indians.

"We can keep her in the back room," Jack said. "She don't even have to show up. It's a party job."

"But who's going to help you?" Lily asked. "What do you know about government? Laws? Parliamentary procedure?"

"Bugger all."

"Don't you think you need someone who does? Somebody who can read and write, to begin with. Smart. Educated. Somebody ambitious, who'll do all the work and give you the credit."

"That's smart?"

"You need Charlie."

"Charlie Whitton! You crazy? She's a Tory!"

"So were we, once. Remember?"

"Jeez. So, what's the difference, eh?"

Lily and Charlotte Whitton had grown up best friends in Renfrew before the war. Both had left at the same time, Lily to go to Ottawa, Charlie to Queen's University in Kingston. In her four years at Queen's, Charlotte Whitton won every trophy and scholarship imaginable and graduated with the gold medal in Arts. (All the smart men had enlisted, some people said.) She should have been the Rhodes scholar, but girls weren't allowed, so she applied for the job of archivist at the Public Archives in Ottawa. The head archivist, Dr. Doughty, summoned her for an interview. She had by far the best qualifications, he said, and on merit alone the job should be hers, but a returned soldier had also applied for the job, a university man who had given up his degree to fight for his country, and wouldn't it be the square thing to let him have the job?

Charlie said yes. She went into social work. She never forgave herself, or archivists, or men.

"When I'm prime minister, I'll kill the bastards," she shouted at Lily on the phone.

"Look, Charlie, it's a very small job, just a secretary, really, but it's a foot in the door, you may have to write some speeches...."

"Hooray!"

"And deliver them too, for all I know."

"Do you think they'll let me?"

"Remember, they're Grits."

"Shits?"

"You can't go on and on about our beloved King and Queen...."

"Is King queer?"

"No!"

"How do you know?"

Apart from her gorgeous girlfriend, Margaret ("Behind every great woman," Charlie says, "there's a woman"), Charlie's passion was politics. She and Ottawa fell in love. Even Willie King was moved when Charlie kissed the cornerstone of the Peace Tower, laid by the Prince of Wales two years before, as if it had been the Prince himself. Charlie's instinctive theatricality suited her for life in Ottawa, where everything was done for show. She was plain, and therefore attractive to women, honest, funny, and she possessed an apparently inexhaustible supply of dirty jokes. Charlie had decided very early in life to be a man, and had learned these jokes as part of what she conceived to be her masculine armament, along with her cropped hair, tailored suits, flat shoes, terrible temper and a command of profanity that equalled her new boss's. Charlie's dirty stories, told in her loud, rough voice, created a sensation, and in a matter of days the new secretary in Interior, Mines & Indians was the talk of Parliament Hill.

Charlie made the Ministry a model of efficiency. She hung a map of the Interior on the wall, so everyone would know where it was, and put Miss Coutu to work counting the Indians, a task she performed with alacrity, coming up with a total of 195,026.03. There were a lot more

Indians than anyone had thought. Charlie discovered that the Indians were not disappearing as Mr. Scott maintained through some inevitable process of evolution, but because of TB, syphilis and starvation, and because the government was bribing them to give up their Indian status. When the Hon. Mr. Coolican asked the Prime Minister to build hospitals on Indian reserves, Mr. King looked puzzled. "But Indians don't vote," he said. Mr. Scott, whose beautiful poems about dying Indians had made him famous, said they were better off dead.

"Whoever runs this country," Charlie said, "it's the same old balls-up."

It sure as hell was. What had gotten into Willie? His cabinet was the same bunch of bums he'd sworn to get rid of! Honesty had never been Willie's strong point. It wasn't that he told deliberate lies, only that the truth was whatever suited him best at the time. Nobody expected Willie to be honest, but everyone, *everyone* expected him to be radical, or at least *liberal*. Reform. Progress. Enlightenment. He'd preached nothing else for twenty years! Where was it now? Had Willie's whole ideology, his *career* simply vanished into the cold, white interior of his soul? Was Willie screwing up *from the very beginning?*

The first week of March, Lily went to Toronto to shop. She had to admit she looked pretty "bushed." Flannel shirts and gumboots might be okay for an *aparatchik*, and she was almost a Communist ("Why not?" said Esselwein), but a little *outré* for a state dinner. (Did the Russians have state dinners? In gumboots?) At The Room, in Simpson's, she was taken aback to find she was expected to look like a sausage, but the salesgirl assured her that waists were "out" and taupe was "in" and the whole look would come together once she had her hair bobbed and her cheeks rouged. Lily resisted a finger wave, not wanting to overdo the sausage effect, and settled for a Chinese pageboy à la Louise Brooks. Four hours and $2,000 later, she headed back to the King Edward Hotel feeling like a Shanghai streetwalker.

Nobody noticed. Money was floating out of one of the hotel's upstairs windows. In front of the hotel, a mob of men was blocking King Street, everyone gawking up, mouths open, arms raised, bellowing and surging this way and that as the bills fluttered here and there on the wind.

"Hundred dollar bills! Hundred dollar bills!" screamed the man beside her, waving his arms. "C'm 'ere! C'm 'ere!" The mob moaned as the bills settled out of reach on cornices or drifted away over the rooftops. A streetcar clanged its bell impatiently. In the distance Lily could hear the faint wail of sirens.

"Jack, you're causing a riot out there!" Lily pulled him in and slammed the window.

"Who're you?" he said. swaying on his feet. He stared at her glassily. "Wanna fuck?"

Lily's room in the Shadow is filled with flowers. They're all from Willie. It smells like a funeral. A good omen, or bad?

He sends his car for her. It's a very big, black Buick. Willie never used to have a car. Sir Wilfrid Laurier always took the streetcar. She feels like a fool in evening dress at eleven o'clock in the morning. The wheels of the car spin and slide in the slush. Ottawa is grey. Grey sky, snow, stone, people. Shabby men crowd the sidewalks. They stare at the car with baleful eyes and spit in the gutter.

"Is there a strike?" she asks the driver.

"No, miss. It's always like this, now."

Laurier House is full of important people all dressed up and feeling foolish. Nothing has changed. Lily feels she hasn't been away from Ottawa more than ten minutes. She looks around anxiously for Mrs. Freiman. Where can she be? The Freimans never miss an opening of Parliament or a do with the Governor-General. Lily feels a little lonely, and somewhat conspicuous in her Schiaparelli. She'd forgotten that Ottawa women never wear "imports." Now that Denison Couture is closed, and dear Flora dead, it is obvious they are in very deep trouble.

Just after noon, more than half-an-hour late, Willie comes downstairs. He's wearing his Windsor uniform, purchased in 1908, when he was forty pounds lighter. How did he ever get into it? White silk stockings, velvet breeches, a tricorn hat, gold braid strewn about like spaghetti: Willie looks like Fatty Arbuckle playing Bonnie Bobby Shafto. His face is red, and very unhappy.

"You have nice legs," Lily whispers, trying to cheer him up. Willie scowls at her.

Later, in the Senate chamber, watching Willie seated at the foot of the throne as Lord Byng stumbles through his speech, Lily marvels at the cunning of the English kings who humiliate their prime ministers, *on their own ground,* by making them dress in servants' livery. She will tell Willie never to wear it again.

(He won't, and this small revolution, the cause of anguished correspondence with the Colonial Office, will be Canada's first message to the King that the Empire is, indeed, dead.)

In the drawing room, as Lily feared, Lady Byng, resembling even more an obscene parrot, is waiting for her.

"Awk! A familiar face at last!" Memsahib places a talon on Lily's wrist. That touch, and the scent of spring violets on Memsahib's gown, brings back in a rush the most painful week of Lily's life, four years before, in London with Talbot during the war. Before Vimy, before Passchendaele, before before before before.

"Splendid young chap," says Memsahib, giving Lily's arm a little pinch. "Heroic death, I'm sure. Now, come and give me all the gossip."

Lily is led away. Cross Memsahib at your peril. "Memsahib" is Lady Byng's own choice, a souvenir of her salad days as an army wife in India, and it is characteristic of her serene obtuseness that it never occurs to her that generals and cabinet ministers, not to mention friends, might resent being treated like houseboys. For Memsahib, to speak is to insult. She radiates rudeness like x-rays. Yet, in spite of snubs and shrieks and puzzling, increasing solitude, Memsahib retains a firm conviction that she is always, in every circumstance, right.

Memsahib's firmest conviction is that her husband, "dear old Bungo," is a *"naif"* of such innocence and unworldliness that he is constantly being put upon, or put down, by hordes of unscrupulous rivals. It is therefore her job, "the wily old Greek," as she calls herself, to fight off these vipers with the tactics, inherited on her mother's side, of an Athenian street pedlar. During the war, Memsahib's forays on his behalf created acute embarrassment for Bungo, an officer of unusual tact and discretion, and wrecked his career to such an extent that his popularity within the Canadian Corps was based on sincere compassion. Bungo banned all women from the front, in an effort to keep Memsahib at home, but she went tootling off here and there anyway, dispatching a barrage of telegrams to Vimy, or Cambrai, or wherever Bungo was fighting the war, ordering him to join her in Brussels, or Paris, or Boulogne, *immediately!!!!*

To send a British general to Canada now is risky; to send Memsahib is an act of war.

"Lord Byng and I are ideally suited for this position," Memsahib whispers at dinner to the Minister of Justice, Sir Lomer Gouin. "We both *detest* politics!"

Memsahib looks around in triumph, but Lord Byng is staring at his plate (as always) and the rest of the table is shrouded in a strange, cold fog. Memsahib breaks the silence herself.

"Politicians, I have always said, should be avoided, like the French."

Sir Lomer wipes the grease from his thick lips (not only French, but Creole!) and bows graciously over the lamb chop.

"And what fault, Madame, do you find with the French?"

"Why, they'll rob you blind!"

"In Canada," Sir Lomer smiles, "we say that about the Jews."

Everyone laughs.

Cigars and port arrive. Lily rises from the poisoned well with relief, only to find herself ambushed in the sitting room.

"What do you make of Mr. King?" Memsahib hisses in her most confiding way. "Bungo is *baffled.* Mr. King does not shoot, or fish. He does not golf! He does not play billiards or cards, nor does he smoke, or drink. Tell me, my dear, what does Mr. King *do*?"

He chases women, Lily is tempted to say.

"He reads a lot, and writes. He writes books."

"Awk! A new Disraeli!"

"Oh, no, not novels, books about...(what were Willie's books about?)...politics."

"Awk! Mussolini is a literary man too, did you know? You can tell by his head, simply bursting with brains! The resemblance *is* quite striking. Mr. King must have his head read. Bungo is a great believer in bumps."

Bungo is in the ballroom, getting quietly pissed. He looks just like the Nob. (Does Bungo write letters? Is he, too, a literary man?) The ballroom seems smaller and shabbier than Lily remembers it. She glances towards the window where she first saw Talbot standing in the sunlight, but it's dark now, and the drapes are closed. The lights have gone out, haven't they, not to be lit again. How prophetic that remark was! And how appropriate that the "barracks," as they called Rideau Hall during the war, should still be occupied by a famous British general, the ballroom a bivouac for his troops. Occupied Territory. But then, Ottawa has always been occupied, hasn't it?

Among the crowd of men in khaki, Lily recognizes Bill Herridge. His mother, poor, mad Marjorie, was Willie's first *affaire.* Does Bill know? It's Major Herridge now, MC, DSO, twice wounded, a hero. (Who'd have thought he had it in him?) It was Major Herridge who took Talbot's job on General Byng's staff after Talbot offered to return, or was ordered back, to the front. Talbot disliked General Byng. The feeling, apparently, was mutual. Lily wishes she'd brought her pistol. She would place it in Bungo's ear and pull the trigger. She wishes Esselwein were here.

"I'm practising law," says Bill, whirling her around the dance floor. "Bored out of my skull. Oh God, I miss the war!"

"Why don't you try politics?"

"That's what Bungo says. Organize the country along the lines of the Canadian Corps. The old fighting spirit, eh? Leadership, discipline, patriotism, that's all it takes, and balls, *balls!* Think what we could do, eh? Christ, look at Mussolini!"

Later, in the car, Lily says "I don't think civilians should be permitted to wear uniforms."

"My feeling exactly," says Willie. "Who is Mussolini?"

They sit up very late in front of the fire in Willie's study, a cosy little room at the very top of the house full of all his favourite, familiar things, the portrait of Mother by the window, as if she were looking out, the photographs and curios and little silver boxes arranged around the room, each in its proper place, the fire and a candle the only light in the room. Willie opens a bottle of brandy in honour of his first Throne Speech (What on earth had it said?), and they toast the Liberal Party, Jack, Mother and all the Dear Ones gone before, Grandfather, Sir Wilfrid, the King, Mr. Legion, and each other. Lily feels she should tell the truth about Mr. Legion, but her tongue is too fuzzy to get the words out and after a while it doesn't seem to matter. They laugh a lot and sometimes they sit for a while not saying anything, Willie's tongue being fuzzy too, just as comfortable with each other as they had been before, before, and Lily decides that she has been stupid to run away, and when she cries, he wipes the tears away with his fingers, his hand, for once, not cold, and she is determined that if he asks her to stay, she will.

But Nicol, the valet, comes to say the car is ready, and Willie sees her to the door.

When she returns the next morning, the telephone is ringing. Willie is shouting at McGregor, who's forgotten something, and the Movieola people arrive to take moving pictures and make Willie go outside without his scarf, and a water pipe bursts, making a big, brown stain on the ceiling exactly where it had been when the Lauriers lived here, and she accidentally knocks Lincoln's stupid plaster hand off the hall table and breaks a finger.

How could anyone who loves privacy as much as Willie live in this madhouse? The furniture makes it look like a railway station, or a museum, formal and unfamiliar, as if it belonged to someone else. In the drawing room, stiff chairs are set in a perfect semi-circle and Sèvres vases stand like spinsters in the corners. The dining room is a black hole of mahogany and ancestors.

"Who *are* all those gloomy people?" she asks.

"I haven't the faintest idea," Willie says.

"But where did all this stuff *come* from?"

"Um...Mr. Larkin...England, I believe, very reasonable prices ...auctions...Mr. Larkin...I make it a policy not to inquire too closely into party finances...so generous, Mr. Larkin."

"You mean it belongs to the party?"

"Oh, no! No! It is mine! *Mine.* I have made that very plain. It is the same with the house, it all belongs to me *personally*, as leader of the Liberal Party, not, as some may think, to the party leader, whoever he may be, in future."

"And now you have a house, you need a wife to put in it."

"Now that you mention...."

"Rex! Look what I've brought you!" A plump, pretty woman bursts in the front door, a bundle of pale brown fur under each arm.

"Look! Aren't they dears?" She deposits the two balls of fur on the floor. They scamper around Willie's ankles, yapping furiously. Willie stands stock still.

"They won't bite Rex. They're only pups." She scampers about after them, clapping her hands. There is something about her high-pitched laughter and girlish manner that remind Lily of a summer afternoon, years ago, at Kingsmere, and the way Willie's mother laughed, and clapped her hands, and pinned flowers in her hair, like Ophelia. This, however, is Mrs. Patteson, wife of Mr. Patteson, manager of the Bank of Montreal, old friends of Willie's from the Roxborough Apartments. How strange that she and Lily have not met before!

"Which one would you like, Rex?"

Willie stares at the scrapping puppies.

"They're brothers, you see, and I thought if we got one, and you got one, they could keep each other company on our walks."

No dogs in my house, Lily mutters to herself. Then she remembers it is not her house.

"I . . . I don't . . . ."

"Isn't he the cutest little fellow?" Mrs. Patteson scoops up a pup and puts it in Willie's hands. It shivers, looking up at him with bright, imploring eyes, and licks his thumb. Willie quickly puts it down again. It squats on the rug, a dark stain slowly spreading out underneath its tummy. Nicol, wearing a look of infinite disgust, is sent for a towel.

"He likes you, don't you sweetheart?" says Mrs. Patteson, scratching the pup behind the ears.

"What *is* he?" says Willie, looking dubious.

"Oh, they're both terriers, wire-hairs, Irish, from the same litter. What shall we call them, Rex?"

"How about Industry and Humanity?" Lily says sweetly. "Graft and Corruption? Chaos and Disorder?"

Willie gives her a stern look.

"Pat and Mike?" he says tentatively.

Or Sex and Rex, Lily thinks, wondering if Mrs. Patteson scratches Willie behind the ears too, and pats his head, woof woof.

"Look, he answers already!" One of the pups waddles over and nips Willie's sock.

"I'd like to keep the post office," Lily says as she puts on her coat.

"Post office?"

"It was a Conservative appointment . . . ."

"Oh. Yes. I pay no attention to pat . . . to constituency matters. The Doctor . . . Senator McDougald . . . mentioned someone, a Mr. Essel . . . ."

"Esselwein?"

"I have made no promises. I am sure something can be arranged. A Jew . . . ."

"Esselwein!"

" . . . won't do."

10

Jeepers, why was she so cheesed off? The post office was just a crappy little job, but it would have made a perfect cover.

"I thought we were supposed to share things," he complained.

"Sharing, Esselwein, isn't stealing."

"We share the movies."

"You just play the piano."

"You can't show the *Perils of Pauline* without a piano player. It doesn't make sense."

"*I* bought the projector."

"*I* sell the tickets. Don't complain, already, we're making a killing."

"All you ever talk about is money!"

"All you ever do is spend it!"

What sort of crazy communist argument was this? Lily was right. Esselwein knew he had an amazing talent for making money. He couldn't help it. If he bought a raffle ticket, he won the prize. If somebody dropped a nickel, Esselwein stepped on it. He sold his radios as fast as he could build them, for as much as he wanted to charge. Should he hire an apprentice? Open a shop? It was embarrassing. He was a born capitalist.

Esselwein figured the movies would be terrific propaganda. They were mostly about poor people who got screwed by the system, or who screwed it back. You didn't have to know English and you could laugh your head off. Wow, was he ever right! Charlie Chaplin and the Keystone Kops played to packed houses in the Union Hall night after night. Maybe he shouldn't charge admission, but they had to cover their costs, and if you didn't charge something, the place would be full of kids. They were clearing over $400 a week. Esselwein bought a big, steel strongbox. He put it under his bed and felt like Scrooge.

What to do with the dough? As a *bona fide* Red, he couldn't put it in the Imperial Bank, could he? He gave a small sum to the Liberal Party ("The Prime Minister needs a new teapot," scowled the Hon. Mr. Coolican) and sent a large donation to the Communist Party in Toronto. Lily thought this a wonderful idea, at first.

"Where's the receipt?" she asked later, when she was doing the books.

"Do you expect a receipt from *revolutionaries?*"

"But how do we know if they got the money, and what they spent it on?"

"We don't."

"But don't they have a budget?"

"Communists never think about money, remember?"

"But they have to eat!"

"They probably ate it, then. Spector's always hungry."

"That doesn't sound very romantic."

The truth was that, without Esselwein's cash, the Communist Party of Canada would likely have collapsed completely. The masses had not rushed to the Red Flag, possibly because the Party remained so secret nobody could find it. Even Esselwein, now in his Liberal disguise, had failed to sign up a single recruit. Lily knew the truth, but when he asked her to join the Party, she laughed.

"Is there dancing?"

"Come off it, eh."

"Let's go to the ballroom at the Waldorf instead...."

"*C'mon.*

"Oh, everybody's doin' it, doin' it, doin' it, everybody's doin' it....."

To satisfy Superintendent Smythe of Intelligence, Esselwein has to invent most of his secret reports. His success as a secret agent depends on the success of the Communist Party of Canada: if it fails, he fails, and it's back to the horse barns in Regina or, worse, the Interior. So Esselwein exaggerates a little here, embroiders a little there, skilfully creating the impression that, while still young and disorganized, the Communist Party is a seething ferment of invisible agitation. Maybe it is. Who knows?

Smythe loves secrecy. Esselwein had wanted the post office job only because it would have made communications with his superintendent a little more rational. He would have been able to write out his reports, address them to the drop and slip them into the mailbags, without anyone being the wiser. As it is, he has to type each report single-space on onionskin, in code, fold the paper into a rectangle precisely two inches by one, conceal the rectangle in a tobacco pouch containing a particular brand of tobacco, take the train to Toronto and leave the pouch by the cash register in a certain restaurant, specified by Smythe in his previous orders, at exactly 16:05 on the third Friday of every month. Esselwein had tried to explain that his regular absences might cause talk, but Smythe replied: "Order is less noticeable than disorder."

Smythe follows his own advice to the letter: he arrives at RCMP headquarters at precisely 09:00 every morning, lunches daily at the Rideau Club, and leaves at exactly 16:00 for a round of whist and whiskey at the Chàteau. His civilian costume is equally inflexible: a monocle, a grey fedora pulled over one eye, a khaki trenchcoat and boots with spurs that clink as he walks. (The difference between Canada and Germany, Esselwein decides, is that such a costume inspires not terror, but disbelief.)

As a junior officer during the war, Smythe had been assigned to the prisoner-of-war camp in Amherst, Nova Scotia, and had been there in April 1917, when the infamous Leon Trotsky was briefly interned on his way from New York to Russia. Communication had been slight, since Trotsky only shouted Russian invective, but Smythe came out of it an expert on Bolsheviks — all of whom, he was convinced, were Jews with spectacles and wild, black hair. (Smythe's own analysis was later confirmed by the infamous pamphlet, *The Protocols of the Wise Men of Zion,* and he saw to it that copies were distributed to all cabinet ministers and members of the press gallery.) When, following the October Revolution, questions were asked in the House as to why Trotsky had been released, and not shot, Smythe replied that Trotsky had been released on purpose in order to sow seeds of dissension within the Communist Party, and it was he, Smythe, who had cunningly planted the bacillus of democracy in Trotsky's brain. Then it was dismissed as a feeble excuse, but now, with Lenin dying, and Russia in chaos, and Trotsky and Stalin at each other's throats, Smythe is a hero. His more extreme eccentricities, such as using the poetry of Duncan Campbell Scott as a code, thereby forcing his agents to compose their reports in verse, are cited as evidence of genius.

Smythe currently believes that the Prime Minister, Mr. King, is a

Bolshevik. Esselwein's job is to prove it. "The Reds aren't *that* hard up!" Esselwein protested. "Incompetence is an insidious weapon," Smythe replied. "Mr. King is the poison gas of politics."

"Maybe I should assassinate him," Lily says.

"King's not worth it." Esselwein shrugs. "he's too . . . *bleh.*"

"The Czar was sort of *bleh,* wasn't he?"

"That's different. The Czar was the Czar."

"Willie'd love to be shot. Right there on Parliament Hill, in the snow. There has to be snow, doesn't there? You want the effect of the blood. We could invite the Movieola people. Willie'd be famous. He's always wanted that."

"So would you. And dead."

"You know, Esselwein, we'd be *history!*"

The idea of assassinating Willie didn't begin as a dream, or a thought. It came as a picture, crystal clear, perfectly complete, *click.* There he is in his racoon coat lying in a snowbank; there I am, in black (assassins always wear black), with a revolver pointed at his heart. The next picture is a courtroom. I am in the prisoner's box, making a brilliant, impassioned speech proving that it was absolutely necessary, completely *right*, that Willie be killed. I am so convincing that everyone in the courtroom stands up and cheers. I am acquitted.

It's not my story, really. It's Vera's. Esselwein told it to me. It happened a long time ago, in St. Petersburg. She was just a girl, a student. She shot Trepov, the head of the St. Petersburg police. At her trial, the evidence of police atrocities so shocked the jury that Vera was acquitted. She is still alive, an old lady now, in London, a revolutionary, but out of favour with Lenin. Everyone is out of favour with Lenin.

The picture won't go away. I'll forget about it for days and weeks on end, then, *pop,* there it is again. Why am I so murderous? Freud would say I was in love with Papa. Maybe I was. So what? I am still murderous. The past doesn't go away. It gets closer. It turns into dreams, and memories, and pictures, so it's impossible to tell what happened, or didn't, or hasn't happened yet. Maybe I'm normal. Everyone is murderous. Esselwein says most of his friends have been shot by one faction or another, or each other. The revolution is drowning in blood. Shoot or be shot. Vera or Rosa; an honoured old lady or a corpse in a canal. It's not hard to choose. Trouble is, once you start, how do you stop?

I practise an hour a day shooting tin cans off a rock back of Essel-wein's shack. Esselwein is alarmed. He's right, though. Willie *is* too banal. This isn't Russia. Russia is romantic. This is Canada.

"Hey, you guys, we've got to do *something,*" Esselwein says at the next meeting of the Party in the attic over Grossman's Deli on Spadina Avenue. "How about a little agitation, eh? An assassination or two would liven things up."

"You have fallen into the error of Luxemburgism," says Comrade Custance, with a look of distaste.

"Rosa? Rosa's only mistake was to get herself killed. I can tell you, nobody in this room is in danger of being beaten to death for an excess of revolutionary fervour."

"Your spontaneity is showing again, Esselwein," Spector sighs. "Stalin says..."

"...capitalism is on the upswing," finishes Custance.

"The time is not ripe," Spector continues.

"...for international revolution," beams Custance.

"The Soviet state is in peril..."

"...we must defend it."

"Stalin has announced a new line..."

"...socialism in one country."

"But *which country?*" cries Esselwein.

"Why, Russia, of course!" says Custance.

Oi. What do you do with a shit like Stalin? A potato. Dictatorship of the potatoes. Is that the future? Goons. Thugs. Who knows what the party line is? It changes every two weeks, depending on Stalin's mood. Does Stalin care about Canada? Are you kidding? By the time the party line reaches Grossman's Deli, it's already been changed three times. So Spector the Soothsayer paws through his pamphlets, searching desper-ately for omens and revelations. Comrade Custance broods over Lenin, capturing Lenin's infuriating irascibility without a shred of his insight, and Chairman Macdonald, who believes everything he reads, is totally confused by the dialectic, which demands he believe two completely opposite things at once. What is to be done?

"I've got a surprise," Esselwein says, placing a big cardboard box on the table. He unties the string and gingerly take out a smaller box. This one is polished mahogany, with bright brass knobs and a grille that looks like a face.

"This is the Marx II," he says proudly. "It's my new shithot compact model. Everybody's got one in Kirkland. Listen."

He plugs it in. Suddenly the room is swinging to the sound of Jimmy Pepper's Good Tyme band coming to them *live* from the Palais Royale at Sunnyside Beach.

"Tea for two, and two for tea, it's me for you, and you for me . . . ."

Esselwein turns the volume up. Comrade Custance covers her ears. Esselwein flicks the sound off.

"How many people you think are tuning in to Jimmy Pepper tonight, eh? Ten thousand? Twenty thousand?"

"Is this a paid advertisement?" says Miss Custance.

"And how many copies of *The Worker* did we all sell this month? A hundred? And how many leaflets did we hand out? A thousand?"

"But this is CFTA!" Spector cries. "It's crap!"

"Sure it's crap. But it's reaching the masses, isn't it? Are we? No. But we can. We can have our own radio station, a Communist radio station."

"With *dance* music?"

"Radio doesn't have to be music. They just play music because they have nothing to say. But we have lots to say, eh? We can say anything! To everybody!"

The inspiration for a radio station had struck Esselwein one night like a bolt of lightning (*Was* it a bolt of lightning?) He was testing out the Marx II without much luck when out of the blue a voice came through as clear as a bell:

"Good evening, ladies and gentlemen. Welcome to Radio CNR, the voice of the Canadian National Railway. We are now leaving North Bay, en route to Kapuskasing, Prince Arthur, Fort William, Winnipeg, Saskatoon, Edmonton and Vancouver. We hope you enjoy the next hour of orchestral music, brought to you courtesy of the CNR. A special welcome to our northern Ontario listeners in Sudbury, Timmins, Hailey-bury, Cobalt, Temagami, Smooth Rock Falls, Porcupine and the gold capital of the world, Kirkland Lake, home of our sister station, CKL."

"That's me!" Esselwein screamed, jumping up. "That's *me!* I'm on the national network!"

Until then, Esselwein's broadcasting had been limited to casual chatter with other operators spotted around North America. He often talked to the CNR boys. The CNR signal came through loud and clear every night between ten and eleven o'clock when the transcontinental passed by to the south. Esselwein could almost see the lighted windows of the radio car as the train thundered through the night, thirty smiling faces wearing haloes of headphones, toes tapping to an identical beat, while miles to the north, in the lighted windows of Timmins and Temagami, strangers wore the same rapt smile and tapped to *exactly the same beat.*

Everybody in Kirkland heard the message. "*We* were on the radio!" they said, amazed. It was the talk of the town. After that, the town shut down every night to listen to the radio. Harry Oakes bought an RCA. It was twice as big and three times more expensive than any other radio in town. (Some said it was gold, but it was only oak.) Harry put up the tallest aerial in town. Once some more proletarian aerials had been surreptitiously hitched to Harry's and strung like cobwebs from roofs to clotheslines to mine shafts, the town lit up in a thunderstorm like Times Square. On warm nights, with the windows open, Kirkland Lake sang with a single voice.

Why not my voice? Esselwein thought. Maybe radio CNR *was* just like CKL, and CHCH, and CFTA. On his next visit to Toronto, Esselwein dropped into CFTA. Sure enough. CFTA was nothing more than a very harrassed young man (CFTA said *har*rassed, not, as in Kirkland Lake, harr*assed*), a microphone, and one jesus big electrical generator. Through his friends in the Railway and Trainmen's Union, Esselwein soon acquired, courtesy of the CNR, enough components to build his own broadcasting station. He named it CFWU, Choose Freedom Workers Unite, and blew the town on its ear by breaking into the CNR's orchestral concert with his own baritone version of the Volga Boat Song. Everybody has a chance to talk or sing or play the fiddle on CFWU, but Esselwein does the news. It is all about people in Kirkland Lake. Nobody ever misses the CFWU news.

"Radio can reach people everywhere," Esselwein says, waving his arms. "Pretty soon we'll have a radio in the kitchen, in the bathroom, in the car!"

"I don't own a car," says Chairman Macdonald.

"A radio in every office, in every lunch pail, in every pocket!"

Esselwein is swept away by a vision of a world in headphones, swinging to the same beat, until one day the music stops and the announcer says: "Workers of the world, unite!" and the world puts down its work and says: "Okay!"

"Workers can't afford radios," says Miss Custance.

"We'll make our own. Sell them cheap. We can make our own equipment, our own programs, our own...."

"Sell?" Spector blanches. "Surely, the seeds of capitalism...."

"We sell newspapers, don't we?" says Esselwein. "Crappy newspapers smuggled all the way from Moscow in a dozen different trunks, valises, coat pockets, shoes, hatbands, armpits and assholes, for all I know. By the time the things get here we're preaching exactly the opposite of the Comintern line. Look, you guys, with radio we can *talk* to Moscow."

"But Comrade Esselwein," Spector smiles. "Russia has not yet invented the radio."

11

Harry Oakes began to fill up Kirkland Lake. He offered no explanation. "It's my lake," he said. "I'll fill 'er up if I have a mind to."

Every day tons of rock slimes from the Lakeshore mine, which had formerly been dumped into a swamp south of town, were dumped directly into the lake. The beach where children played disappeared. The tea-brown water turned milky grey. Dead fish stank on the shore. No one swam. A rumour went around that when the lake was gone, Harry would have the town renamed "Oakes." It seemed as logical a reason as any, but Lily knew it was just another skirmish between Harry and Jack: without a lake, GNOME Air couldn't fly.

Jack Coolican purchased the remnants of the Canadian air fleet in the summer of 1924. The Prime Minister was on another of his economy drives. Having reduced the Canadian army to one thousand men (almost all officers) and a single, obsolete tank, he decided to eliminate the air fleet altogether. "The aeroplane," said Mr. King, "is much too inefficient to be of any practical use in modern times."

The air fleet consisted of the flying boats that had quashed the Kirkland Lake riot in 1919. Jack thought they might be useful in the Interior and got them for a song. "The Prime Minister is scared shitless of heights," he explained.

Jack didn't feel too terrific himself the first time he sat in a flying boat on the smooth, glassy surface of Dow's Lake outside Ottawa. The flying boat did everything backwards. The propellor was in the rear (stern?), the engine was overhead under the wing, the fuel tank was underneath in the hold, and the passengers sat out front in the bow (nose?)

"What do you think this is, fish or fowl?" Jack asked, flapping his arms in encouragement.

"Neither," said the pilot, Jack's seatmate in the House of Commons,

Bartholomew Bandy. "It's a whale with expectations."

The gas tank was connected to the engine by a pump. The pump was operated by a windmill. When there was no wind, the pump was operated by hand. There was no wind.

"Pump! Damn you! Pump!" yelled Bandy.

Jack pumped until sweat fogged up his goggles.

"Crank!" screamed Bandy. "Crank!"

Jack cranked. The engine coughed, and the propellor turned over lazily. *Pump pump, crank crank.* Finally, it caught, and the flagship of the fleet, G-CAOS, lumbered out into the lake.

CAOS cleared the Dominion Experimental Farm at the far end of the lake by less than fifteen feet, spooking the sheep into the roses. (The spooked sheep were later donated to the Prime Minister's country home at Kingsmere, where they added a bucolic touch until the following year, when Jack landed CAOS on Kingsmere, causing the sheep to stampede towards the ruins Willie had erected at the edge of the pasture and to leap, loyal Liberals all, through the empty windows of parliamentary democracy into oblivion.)

"Hey, there's nothing but water down there!" Jack said.

"Thank God!" yelled Bandy.

They hit rough air over North Bay. CAOS came down into three-foot waves. A wave caught a wing-tip and CAOS skewed sickeningly to one side.

"Run!" screamed Bandy.

"What d'you mean, *run?* Run *where?*"

"Onto the other wing! Weight! Balance!"

Clinging to the struts, Jack crept out, the wing bending and shuddering under his weight. He was more than thirty feet out, near the tip, standing alone, it seemed, in the middle of the lake, when the opposite wing gradually rose from the water and CAOS straightened out.

"Run!" screamed Bandy. "Run!"

"*Where?* Run *where?*"

"Back! Get *back!*"

Jack scrambled up and down the wing like a wet dog until CAOS finally landed, with a terrific *whump*, on the beach, and Jack was thrown into the water. The whole town was watching.

"Will ye have a wee drink?" winked a grizzled railroader, holding out a bottle.

It was the Doctor who suggested, when Jack took him up for a spin, that CAOS would fly much better with a cargo, and that CAOS and her sister ships, CAUK, CARP, CANO and CANT, could carry among them nearly five tons of freight, and that Manitoulin Island, a wilderness of hidden coves near the American border, was an easy hop from North Bay, and that the contents of a freight car, forgotten on a siding near the North Bay beach, could be in the holds of Manitoulin fishing boats within hours, and the boats in American waters by nightfall. As well, the population of Manitoulin Island was mostly Indian, and did not the Minister of the Interior, Mines and Indians have a responsibility to bring prosperity to the native people?

"I dunno," said Jack. "I'm an Honourable now. I ain't no fly-by-night bootlegger."

"You don't fly at night," the Doctor said patiently. "There is absolutely no risk. The Coast Guard on the Great Lakes has been reduced to a single boat, another of our Prime Minister's admirable economies, and everyone else is on board, so to speak, including, unwittingly, the Prime Minister himself. Dear Mr. King is an innocent. I am always delighted to have a man of such temperance and probity as my guest in Atlantic City. Mr. King's private railway car never fails to arrive with a cargo of excellent Crown Royal, and returns north so full of cocaine that those 'in the know' call it the Snowball Express. Were Mr. King's appetite not so insatiable, and were he willing to recognize our friendship in, shall I say, a more *material* way, I would not be forced to expand my import-export business."

During the summer of 1924, a sudden fashion for lilac suits, white neckties and diamond pinkie rings swept through Sudbury, North Bay, Timmins, Temagami, Kirkland Lake and all the other little places in northern Ontario where CAOS and her sisters touched down. A lot of people who didn't seem to have a pot to piss in bought snazzy cars and took cruises on the Cunard Line. Jack said the flying boats were "exploring the Interior."

"The Interior is west," Lily said. "You're flying south."

"Mr. Legion likes North Bay. He's very popular there."

Lily met Al Capone. He was pretty, and painfully polite. She liked him. Shoot, or be shot. No bullshit about Al Capone.

"Stalin is right," Esselwein said. "Capitalism is on the upswing."

"It's just Coolicanism," Lily said. "Have a drink?"

The exact content of GNOME Air's cargo was not discovered until

June 1925. The Deputy Minister of Indian Affairs, Duncan Campbell Scott, putting the finishing touches to one of his beautiful poems of pagan passion, visited Manitoulin Island by canoe, and found his simple children of the forest drunk as skunks.

The Hon. J. Rudolphus Coolican expressed astonishment. Mr. Scott was immediately dispatched on a six-month tour of the Interior to investigate drunkenness among the Indians. Mr. Scott said the Hudson's Bay Company was to blame. The following week, when the United States Coast Guard impounded, at gunpoint, a Canadian fishing boat carrying nothing but fish, it was clear the whole thing was a Yankee plot. The Hon. Mr. Coolican was elevated to the Senate. He was relieved to find it contained neither Indians nor poets.

"Water," the Doctor observed, peering out of CAOS at Niagara Falls, "is a much safer investment."

With Kirkland Lake still only half filled up, Jack taxied his flying boats, one by one, into the middle of the lake and set them alight. They burned like golden dragonflies.

"Liquor?" said Jack when the RCMP smuggling squad arrived. "Not me, hell, I'm into hydro!"

12

"He's coming," Mum said.

"Who?"

"Houdini."

"Here?"

"I invited him. He needs his mother."

Esselwein had seen the announcement in *Popular Mechanics:*

"The *Scientific American* is offering a prize of $2,500 to the first person able to produce a psychic photograph under its test conditions. A further prize of $2,500 will be awarded to the first person able to produce a visible psychic manifestation. Harry Houdini, the magician and expert of psychic quackery, will double the reward out of his own pocket if he is convinced the spirit manifested is that of his mother."

"But Mum, you've never produced a 'psychic manifestation,' whatever that is."

"A psychic manifestation is merely a moment of illumination, like a photograph. Houdini's mother, at the moment, is in the vest pocket of his suit coat in the closet. She needs only to be illuminated."

Sure, but how? The photograph in Houdini's pocket was just a dog-eared old snapshot. Any kid could take a psychic photograph. Lily had made one herself once, by accident. It was a photo of a child in a coffin, the dead boy's face in the centre of the picture; but when she developed the negative, the boy's face reappeared surrounded by a halo, floating in the right-hand corner, looking down at his own body. She'd almost fainted. It had just been a double-exposure, although some professionals used screens and gauze and trick lighting. It was amazing what you could do with cotton batten. "Some people will think any blob is Great-Aunt Hattie," said her employer, Mr. Sims. "You can show the same blob to ten different people and come up with ten different loved ones." A blob wouldn't satisfy the great Houdini.

News of the seance (Mum preferred to call it "tuning in") created a sensation. Reporters from the *Star* and the *Telegram* and the *New York Times* descended on Kirkland Lake like locusts. Lily came downstairs one morning to find that the obnoxious Sinclair had spread his sleeping bag on the floor of the post office and was snoring happily. When she poked him, and ordered him out, he shouted that the post office was public property and he was as good a taxpayer as any. Constable Dempster had to remove him bodily for interfering with the Royal Mail. Sinclair then erected a tent outside the front door, set up his portable typewriter, and informed the world that the plain, concrete road by which he camped was paved with gold.

"You're doing it for the dough, ain't ya?" Sinclair shouted at Mr. Legion.

"Is money all you ever think about?" Mr. Legion replied calmly. "You can't be very well paid."

"My salary is none of your damn business!" Sinclair screamed.

In New York, Houdini gave a statement to the press: "As I sat alone by my mother's deathbed," he said, "I spoke one last word to her. Only she and I know what that word is."

"Do you think she spoke Italian?" Lily said. "What if she wasn't Italian, but only married one?"

Mum seemed perfectly confident. Lily had faith in Mum's unusual gifts. She seemed to possess exceptional empathy, but there was no way Mum had been hovering over Mrs. Houdini's deathbed.

"Look, Mum, even if you get the word right, Houdini can *say* it's wrong. It's a trick."

"Of course it's a trick."

Meanwhile, the world was waiting on their doorstep. Sinclair claimed in the *Star* that Mr. Legion was the last survivor of the charge of the Light Brigade and had picked up his hocus-pocus in Egypt, from an astrologer. Every quack in Canada wrote to claim an intimate, top-secret acquaintance with the late, lamented Mrs. Houdini, Sr., send payment by return post please.

"But what if he recognizes you, Mum?"

"Do I look like a crazy lady?"

"You look like a banker."

The seance would take place in Mr. Legion's room behind the post office. After a lot of experimentation with the window blinds, Lily figured that if the sitting took place on a sunny afternoon, she might be able to reveal Houdini's mother in the window. As for the rest, well, the press would make it all up anyway. Sinclair had interviewed everyone in town, but he only wrote about himself.

Fame had one advantage. Only a few days before Houdini's visit, Mr. Legion received a letter from Saranac Lake, New York:

Dear Sir,

I am a medical doctor. I am not a spiritualist. When my colleagues in the medical profession identified the 'ectoplasm' produced by a famous medium as a fresh sheep's pancreas, I believed them. However, the notice in the *Times* about your contest with Mr. Houdini aroused an irresistible urge to interfere.

Among the six of us breathing ourselves to death here is a man named Bernard Weiss. Bernie is a Jew. He was a shoemaker in New York City before coming here last year. Bernie is such a quiet, unassuming little guy you'd never know his brother is the famous magician, Erich Weiss, *alias* Harry Houdini. The physical resemblance is quite striking.

Bernie and I discussed his magical brother several times this year, long before the contest was announced. We have no reason to deceive each other here. Erich Weiss has not written to Bernie, or come to visit him, or sent a single penny of the five thousand dollars he promised to pay for his care. Bernie's view of his brother is quite different from the usual sycophantic hysteria. You might find it interesting.

> Yours truly,
> Norman Bethune, M.D.
> Trudeau Sanitarium, Saranac, N.Y.

My dear Miss Coolican,

I am happy to answer your request for more information about my brother Erich (Houdini is just one of many names he had taken since he was working with circuses as a mind-reader, contortionist, juggler, and so on). I regret that much I say will not be news since I have not seen my brother since ten years. I think he likes to forget he is mortal like the rest of us and no matter how many times escapes death by trickery some day he will not. He does not know himself what is truth and what is lies.

If Erich lies only about himself I do not mind, but I am ashamed when he says to the world that our poor father was a rabbi with many university degrees. Our father was a simple man. He could not read or write. We spoke only Yiddish at home. It is not to be ashamed of. They were immigrants. Erich was born in Budapest. He was smuggled into the United States under our mother's skirt. She always said his seasickness was judgment for that. I think he must be crazy jumping off these bridges in handcuffs and chains and so on. He is no longer young. Well, it makes him rich. I do not grudge. Dr. Bethune is looking after me. A good doctor should be more famous than a fake, eh?

I am sending a little snapshot of us all. That is Erich on the left, I am second from right. It was taken just after our mother died. We had to hold the funeral off for a week so Erich could come from England. Even so, what a show he put on! Such weeping and tearing of hair! He was ashamed to be doing tricks when she died.

Please excuse me if I have disappointed you. At my time of life it is hard to have illusions.

With all respects,
Bernard Weiss

CNR Telegram to:
Miss Annie Buller, c/o *The Worker,* 165 Spadina Ave., Toronto:

COME KIRKLAND NEXT TRAIN

Signed: ESSELWEIN

Annie's Yiddish was no hell, but it would have to do. CFWU could broadcast her voice from Esselwein's shack to a speaker hidden in the ceiling light of Mr. Legion's room. Houdini would reply into Mr. Legion's star-shaped microphone. The microphone had no cord. It was just a prop, but Mr. Legion said it improved communication one hundred per cent. Esselwein goosed the mike with the best battery he could find, hid a second microphone in the stovepipe, strung a lot of copperwire clothesline around the kitchen, and hoped for the best.

Houdini arrived with a trainload of Movieola people the day after a freak blizzard dumped nearly three feet of snow on Kirkland Lake.

"It's August," Houdini said. "This can't be snow. Find out what it is."

By the time Houdini reached the post office, his snakeskin shoes were soaked through and his trouser cuffs were full of slush. He was in a bad mood.

"Hey, look here Mr. Houdini," yelled the obnoxious Sinclair, "this is just a publicity stunt, ain't it?"

Houdini pulled an all-day sucker out of Sinclair's left ear.

"Stick it up your ass, kid," Houdini said. Everybody laughed.

Houdini posted two goons at the door to keep the crowd back. Two more began to take the room apart. They inspected Mr. Legion's microphone for wires. They overturned the table, tapped the legs and searched it for secret compartments. They went through the cupboards and threw all the pots and pans on the floor. They dumped the potato bin, groped in the flour and even looked into the burning stove. (A hundred yards away in his shack, Esselwein was nearly deafened when they banged the stovepipes.) They rapped the walls and tapped the floor. They even dumped the slop pail.

Houdini's eyes buzz the room like black flies. What's the catch? Where's the scam? He wants to get the hell out of here quick. His feet are freezing. His gout is killing him. He's not as young as he used to be. What the hell is he doing here anyway? Some old geezer in the boon-docks hears voices. Big deal. Who can con the great Houdini? Most mediums are sexy broads who lift their skirts in the dark and pass off a good feel of pussy as a "psychic manifestation." Crowd loves it. Whatever this old duck offers, it ain't pussy. *Feh.*

The crowd is roped off on the other side of Government Road. Houdini locks the door from the inside. He is ready to take his place when Sinclair's round, freckled face rises like the moon over the window sill. Houdini yanks down the shades. The room is bathed in a soft, yellow glow.

"The guy's a phoney, if you ask me," Sinclair screams outside.

Mr. Legion is already seated near the stove. He is hunched over, holding a handkerchief to his lips to stifle a racking cough.

The cough gives Houdini the creeps. If he'd known the old bugger was about to croak he'd never have come. He edges as far away as possible, drumming his large fingers impatiently on the table.

"So, are we ready?"

Mr. Legion looks up. His large, melancholy eyes are bright with fever. His thin shoulders are bent, his chest hollow and his face a strange yellow. He speaks in a rasp.

"Ah, Erich, always in a hurry, eh? You have come to visit me at last. Why not stay a while?"

"So you know my name. That's not difficult." Houdini wipes his palms.

"You have many names, Erich. In the early days it was hard to keep track. The Amazing Merlin, Weiss the Wizard, Ernesto, the Incredible Vanishing Man, Marvel the Mind Reader, *oi*, there were so many. Perhaps there are more."

"What did my mother call me?"

"Mostly she called you a *shmuck*." Mr. Legion's dry, mirthless laugh ends in another fit of coughing.

"You're lying!" Beads of sweat stand out on Houdini's face. His hands are trembling. "She loved me! *She loved me!*"

"How do you know, *shmuck?* Were you ever home? You take an Italian name and pretend you are not a Jew. You show yourself on the street naked, like an ape. You dress up in a straitjacket like a crazy person. You jump into rivers to show you do not fear the water. It is the stuff for children. A hundred times you go into a trunk, a coffin, and rise from the dead. Big deal, eh? But when Mama is dying, you run away. *Feh!*"

"No! No! *It's not true!*"

Houdini's anguished cries can be heard clearly in Esselwein's shack. The only other sound is a terrible, rattling cough.

"When do I get my turn?" Annie whispers.

"Shhh!" says Esselwein. "There's somebody else in there! Somebody with a Brooklyn accent!"

The spasm subsides. Mr. Legion removes the handkerchief from his lips. It is spotted with blood.

"When Mama died, you were doing tricks at Covent Garden. Not even the great Houdini can be in two places at once. There is no deathbed 'word,' *shmuck*. Shame you bring us in life, now you make a *schtick* of the dead!"

Houdini bows his head and covers his eyes with his hand.

"It's a living, Bernie. I mean no harm."

Bernie sighs.

"Look at your shoes, ruined! Five days I work to make those shoes, stitched by hand, fifty dollars even for the skin."

"I'll pay, Bernie. Promise. Double. Whatever you ask. Next week for sure, eh? I've been busy. We'll get together, have a good time, Cotton Club, shoot the works, on me...."

Bernie is silent. His face is ashen. He is staring over Houdini's shoulder.

"Mama?" he whispers, rising from his chair.

Houdini turns. There, in the golden light of the blinded window, shadowy but unmistakeable, is his mother's face.

Esselwein is nearly deafened by the crash. Then, the sound of splintering glass. Then, silence.

"When do I get to say something?" Annie whispers.

"Somebody's changed the script," says Esselwein, running to the door.

The spectators have broken through the rope and are trampling the snow on the west side of the post office, shouting and waving their arms. Only moments before, Mr. Legion's microphone had come flying through the window. Sinclair had been knocked out cold. The microphone is now buried in a snowdrift.

Inside, Mr. Legion is sitting by the stove, startled, but perfectly calm. Houdini has disappeared.

MAGICIAN VANISHES INTO THIN AIR! yells the reporter from the *Telegram*.

"No," said Mr. Legion. "He ran out the door."

When pieced together, the window blind still showed the image of a woman's face. It was bundled up carefully by a representative of the *Scientific American*, but by the time it was unwrapped in New York, the image had disappeared.

"Spirits don't hang around forever," Lily said, but she didn't get the prize. (Years later, when Mr. Land invented the Polaroid camera, and made a fortune, Lily kicked herself for not having the sense, having turned a window blind into a roll of instant film, to put the goddamn thing into a camera.)

Mr. Legion was asked if Houdini's mother had spoken the secret word.

"Of course not," he said.

The *Star* ran a photo of Sinclair with his bandaged head on the front page. The caption read: "HOUDINI HOKUM: STAR REPORTER RISKS LIFE TO EXPOSE TRICK."

Houdini, buttonholed the next day at the funeral of his brother, Bernard, made no comment.

Whispers began that Houdini performed his magic with the aid of keys taped to the soles of his feet and lockpicks concealed in his hair. His audiences dwindled. He disappeared from the headlines. One year later, in Montreal, Houdini was playfully punched in the stomach by a student at McGill University. Houdini died on Hallowe'en from a ruptured appendix.

"McGill is a very dangerous place," commented Christina Coolican.

(This remark, noted by the Prime Minister in his diary, and repeated by Mr. King to his secretary, McGregor, and by McGregor, in the strictest confidence, to the Deputy Minister of External Affairs, O.D. Skelton, and by Skelton to Ernest Lapointe, the Minister of Justice, and by Lapointe to Superintendent Smythe of the RCMP, and by Smythe to the Friday lunch crowd at the Rideau Club, and by Willis O'Connor, aide-de-camp to Lord Byng, to Lady Byng, and by Lady Byng to Chief Justice Sir Lyman Duff, and by poor, drunken Duff to the Prime Minister, who said, "Exactly so, I suspected it all along," caused the President of McGill, Sir Arthur Currie, former commander-in-chief of the Canadian Corps, to be investigated for subversion, libelled by the press, forced out of his job and buried, five years later, a suspected traitor. In the meantime no McGill graduates were hired by the civil service or taken on the Prime Minister's staff. When one of them finally asked, twenty years later, no one in Ottawa could remember why.)

Mum did not discuss the Houdini incident. Lily was as puzzled as everyone else, but when Willie called an election the following week, she tried to put it out of her mind. She received a telegram signed WLMK. It said simply: HELP.

MEANWHILE, IN OTTAWA:

HELP! HELP HELP HELP! HELPHELPHELPHELPHELP!

I must get a grip on myself. I haven't lost the election yet. There is still time. Time, plenty of time, time to cover things, clean things up, time for our own investigation, time to bury, time for revisions to the Customs Act, nothing need come out, our own investigation will lay the blame elsewhere, there will be time to wash our hands of the whole affair, launder, pure, Ivory Snow, shhhh!

I have instructed Nicol to remove the cases of whiskey from the cellar. An unnecessary precaution, no doubt, but better to be safe. Nothing in this house has been smuggled into the country, or obtained in any unethical way. The Doctor has assured me of that, and the few things I have brought back from New York in the way of furnishings and knick-knacks cannot come under suspicion, all being gifts. Perhaps I have been too accepting of the Doctor's hospitality. It is well-meant, but it has led to misunderstandings in some quarters. I have spent too little time in the House, and have fallen behind in the correspondence. Had I been more vigilant, these vicious rumours would have been scotched before they got started. The Big Interests are behind it all! There are men who will stop at nothing to see the party defeated and myself destroyed. Their slanders reach into high places. Only yesterday, His Ex., Lord Byng, took me aside and said "I would have more confidence in the success of your government, King, if you had some sort of policy."

"Sometimes no policy is the best policy, Your Excellency," I replied immediately. That stopped him! He had no comeback to that! How ignorant these Englishmen are of the need to steer a middle course between the Scylla of Socialism and the Charybdis of Reaction! To move too precipitately in either direction is to run upon the rocks, to plunge the country into chaos, or the deathgrip of Toryism. I admit that I have not followed through on the great reforms of the Liberal plat-form, especially those affecting the poor, the cause closest to my heart, but to move too quickly in this direction would antagonize the more conservative elements in the party, and create exactly the kind of friction that would bring certain defeat, and the triumph of Toryism, and where would the poor be then?

Have we not opened our gates to the poor of Europe? What a shining example the foreigners have set us! They accept the meanest work, and toil without complaint for a pittance. Their industry and frugality, if followed by others, cannot help but bring prices down, a boon to us all. This year alone, by the most relentless economy, I have managed to save the government of Canada $50 million. This practice, if continued in future, will eliminate the last vestige of waste and remove entirely the need for an income tax, a discouraging burden on those who contribute the most to the nation's financial health.

I believe that I have led an honest and just administration. I sometimes fear I do not have the intellectual equipment essential to my part, but the saving grace is the lack of greater equipment in others. Possibly some mistakes have been made through selfishness, or greed, or inexperience, yet, as the Doctor has pointed out, the liquor traffic is simply a form of free trade, and are not a majority of the members of the House, indeed, a majority of the voters, in favour of free trade? Why, "free trade" is the cry of the horrible Progs, and the Progs promise the *most rigorous* morality, if elected. What, then, can be immoral about the liquor traffic?

It is true that Coolican is a vain, egocentric fellow, but honest, I believe. He is headstrong, and liable to put a foot wrong through impatience (I was much like that at his age), yet he has progressive ideas and just the right touch for the Interior. Of all the men, I believe he and the Doctor are the best to trust, being wealthy themselves, with nothing to gain, and having helped so freely in the past, and offering to help now. Coolican will be safe in the Senate, and he is most helpful in matters of pat ... constituency affairs. It will be a question of finding a suitable replacement, not that Essel person, and showing that we are behind him in a concrete way. A public building, at this time, would not go amiss in Temiskaming.

.

The following week, Senator J.R. Coolican announced that construction would begin immediately on a new $3.2 million post office in Kirkland Lake. It would be designed along the lines of a medieval castle, and built entirely of stone.

"Willie's trying to lock me up again!" Lily said. "He's getting closer, *tick, tick, tick.* Willie is my fate, Esselwein."

"We could fly to Russia."

"We're Trotskyites. We'd be shot."

"That's true."

Esselwein seemed sad. There was something nostalgic about him, something uncanny. It worried her. The Irish would say he was "away." Is that what Communism did to you? When Lily tried to think about the proletariat, she imagined a lot of little people who came out of the

ground and danced by the light of the moon. Anyone who danced with
the faeries went mad, and fought with the waves of the sea.

Why should she care? Is she in love with him? Lily had given love up,
she thought. She prides herself on being cynical. Esselwein says she's the
only unsentimental woman he knows. Is that a compliment? Esselwein
tries to be hard-boiled, but he is really very sentimental — no, not
sentimental, emotional. He *feels.* Esselwein is the only unselfish man
Lily knows. She enjoys just being with him, he's so full of energy and
optimism. Esselwein believes. Lily doesn't. He says she always sees the
fly in the ointment. But the fly is *there,* she protests. Esselwein, of course,
says that the fly improves the ointment one hundred per cent, and
slathers it all over, while she says "Ech" and throws the whole damn
thing out.

Is he in love with her? They make love, but that's not the same.
Mostly they talk politics. They argue a lot. Esselwein is always so
passionately *right* about everything, Lily can't resist poking fun at him.
Then she feels badly about it. She cares more about politics, and people,
than she lets on. For Esselwein, the struggle is everything.

"We are *engaged*," he said last week. Did he mean it personally, or
politically? Oh, Esselwein, don't let the mermaids get you!

Esselwein disappeared the next Friday. He went to Toronto, as usual,
and didn't come back. His shack was unlocked. Nothing was missing.
He didn't even take his toothbrush. A search party combed the bush for
miles around. They found the skeletons of the three Finns, each with a
hole in its forehead. That was all.

Every evening Lily went to the shack and waited. He would be back.
Esselwein wouldn't leave, just like that, without a word. At the end of
the month his copy of *The Worker* arrived. She opened it.

"POLICE SPY EXPOSED

John Esselwein, of Kirkland Lake, Ont. is now known to
have been planted by the fascist police...."

Lily read the story twice. She wondered what Lillian Gish would do,
under the circumstances. She sat down and wept.

13

"But Mr. King, you have only one hundred seats. The Conservatives have one hundred and sixteen. Surely you have lost!"

"Oh, no! No no no no no, Your Excellency! The setback was unexpected, I admit. The election results have been a great disappointment...."

"But you have lost your own seat, Mr. King!"

"Oh, I shall find another."

"Your entire cabinet is gone...."

"Good riddance, I say. They were a poor, weak lot. The responsibility for our de... for the Liberal *reverses*, rests squarely on their shoulders. I intend to bring in some new men. The horrible Progs... the Progressive Party...will come in with us, the Labour men too...."

"But you will be at their mercy, Mr. King. You will have to fetch and carry for them. The country will say you are clinging to office at any price...."

(I am! I am!)

"Mr. King, you're in a bit of a sticky wicket, aren't you? Why not give the other fellow a chance at bat? Be a good sport, eh?"

(What is the fool talking about? Why do Englishmen always change the subject? How I feel the lack of a proper background at times like these! If only Massey were here, Vincent always knows about these things.)

"I believe I can carry on, Your Excellency. No party has a clear majority. The horrible... the Progressives will not support the Conservative Party. A Tory administration would be defeated in a matter of

... (That's it! That's *it!* I'll quit, and dump the whole mess on the Tories! Let them suffer in the shallows and miseries. They're bound to run aground. Then, in a matter of weeks, or months, I'll come sailing back into office on a wave of popular indignation. Let them have the government, but give me the *people!*)

"The Conservatives deserve a chance, don't you think, Mr. King? It would be *undignified*, don't you agree, to appear too *desperate* for office...."

(But I am! What does the fool think politics *is?*)

"It *would* be a terrible strain, Your Excellency, my nerves...."

"A good rest, Mr. King, a decent interval...."

"...a return to the scholarly life."

"...the honourable course."

"I'll do it. I'll resign tomorrow."

"Bravo! Good chap! I knew you were a gentleman!"

(Gentleman? Me! A Gentleman! Ohhhho, I *am* a gentle man! For he himself has said it, and it's greatly to his credit, that I *am* a gentle man! OHHHHHH, I AHAHHAHHAHHAMMMMM a *gentle man!*)

I came home and went to bed for a little rest, feeling much relieved. I am sure Lord Byng was right. He is a man of great spiritual strength and power. I am truly grateful for his friendship. After a little supper I called C at the Château and told her of my decision to resign. She seemed quite alarmed. She said that if I resigned now, and the Tories came in, 'everything would come out,' and that her brother, and several others, might go to jail, and my own name would be dragged through the mud as a result of the furnishing of Laurier House, no duty being paid, etc. etc.

I admit this put a whole new complexion on things. Clearly the Big Interests are at fault, and the Jews. They have ganged up against us. I am told that Mrs. Freiman lined up all the Jews in Ottawa against us, then went to Winnipeg and lined them up there! The cry was that our government had tried to keep out the Jews! Well, no wonder! They are an untrustworthy, moneygrubbing lot. No Jew will ever be part of a Liberal government as long as I'm Prime Minister! (Ah! Prime Minister!)

MEANWHILE, IN THE HOUSE OF COMMONS:

We're burning everything.

"To think I went to Queen's for this!" Charlie says. "Let's hope the Indians can remember their treaty numbers."

At least Jack never had much truck with paper. Who could believe there'd be so much of it? It seems that the Doctor's import-export business involved the Minister of Customs and Excise (of course), the Department of Internal Revenue, the Coast Guard, the provincial police, the Canadian National Railway, the Bank of Montreal and most Liberal MPs in Nova Scotia, Quebec, Ontario, Saskatchewan and British Columbia, not to mention Willie.

"The Tories are into it up to their eyeballs," the Doctor says, but he looks worried.

The Tories have spies outside. (Are you there, Esselwein?) We have to keep the doors locked and the blinds drawn. The temperature in here is 120F. The furnace is red as a hot coal.

"Maybe we should burn the whole place down," I say. "It's simpler."

"Are we going to burn the House of Commons down every time some prick slams his pecker in the door?" says Charlie.

"It could become a tradition, you know, like the Vikings. Willie likes Wagner."

"It could become expensive. He wouldn't like that."

"Oh, he wouldn't mind, as long as he didn't have to pay for it himself."

At midnight I go for a walk along the Canal. The wind smells of snow. Talbot was killed eight years ago today. Funny, I'd forgotten. Is that a good sign? Tomorrow is Hallowe'en. What will Willie wear? I walk by Laurier House. The light is on in Willie's study. There's no smoke from his chimney.

ON HALLOWE'EN,
THE PRIME MINISTER CONSULTS HIS ORACLES:

I had Mr. and Mrs. Vincent Massey to lunch. Vincent is quite cast down over his loss in the election campaign. He is indignant over Tory methods, the lowness of the campaign, the cynicism of it all. His use of a limousine to attend meetings, etc. had been totally misrepresented. It was only a convenience, not "showing off." He says his income has dropped by one-fifth, loss of directorships, bridges burnt, etc. I told him my plan to resign. I said I had given my word to His Excellency to do the 'gentlemanly' thing. Vincent strongly approves. It is a blessing to have someone who shares the spiritual side of public endeavour. Massey will be a tower of strength. I mentioned I would try to get him a seat in Saskatchewan.

At five p.m. I called on Sir Campbell Stuart, President of the Bank of Montreal, and went for a walk with him. He told me the bank had put nearly $1 million into trying to elect French-Canadian Liberals. The French-Canadians will strongly oppose my tendering any resignation. I have to safeguard the party's interest, of which I am the leader, and not surrender to give an opponent a more strategic position. I believe now the country expects me to carry on until Parliament meets. I have had great help and comfort from the spiritual influences around me.

THE PRIME MINISTER MAKES UP HIS MIND:

I slept better last night, tho' restless with a heavy cold. The butler gave me some medicine for rubbing on my chest and neck. It made me frightfully giddy, causing my eyes to bulge out and my whole face to become scarlet. I had great difficulty seeing. I drafted my letter of resignation to His Ex., asking him to call on Mr. Meighen and the Conservatives. I did not have it quite complete by caucus time this afternoon.

It was about three p.m. when I went into caucus. All members were present except three. They were in good humour, but showing signs of a little weariness. I opened discussion on the question of tendering resignation. Not one, save Vincent Massey, would hear of it! They were all for holding to office! I confess that certain arguments presented had been absent from my thoughts:

1. duty to the party
2. Meighen's unscrupulous methods
3. possible criticism that because I had been defeated myself, I was unwilling to stand up to the situation.
4. the right of Parliament to decide.

At six p.m. I went to Government House to see His Ex. I told him I had decided to carry on. He seemed disappointed. He said that in his own opinion, Mr. Meighen should be called on, but he would accept my advice.

The Doctor came to dinner. He spoke of getting men into the Cabinet who would be true to me. I asked him if he would come in, and he said he would.

When I woke about four-thirty this morning, there came to me the idea of summoning Parliament at once to decide the question of control, to adjourn the House as soon as the vote is taken and to spend a month or two covering, *cleaning* up. I felt this was an inspiration from the loved ones who are watching round about. I am sure we shall be able to carry on even better in some respects than the last few years. All this is bringing the Liberal Party together. It is giving me a recognized place in Canadian affairs as a leader who has to be reckoned with!

"But he said he was going to resign!" cried Mr. Meighen.

"Yes, he did, didn't he?" said Lord Byng, scratching his head. "But then he didn't, did he?"

14

Mum and I have a nice suite on the sixth floor, overlooking the river.
The Englishwoman in the next room reads palms, and the swami across
the hall does astrological charts, so obviously the Château has decided
to put all Willie's soothsayers together in one place. He seems to need a
great many. I guess he does. I am a Scorpio, Willie a Sagittarius. This
seems to be very bad news indeed. Mum resents the competition and
refuses to leave her room. Just as well. She's taken to wearing a loose,
white shift and going barefoot. She's always been very particular about
shoes, being Scotch, and not wanting to be thought bog Irish. We are
into a new phase. Could it be the Ku Klux Klan? I should make a movie.
We could call it *Death of a Nation.*

The horrible Progs (or the fucking farmers, if you prefer) are directly
below us on the fifth floor. They all wear brown suits, and smell of
mothballs and manure. They tie up the elevators day and night running
up and down between the Liberals on the fourth floor, and the Tories on
the third. The House opens next week, but they can't decide which bribe
they're going to take, from which side. Mr. Meighen has promised them
all the Senate, and a railroad for each constituency: Willie has promised
them seats in the Cabinet, and old age pensions. So far it's a draw. They
won't take money. Farmers are funny about money. As soon as they get
some, they spend twice as much buying land, or livestock, or machinery,
and go deeper in debt. That's why Vincent Massey, whose grandpa
invented the combine, is able to buy controlling interest in the Liberal
Party and why the Progs snuffle around his ankles like pigs smelling
swill.

"They won't even take cash!" says Vincent, amazed. Vincent is
accustomed to buying things. On a trip to Moscow a couple of years ago

he picked up, for peanuts, a priceless collection of revolutionary art. His wife Alice smuggled it all out under her dress, along with several dozen of the Czar's table napkins. The Masseys think it's a huge joke. Serve the Bolshies right, eh? The Progs hate Vincent. Everybody does. He has the charm of a cadaver.

"Try sex," I suggested.

Sex hasn't worked either. It's not for lack of interest (Check the stock, eh boys! Woo! Woo!), but the Progs bunk in two to a bed (One at a time, eh mister?) and no hoor is going to hoof it up five floors (Stuff it up your arse, mister!) and there aren't that many hoors committed to Liberalism, fond as they may be of certain Liberals.

Willie phones me twice a day, every morning when he wakes up, and at night when he goes to bed. Should he wear the blue suit, or the grey? (Buy one that fits, for God's sake!) Can I arrange for a plumber to fix the shower? Should he fire McLeod, the butler, for getting into the whiskey? Will I invite some Progs for dinner, and arrange the flowers? He seems quite cheery. He has decided the smuggling scandal is nothing more than Tory propaganda. "I can't find a shred of evidence," he says. (I hope not!)

Charlie Whitton has been sacked. The story is that she leaked "classified" information to the Conservatives. Willie now holds Cabinet meetings in the middle of the night, in secret locations, and has ordered all his ministers to fire their female secretaries. I tell him the gossip and try to calm him down. At night I talk him to sleep. It started as a joke. One night he asked what I had been thinking about when he called. I said I'd been thinking about the ladder in my stocking, and that I would have to buy a new pair. What colour was the stocking, he wanted to know. Oh, oh. I'd completely forgotten his obsession with underwear! So now I undress for him, on the phone. Not really, of course. Who can talk on the phone and undress at the same time? It's easier to lie in bed naked and make it all up. I have invented a wonderful wardrobe of sexy lingerie! Willie likes red best. I always start with the shoes, then the slip. ("What does it feel like? Soft? Slippery? Oh! Oh!") and go on, very softly, very slowly, from there. He blows up when I get to the garterbelt, and undo the garters, one by one. We'll progress from there, I imagine, with time. It's a lot of fun. Move over, Scheherazade!

I am, appropriately, in charge of the Woman Question. The Woman Question occupies the second floor of the Château. It consists of five very large ladies from Alberta, all of whom want to be in the Senate. Their spokesman (ulp, spokeswoman) is Mrs. McClung, who got the vote for women during the war, and brought down a government doing it. Mrs. McClung, moreover, is Temperance. She's not a patch, however, on Magistrate Murphy. Emily Murphy is three hundred pounds of solid determination. She's a police magistrate in Edmonton. Mrs. Murphy can spot a hooker at a hundred yards. She's written an exposé of dope smuggling. Mrs. Murphy and Mrs. McClung are very big on Vice. Willie is terrified of them. I can't blame him. So am I. So are the senators.

I had a little tea for them yesterday. I invited Miss McPhail, the only woman MP in the House (a Prog, but she smells nice, and I like her), Mrs. Freiman, and some young Liberal women. (We are forbidden to entertain the enemy at this point.) I explained that Willie saw no reason why women should not be in the Senate, but that he was without a majority, and without a seat himself, and powerless to act "at this time." They were all very friendly and sympathetic. Someone had told Mrs. Murphy that women could not be in the Senate because we are not specifically defined as "persons" under the constitution, and they are organizing a delegation to appeal to the Privy Council in London. (What are we, fish?)

Willie came late. He smiled a lot, and shook hands all around, and asked after everyone's children, by name. He told Mrs. McClung she had a purifying effect on public life, and compared Mrs. Murphy to Joan of Arc. He was especially nice to the Progs, since they have ten seats in Alberta, and the Liberals have none. He did not call Mrs. McClung a troublemaker, or suggest to Miss McPhail she'd be better off on the farm, or hint that as long as he had a say in the matter, a fish would make it to the Senate faster than Emily Murphy. Willie drank a cup of tea and nibbled on a slice of toast.

"There is a time for everything," he said, patting the bald spot in the middle of his hair.

(If he's going to appoint a woman to the Senate, why not me?)

"How much does it cost?" Mrs. Freiman asked after the others had gone.

"Who *wants* the Senate?"

"Everyone, it seems."

"But you have everything, Lillian. You run Ottawa!"

"We've been dropped. Archie and I are no longer on the 'list.'"

"Oh, Memsahib...."

"We are no longer on any 'list.' It is not for us I care. It is for our people. For years we were the only Jews to be asked to 'official' things. Now there are none. Can you tell me, what terrible thing have we done?"

"Why, nothing, I have no idea...."

"We give to everything, the Red Cross, the hospitals, charities, even to political parties. To Mr. King's private fund, Archie subscribed $25,000...."

"Good God!"

"It is nothing. For ourselves, we do not ask. We ask only for the children. We ask to bring twenty little children to Canada, war refugees, children who have no homes, no families. We ask to bring them here, to our own homes, to be our own children. We do not ask for money, or time, only permission. What is the answer? There is no answer. 'Oh, Mrs. Freiman, you have come to the wrong department!' 'Oh, Mrs. Freiman, we must have a request in writing!' 'Oh, Mrs. Freiman, you will have to see the Minister of Immigration!' 'Come back next week, Mrs. Freiman, next month, Mrs. Freiman, next year, Mrs. Freiman!' Yet all this time, every day, boats are docking at Halifax, at Montreal, with *thousands* of refugees from Austria, from Holland, from Russia! There is only one difference — they are not Jews!"

"Oh, I'm sure there must be some...."

"I am not giving up, I *cannot* give up but it seems the harder I try, the worse I make things!"

"It's not your fault, Lillian."

"You see, if we give *more* to good works, we are accused to 'buying our way in,' if we give less, we are 'hoarding.' If we speak out, we are 'pushy,' if we keep to ourselves, we are 'sneaky.' I try to be always pleasant, polite, to keep my feelings inside. It does not work. Others are not pleasant to me. What do we do?"

"I don't know."

"Do you know what they are saying? They say that Freiman's Department Store sells 'Jew junk.' They say that Zionism is a secret society, a cabal, a conspiracy to take over the world. Lily, they say we are Communists!"

"You!"

"And Mr. King, too!"

"Willie!" (God, what are they saying about me?)

"Of course, he and Archie have been friends for years, ever since Mr. King came to Ottawa, before we were married. Archie always says Mr. King is the only *true* liberal. Archie delivered the entire Jewish vote for Mr. King at the convention, when he was chosen leader, not to mention contributions to the campaign, not that Archie would ever bring the subject up, or put himself forward, like the Doctor, or Mr. Massey, but he is a hard worker, and has a good head for figures. . . ."

"And you want your twenty homeless children?"

"Oh, Lily, there are hundreds! Hundreds of homeless children! Everywhere the doors are locked against the Jews! Those doors can only be opened *from the inside.* If it takes money, I will pay. I will pay *anything.*"

"It's more than that. It depends on who you are, you know, Irish, Catholic, French. . . ."

"Jewish?"

"Then you have to wait until some old geezer croaks and an Irish, or Catholic or French seat opens up. . . ."

"But there are no 'Jewish seats.' There are no Jews in the Senate."

"No."

Mrs. Freiman put her teacup down and looked at it a moment. Then she stood up abruptly and looked at me. She spoke softly.

"The terrible thing is, *we have nowhere to go.*"

I asked Jack if Willie would appoint Archie Freiman to the Senate.

"Christ no! He's a Jew!"

"Do you think there's a conspiracy, a Jewish conspiracy, to take over the world?"

"This world? Who wants it?"

"But Esselwein's done quite well. He's got this country by the balls."

"Esselwein's not a Jew. His name is Leopold. Sergeant J., for Jackass, Leopold. He's a Kraut."

I sat down and thought of all the creepy, conspiratorial people I knew. Not one of them was a Jew.

"Perhaps Vincent Massey is going to take over the world," I said.

"Don't laugh," said Jack.

Parliament opened the first week of December. Willie won his first vote of confidence by a majority of one. The next vote he won by two, but on the third vote his majority slipped back to one. It was a different Prog every time. You never knew which way they would go. Neither did they. They had a lot of trouble understanding the difference between Liberal and Conservative, no matter how often it was explained to them, by both sides, and they tended to fall asleep during debates, and forget which side they were supposed to be on. They couldn't see the point in all the jumping up and down and hoohaw over this and that when things could be worked out a lot quicker over a cup of coffee. The Progs drove Willie nuts. Just when he'd have them all lined up, one of them would phone the wife back in Pincher Creek or Three Hills and get a whole different story, and change his mind, and spook the rest.

Potatoes, Lily thought, watching the Progs from the gallery. A sack of potatoes. Esselwein was right. Oh, shit! What a sucker she was! At least she hadn't joined the Communist Party. That was close. But what doesn't he know? And who has he told? Funny, all that talk about overthrowing the State, and he can dump this government any time he wants, now. What's he waiting for? Pig. She'd seen him a few weeks ago, she was sure of it. It was just a glimpse, but she recognized the walk, the bent head and short, purposeful strides of a man who knows exactly where he's going. She'd hurried to catch up to him, but he turned a corner and disappeared. I'll get you yet, pig, she thought.

Lily's lost weight. Just as well. Never too rich or too thin as they say. Bad enough to look like a bratwurst, but a burst bratwurst, ugh. On the other hand, Mussolini has created a fashion for short, squat men. It's very strange. Ottawa doesn't like Italians. They're sex-crazed. Maybe it's because Mussolini strikes poses, as if he were a statue, and dresses like a bit player from *The Barber of Seville*, so people here think he's cultural. Does he wear cologne, and pick his nose, like Al Capone? Don't complain. Willie is in fashion too. Her official portrait of the Prime Minister, showing Willie with teeth clenched and a far-away look in his eye, is admired everywhere. Even Willie commented on the likeness.

Mum has been taken up by Memsahib, who says Mum reminds her of a yogi she knew in Poona who could walk on fire and fly through the air. Mum does neither of these things, but Memsahib is delighted to have someone to talk to, or talk at, in the afternoons, when Bungo has his nap. Memsahib considers herself very spiritual. Lily too has been taken up, much against her will, as a result of a casual reference she made in the course of conversation to "Mr. King and his dog, Patronage." Memsahib considers herself a wit also, and has gathered around her, as the Rideau Hall set, a group of bright young things who behave like characters in a novel by Evelyn Waugh.

Since Memsahib mistakes wit for malice, she also likes to invite people who hate each other, and provoke them into a fight. Willie is often invited with Mr. Meighen, but usually makes his excuses, and when he does come, proves to be utterly witless. Mr. Meighen is, Memsahib's star boarder. Mr. Meighen is brilliant (everybody says so). You can tell because he makes you feel so dumb. Mr. Meighen knows he's brilliant (everybody says so), and he never misses a chance to show how much smarter he is than you are. Fortunately, Mr. Meighen doesn't talk to women, who have no brains at all.

The rest of the "regulars" are out-of-favour politicians with grievances, and bitter ex-officers dying for a war. At dinner, reputations are served up, cut to ribbons, with relish, and the juicy tidbits are carried off, still hot and steaming, to those most likely to choke on them. If Lord Byng considers the conversation indiscreet, or the guest list undiplomatic, he gives no sign.

"Bungo *hates* people," Memsahib confides. "Without me to smooth the way on the social side, he'd be completely lost!"

Bungo likes women. Lily often feels his eyes following her as she moves about the room. Lord Byng's eyes are large and blue. They are fringed with dark lashes and have interesting crinkles at the corners. Sometimes he asks her opinion, and tells little jokes, his eyes smiling as if to say, "If only we were in another country, and the bitch was dead!" His eyes follow Miss Sandford too. Eva Sandford is Memsahib's lady-in-waiting, a hearty English girl, young, not pretty, but good fun. Eva fetches Bungo's pipe, and often sits beside him in the evenings when he reads the papers. He touches her arm from time to time, and becomes agitated if she leaves the room for long. Watching them together, you'd think they were alone. The intimacy is so striking, Lily sometimes wonders if Eva isn't the offshoot of an old indiscretion, or whether a *ménage à trois* is now "the thing" in vice-regal circles.

Bungo does not like Willie. King is a cad, although Bungo is too much a gentleman to say so. Instead of handing the country over to

Meighen, like a good chap, the bounder tucked it under his arm and ran off down the field with it! Now they have a mess! Bribery, drunkenness, horrible Progs everywhere, Bolshies, thugs, political women from the west, with hairy lips, who shake hands! Where will it end? But at least King isn't a scoundrel, like Meighen.

Bungo was shocked when Memsahib began reading aloud, after dinner, a scurrilous new novel, *The Land of Afternoon,* by a Gilbert Knox. It revealed the steamier side of Ottawa political life in alarming, and accurate, detail. (Even the Governor-General was in it, but it was obviously old Connaught, poor bugger.) It was the usual trash, an *amour* between an up-and-coming politician and his plain but socially prominent secretary. Bungo would have paid no attention, except that the politician was Meighen to the life, right down to the supercilious sneer, and Memsahib had had the plain but socially prominent secretary up for dinner a dozen times!

Meighen! Meighen had a poker up his ass and ice-cubes for balls! It was a clear frame-up, a straight case of libel. Nobody had ever heard of this "Gilbert Knox." Bungo took Meighen aside and advised him to sue the blue blazes out of the publisher.

But Meighen didn't sue. Then the rumours started, how Mr. Meighen always worked far into the night, and often slept on the couch in his office, and didn't see his family for days on end, and was *so* dependent on Miss K. to see he had the right papers, and that his socks matched, and wasn't it amazing that no one had guessed! Meighen's only reply was to say that he did not read novels, and had no intention of reading this one.

Who was "Gilbert Knox"? The question obsessed Ottawa. It was certainly a pseudonym for someone "in the know." "Why, he must be one of us!" Memsahib cried. "He's sitting in this very room!" That made everyone uncomfortable. A $5,000 reward was offered to anyone revealing Knox's true identity. There was speculation that it must be clever young Spry, who had scandalous views, but then it could be bright young Forsey, who had even more scandalous views. Some whispered that it was Memsahib herself! No one doubted for a moment that the book was perfectly true. As for Mr. King, since no one wrote a novel about his sex life, he was presumed not to have one.

Sex was always a safe topic of conversation in Ottawa. Hardly anyone indulged in it, whereas, when it came to corruption, everybody had a thumb in the pie. There was never a whisper about the Doctor's import-export business, or about Senator "Chaos" Coolican's flying boats; and when the Tories finally broke the smuggling scandal in the House, all they could come up with was an obscure custom's officer in Quebec, a Mr. Bisaillon, who had deposited some unusually large amounts of money in the personal savings account of the Minister of Customs. The minister had long since been appointed to the Senate, where he was dying of acute alcohol poisoning, and Mr. Bisaillon had been fired years ago. Lily almost wept with relief.

As soon as the public learned that the Liberals were behind bootlegging, Willie's popularity soared. He'd made such a mess of Canada, rum running was almost the only way to make a decent living. Everybody was doing it. The country slept by day and danced by the light of the moon. Willie himself whirled off to Saskatchewan, where he found a vacant seat in Prince Albert, and shimmied back into the House on a wave of potato whiskey. The Conservatives, faced with a long list of their own party faithful engaged in the import-export trade, decided that perhaps the indiscretions of Mr. Bisaillon were taking up too much of Parliament's time, and gratefully accepted the offer of an anonymous donation to settle the party's debts.

"Cost me a million bucks," the Doctor said. "Cheap at the price."

Senator Coolican, who had never before been on anyone's "list," became the toast of Ottawa.

"Too bad *you* didn't get his looks," said Memsahib, making googly eyes in Jack's direction.

Jack was the only man in Ottawa to wear a pink suit. He drove a cream Buick roadster that made women weak in the knees. He used coarse language in the presence of ladies. He wore a black kid glove on his left hand, where a steel claw replaced the fingers he'd blown off before the war, and sometimes, under his jacket, he carried a gun. Jack had dined with Al Capone, and lived. He had shaken hands with Jack Dempsey, and golfed with Douglas Fairbanks. He called the Prince of Wales "David." With his vague resemblance to Valentino and his look of weary dissipation, Jack could have had the pick of any girl in Ottawa, and did, although if he ever explored the Jello quivering beneath Memsahib's *crêpe de Chine,* he never let on.

Jack took Memsahib to hockey games. Hockey was her passion. She never missed a game, kept scorecards on all the Senators, and swore like a sailor when they lost. Jack and Memsahib made a striking couple, the hood in the white hat and the banshee in beaver, her diamond earrings swinging wildly when she screamed. Memsahib donated a trophy for "the most gentlemanly player." It was her best joke. After the disaster, the Lady Byng Trophy would be Canada's only happy memory of the Byngs, although Willie always said Bungo brought it all down on his own head.

The crisis began with an incident at dinner following the opening of the House. Almost no one noticed, and its significance didn't emerge until later. Willie was seated at the head table, next to Eva Sandford. The soup had barely been served when Miss Sandford suddenly flushed and moved her chair slightly away from the Prime Minister. A moment later, she flushed again and bit her lip. She moved her chair again, and turned her back on Mr. King. Then Willie doubled over and uttered a faint cry of pain.

"He pinched my thigh!" Eva Sandford told Memsahib later. "Then he pinched it again!"

"No!" cried Memsahib.

"I kicked him," said Miss Sandford. "Hard."

Memsahib swore never to have "that man" in her house again. (It's not your house, Lily was tempted to say, but didn't.) No one asked the Prime Minister if he had pinched Miss Sandford, and no one suggested he apologize. Pinches were an occupational hazard in Ottawa. Lily had a run-in with a chief justice that left her black-and-blue for days. What's the fuss? Older women considered a pinch a compliment. Was Memsahib jealous? Willie had clearly pinched the wrong thigh.

Bungo threatened to horsewhip his Prime Minister. He was restrained only by the memory that he had threatened the Prince of Wales with the same thing last year, when the Prince toured Canada totally sloshed, or stoned, or both, but the King, while sympathetic, had not been encouraging. God, Bungo missed the army! Send the farts to the front! Let them get fucked at the front! But where's the front? Oh God, where is the front? Why is he here in this goddamn cesspool? Stinking sinkhole! Stinkhole! A pervert and a fornicator! What is to be done? Who's running this show? Why, *he* is, goddamn! He's in charge here! He'll do something! He'll blow the whistle, goddamn!

15

The Château Laurier Grill is a great place for a conspiracy. It is Lily's favourite place in Ottawa. She eats here almost every night (Mum prefers room service, materializing loaves and fishes simply by speaking a few words on the phone), and she always sits at the same table, the last banquette on the right, by the band, with an excellent view of the room. It is Senator Coolican's table, in fact. Lily never lacks for company. When the House is in session, as now, the nation's business is transacted over brandy and cigars in the Grill, and during times of political crisis, as now, the Grill is as busy as a hoorhouse on payday. The velvet banquettes are crowded, the air smells of sex, and the whispered seductions are so crude that acts of mutual buggery might as well take place right there and then.

The Grill is a subterranean room, dark green, with potted palms clustered here and there. The light is murky, the air thick. Lily feels like she's sitting in a grotto at the bottom of the sea. She loves to watch the slippery, shadowy creatures floating past, arms flung around shoulders or raised in greeting, hands waving glasses, lighting cigarettes, hands shaking hands: schools circling, circling, forming a pattern around a table, then dissolving to reform somewhere else, the little French-Canadians, as alike as minnows in their black suits, darting swiftly here and there among the palms, the lumpen Progs herded together in the centre of the room, walrus on a rock, snoozing in a pool of light, the low murmur of conversation ebbing and flowing around the music, the sudden ripple as a great Liberal leviathan enters the room, an eddy of respectful space forming around him as he moves heavily, deliberately, among the tables, nodding serenely to left and right, acknowledging friends with only the faintest flicker of his fingers.

From time to time Lily wonders what sex would be like with one of these old bulls. They are all carefree bachelors again, wives safely dead, or left behind in Halifax or Saskatoon, and they drink the nights away in each other's rooms. They are just old farm boys, mostly, worn smooth by the rough and tumble of politics. They smell of shaving lotion, thick necks clipped and pomaded in the Château barbershop, gnarled hands softened by rosewater, hard faces ruddy with good food and browned, in winter, by the Château sunlamp. They think slowly and speak softly. They treat Lily with the exaggerated courtesy older men reserve for women not their wives, a humourous, flirtatious attentiveness. She is a woman to flatter and cajole, to kiss on cheek or hand. But she is also a pump to prime, a means to an end. She's stuck with the role of spinster sister at the moment, Cerebus at the gate to Hell, woof, woof.

Willie never goes to the Grill. He never goes anywhere except, occasionally, to the House. Is it her fault?

Their nightly conversations on the phone have progressed beyond the garterbelt now, and sometimes go on for an hour or more (with a lot of heavy breathing at the other end). Lily finds this erotic arrangement more exciting than regular sex, biff, bam, thank you ma'am, and Willie is a hell of an audience, but what do you do when the Prime Minister can't get his hand off his pecker? Willie now spends most of his time in bed, "dreaming," and the rest of his time having his dreams interpreted, or his chart cast, or his tea leaves read, or writing it all up in his diary. It seems to be only a matter of time before the government falls, or Willie goes mad. But the government has already fallen, pretty much, hasn't it? And Willie *is* mad.

Tonight the Grill is almost empty. Another emergency vote in the House. Lily hates eating alone. An empty chair is an invitation to a bore, and she's apprehensive when she sees Bill Herridge weaving unsteadily towards her. Bill has been drunk almost constantly since his wife died. Why should he care? Ruth left him millions, and he didn't give a damn for her when she was alive. There's hardly a night when Bill doesn't turn up with a new date, a pretty girl with long legs and tiny little tits who says "boop-doop-a-doop!" and giggles when Bill kisses her. No doubt they are all Young Canadians. Bill is busy organizing a League of Young Canadians, cold showers and calisthenics from what Lily can figure out, a civilian Canadian Corps to save the country from corruption. Everybody calls them the "Krime and Krap Kids."

"I killed my wife, have you heard?" Bill says, sliding in beside her.

"It was TB, I thought."

"Nope. Ruth died of a broken heart, that's what they say. Old Bill did her in, the bugger."

"Ruth was sick a long time."

"Yeah. We're all sick, aren't we? Whole damn country's got the clap. Caught it from the PM."

"Come on. Willie just *thinks* he's got VD. It's part of his neurosis."

"Yeah? I hear it's terminal. Real quick, a bullet in the brain, right there on Parliament Hill, a little blood on the snow, a Colt .45 and a mysterious lady in black."

Bill's eyes are looking at her intently now. They are perfectly in focus.

"Who told you that, the RCMP?"

"Not much Smythe don't know."

"It was a joke."

"Not to us. We're serious."

"Who's 'we?' "

"Me, Smythe, the Chief of Staff, Great War Vets, the League, Tories, Grits, everybody who wants a clean, honest country."

"And you want me to assassinate Willie?"

"It's the only way to get him out of there. He's pulled a kind of Cromwell stunt, taken over Parliament, bribes the MPs to vote for him, what can you do? Democracy's dead. We've got a creeping Jesus little dictator. Somebody's got to step in and save the country, that's what Bungo says."

"Bungo!"

"Sure. It's his idea, pretty much — not bumping King off, that's my idea — but grabbing hold of the country, you know. It's us or the Reds."

"Reds! I haven't seen a Red since I came to Ottawa."

"Right! They're invisible, that 's what Smythe says. They're all busy boring from within, banks, business, politics, everywhere, like termites, just waiting for the big word from Moscow, then pow! The Reds look just like the rest of us, did you know that? That's what makes them so dangerous. Smythe says there thousands of Reds, maybe hundreds of thousands, coast to coast. That's who's propping King up, the Reds and the Jews."

"But if I bump Willie off, as you put it, the Liberals will just choose someone else!"

"Nope. We're goin' to change everything, the works. The old party system's had it. Kaput. Look at Meighen! He's worse than King! Nope, we're goin' to organize a one-party system, a national government, bring in the best guys from *all* parties, conscript the best brains out of business, industry, finance, labour, put everybody to work *together*. No more bloody bickering — organize the whole country along military lines, each neighbourhood a company, with a captain and junior officers. Universal registration — find out what people can do, put them to work, get the unemployed going building roads, airstrips, everything run according to plan, rational, efficient. Boy, just you watch! We'll show those damn dagos a thing or two. We'll show 'em the *new* democracy! Hey, that's kind of nice eh? 'The New Democracy.' "

"And when is all this supposed to, um, happen?"

"Early June, maybe sooner, Meighen's going to propose a motion of censure against the government over the Bisaillon affiar. Pretty tame stuff, but the Progs'll go for it. Once the motion of censure passes, King's a dead duck. He'll either have to resign, with shit on his head, and give Meighen control, or try to carry on. Of course, he'll hang on. That's where you come in. A dramatic assassination, in public. The army will move in, Bungo will declare a state of 'apprehended insurrection,' I think that's the phrase, invoke the War Measures Act, and we're home free."

Lily shuts her eyes a moment. The picture has changed. Instead of snow, there is green grass. Willie is lying on it, a small hole in his head, but instead of just the two of them, there's a big crowd of soldiers and police, and Bungo is there in the background with a smile on his face, and instead of just one body, one black shadow on the ground, there are two. The second is her own. Shoot and be shot. Of course. Blame the Reds. She is a Red after all, isn't she, or so Smythe will say later. How neat.

"I don't think I can do it without snow, Bill."

"Christ, what difference does it make?"

"It's in black-and-white. Green spoils the contrast."

"Jesus, you artsy types! You drive everybody nuts!"

"The Italians are artsy, Michelangelo, Leonardo, Dante...."

"Yeah, the *Duce's* goin' to get rid of a lot of that stuff. Into the garbage. Out with the old Rome, in with the new!"

"And who's to be the New Democracy's Duce? You?"

"Could be. General MacBrien wants a crack at it, the shit. You need somebody with a lot of popular appeal, though, somebody to keep the masses happy, you know, bread and circuses. . . ."

"Movies?"

"Hey, yeah! Great idea! We'd make a great team, you and me, brains and balls! You're not a bad lookin' dame for your age. You just need a little sparkle, some glitter, you know — ritzy clothes, diamonds, a little flash. If you got it, flaunt it, I always say. No need to look like a funeral, eh?"

"I like black. Besides, I never know when I might want to shoot someone, do I?"

"Good girl! You're on, then?"

"I'll think about it."

We were leaving for Atlantic City the next day. I woke up in a panic. Did I dream it? Did Bill? Was I drunk? Was he? What to do? I packed in a daze and got to the train early. The red cap said Jack was in Willie's car, at the back, with Mister Massey. By the time I walked down, I found that events had preceded me.

"Esselwein!"

"That's our new steward," said Vincent.

"But it *is* Esselwein! Jack, you must recognize him!"

"His name is Leo," said Vincent.

I looked at Leo very hard. He stood at attention and looked over my left shoulder. This man was thin, even skinny. His hair was cropped very close, almost shaved. He didn't wear glasses. But the ears! Those satanic little pointed ears that Esselwein always kept covered with a hat, except in bed.

"This man's a Bolshevik, or used to be," I said. "He's a cop. He's a spy, a stool pigeon, a fink, a creep. He's a Jew."

Vincent looked alarmed.

"He's a Kraut," said Jack "Say something, Leo."

"*Danke shoen.*"

"He's a steward," scowled Massey.

"Okay, then, Leo. I'll have a cocktail. A Pink Lady, please Leo, straight up."

Leo cleared his throat and shifted from foot to foot. Then he raised his hands helplessly, palms up.

"Excuse me," he said in German-accented English. "I do not know."

"See! Esselwein never could handle a drink."

"I thought you said he knew his liquor," Vincent said to Jack.

"Only in bottles."

"He's a fascist."

"You aren't a Jew, are you?" asked Vincent.

"Okay, so he *is* a cop," said Jack. "Keep it under your hat, eh?"

"Esselwein, you are a shit."

He smiled.

"We understand there may be a plot to kill the Prime Minister," said Vincent.

"Kind of a coop," said Jack.

"So I hear."

"You *do*?"

"It's all over town. I'm sure Leo can tell you all about it, can't you Leo? When it comes to conspiracy, Comrade Esselwein is very capable."

16

Finally, the snow melted. Ottawa turned from grey to brown and then, very slowly, to green. The motion of censure against the Liberal government was tabled in the House, as expected. But Willie conjured up so many amendments, and amendments to the amendments, that the Progs became hopelessly confused, and things bogged down completely. The Progs were desperate to get home to seed the crop, and thought of nothing but the weather.

A testimonial dinner was held in Lord Byng's honour on April 9, 1926, the ninth anniversary of the Battle of Vimy Ridge. Hundreds of Byng's Boys came to Ottawa and got very drunk. They presented their old commander-in-chief with a Buick sedan. Lord Byng thanked them and wept. After that, nearly every regiment in Canada held a memorial dinner, or a reunion, or a parade. Militia units that hadn't drilled since the war were suddenly ordered out on maneouvres. Everywhere, the streets were filled with marching feet and the sound of the pipes.

Bill Herridge (Major Herridge, he insisted now) wore his old uniform all the time. So did several of the other Rideau Hall "regulars." It gave Lily a strange sense of *déjà vu*, as if it were 1914 again, and the war had just begun. Bill never spoke directly about "Operation Fat Boy," as the *putsch* was called, but Lily could tell from all the late night meetings, the secret signals and knowing looks, that things were progressing. General McBrien walked on tiptoe, and looked over his shoulder before saying as much as "Hello." (Oh, Big Peter, where are you now?)

Lily anxiously awaited her "orders." Jack told her not to worry, play along, everything would be okay, but she had nightmares. Bill seldom let her out of his sight. They became a "couple" — tea dances on Wednesdays, bridge on Thursdays, Sunday drives up the Gatineau, cocktails every afternoon at five, then dinner out, with one of "us." Bill was good company. He was the Charleston champion of Ottawa. He mixed a good martini and told a good story. He was a good lay. This had endeared Bill to Bungo during the war, when Major Herridge had been the Corps HQ'S chief procurer, snatching downy-cheeked young adjutants out of public school before some other commander's pimp grabbed them.

" 'Suck or die!' I said. The kids did okay. Some of them made brigadier."

(God, Willie did pinch the wrong thigh!)

Bungo seemed puzzled about "Fat Boy." He was desperate to do the "right thing," When the government of Canada had in effect ceased to function, he'd cabled the Foreign Office for advice, but his cables had never been answered. He'd consulted the precedents, only to find that Canada's first prime minister, Macdonald, had set a precedent for chicanery and corruption as yet unsurpassed. Canada was clearly being unBritish, but when it came right down to it, Bungo has only the vaguest idea what being British actually meant.

Life held little mystery for Bungo. He'd made a complete botch of school, and had been put in the army because he preferred the company of horses to men. After a military career distinguished by a combination of stubbornness and recklessness that had nearly lost the war, Bungo had been sent to Canada to suppress Bolshevist agitation among the lower classes. Lower classes! God, his *Prime Minister* was a Red, a traitor, a degenerate! Bungo would gladly have put a bullet in Mr. King's little pea brain. The trouble was, he had no orders. Bungo had never in his life done anything without orders.

Lily noticed that Bungo often shook his head and rubbed his eyes with his fingers, as if he had sand in them. Perhaps the sand came from his brain. Bungo's brain resembled the Mojave desert, flat, and beige, with a thatch of dry sagebrush here and there. In the middle of the desert was a stockade, and inside the stockade were the White Men; outside the stockade, hiding in the gullies and crouching behind the sagebrush, were the Natives. In between, Memsahib lived in a gaudy striped tent, with fluttering pennons and skulls on spikes, and urged both sides on to battle with ferocious screams.

Memsahib had coined the code name for "Fat Boy." She never called the Prime Minister anything else, except "That man." She developed the

fixation that Willie, by indecency and incompetence, had besmirched
Bungo's reputation, and as a consequence, Bungo would not "get
India." Memsahib made "getting India" sound wonderfully horny, like
getting laid, and she was obviously dying for it. A show of strength
against the junglees in Canada would certainly "get India" in the bag.

The Fat Boy, meanwhile, spent more and more time with Mum. Lily
was a little alarmed. It looked like Mum might be getting religion again,
and Lily was careful to hide the cigarette lighters. Mum sewed strange,
coloured patches on her white shift, and bound her head in a turban,
and whirled around the room, her right arm aloft, crying "Death to the
Infidel!"

Willie interpreted infidels to be Tories. "A religious note is exactly
what is needed at this time," he said.

Most of what Mum said was gibberish. Lily could make no sense of it
at all, until one day she heard, in the cadence of Mum's chanting, a
familiar old riverman's shanty that Papa used to sing. All of a sudden
Lily could see the Nile, and little white boats full of redcoats, and Papa
on the riverbank with the other shantymen, pulling the boats up the
river to Khartoum, while in the desert not far away, dervishes whirled
and shook their spears. God, Mum was the Mahdi!

"What do you think she means, 'Take Khartoum?' " Willie asked.

"I think it means Bungo's up the creek, without a paddle," Lily said.

"Operation Fat Boy" was scheduled for July 1, 1926. It was Dominion Day, a national holiday, and the country would be at the beach. By
the time anybody noticed, or cared, Canada would have New Democracy, and the trains would run on time. ("But the trains already run on
time," Lily protested. "You could set your watch by the T&NO.") Lily
had her gun loaded. The shells were blanks, she had a bulletproof vest,
courtesy of Al Capone, which she didn't tell Bill about, and she'd lined
the inside of her hat with steel, so she could hardly hold her head up.

It was not the kind of revolution she had in mind.

On June 26, Memsahib held a fancy-dress ball. She'd found an old
powdered wig in the Rideau Hall attic, and conceived the idea of a ball
based on characters from the American Revolution. Willie came as mad
King George III. "A striking resemblance!" Memsahib cried, leading
him triumphantly around the ballroom. Memsahib was Marie
Antoinette. She was always a little vague about her revolutions. "But I
know one when I see one!" she said. Bill was George Washington, and

Lily went as his slave, a barefoot black mammy with a calico kerchief and a ton of greasepaint. The band played tunes from the Broadway hit, *Shuffle Along*, and they brought down the house with "Swanee, Swaneeee, How I luv ya, how I luv ya." Even George III danced all night and sang his heart out.

The next day, at noon, when Bungo was still nursing an appalling hangover, he was astonished to find Mr. King ushered into his study. Mr. King looked ghastly.

"I can't go on," croaked Mr. King, and sank into a chair.

"Are you ill, man?" said Bungo. Had somebody poisoned the little fart? That wasn't the plan, was it? What the hell was going on?

"I am quite at the end of my strength, Your Excellency. The House is in chaos."

"Well, that's been plain for some time, hasn't it, Mr. King?"

"I believe an election is the only way to clear the air."

Bungo felt a shell whizz close by his head, leaving a frightening vacuum. Election? Who said anything about an election? Where the hell was Herridge?

"An election eventually, Mr. King, but what about the motion on the floor of the House, a very serious motion involving illegal activity on the part of your administration? Surely you must face the music!"

"I have decided to take my case to the people, sir. I believe I have their confidence, and will be returned with an increased majority. I thought August 28, for an election date, or perhaps the following week...."

"Are you asking me to dissolve Parliament, *now*?"

"Yes, Your Excellency. At two o'clock."

The shell exploded in the back of Bungo's mind, filling his head with smoke.

"No," he said, "I won't."

"But you must!"

Mr. King jumped up and began to dance nervously around the room, his little hands waving wildly in the air. Bungo resisted the urge to hit him.

"My advice, Mr. King, is to accept defeat like a man."

"But if I *am* defeated in the House, an election is inevitable!"

"Not at all. I shall feel obliged to call on someone else."

"Not Meighen!"

"But there *was* an agreement, wasn't there, Mr. King? Didn't we have a sort of gentlemen's agreement to give Mr. Meighen a 'go,' in the event you were unable to carry on?"

"I *have* carried on."

"Then why are you running away? Why not accept the verdict of the house?"

Mr. King was leaping up and down now, his face quite contorted with rage.

"You *must* do as I say!" he shouted. "*I am Prime Minister!*"

You're a twat, Bungo thought. He rubbed his eyes with his fingers. The smoke was lifting now. He blew the last of it out through his nostrils.

"No," Bungo said. "I won't."

Early the next afternoon, while Bungo was still at lunch, Mr. King returned to Rideau Hall. He was dressed in a morning coat and striped trousers. In his left hand he carried a top hat and white gloves, in his right, a long white envelope.

"My resignation," he said, handing the envelope to Bungo with a little bow. Then he turned and ran down the steps as fast as his little legs would carry him and hopped into a waiting limousine.

A few moments later, Mr. King rose in the House of Commons to announce that he had submitted his resignation to the Governor-General, and Canada was without a government. He gave a little bow, turned, and ran down the steps, *trip-trap, trip-trap,* and hopped into a waiting limousine.

"Kingsmere, Leo," he said. "Quickly!"

General MacBrien was golfing at the Country Club. Major Herridge was in a bar in Hull. Lily was in the bathtub.

Bungo summoned Mr. Meighen and asked him to form a government. Meighen accepted with almost indecent haste.

"But what about New Democracy!" shouted Bill.

"Meighen should have a go," Bungo said. "Fair's fair, eh?"

Meighen's Conservative government lasted two-and-a-half days. At midnight, on July 1, a befuddled Prog, wakened from a deep sleep by the Speaker's voice, voted "Aye" instead of "Nay," and the government

fell. Mr. Meighen asked Lord Byng to dissolve the House and open the
way for a general election.

"Why, I guess so," said Bungo, Looking puzzled, "Why not, eh?"

THE NEXT DAY, AT LAURIER HOUSE:

An election to him! And not to me! Me! Me! It's absolutism! A
return to autocracy! We are no better than, than *Newfoundland!* An
Englishman, a foreigner, who knows nothing of the country, *presumes*
to think for the nation and exercises a royal prerogative! It is the old
aristocratic prejudice that the Tory party has some sort of divine right to
rule, and that the way must be made easy for them, and stumbling
blocks put in the way of the opposition. The advice of the Tory prime
minister, who governed for two-and-a-half days, is accepted, while the
advice of a Liberal prime minister, a *true* representative of the people,
who governed for *six months,* is rejected!

I have seen it all coming from the very beginning. First, the State
dinner was postponed, a clear sign that His Ex. had no confidence in the
survival of our government, and when we *did* stay in, the dinner was
cancelled! His Ex. gave some lame excuse, first about servants being
overworked, and then that Queen Alexandra's death ruled it out, but I
really think it was done to save money, and to let the government down.
I felt greatly annoyed and incensed. No expense was spared for Her
Ex.'s fancy dress party! All along their attitude to me has been less than
gracious. Last November 19, I attended a hockey game in the Audito-
rium at Her Ex.'s express insistence, in the way of lending patronage. At
both the first and second intermissions, I spoke to Their Ex.'s. I felt that
they not only might, but *should* have invited me into their box. After all,
I was PM of the country, and His Ex. a *visiting* governor. The fact that at
the time there was a difficult situation only made me more indignant
that they had not the courtesy to recognize the situation as meriting a
little graciousness. The box was full of a lot of people from England,
who adopt a sort of superior air towards those of us in Canada. It is a
Tory air of superior knowledge and station that makes a man with red
blood in his veins feels a deep resentment, that 'tranquil consciousness
of effortless superiority' of which Asquith spoke. I feel real indignation
at attitudes that spell 'colonialism' for Canada. If we are going to have
self-government, we are going to have it in its *entirety*, without anyone
sent from England to 'umpire' our behavior!

It's all a Tory conspiracy, I can see that now. Government House is nothing but a Tory preserve, a bastion of privilege, Tory influences at His Ex.'s elbow day and night, the Tory attitude that only 'certain' people have the right to govern. It all comes from His Ex.'s desire to 'save Canada,' but he has brought it all down on his own head. I told him Meighen couldn't govern. 'I am of a different opinion,' he said. 'The Governor-General does not have opinions,' I told him. 'He simply accepts or rejects the advice of his first minister.' Never, until now, has a governor-general of Canada refused his minister's request for a dissolution! I told His Ex. straight out that if he refused me, and granted a dissolution to my opponent, that I would not answer for the consequences. It would become an issue in the election and do no end of injury to the British Crown, and all parts of the Empire, and I would stand out for the rights of the people vs. the Mammon of unrighteousness and remain true to my tradition, my name, and my cause.

Meighen has doomed himself forever! He has given us a great issue to take to the people, the one true issue of democracy, the noble cause of responsible government! It was Grandfather's great victory, and it will be mine! Mine! I cannot help but feel the loved ones have been guiding me through all this. Last night, when I completed writing my diary, I went and looked at the painting of dear Mother, then I looked at the lock of her hair and her wedding ring, and, putting these down, went over to the piano, which she played over and over again, and which she had bought herself with money earned from pupils she had taught, and I sat down to play some hymns myself. I began by playing 'God of Bethel' and went over the words, 'God of our fathers.' I felt I must take the Bible down to receive a message from Mother. I took out the large volume, put my hand on the page and my finger at certain words, all without knowledge of what book I was opening to. When I looked down, this is what I read: 'The God of thy fathers hath chosen thee . . .' I could scarcely believe my eyes! I looked up a dear Mother's face in the painting. Then I looked again at the Bible, and my eyes fell on the words, 'And at the same hour I looked up.' What could be plainer than that? I felt that Mother would wish to help me now, when I most need it, and her wish would be the will of God.

Bungo sandbagged himself inside Rideau Hall. He kept his head down, and hoped the Fat Boy would shoot himself in the foot. Bungo was satisfied that he'd done the "right thing" — he'd got the little bugger out of there, hadn't he? — and immensely relieved that he hadn't had to "blow the whistle" after all. Bungo was perfectly satisfied that only a fool or a knave would vote for King, and that Meighen, while a rum sort, at least was not a traitor, or a crook, and that Canadians, being decent people on the whole, would do the decent thing and vote Tory.

Nobody understood exactly what had happened, except that Willie King had pulled a fast one. He'd put one by old Byng and got the election he'd wanted all along. You had to hand it to the guy. Maybe he was smarter than he looked, eh? In the excitement of a new election, the smuggling scandals were completely forgotten. The whispers were all of conspiracy, and insurrection, and a *coup d'état* which almost happened, or didn't happen, or might have happened, or could happen yet, or was almost certain to happen.

Lily was impressed. Willie had always been a good dancer, better than Bill, as it turned out. Poor Bill. New Democracy vanished like a pipe dream. Why, nobody in all Ottawa knew anything about it!

Memsahib did not "get India." Someone else was made Viceroy. In October the Byngs would return to England and oblivion. Memsahib blamed it all on the Fat Boy. Willie, by dark design, had blotted Bungo's copy book, ruined his reputation. Up to that point, Bungo had felt quite secure, even cheerful, about his reputation. But by the time Memsahib had finished with him, Ottawa was convinced that Lord Byng was a broken man and a total balls-up as governor-general. Memsahib's venomous attacks on the former Prime Minister and Liberal leader won Willie everyone's sympathy. Lily came to understand how badly Willie's pride — a nervous, bloated thing at best — had been bruised by the Byngs. "He's not a gentleman, he's a politican," Lily told Memsahib. But Memsahib listened only to the sound of her own voice. Lily decided that the English started wars simply by being uncivilized, and that the Empire was built on bad manners.

How stupid the English were about Canada! They were always so delighted to arrive and find that Canadians, on the whole, were white, and spoke English, like themselves. But they never stopped to ask why all these lovely British subjects were over here instead of back there, and whether they had come of their own free will, or had been forced into the sea at bayonet point to make room for English sheep and English slums,

and whether the murderous rage that took Vimy Ridge might have
more to do with being dispossessed than with any affection for the King,
or Byng, and if the Kaiser wasn't around to kill, then the King, or Byng,
would do just as well. To the English, we were simply a plain, mud-
coloured people, good-natured, brave enough, but rather lazy and
backward and in need of shaping up. They did not see, beneath our
polite and inoffensive faces, our cruel and cunning peasant soul. Or
realize that they had entered enemy territory: the land of Goliath, and
Delilah, the Not-Chosen. And that Willie King was the quintessential
Canadian.

Lily gave a $5,000 cheque to Andrew Haydon, the Liberal Party
bagman, and specified that the money be used expressly to buy votes, so
that it would end up where it belonged, in people's pockets.

"Let's hear it for chaos," she said.

The election was a hell of a fight — barbarian vs. Philistine, Imperialist
vs. colonial, gentleman vs. cad, soldier vs. slacker, decency against dirty
tricks. Mr Meighen, feeling left out, campaigned in splendid isolation on
the tariff. Memsahib shot poisoned arrows in all directions and threw oil
on the flames. Young Forsey published a book proving that Bungo had
been right, but for all the wrong reasons. Bungo dug in at Rideau Hall
and prayed for reinforcements. But the Ottawa was a long river, and
England very far away.

Willie emerged from his tent clad in the snow-white garments of
political innocence, weeping crocodile tears of outraged modesty. He, a
virgin prime minister, had been jilted at the very altar of democracy by
big, bad Byng, a Bluebeard among governors-general, who had seduced
him, beguiled him into thinking that it was a love match, then cruelly
thrown him over for an ugly Tory stepsister, and now Parliament, pure,
precious Parliament, was stretched like Iphigenia on the altar of Aga-
memnonian autocracy!

Willie the Apostle whirled through the country blowing the ram's
horn of responsible government. He unfurled the banner of Liberalism,
called on the people to come out of the wilderness of colonialism into
the promised land of nationhood. Wild and reckless, passionate, aflame
with righteousness, Willie was master of the feint, the ruse, the ambush.
He blinded his enemies with mirrors. He hid behind smokescreens of

innuendo and fired volleys of half-truths at the barbarians holding out in Rideau Hall. Willie bit and kicked and gouged. He kneed Bungo in the groin and stabbed him in the back. Ablaze with divine desperation, Willie leaped and danced around Parliament Hill, his followers pounding their spears against their shields, until, on September 14, 1926, the people rose, and walls fell, and Willie emerged triumphant, carrying aloft, on the tip of his bloody lance, the severed head of General Byng of Vimy.

THE NEXT DAY,
AT LAURIER HOUSE:

We have won a great victory, a clear majority of 40 or more, if the Progs stay with us. I get the most satisfaction out of Meighen's defeat in his own riding. This will mean his finish as leader of the Tory party, and a great thing it will be. He lowers the whole tone and standard of public life. I believe he is suffering from TB and has not long to live. I am told Lady Byng is hysterical. Lord Byng dreads having to call on me. Has there ever been a governor so arbitrary and tyrannical? This is the sort of trash that comes out to Canada to *govern*!

When I came back to the house at four-thirty a.m., I kissed the lips of the marble bust of dear Mother and came up to the library where I prayed very earnestly that I may be a saviour to men in some way. I believe I have been borne up by a heavenly power, saved by grace. Only yesterday at Kingsmere, a little bird came and perched on the side of the birdbath, looking at me and drinking the water. I remembered how in her last days Mother often thought of herself as a bird, and wondered if it wasn't a message to me. I noticed particularly the scarlet head. I thought of the Holy Grail, the light in the church window at Mother's burial, the scarlet glow as the bird dipped its head, and it was as if I must be assured of Mother's nearby presence. I felt very happy, a Knight Errant radiant in the heavenly light.

I decided to purchase the woods and little stream adjoining Kingsmere. I will offer to buy seventy acres for $4,000. It is a heavy price to pay, but it will keep the Jews and other undesirables out, and will make a splendid gift to the nation. Now I feel more like a gentleman.

I went to bed greatly pleased and with little Pat as a companion at my side. He seemed to understand all was well.

17

The Byngs left Canada in the rain. Nobody came to see them off, only the Prime Minister, Mr. King, who wept and wrung his hands, and said it was all a terrible misunderstanding. Lady Byng swelled up like a puff adder, but didn't strike. So Lily was told. She had not forgiven Memsahib for the rumour about her pregnancy, followed, within weeks, by the rumour about her abortion. She felt a little sorry for Bungo. He was a decent man. But on reflection, among all the reasons for revolution, decency would do as well as any.

Mrs. Freiman was allowed to bring two Jewish orphans into the country. Archie Freiman was not appointed to the Senate, nor was Mrs. McClung, or Magistrate Murphy, even though they had won their case at the Privy Council, and women were now officially "persons." Instead, Willie appointed Mrs. Wilson, an Ottawa heiress and socialite, who was young and handsome and not afflicted by reforming zeal, or opinions of any kind. Unlike Mrs. McClung and Magistrate Murphy, Mrs. Wilson gave splendid dinner parties in the Prime Minister's honour, and sent around fresh game and barrels of Malpeque oysters, in season, to Laurier House.

Willie lost interest in the country, now that he'd seduced it. He devoted his time to his dog, Pat, and the faithful Mrs. Patteson. The three of them were seen everywhere in Ottawa. There was speculation about which one he took to bed, until Nichol, the valet, confirmed that it was indeed Pat.

Usurped by a dog! Now that was grounds for divorce! But the divorce petition would have to go to the Senate, and Lily could just imagine Jack and all his friends rolling around the aisles in fits of laughter, and the terrific dirty stories they'd tell about her for the rest of their lives, and hers. Thanks, but no thanks.

Willie devoted himself to the destruction of Ottawa. He began with the row of lovely old mansions on Wellington Street to the west of Parliament Hill, facing the river. They had once been the homes of Ottawa's first families, but had gone to seed, and were now charity homes for Orphans, Incurables and Friendless Women. The ceaseless procession of the ragged, the dying and the pregnant past the Prime Minister's East Block window offended his sense of justice. Why, what could be more fitting than a new Justice Building, a monument, in the gothic style, to his love for the common man, right there on the bluff? And beside it, in the garden where the Incurables now sat under the lilac trees, a new Supreme Court of Canada!

"Ottawa requires a vista," Willie said, waving his pince-nez.

Once the great stone houses were knocked down, and the debris carted away, and the lilacs uprooted, and the gardens trampled, and everything made flat, the vista that emerged was a view of the E.B. Eddy Pulp and Paper Mill across the river. We could always smell the E.B. Eddy Pulp and Paper Mill, but now we could see it too, with its enormous water tower advertising toilet paper, and its pall of stinking yellow smoke that lent Ottawa the aroma of rotten weiners.

"A pillar of cloud by day," Mum said, squinting into the western sun.

Sure enough, that night the Russell Hotel burned down.

The Russell was a fleabag, an old den of ill repute in Second Empire style, but it had been beautiful in its day, and the heart of Ottawa. Everyone felt a pang except Willie. He persuaded the City to tear down the old Russell Theatre next door on Elgin Street, and said that once the surrounding slums and saloons were swept away, Elgin would become a great boulevard, a Canadian *Champs Elysées*. The Federal Improvement Commission bought up whole neighbourhoods, and everywhere buildings came tumbling down, clouds of dust, heaps of rubble, naked rooms shrinking from the sun. Back alleys, garbage bins, fire escapes and blank, brick walls were suddenly exposed to the full glare of public scrutiny. The owners of some buildings held out, from nostalgia or greed, so new construction could not begin, and when the dust settled, Ottawa was a city of parking lots.

After old Corktown was flattened, and the Irish moved to some other slum, everyone could see that the railway yards ran alongside the *Champs Elysées* on the other side of the Canal, and the Canal itself was a sewer. Everyone could see, too, that the *Champs Elysées* began in a bottleneck, and ended in the river, and that the main post office stood right where the *Arc de Triomphe* should be. By the time the Justice Building was opened, and Wellington Street widened and stripped of its trees, Ottawa was as bald and bleak as the Interior in January, and just as cold.

Kingsmere too was razed. Lily was shocked. Willie had the pines chopped down and the brush cleared away. The pasture was now a rolling green lawn with beds of petunias, and the wild raspberry patch was paved with flagstones. A broad driveway, bordered by a neat stone wall, swept up to the cottage where Willie was waiting for her in knickers and tweeds beneath a new classical portico supported by white pillars, beaming with delight at having transformed this corner of a foreign field into an illustration from *Country Life*.

He led the way down a whitewashed path to a meadow, where the stone arches they'd salvaged from the burnt-out Parliament Buildings during the war had at last been erected in the form of a ruined cloister. Here the grass was rough and overgrown with weeds, as if the ruin had been there for ten centuries, not ten months.

"I wonder if I shouldn't enlarge it a little," Willie said. "I am thinking of adding another wall here, and possibly a small chapel, for quiet meditation. A rose window would give the right effect, don't you think? Without the glass, of course, no hope of that, wreckers being what they are, no sense of history, just knock everything down, bang, bang. Like the old Perley house on Wellington, you know, the Incurables, just complete rubble, nothing at all worth saving, and the old Parent house too, it was just by the purest coincidence I was passing by, and managed to salvage the bay window, and Godfroy Patteson was able to speak for the coat of arms from the Bank of Montreal..."

Willie paused, and Lily felt she ought to say something, but couldn't think of a thing. It didn't matter, because Willie clasped his hands and sank to his knees, and bowed his head, and prayed aloud. He thanked God for guiding his steps to the highest office in the land, where he had been able to fulfil his life's ambition, to help the poor, and by doing so had been able to erect this modest shrine, this little altar in the wilderness. He thanked God too for sending the dear friends who made it possible for him to improve this humble property, at a cost completely beyond his own means, although he wished that the big pine by the house had not been cut down, and that the house itself did not smell of sour milk. He prayed that the pheasants would not be eaten by wolves, and that Pat would not chase the new lambs, and that the lambs would not eat the petunias, or leap off the cliff. He prayed that he'd have the strength to carry on, and set an example to the nation, and not lose control, and break down with the strain.

"Amen, darling," Lily said. "Now let's go in for tea. I'm frozen."

A SHORT TIME LATER,
THE PRIME MINISTER GOES ABROAD:

Today I went to call on M. Mussolini. I confess I had no intention of doing so at the outset, but I have become enthused at the manner in which this country has been brought together and is going ahead, the order of it all, the fine discipline, the evident regard for authority and for M. himself. It is a government by a young man and young men. As I approached the offices, I was held up by police, not allowed to make headway anywhere 'til full explanation given. I saw what government by a dictatorship meant, but when one hears how he came with his blackshirts to the King, offered his services to clean up the gov't and House of Representatives filled with Communists, banished them all to an island, cleaned the streets of beggars & the houses of harlots, one becomes filled with admiration. It is something I have never seen before and one feels it in one's bones. I had a very pleasant talk with his private secretary who said that he thought M. would wish to see me. I feel the deepest sympathy for the man. I know what his work is.

THE NEXT DAY:

I was up and dressed at seven-fifteen a.m. full of interest at the thought of meeting Mussolini. Had breakfast in the large dining room, then went with the guide to see an antique establishment, very fine, but very expensive, then to the home of a friend of his who had an immense collection of velvets & runners, silks, plushes etc. I found the prices very high. I could not resist purchasing the coat of arms from some old flag, said to be 18th century. Paid $20 for it. Then I bought for $50 a gold velvet cloth. Later, I negotiated to purchase another heraldic design. He asked $3. I jumped on him rather hard, and he came down to $1 or nothing. It was unfortunate, as I liked the man very much, but it seemed to me a holdup at the time.

I called on Mussolini at ten-thirty a.m. There were too many secret police, secretaries and messengers to pass. When I was shown into his office, he came forward from his desk where he had been writing & with a smile and a hand outstretched greeted me in a friendly way and showed me to a seat behind his desk. He took a chair in a position just opposite, the light falling on my face & his being between me and the windows. He said 'How are your relations with England?' He was interested in our self-government. When I explained that we were as free as Italy or any country it seemed to surprise him. He told me that in Italy they were mostly concerned with 'streets and agriculture.' I spoke of the fine appearance of the country, its evident progressiveness under his regime. Then I got up to go. I wished him well & the necessary strength to carry on his work.

The impression he made on me was a very real & vivid one. He was more sparse in appearance — very dark — eyes very dark — with large white showing. There was evidence of sadness & tenderness as well as great decision in his countenance. His hand was softer than I expected to find it. It seemed like a hand most given to office work. The head was a Napoleonic one in shape — a Roman through & through, I should say. He has won his way deservedly to his present position, a truly remarkable man of genius, fine purpose, a great patriot. I would not have missed this conference for anything.

Unfortunately the books I bought yesterday had missed being delivered to him. I learned later that M. Mameli, his secretary, to whose care they had been entrusted, lost his wife yesterday in a railroad accident, about the time we were talking together.

Leo the steward was dismissed after the election campaign. He'd done his job. Not a whiff of contraband liquor or heroin or cocaine was found in Willie's railroad car. ("Who would smuggle snow?" Willie complained. "It would melt, wouldn't it?") I had almost forgotten about Leo (Is that a good sign?), when I suddenly found him walking beside me on Sparks Street, in a snowstorm.

"Trotsky was exiled from the Soviet Union today," he said. "I have some shampanski. Would you like to share it?"

"Sure."

Leo lived in Lower Town. The apartment was cheap and shabby, but his bedroom was, as always, neat as a pin. They learn that in the police, don't they?

"Where's the radio?"

"In there." He pointed to a closed door. "Sorry, top secret."

He opened the window and took a bottle of champagne off the ledge. It was almost frozen when he opened it, the cork made a hole in the plaster ceiling. We drank out of teacups.

"The revolution is dead," said Leo, raising his cup. "May it rest in peace."

"You don't sound very happy. You should be, shouldn't you?"

"Six years of my life I spend subverting the Communist Party of Canada, and what do I find? They do the job better without me! Once all the Trots are purged, the party'll be down to two Stalinist lackeys, a secret agent, and a running dog."

"But you helped make them Trots. I mean, they might all have been Stalinists."

"Or Zinovievists, or Bukharinites, or Kalininists, or Luxemburgers, or Molotov cocktails, who knows? By the time the Russians pin a label on something, it's turned into something else. 'Socialism in one country,' what is that? Nationalism, of course. Leninism is just 'Capitalism in one country.' And Stalinism is Czarism. 'Come, come, Comrade Trotsky! What is this talk of revolution? Who is there to give power to? The *kulaks*? They are corrupt. The peasants? The peasants are potatoes. The workers? The workers are ignorant. Comrade, *we* are the revolution! And here we are! It is *ours*!' "

"Stalin sounds a lot like Willie."

"Sure. Smythe thinks King's a Red, eh? Trouble is, Smythe has it all backwards. Stalin is a Philistine. They'd get along like a house on fire."

"But Willie doesn't go around exiling...sorry, I take it back. He's just more subtle about it."

"You ain't seen nothin' yet, kid."

Leo opened another bottle. He was quite drunk. It wasn't like him. (Was he going to fall asleep?) His face was hard, tense, and when he rubbed his eyes I thought for a moment he was going to cry. I had forgotten Esselwein had feelings. Or that I did.

What was I doing there, with a man I should hate? Funny, but it didn't seem to matter. The room was warm, and smelled faintly of borscht and bread, just like the shack at Kirkland Lake. I took my shoes off and curled up on the bed. After a while, the only sound was the snow.

18

Willie discovered radio. He found that he could speak to thousands of people without having to leave Laurier House, and nobody could see him! After all those years of reading Tennyson's *Maud* aloud, to friends, he was at ease in front of a microphone. His harsh, high voice jolted listeners upright in their armchairs. Mr. Leopold, the CNR's brilliant young wireless engineer, explained to the Prime Minister that he could speak to the whole nation *at once*, if he liked, and on July 1, 1927, Canada's Diamond Jubilee, the nation was linked from coast to coast by the longest radio network in the world.

At twelve noon, a children's choir in Halifax began to sing "O Canada" on the national network. The chorus was taken up, in French, by a choir in Quebec, the next verse was sung by children in Toronto, then in Winnipeg, Regina, Edmonton, Vancouver, until ten million people were singing together from sea to sea and there wasn't a dry eye in the whole Dominion.

Otherwise, the day did not go well. Charles Lindbergh flew up in the "Spirit of St. Louis." Willie introduced Lindbergh as "a young God," and everyone fell in love with him, but the old God must have been put off, because an airplane buzzed the Peace Tower during the celebrations, and Willie's speech was drowned out by shrieks and moans as the pilot flew upside-down over Willie's head. All that the radio audience at home heard was the drone of a giant bee. The pilot crashed on landing and was killed. He was an American airforce officer. Willie gave him a state funeral, with full military honours. Ottawa was draped in mourning, and American flags.

When the not-so-young God, the Prince of Wales, arrived the next week, he was furious to find himself completely upstaged. He took his revenge by dressing like Charlie Chaplin. He carried a walking stick that he twirled continually, so nobody could get near him, and said nothing, so nobody could speak to him. He spent the night with a certain married woman, with whom he had danced every dance at the state ball, and had to be carried back to Rideau Hall at sunrise, sound asleep, by Scotland Yard. His younger brother, the Duke of Kent, propositioned the debs and made obscene suggestions to their escorts, and had to be locked up after he was found mooning at spectators through the windows of the royal train.

Willie was horrified but undeterred. He accompanied the Princes across Canada on their royal tour. At each stop, he skipped into the station early and waited in the very front row, hand outstretched, to be the *very first* to welcome Their Royal Highnesses to OttawaToronto WinnipegReginaCalgaryEdmontonVancouverVictoria.

"What, you again, King?" the Prince would say, and twirl his stick.

Apart from brandy, and cocaine, which he carried in his shirt cuff so that by casually resting his head on his hand, or rubbing his nose, he could get a good snort, the Prince had only one desire.

"I want to go to Hollywood," he said.

"No," said the King.

Cables flew back and forth between OttawaTorontoWinnipeg ReginaCalgaryEdmontonVancouverVictoria and London, but the King held firm. Hollywood was full of prostitutesdopefiendspervertsJews. The Prince had to settle for Harlem, where he, and the Duke of Kent and Lily, and Senator Coolican, and Dr. Bethune were entertained at the Cotton Club by the aristocracy of jazz. Later, at a party, they met Bessie Smith. Bessie was about as pissed as the Prince. She seemed to think he was a honky act from some downtown club.

"Why, you jist show me your whale, white sugar," she drawled, "and ah'll show you my black bottom!"

Lily came home with a terrific idea.

"Vincent, we should set up a movie studio, right here in Ottawa. We've got everything, scenery...."

"Do you mean make *fillllmmms*?" Vincent said, curling his lip.

"We could get the Prince of Wales. He's dying to be in movies."

"That's about his speed, isn't it?"

"He could play himself, you see. He'd be a smash! Then there's your brother: he's an actor, isn't he?"

"Raymond is on the *stage*. That's quite embarrassing enough."

"But you said you wanted to encourage the arts in Canada!"

"My dear lady, whatever persuaded you that *fillmms* are art?"

What the hell are the Czar's table napkins then? Obviously art was whatever Vincent happened to own. Lily decided to try the Prime Minister. Willie adored Mary Pickford, and she *was* Canadian.

"Willie, I want to make a movie with the Prince of Wales...."

"Oh, God."

"It's a terrific story, about a revolution."

"No! No!"

"I mean, more of a popular uprising."

"Grandfather?"

"I thought something a little more contemporary...."

"Mother is very photogenic."

"It's about a girl, who always wears black, and a Russian, who isn't, and Finns with yellow eyes, and Mounties, you have to have lots of Mounties, and flying boats. Don't you remember? Wouldn't that be terrific? Someone could even play you, Willie."

"Barrymore?"

"Well...."

"Fairbanks? There's quite a striking resemblance, in the chin...."

Willie became excited, and rushed out to see both the movies then playing in Ottawa. Actors with black moustaches and wavy hair were out for Willie, and Fairbanks was too swashbuckling. By the time the field was narrowed down to Fatty Arbuckle, Willie decided to play the role himself. Once he got finished outlining the script, *The Triumph of Willie King*, choosing the rest of the cast (Mother, Father, Little Bell etc. etc.) and drafting the forty-five minute speech he would deliver at the end, Lily realized it was hopeless. It didn't matter anyway. Willie had just sold control of the Canadian movie industry to a Mr. Nathanson of Famous Players, Hollywood.

Jack and the Doctor divided Canada between them: the Doctor took the water, and Jack got the rock. The Doctor started with the St. Lawrence River. For $20,000, he bought the Beauharnois rapids near Montreal. As water, the rapids were worthless, but with a hydro-electric dam, and the entire St. Lawrence River diverted through the Beauharnois channel, the Doctor could provide enough electricity for all Quebec and half the New England states. A development of this size required government approval, and since the Prime Minister knew nothing about hydro, and cared less (he preferred a cosy fire), it seemed logical to appoint the Doctor to the National Advisory Committee on the St. Lawrence Seaway — a position, the Doctor was quick to point out, with no financial remuneration at all.

As soon as the Beauharnois project became public, the Doctor was rushed off his feet by all the Montreal millionaires who routinely blackballed him at the St. James Club. Within weeks a new syndicate was formed consisting of Quebec's leading financiers, and the Doctor was paid $300,000, plus 80,000 shares,for the rights to Beauharnois. He was pleased to report to the Prime Minister that support for Beauharnois was overwhelming. When the National Advisory Committee recommended that Beauharnois proceed, its shares tripled in value. Each member of the syndicate made a million dollars. The Prime Minister himself declined the Doctor's offer of shares, saying that as guardian of the public interest, he would be unwise to become too closely involved with a private venture.

GNOME sold its shares in the Rainbow Mine for $40 each. The next week, the shares were down to fifty cents. It was rock, after all.

"Hell," said Jack. "I'll mine Toronto."

The first brokerage office of Coolican Ltd. opened in a store window on Bay Street. Jack's desk was right out there in the middle of the floor, next to the phone and the tickertape, with the big chalkboard up behind where everybody could see it. It caused a sensation. In Toronto, dealing with money right out there *in public* was unheard of. It was better than peeping through the window of a cathouse. The very first day, men were lined up three deep on the sidewalk, noses pressed against the glass. The second day, they were three deep inside the office and spilling out onto the street. By the end of the month, Jack took over the whole ground floor and opened offices in Winnipeg and Calgary.

Coolican Ltd. traded only in minerals, oil and gas. The stocks were speculative, but cheap, and bought on credit. For a few bucks down, anybody could own a stake in the future, way up north, or, way out west, and hope like hell it panned out. Usually it did. The numbers on the magic chalk board went up and up and up. Some stocks doubled in value, then tripled, then went up by leaps and bounds. Men quit their jobs or were fired, and spent the whole day on the trading floor at Coolican Ltd. staring at the board. A $10 investment became $100, then $1000. You could make more on the market in a month than most people made in a year. Only a fool would keep his money in the bank at three per cent, and the chickenshits who cashed in, and took their profits, saw the stocks climb higher and higher yet. Soon everybody was into the market, even the Communist Party of Canada, whose office was upstairs, and nobody was getting out. Within a year, Coolican Ltd. had forty offices from Halifax to Victoria and was rumoured to be doing more than a billion dollars a year in business. Coolican Ltd. was bigger than the Bank of Commerce.

Jack moved out to Alberta. He pumped five million dollars into the Turner Valley oilfield, four million into mineral exploration in northern Alberta, and spent another million flying around in his old friend, the Interior. From the air, the Interior looked just like it did on the map, white, with the Hudson's Bay Company posts sticking up like pins. Snow. A lot of snow. What do you do with snow? Jack bought a fleet of airplanes, with skis, and started an airmail service down the Mackenzie River to the Arctic Ocean. He was the first man to fly across the Northwest Passage. Hollywood made a movie about Jack called *White Dawn*. It was shot in California with Ronald Coleman and Ivory Snow. It bombed at the box office. "Snow doesn't sell," Hollywood said.

ONE WEEK LATER:

Wall Street crashed. The crash didn't seem too important at first, one of those crazy things the Americans do from time to time, and the stock market actually rose for a while, as speculators rushed to buy up blue-chip stocks at bargain prices. The Prime Minister, who had all his money in the bank, or government bonds, took no notice of the crash at all. If people were foolish enough to gamble, they deserved what they got, and if the odd broker went broke, well, that was the game, wasn't it? However, on November 1, 1929, as Mr. King was walking down King Street in Toronto (a coincidence?), he was nearly crushed by a man leaping from the roof of the Bank of Commerce. The sight of the body lying at his feet, so broken and squished-looking, scared him.

It was business as usual at Coolican Ltd. In fact, business picked up as clients transferred their money out of the sinking American market into Canadian stocks. As other brokerage houses went bankrupt, Coolican Ltd. remained calm. It was only when the market continued to slide, and money began to disappear altogether, and factories shut down without notice, and beggars crowded the street in front of city hall, that Coolican Ltd. began to look suspicious. It was whispered that Coolican Ltd. had never purchased the stocks its clients ordered at the peak of the market, but rather had invested the money in oil wells and airplanes. Then, when the market fell, and people had to pay up at inflated prices for stocks that were virtually worthless, Coolican Ltd. made a killing.

Senator Coolican said it was all crap, that he'd never had a complaint from a customer, or failed to deliver a stock on demand, or been reprimanded by a government inspector. He hadn't broken any laws because there were no laws. His business was his, so buzz off.

Who had the money, then? It had to be somewhere, didn't it? Money didn't just disappear. If it wasn't in the stock market, or in the bank, or in the pants pocket, it had to be in *somebody*'s pocket, didn't it? By Christmas, the suspicion became a certainty: the money was in Senator Coolican's pocket, and he had stolen it. Coolican had caused the Crash.

In Edmonton, Jack didn't pay much attention to the rumours. A lot of big guys had gone down, he hadn't. You could figure they'd be bitter. So the *Financial Post* "exposes" the stock exchange as a big swindle. Big deal. Where was the *Post* when the market was taking off? Kissing its ass, that's what. Jack knew where his money was. It was in Alberta. There wasn't much to Alberta but dirt. What a piss-poor place! But *under* the dirt, that was something else. He'd staked most of the province, whatever wasn't already mortgaged to the Bank of Commerce.

Jeez, did they hate the banks out here! That was why they loved him. He wasn't a bank, but he had money. Funny guys, the Progs. He had to keep it quiet he was from the East. They hated the East too, even though they were mostly born there. Maybe that's why they hated it. So Jack wore cowboy boots and a string tie, and pretended he was from Montana, like everybody else.

Not the Premier, though. Mr. Brownlee looked like a lawyer from Ontario. Which he was. It made him none too popular with the Progs, who hated lawyers worse than bankers, but Brownlee looked smart, and God knows they needed a smart guy to run Alberta, so they let him run it. Brownlee was okay. Not exactly a barrel of laughs, but he'd given Jack encouragement, and the little boom Jack had created in Turner Valley, while it hadn't amounted to much, made them both pretty popular. When they do strike oil, baby, look out!

On January 2, 1930, Premier Brownlee held a testimonial dinner in honour of Alberta's Citizen of the Year, Senator J.R. Coolican. In his speech, the Premier called Senator Coolican "the most dynamic man in Alberta" and the key to the province's prosperity. One week later, Premier Brownlee ordered Senator Coolican arrested and charged with stock fraud. Jack was imprisoned in Fort Saskatchewan.

The offices of Coolican Ltd. remained open. Senator Coolican was out on bail the next day. He assured everyone that he had followed customary brokerage practices, and should not be made a scapegoat for others' failures. He was still in business, wasn't he? If he was crooked, well, why didn't the cops close him down?

"If Coolican Ltd. is forced to close its doors," he warned the Edmonton *Bulletin*, "Alberta will go broke."

The offices of Coolican Ltd. remained open. When the Alberta legislature met in March, Premier Brownlee introduced legislation prohibiting bucketing, and short selling, and various other customary practices on the Alberta stock exchanges. The bill passed unanimously. Under this new legislation, Senator Coolican was committed to stand trial in June.

The trial lasted three weeks. On June 23, 1930, Jack Coolican was found guilty. He was sentenced to one month in jail, and fined $250,000. The next morning, Coolican Ltd. was mobbed by hysterical shareholders desperately selling. The following Monday, Coolican Ltd. closed its doors. The Crash was over. The Depression had begun.

IN OTTAWA,
THE PRIME MINISTER IS AFRAID:

This morning I had a very vivid dream. I seemed to be sleeping at home in a room in the back part of the house. In the front part, mother and father were evidently sleeping. It was towards morning. I was suffering in mind a little about an examination I had to take. It was a dream I not infrequently have had, of having an examination to pass for which I am totally unprepared. It cost me great mental anxiety, and always carried with it a feeling of being exposed. I was wondering how this examination could be managed, and so was lying partially awake.

Suddenly dear Mother came to my room and slipped quietly into my bed beside me, as if not to alarm me. I was conscious that she knew I was worrying about the examination and did not wish to disturb me, but there was something important. Then she told me in a very quiet way that there were voices in the house, and that Father was sure there was someone in. As I listened, I heard Father begin to call out, as if to ask who was about. I tried to get out to go to his room, but found myself held down by a paralysis of fear, but still more by the bedclothes, which had bound themselves around my body as I was trying to get out. I heard Father call much more loudly, almost as if the intruders had reached his room and he was about to grapple with them. There was real alarm in his voice, so much so that I was genuinely pained in my heart, pained to the extent that I awoke at that moment, mightily relieved to find that it was a dream.

ON DECEMBER 17,
HE DREAMS OF DEATH:

My fifty-fifth birthday. At the time of wakening this morning, I was struggling with my passions, having slept perhaps a little too long, and under too many coverings. There are times when I suffer from an inner fire, and my passions seem to tear my very skin apart. This distressed me very much, for I remembered it was my birthday, and I wished my thoughts to be pure and calm. Then I began to reflect on the vision I had just before waking.

I seemed to be in a great crowd of men, indeed, I was in Parliament. I recall saying in answer to someone, who had spoken in an insinuating way, 'The Hon. gentleman has said either too much or too little.' It seemed to me he was pretty much alone in the effect of his words, that the House was with me, and that the members greeted his utterance in silence. Later, I was in a hallway, with all the members coming out a passage, sort of down an incline. They were rough and jovial, as Members of Parliament in a large part are. I decided to join them as they were going on a drive, a sort of tally-ho. We all got aboard a caravan to take us on our journey. We went quite a little way, then came to what seemed to be the journey's end. It was as if we had passed out of a crowded city to the outskirts, and right out to an edge where even the streets ceased to be.

We came to a sort of sand stretch. There were no roads. It seemed to be a beach, a bridge to the right where pasengers might go to a sort of ferry, the water beyond. I did not see the water. What I saw was the sand stretch, and in the centre of it, the figure of a woman with a pencil in her hand. She seemed to be full of life and vigour, to be a guardian placed there to see that no one drove past. Beyond her was a beautiful grove of very deep green trees, like the cypress tree. In the grove, there was a gathering of persons in black and white, arranged like a choir. They seemed to be singing. Most, if not all of them, were women, and I thought they were Mennonites, or some sect that stood for peace. It seemed a place of great contentment. The figure in the foreground with the pencil seemed to be very happy, sort of rejoicing, tho' making it clear none of us was to drive any farther.

I felt that I wished to leave my companions and go and join the choir, so I got off and approached the solitary figure with pencil in hand. She seemed to welcome my going by, that it was all right to go on, but I had to go on foot, and alone. The others turned to drive back. I did not see any more of them. I passed the figure guarding the sandy area. As I journeyed on over this arid waste, happy in heart and realizing I had left all the evil for the good, I awakened.

PART II

WAY OUT
WEST

19

Vivian brakes gently, allowing the Macmillans' old Model-A to coast to a slow, dignified stop on the edge of the dirt road. Dust plumes up from beneath the wheels and drifts lazily across the scorched grass of the Pattinsons' lawn. Should she honk? It may seem disrespectful. She'll wait. Besides, Vivian's peeved at not being invited to lunch. So it's the Premier of Alberta. Big deal. She's the Mayor's daughter, isn't she, and perfectly grown up, and deserves to be treated better than a hired girl, sitting out here sweltering while the big shots take their own sweet time. By the time they get to the picnic it'll be half over and she'll have to listen to a lot of boring speeches.

It's dumb idea anyway, taking Mr. Brownlee in their beat-up old wreck when he's got a perfectly heavenly limousine of his own. She saw it in front of the hotel, a black Studebaker a block long, but Mr. Brownlee said he didn't want to drive it to a railwaymen's picnic, given the times, and then Mr. Pattinson got scared his new Packard might be taken the wrong way, him being a Labour MLA, the working man's friend and all that garbage, so it's the Macmillans' Model-A, 'though any car at all is a luxury in Edson 'cause the railwaymen all ride the train for nothing.

Vivian peeks into the rear-view mirror to see if there's a smudge on her nose. Her nose is much too long: a classic nose, Mama says, but Vivian would much rather have a tiny, tilted nose like Gloria Swanson, and long, straight blond hair instead of the mop of frizzy curls she cuts short out of sheer exasperation. In Edson some people say Vivian Macmillan is pretty enough to be a movie star. But how do you get to be a movie star in Edson, Alberta? Jeez, she's eighteen and can't even wear makeup.

Is she fed up with Edson! What a hole. She's bored out of her mind. She doesn't even have a boyfriend. Boys think she's stuck-up. They're all apes anyway. Last year Carl, her Latin teacher, took her out. He proposed to her at Christmas. Carl was okay, but a real stick, and when he talked about going north as a Baptist missionary, and living with the Indians, Vivian got scared. "I'm too young," she said. "I can't even boil water."

Vivian has other plans. She is going to be a famous pianist. It's been part of her imagination as long as she can remember. Mama won't allow her to lift a finger around the house, to protect her hands. At first Vivian pictured herself in a black velvet gown, with a train, alone at the piano in the middle of an immense stage, but then her dad took them to the Jasper Park Lodge, and in the lounge Vivian saw a woman playing dance music in a dress with sleeves that sparkled as she moved her arms, and Vivian decided right then and there that her idea of perfect heaven was to play Broadway show tunes in the lounge of the Jasper Park Lodge. She would wear beautiful gowns covered with sequins, and fall in love with a handsome count with slicked-back hair who would whisk her off to some exotic foreign place, and she would return to Edson years and years later, remote and tragic in luxurious furs, for her mother's funeral.

Vivian was all set to go to Edmonton to study piano at Alberta College. She'd even applied to audition for the CFUA talent contest. Then Carl proposed. Her dad had a fit when she turned him down. Her dad was a Baptist, and he didn't want his daughter marrying a rail-roader, like himself. "If you're too damn young to marry," he roared, "you're too damn young to leave home!" And that was that. So now Vivian studies piano with her old teacher, batty Mr. Hopper, sleeps late in the morning, and lies awake half the night listening to jazz on the radio. Her life is ruined.

Vivian licks the tip of her little finger and smoothes it along her eyebrows. It *is* something to be going on a picnic with the Premier, even if he is old, and married. Maybe he'll fall in love with her, and they'll elope, after his wife dies. Vivian bites her lips to bring up the colour and practises her smile.

John Brownlee fiddles nervously with the pack of Players in his pocket. Do I dare? The meal is over. Mrs. Pattinson's pie crust rests like a stone in the pit of his stomach. Why do they continue to sit here in this stifling room, making the obsequious small talk that irritates him almost to violence? Let's get out of here! he wants to shout. Let's go outside! Let's go! Instead, John Brownlee sits silent and rubs a cigarette to shreds in his pocket.

Was he born in a room like this? Or has he been in so many, all alike, that he seems doomed to live here? The room is always small and airless, with varnished oak trim and green wallpaper. In one corner there's always a bookcase, in another a radio. There's a fern on a stand in the window, and facing it, red and swollen as raw liver, a sofa; beside it, a matching armchair, with a lamp and ashtray. The room speaks of propriety. It stinks of righteousness. It is Ontario.

Oh, God, if only he could sweep it all away with a thrust of his arm! If only he could cut away the rotten, decaying flesh and scour Alberta as pure and white as a bleached bone! But everywhere he turns there is another door, and beyond the door, another airless room, a room full of complacency, and compromise, and fear. His own fear.

God, he hates politics! It's ruined his life. How did he ever get into this hole? Only nine years ago he was an up-and-coming young lawyer in Calgary, perfectly content to leave politics to his senior partner, R.B. "Bonfire" Bennett, the Conservative MP for Calgary West. Through long hours and painstaking attention to detail, John Brownlee built up a solid practice among the local farmers. His modest manner, and modest fees, made him a favourite with the United Farmers of Alberta, and he was acting as their solicitor when, to their own surprise and everyone else's, they swept the Liberal government out of power.

He'd been home, asleep, on election night, and had been awakened at two a.m. by a group of newly-elected UFA members frantically beating on his door. They had not expected to be elected. They did not *want* to be elected. They had campaigned on a platform of moral reform, arguing that all government was crooked, and now they *were* the government! Half the new members were for resigning their seats immediately, especially since it was haying time, but the Lieutenant-Governor wouldn't hear of it. Not one member of the new government had a day's parliamentary experience: in fact their mistrust of the democratic process was surpassed only by their ignorance of British law, parliamentary procedure, and, in some cases, the English language. They didn't even have a leader.

What was to be done? Out of compassion for their predicament, and a genuine fear that this peasants' revolt could lead to the collapse of democracy in Alberta, John Brownlee agreed to serve, temporarily, as attorney-general. He regarded it as a personal sacrifice, an act of charity, and intended to leave once the machinery of government was running smoothly. What a joke! Oh, the farmers were honest, good-hearted men. They wanted to accomplish miracles, and spend no money. They wanted to reform the government, and pass no laws. They were intimidated by debate, baffled by gobbledegook, enraged at not being able to do, immediately, exactly what they wanted. Most of them washed their hands of the whole business and went back to the farm. The Premier took to the bottle. No one could be found willing to replace him. In 1925, at forty-one, Attorney-General John Brownlee became, reluctantly and by default, Premier of Alberta.

Small thanks he gets for it. Alberta is not Utopia. He is to blame. No matter how fair and frugal his government, how compassionate towards the unfortunate and severe with the profligate, John Brownlee cannot make the rain fall, or the wheat grow. He cannot even sell the wheat, confiscate the Bank of Commerce, or take over the railways. He is not a Bolshevik. Nor are the farmers. Almost to a man they would lay down their lives to defend the tiny patch of land that is slowly starving them to death. John Brownlee respects their courage. The puritan in his soul admires their perverse tenacity. God's country, Alberta. A Methodist God.

He knows this country. For five years he has forced himself to visit every corner of it. He has spent weeks on the wooden seats of railway cars, jolted by buckboard over miles of arid desert, slogged through mosquito-infested swamps in mud up to his knees, huddled in log shacks to wait out thunderstorms and blizzards, slept in verminous beds, and willingly gone hungry when he saw children doing without so he could be fed. He has shaken a million hands, how d'y'do, how d'y'do, sat silent through endless litanies of insoluble grievances, forced himself to speak in crowded halls, hands shaking as he read from his papers, the farmers cold as stones. He has tried, in his patient, logical way, to explain that the prosperity they had all been faithfully promised by the government and the banks and the railways — promises that had persuaded them to abandon their old homes hundreds and thousands of miles away, promises that had reduced them, in God's wilderness, to a state of semi-savagery — that this prosperity would now be achieved only through their own toil, and it would not even be theirs, but a gift to future generations.

They hate him for it. They hate his blue gabardine suit that is always clean and pressed. They hate his white shirt and polished black shoes. They hate his city skin, and his soft city hands, his university degree, and his salary of $3,000 a year. He is not one of them. In this country of nomads and refugees, fortune-seekers and trouble-shooters, Ukrainian peasants, German burghers and Mormon fanatics, he, John Brownlee, a Canadian, is a foreigner, an outsider, an egghead, an Easterner. The Enemy.

He hates them too. The people, on the whole, are vulgar, selfish and cruel. In the countryside, away from Edmonton, he feels as if he has been sucked back into some primitive, Neanderthal age, an age when men lived in burrows in the earth and communicated through grunts and blows. It's not their fault. But sympathy alone cannot overcome his horror at seeing half-starved, barefoot children roped behind a plow, or subdue his anger at the people's ingratitude. More! More! More! Whatever he does, it is never enough. His toil merely shames their helplessness, and inspires their rage. Do something! Do something! Something!

What?

He has done his best. Things could hardly be worse. He never had much of a head for money. Now everybody's money is gone. Is it his fault? Has he made some terrible mistake? Everything has gone wrong. It seemed perfectly obvious that once the stock market was cleaned up, and the culprits behind bars, things would return to normal. Mr. Brownlee even called an election on the heels of the trial, he was so certain of public acclaim. But in court, John Brownlee was humiliated when Senator Coolican described his long and friendly association with the Premier, and the substantial loans the government of Alberta had made to the various enterprises of Coolican Ltd. Coolican seduced the court as sweetly as he had seduced the Premier himself. He concealed nothing, admitted nothing, explained everything. He baffled the lawyers with Bay Street jargon, tossing off figures of ten and twenty million as casually as other men would flip a dime. He thrilled the jury with stories of his adventures in the Arctic. He dazzled the press with his nerve. The *Bulletin* ran Jack Coolican's picture on the front page. The next morning, women were lined up at the courthouse door waiting for seats.

When Jack Coolican smiled at the court stenographer, she became too flustered to continue. As the trial dragged on, whispers began that this nice young man was being persecuted, that it was all "politics" and personal vengeance. Public opinion shifted in Jack Coolican's favour. When the verdict was read, Senator Coolican shrugged. He wrote out a cheque for $250,000 on the rail of the prisoner's box. He wrote out another for $100,000 bail, pending appeal, and walked out of court a hero.

Alberta is ruined. Everything's lost. It's all his fault. There is nothing to be done. John Brownlee went to Ottawa to beg a loan from the Prime Minister. "Not a five cent piece!" said Mr. King. Nothing to be done. Only an election to be endured, another airless room, with the windows closed, and a picnic. Picnics remind John Brownlee of his boyhood in Ontario, swarms of strangers, stupid games, being sick from too much food, the white tent in the middle of the field, its walls cracking with the wind of God's wrath, the hot stench of salvation, fear of hellfire, the death of eternal damnation. Picnics inspire in John Brownlee an over-whelming, paralyzing conviction of sin.

He had never been saved. He lied about it, out of shame, and was chosen for the ministry. But God struck him mute. He was too frightened to face a congregation. Will he be able to speak today? What will he say? Will he lie again, and say "Trust me, all is well"? Or will he stand up and shout "Blame me! Blame me! For I have sinned, O Lord, I have sinned!" Will he beat his breast and cry out and hear the comforting chorus of "Amens" from the crowd, and the preacher's reassuring call "Repent ye and be saved! Repent and be saved!" Will he be able to weep, and bow down on the sinner's bench, and be cleansed of his guilt?

John Brownlee's hands are cold and his mouth is dry. He needs a cigarette.

"Viv's here," says Macmillan.

"Let's go, then," says the Premier, jumping up.

"Mr. Brownlee, Vivian. Vivian, Mr. Brownlee. How d'y'do. How d'y'do."

Vivian smiles. Her teeth are white and even. She has tiny freckles on her nose. Her legs are long and slender and her slim arms bare to the shoulder. Her skin is golden, like her hair. She is wearing a white dress with tiny blue flowers that match her eyes, eyes as wide and blue as the Aegean Sea where this morning she must have arisen in a cloud of foam. John Brownlee leans against the car to catch his breath.

"Are you okay?"

He nods and smiles. So this is what they mean by a "knockout." He wants to laugh out loud, but he is too astonished to make a sound.

Mr. Brownlee sits beside Vivian in the back seat. It's cramped, and she's amused at the way his long legs are doubled up almost to his chin. He's not as old as she'd imagined. His hair's quite black, except at the temples. The gray looks very distinguished. His forehead is deeply furrowed between his eyes, giving him a look of anxious concentration even when he smiles, and the muscles of his jaw are beginning to sag in a way she finds fascinating. It's a shut-in, secretive face, a suffering face, and Vivian feels a rush of sympathy for the terrible weight of responsibility Mr. Brownlee must be carrying. Imagine, running a whole province! Vivian has never met a premier before. She's impressed.

She's flattered, too, when Mr. Brownlee calls her "Miss Macmillan," and offers her a cigarette, and lights it for her. He smiles at her, and asks her so many questions about herself she feels like a dummy.

"I'm just sort of sitting around," she shrugs.

"Vivian is studying the piano," Mama says from the front seat.

"Damn waste of time." Good old Dad.

"Well, there's nothing *else* to do in Edson!" Vivian snaps.

"Why don't you come to Edmonton?" Mr. Brownlee looks right into her eyes.

"Oh, I'd love to . . . ."

"Too damn much money."

"Can you type?" asks Mr. Brownlee.

"Me? Oh, no! I *hate* typing!"

"Work's pretty scarce," says Macmillan, sensing that his daughter is slipping out of his control.

"I think I could promise Vivian a job, Mr. Macmillan. If she took a business course . . . ."

"Viv's pretty young yet. Big place, Edmonton."

Vivian watches her dad's neck swell up in an ominous way. If Mr. Brownlee wasn't Premier, he'd probably get a punch in the nose.

"Oh, I'll take good care of Vivian, Mr. Macmillan. She can call our home her own. Why, we even have a piano. Vivian will be free to use it any time, if she wishes."

That stopped them dead! Imagine her, Vivian Macmillan from Edson, a guest in the Premier's home! Wow, it must be a mansion! And the piano! She can see it already, a concert grand, red mahogany, in a bay window overlooking a rose garden, with sunlight streaming in through lace curtains and a maid in uniform bringing her an iced drink on a silver tray. Wow, she'll be famous in no time!

"I guess typing's not so hard." Vivian smiles at Mr. Brownlee. He smiles back.

"You have a very beautiful daughter Mr. Macmillian," Mr. Brownlee says, leaning forward.

Vivian blushes. She's been told that a hundred times, but hearing it this way, obliquely, in front of her parents, it sounds different, more serious, like ... like a ... proposal.

Holy cow, he's in love with me!

20

The Edmonton YWCA is ghastly. And the food! Ugh. Vivian can hardly make herself eat it. She wishes now she'd gone into residence at the College with the other kids from the country. Here, there's nothing but horrible old maids. Mama chose the Y because it was Christian, and there were no boys around, and Vivian would be spending a lot of time with the Brownlees, where she would meet a better circle of people than the College crowd. But Vivian hasn't heard a word from Mr. Brownlee since the picnic in July. "I'm sure he's a man of his word," Mama said reassuringly. But Vivian is beginning to despair.

Two mornings in a row, as she was walking to the College, the Studebaker passed her, driven by a chauffeur, with Mr. Brownlee in the back. But he hadn't seen her, or pretended not to. Vivian is beginning to think she dreamed the whole thing. It rained at the picnic, and they all got soaked through, and on the way home the car got stuck in the mud, and Mr. Brownlee jumped out to push in his best suit, and pretty soon he was all covered with mud. He looked so funny Vivian couldn't help laughing, and he laughed too, and made oinking noises like a pig. Even her dad cheered up and said John Brownlee was the only premier in the world who'd get more than his hands dirty. Mr. Brownlee said he hadn't had so much fun in years. That night, at the dance in the Veterans' Hall, he danced with Vivian *five* times, and each time told her how beautiful she was. She was embarrassed, being singled out, but everybody was so amazed to see Mr. Brownlee *dancing*, they paid no attention to her at all. Vivian floated home on a pink cloud.

Oh, the castles she's built in the air! She's dreamed about Mr. Brownlee almost every night, and every night he's grown more handsome, more mysterious, more irresistible. Imagine what he knows about

life! And how he's suffered! Vivian has chosen a dozen different trous-
seaus for when they marry, after Mrs. Brownlee dies, and has wept real
tears into her pillow at the sight of Mrs. Brownlee's coffin being lowered
into its grave. She's haunted the post office, and read everything about
him in the newspapers, and brooded so long about whether to write him
a note of congratulation on his election victory that the opportunity
passed by the time she decided against it. Never chase a man, Mama
said.

Just as well. Has she been taken for a fool! He just flirted with her like
he must have done with thousands of girls, then completely forgot
about her. He's just a crummy politican after all. They're all liars, her
dad says. And here she is in this terrible hole that stinks of Lysol. And
she does hate typing! And bookkeeping. And her teacher. And the
stuck-up city girls who go by with their noses in the air. And after it's all
over, she'll only be a secretary!

Vivian is deciding she should have married Carl when she is called
to the phone.

"Hello, Vivian. Do you know who this is?"

"Mr. Brownlee?"

"A little bird told me you were here."

"Oh, yes. For a week now."

"How are you?"

"Oh, fine. I'm just fine!"

She flies around the room finding her best Sunday dress. Tea at the
Premier's! What to wear? Who will be there? All sorts of important
people. She wishes she had some nice store-bought clothes instead of
homemade things, so she wouldn't look like a hick.

Downstairs, Vivian is surprised to find a tall, elegantly dressed
woman waiting for her. She hadn't expected Mrs. Brownlee to be up
and around. Mrs. Brownlee has been an invalid for years, so people say.
Vivian sits in the back seat, behind Mr. Brownlee. They drive across the
bridge and stop in front of a plain, shingled house on 88th Street.
Vivian sits still, thinking they've just stopped here to pick something
up, until Mr. Brownlee opens her door.

"Here we are!"

Well, the house is just a little box, messy too, with dust on the window
sills (Mama would be shocked!) and junk thrown around everywhere.
And the piano! It's an old upright, not half as nice as her own. "I'm

afraid it's out of tune," says Mrs. Brownlee. "I haven't played much recently." The Brownlees' two kids, John and Allan, are there, and two student nurses from the hospital who giggle a lot and leave early. They play Chinese checkers. Vivian is hungry, but Mrs. Brownlee seems very vague about tea. At last she produces some stale biscuits and a store-bought lemon pie. Mr. Brownlee acts as if Vivian isn't there.

She's glad to leave when Mr. Brownlee offers to drive her home. They cross the bridge in silence. Vivian looks down at the river. It's cold and grey, a wild, mountain river that cuts a deep gorge across the flat prairie. The river is the only thing Vivian likes about Edmonton.

"Would you like to see where I work?"

Mr. Brownlee turns off towards the Legislature. Its pale, brown dome stands like a hoodoo against the western sky. He stops the car at the front steps. The massive door is open, but the building is deserted. Inside, it is grey and cold, like the river, and their footsteps echo spookily on the stone floors. Mr. Brownlee's office is a dark, sort of scary room with a big blue rug, a black leather sofa and an ominous, shiny desk. Mr. Brownlee makes her a little bow and gestures towards the tall chair behind the desk.

Vivian sits in the chair gingerly, feeling very small, and stupid. She touches the desk top with her fingertips. It's soft blue leather, with beautiful gold filigree around the edges, and a gold monogram in the middle. She touches Mr. Brownlee's gold pen and lifts the paperweight made out of a buffalo hoof. Otherwise, the desk is bare. How can Mr. Brownlee work so hard and have nothing to do?

"Would you like to work here?"

"Here?"

"Not in this office, necessarily. But here, in the building. In an office just like this."

"Oh, I'm not good enough!"

"That doesn't matter."

Mr. Brownlee smiles at her again. He shows her his own private washroom, and the liquor cabinet hidden in the closet, and the blanket he uses when he sleeps on the sofa if the House is sitting late. It is very quiet. The afternoon sun fills the office with a strange blue light. Vivian imagines for a moment that she has drowned, and finds the sensation pleasant.

A key rattles in the door.

"Who's there?" Mr. Brownlee strides towards the door, frowning.

"Jessup, sir. Cleaning. Is that you, Mr. Brownlee?"

"Yes, Jessup. Working late again, I'm afraid. Can you make it in an hour or so?"

"Certainly, sir. Sorry to bother you, sir."

"Perhaps we should go now, Mr. Brownlee." Vivian is suddenly a little frightened. Mr. Brownlee looks furious! Has she done something?

He strides out of the building, leaving her to scamper along behind, and slams the door after her when she gets in the car. He lights a cigarette, drags on it, then stubs it out viciously against the dashboard. Vivian sits very still and doesn't say anything.

"I'm sorry," Mr. Brownlee says when they stop in front of the Y. "It's my fault. I lost my temper. You see, I'm under a very great deal of strain. Can you understand that, Vivian?"

"Oh, that's okay, Mr. Brownlee."

"I'm very glad you came, Vivian."

"Sure. Me too."

ONE MONTH LATER:

"Do you like going for car rides, Vivian?"

"Oh, sure. It's nice. Yeah, I like it. Wow, 'specially in a car like this!"

Vivian feels quite natural with Mr. Brownlee now. She's been to the house a few times and gotten used to the fact that, except for the car, they live just like ordinary people. She's pretty well over her disappointment, and, like Mama says, beggars can't be choosers.

Edmonton's a kind of scary place. Except for the movies, there's not much to do, and Vivian's afraid to go out by herself. The streets are full of hobos who whistle at her and make nasty remarks when she goes by. Sometimes they block her way and laugh at her when she cries. She's glad to have a safe place to go sometimes after school, and Mrs. Brownlee is awfully nice to her. Mrs. Brownlee's own little girl was born dead, years ago, and they'll never have a daughter of their own. It makes Vivian feel very sad, and determined to be on her very best behavior. Mrs. Brownlee is so educated, so refined. How could Vivian ever have imagined that Mr. Brownlee would be interested in a kid like her?

"Where are we going?"

"Just for a drive. I want to talk to you, Vivian."

Oh, oh. Another fatherly lecture. The College must have phoned to complain about her awful grades. Vivian slumps in her seat.

They turn west on Stony Plain Road and head out past the city limits. They are driving into the wind. Big snowflakes plop against the windshield. They drive for some time, then turn north on a sideroad. Vivian is getting worried. It's after ten p.m. and the Y will bawl her out if she's not in by midnight.

"I guess you've gone out with a lot of boys."

"Me? Oh, no, not really. Most boys didn't... didn't like me. At least not the ones I liked."

"And what *do* you like, in men?"

"Oh...." Vivian blushes. Why is he asking all these personal questions? "I don't know...really."

John Brownlee stops the car on the side of the dirt road and switches off the headlights. They are enclosed in a cocoon of falling snow. It's very dark.

"Do you like this?"

He takes her hand by the wrist and places it, palm down, on the front of his pants. She feels something hard. He presses her hand against it. It jerks. Vivian tries to pull her hand away, but Mr. Brownlee holds it down. He is breathing very hoarsely. Vivian feels dizzy. The thing under her fingers is growing bigger. Mr. Brownlee takes her hand away and holds it in his.

"Do you know much about men, Vivian?"

"No... not really."

"Do you know that men have certain needs, certain physical needs, that have to be satisfied, otherwise the consequences might be... terrible?"

Mr. Brownlee is still holding her hand. His other arm is around her shoulders. His mouth is very close to her ear. He is holding her very tight. Vivian's head is spinning. She doesn't know what to say.

"You know that Mrs. Brownlee isn't well, don't you?"

"She looks okay to me."

"Mrs. Brownlee can't have any more children, Vivian. Another child would kill her."

"Oh. I'm sorry."

"Mrs. Brownlee and I have not been man and wife for ten years, Vivian. I cannot go on. I am afraid I'll break down...and kill Mrs. Brownlee, or myself."

"Oh, no!"

"Vivian, I want you to be my wife, my true wife. I am asking you to save Mrs. Brownlee's life. Will you do this for me? And Mrs. Brownlee?"

Vivian's head whirls. She is elated, excited, curious, frightened. She hadn't imagined it would be like this. Save Mrs. Brownlee's life! Mr. Brownlee is kissing her now in a rough way she's never known before. He is whispering that he loves her. He loves her! Vivian sits perfectly still. She is unable to move or speak. She seems to be floating in the air, looking down at herself as if she were somebody else. A voice in her head says over and over. *This is it This is it This is it This is it.*

"You love me, don't you Vivian?"

"Oh, yes. Yes!"

"I want you to show me your love. Show me show me. Show me, Vivian, show me."

She feels herself being pushed down on to the seat, nearly crushed beneath Mr. Brownlee's weight. He kisses her so hard he nearly sucks the air from her body. Vivian struggles for breath. She feels his hand on her leg, under her dress. It feels very big and cold. It gives her a shock. The hand begins pulling at her panties. She wants to cry out No! No! But she can't breathe, and soon the struggle for breath obliterates everything else. She feels only panic, and pain, then something very big, very sharp, is poking into her crotch, forcing its way into her, pounding, stabbing, a knife, he's killing me, he's killing me!

Mr. Brownlee is saying her name over and over *VivianVivianVivian VivianVivianVivianVivianPleasePleasePleasePleasePleasePlease.* His eyeglasses slip to one side, then fall with a faint thunk to the floor of the car. He pulls back, distracted, Vivian raises one knee and pushes against him with all her might. A car horn sounds. It seems a long way away. It doesn't stop.

"Damn!" Mr. Brownlee twists around and untangles himself. He sits up. The car horn stops. Vivian pulls her skirt down and huddles on the far side of the seat, by the door. She hands Mr. Brownlee his glasses. He puts them on without looking at her. Well, she's really loused things up, hasn't she? Here she'd wanted Mr. Brownlee to fall in love with her, and now that he has, and treats her like a grown-up woman, she behaves like a perfect baby! He must really hate her now!

They drive back into the city without speaking.

THE NEXT DAY:

"Hello, Vivian. I'd like to take you for a drive."

Vivian is stunned. She was sure Mr. Brownlee would never speak to her again. He had been so mad at her last night! He'd stopped the car blocks from the Y and pushed her out, saying that she wasn't good enough to ride with him. She walked for several blocks, too numb with misery to care about the cold, then the car pulled up beside her again and Mr. Brownlee told her to get in, he was sorry, he would take her straight to the Y. Vivian wanted to keep walking, but her good shoes were getting soaked, and Mr. Brownlee was so angry she was afraid to say no. She got into the back seat, and he dropped her off at the door without saying a word.

"I don't think...I..."

"I owe you an explanation, Vivian."

She's pretty much made up her mind to go home to Edson. She's scared of that, too. She'll catch royal hell for throwing up school, wasting all that money, her big chance. Her dad'll kill her. How can she tell them what's happened? They'll think she's crazy. That's what Mr. Brownlee is saying now: "You're driving me crazy."

"I'll pick you up at the corner, nine o'clock. Okay?"

Vivian waits under the streetlight in front of Eaton's. She studies the beautifully dressed mannequins in the window, then catches a glimpse of her own face. *She* looks beautiful too — quite mysterious, with her coat collar turned up around her ears, the heroine in a romantic love story, doomed to die at the end. I am! she says to herself. I am in a romantic love story. I am having an *affaire*! It's true! It's happening to me! Vivian thinks about Jean Harlow, and her white satin nightgowns, and her spun-sugar hair, and all the dark, handsome men who are madly in love with her. Vivian smiles, then pouts, and adjusts her face into a sultry, slightly melancholy expression.

They drive out Stony Plain Road and park in the same spot. Vivian is nervous. She'd rather forget last night. She'd been such a fool. Mr. Brownlee reaches across and opens her door.

"Let's talk in the back seat. It's more comfortable."

Vivian feels silly, just the two of them alone in the back of this enormous limousine, but she doesn't want to object and make Mr. Brownlee mad at her again. She could never walk home from here.

"This is how we met, isn't it?" he says, putting his arm around her. "That was the day I fell in love with you."

Vivian looks down at her hands. She wishes he would talk about something else. He promised on the phone that he wouldn't make her...do...anything. If only he'd send chocolates, and flowers. But that's stupid, isn't it, with her living at the Y, and him the Premier, and she should feel flattered he's singled her out, except when he talks about Mrs. Brownlee she feels so terrible.

"How old are you, Vivian?"

"Eighteen."

"That's still very young, isn't it?"

"I guess so."

"You don't have much experience of life."

"That's for sure." She smiles.

"So when an older person tells you something, you pay attention."

"Yes, I guess."

"Because they know better."

"I...I suppose."

"And you obey your parents."

"Oh, sure! My dad's real strict!"

"Do you remember, going to the picnic, when I promised to look after you, to be a guardian to you?"

"Oh, yes. We were very grateful."

"Was that a lie?"

"Oh, no!"

"And when I say I can't live without you, do you call that a lie?"

"I...no."

"Have I been good to you, Vivian?"

"Yes."

"You know me quite well now?"

"Yes."

"Would I ask you to do something I thought was wrong?"

"No...I don't think so."

"So when I ask you not to be selfish, and do something to help me, to help Mrs. Brownlee, that's not wrong, is it?"

Tears sting Vivian's eyes. She shakes her head.

"Mrs. Brownlee has been good to you, hasn't she?"

Vivian nods.

"Don't you think the right thing is to do something good for her? If I had a daughter, Vivian, and someone who loved her asked her to do something generous, something wonderful, to save a life, I would want her to do it. I would *ask* her to do it."

Vivian takes a deep breath.

"But what...what...what...if I...I...get...."

"Trust me, Vivian. I'll take care of you."

Vivian lies down and shuts her eyes. She can't help crying.

She tries hard not to struggle. She trembles violently when she feels his thing between her legs. He forces his way in quickly, savagely. She clenches her teeth not to scream. She feels only pain. She's being split in half, wider, deeper, cut, slashed, bleeding, *oh help, help, help, oh oh oh oh oh oh oh oh oh.*

She only realizes it's over when Mr. Brownlee abruptly sits up and buttons his pants. She hurts so much she's surprised to see that the car seat isn't soaked with blood. Mr. Brownlee pulls down her skirt and straightens her coat. He smiles at her and brushes away her tears.

"I think I'm the first, aren't I, Vivian."

"Y...y...yes."

"So, you're my girl now, aren't you."

"I guess so, Mr. Brownlee."

21

A FEW WEEKS LATER, IN OTTAWA, MR. KING,
THE FORMER PRIME MINISTER, NOW LEADER
OF THE OPPOSITION, CONTEMPLATES THE
IGNOMINY OF LIFE IN THE POLITICAL WILDERNESS:

Tonight I waited for Senator Cairine Wilson and Mr. Wilson to call for me to take me to Parliament Hill for the Armistice ceremony. It was their own suggestion (Mrs. Wilson's). They never came, & I was obliged to get in a streetcar with the wreath I bought this afternoon. At the city hall, I hailed a man in a car. He drove me to the Hill just in time for me to place my wreath with the others. I was too late to get a rightful place on the platform and did not put the wreath on in the right order.

As I was coming away, I met Mrs. Wilson, who said she was relieved to see me. They had not called because they'd had no word. She was not sure if the fault was her maid's, or the secretary in my office. I phoned Henry, who said he delivered the message to Wilson's butler himself. The Wilsons might have phoned to ask if I had received the message. This is the worst neglect I have met with yet — and this is the woman I appointed Senator! She said they were going to a hockey match. I felt too incensed for words.

Sunday, December 14, 1930:

Dr. McDougald came to lunch and we talked over money matters. He feels quite lost and is worried over Beauharnois. Apparently the company has gone ahead without the plan ever having been approved by the government. It was neglect. In many ways, our ministers were frightfully neglectful. He is afraid the Tories will try to crowd him out, put their own people in. He says the banks are behind it, that they are out to 'get' him the way they 'got' Coolican, that Coolican was perfectly innocent, passed all government inspections etc. etc. I suspect there is some truth in this since the links between Brownlee and the Big Interests, thro' Bennett, are well known. The Tories have stopped at nothing to discredit our government and the Liberal Party. I cautioned McDougald to keep his conversations with me strictly confidential. I am afraid he has taken a big chance with Beauharnois. Too often, the ways of business are those of the highwayman.

Monday, December 15, 1930:

This afternoon I finally decided on the purchase of a Cadillac motor car, eight-cylinder, present-year model, to have the latest finish. The price is $3,700. Mr. Brown, the representative of McLaughlin-General Motors, is letting me have it for $2,500, the difference being the advertising value for the company to have me drive one of their cars. I debated some time on a Buick, it being a cheaper and somewhat smaller car, but I have come to the conclusion that I might be looked on as 'letting down' my position a little. The Cadillac is not pretentious or luxurious, but comfortable and commodious. Getting it at a bargain, the purchase is well worthwhile.

Tuesday, January 13, 1931:

Vincent Massey arrived at four p.m. We talked together in my library for some time. Massey spoke of his perhaps being loaned out to some Imperial mission, to the foreign service in Britian. He spoke also of the Massey Foundation, perhaps organizing a mission to Russia on which he might go with others. He asked if I thought he *could* go back as Minister to Washington, if Bennett asked him. He had declined a Bennett invitation to dinner tonight.

We talked over party matters. He is going to try to raise subscriptions to the Liberal office. Senator Haydon will be a trustee, under my direction, and he will see how the funds are expended etc. I told him something of my outlays for this house, car, chauffeur, etc. and told of having to pay part of office staff and expenses to let him see how completely alone I was. I said I did not want things done for myself, but feel these rich men should take some part in government, should help a party, like a church is helped, if they wish to be identified with it.

Massey wondered if he were made president of the University of Toronto, if that would stand in the way of his appointment to London later. I told him not. One feels that it is all self and position he is after. However, he is the *only* one who has done anything since last July, the others have *all* disappeared.

Saturday, February 14, 1931:

A very serious blow fell today when I learned that Andrew Haydon had had a severe heart seizure at five this morning, great pain, had to have a hypodermic etc. and his son sent for. I pray it may mean only great care & rest for the remainder of his life, but it means that my greatest help in the political field is gone, the one on whom above all others I have relied most since 1919, & one of my nearest & truest friends. It means the touching of the very bottom of loneliness and isolation in *my* work in the political field.

Joan and I exchanged Valentine greetings in flowers. We had a walk together. Very slippery.

Monday, March 9, 1931:

The morning papers announce the appointment of Bill Herridge as Minister to Washington. Certainly fact is stranger than fiction. I own, and live in, the house at Kingsmere which his father and mother owned and lived in; he is going to live in the house I was responsible for purchasing, and to fill the position I was responsible for creating. He would have been just as good a supporter of mine, had I wished to make much of him. He professed Liberal sympathies at one time. He has betrayed and knifed Massey, who was a very close friend, in the most damnable fashion. He is a coward at heart, or he would have spoken to me of his intention to help Bennett in the campaign. It would almost seem that the zeal with which he went into the campaign had something of irritation against myself, possibly for knowing too much of his family. I think, tho', it is all self-seeking. I shall be surprised if everything doesn't come to grief some day. He has had to suffer a lot, and I wish him well. I wrote him a letter saying so this morning, but not congratulating him, or the government, or the country. Bennett will be much criticized by his own party, more so when it appears that Herridge is to be Bennett's brother-in-law. Nepotism.

Friday, April 10, 1931:

I am debating whether I should give Mildred Bennett a wedding present. Certainly Bill Herridge deserves nothing & will get nothing from me. I suppose I should send Miss Bennett a gift, but I see little if any reason for doing so, except a certain conventional etiquette.

Saturday, April 11:

Mrs. Black, wife of the Speaker, phoned to ask if I would propose Miss Bennett's health at a dinner she and the Speaker are giving in her honour this evening. After some hesitation, I accepted, feeling it was the right and the only thing to do in the circumstances.

I gave Miss Bennett credit for the whole Conservative victory, told the PM and Bill H. they both owed their positions to her, etc. In conversation with Miss Bennett, she spoke quite openly about having had a very hard time to decide between two men, Bill being one (and as tho' she was not even yet quite sure, it seemed to me). It did seem strange, her saying this on the eve of her marriage. She made it clear to me that 'ambition' was the guiding star with her and with Bennett. I have come to that conclusion — they are both 'exploiters' — nothing deep, nothing really refined, just aggressive exploiters. I was really a little surprised and not a little disappointed at her general demeanour tonight. She took a cocktail before dinner, at dinner took all the wines as they came along, did not seem to be really serious-minded, kept smiling over at Bill in a supercilious way, as if together they were laughing at everyone else & as if the whole business were a play.

Bill Herridge's speech was a study. He has changed a great deal since I saw him intimately years ago. The lower part of his face, his mouth and chin, have taken on a most unpleasant expression, a sort of slimy, loose, uncertain expression, very sensual in a way. His mannerisms show a great deal of self-conceit and satisfaction. What he said was well-expressed, but it had that Herridge note of bravado about it, nothing open or grand or really happy. It was quite an ordeal for Bill, harder, I imagine, to face the Tories at the table than myself. He thanked me very warmly for what I said about Mildred & pressed my hand very, very warmly. I said to him that the old love was there always, to feel that he could count upon it at any time. My belief is that he will yet come to me in some breakdown or crisis for sympathy, understanding and help.

There can be only tragedy ahead. These two will never be happy for any length of time together. Both are too self-seeking & self-centred & selfish.

There were songs and scotches & sodas etc. after dinner. When I was coming away, Miss Bennett said that if there were not so many present, I might kiss her good-bye. I said that the chance might come on Tuesday, but others urged the present, so I said 'All right.' She leaned her cheek forward & I kissed it.

Tuesday, April 14:

The wedding took place at three p.m. at Chalmers Church. I was not invited to the church and am glad I was not. It relieved me of sending any gift, for one thing, not that I cared about the cost, but I was most anxious not publicly to appear as making a gift in that connection. Also, I think that both Bill and Mildred have acted in a very crude manner, considering what a lady and gentleman would have done.

I went over to the reception at four-thirty p.m. and fell in line with the others. When I shook hands with Mildred, she said "You know my husband," getting a certain amount of fun out of the word. The whole business was snobbery of the extreme kind. The Gov.-Gen'l proposed the bride's health. I thought His Ex's speech very poor, fulsome, & without any delicate touches, kowtowing to Bennett. I also hear Bennett has a cable from the King & one from Hoover. What advertising! All arranged, without a doubt. The reception was a very large one. Everything one heard was in the nature of criticism over size, flowers, motor, etc. Champagne & wedding cake ran out, women stripped the tables of flowers & fought (I am told) to get into the Church.

I called to see Haydon & brought him a rose from one of the tables.

22

A Depression *is* depressing. Freud doesn't have a hope with this one. It's a beaut. A depression feels like stepping into an open elevator shaft

AAAR
 R
 R
 R
 G
 H
 H
 H
 H
 !!

  except that when you expect to hit bottom, you keep right on going. A free fall. Weightless. Lightheaded. A relief, in a way. The phone doesn't ring anymore. Nobody wants to know how I am. And vice-versa. Nobody asks for favours. I have none to give. We are shunned in the street, in case Liberal luck is catching. Nobody wants Mum to "do it" in Times Square. The spirits, it seems, have given bad advice on the stock market. They were dead wrong about the election too. Willie, however, has forgiven the Loved Ones. I think he is secretly pleased to be able to share his unhappiness with so many, and to find that paranoia, at last, is a perfectly reasonable way to deal with the world.

 Waking up is the worst. Find out all the bad news from yesterday, wonder what bad news will happen today. It's like reading the casualty lists during the war. People react the same way. They go into mourning, or become hysterical, or disappear. Nobody asks where they went, or what became of them. Nobody wants to know. Who's next? The silence is spooky. It's hard to breathe. Everything, even the air, seems to have been sucked away. We've been Hoovered.

I still have some money in the bank. Famous Players is doing okay. My RCA shares have dropped from $525 to $65. Will people stop going to movies and listening to the radio? Not me. Will I end up on the street after all? At my age! What's sex selling for these days? Most stuff you can't give away. Nobody'd be caught dead with jewellery, silver. It's now the thing to look like a street urchin, as long as you don't overdo it, and the dress is by Chanel. Not that I go out much, since Bill dumped me. It's amazing what men will do for money. I gave the lovebirds six months. Bill was back in two weeks, on the make, as usual.

"So, how is it, mating with a hippopotamus?"

"Lay off, eh? Millie's a good girl."

"Girl?"

"Okay, so she's my age. Forty-five's not that old."

"An October-October romance. A Hallowe'en prank."

"Don't be a bitch, Lily. You wouldn't marry me."

"I couldn't make you Minister in Washington either, Excellency."

"That's Millie's plum. She's had a pretty dull life as an . . . ."

"Old maid?"

"She wants to live it up a little. You know how she likes the social stuff. Trouble is, Hoover's strictly grape juice. We have to drink at home, with the blinds drawn. It's worth it, though, just to see Massey's face."

"Poor Vincent is among the unemployed, at present. He feels his exceptional talents are being wasted."

"That's exactly what he told Bennett. Tried to get R.B. to send him to Moscow, of all places! Can you imagine? Now Bennett thinks Massey's a Red."

"And what are *you*, now? A New Conservative?"

"I'm a kept man. Isn't that what people are saying?"

"They aren't that kind."

What did Bill want? He obviously didn't come to gossip. I waited for him to get to the point. With Bill there is always a point, but it can take a while to get there. He is a born conspirator. But what conspiracy? Bill adopts like camouflage the characteristics of the people he's trying to impress. As a Byng boy, he affected a pipe and a gruff manner, but as soon as the Prince of Wales stepped off the boat, Just-call-me-Bill turned up everywhere in plus-fours and a canary-yellow pullover, his hair slicked down like fly-paper. Now he has put on a lot of weight, and his chins recede into his neck just like Millie's. I like Millie, really. She's one of those big, sweaty, grownup girls who live to eat and spend money. Obviously, R.B. grabbed the chance to unload Millie's appetites on Washington, and the public purse, in a single stroke, and in the hungry Mr. Herridge he found the perfect sucker. I don't really give a damn about Bill, it's just that all the people who used to feel sorry for poor Millie Bennett now feel sorry for me.

"Did you go to Bermuda this spring?"

"Are you kidding, Bill? I'm broke!"

"I thought the Doctor paid for all that."

"Not for me he doesn't."

"But for others? For Andrew Haydon? Our Mutual Friend?"

"You mean Willie? I don't know. I suppose he does. The Doctor *says* he does. It's no big secret. God knows Willie never paid for anything in his life."

"But you went to Bermuda last year?"

"No. I was supposed to go, but Jack was in ... Alberta."

"But King went? And Senator Haydon? And the Doctor?"

"Sure, as far as I know. It was a 'Party' holiday, to plan the election campaign. What's so fishy about that?"

Bill rummaged in a pocket. He looked so much the plutocrat I thought he was going to produce a monocle and stick it in his eye, but he came up with an envelope and carefully extracted a piece of paper. He handed it to me. It was an ordinary hotel bill. Across the top it said "The Ritz, Bermuda," and underneath, "Account — W.L.McK. King." It was the usual stuff, room, meals, valet, telephone, with the amount owing at the bottom: $288.53. I handed it back.

"So this would be his hotel bill?"

"I suppose. I'm surprised it's not more, they were there a week. So what? Who pays your bills?"

Bill handed me a second piece of paper. It was a voucher, on the Doctor's stationery, claiming the $288.53 for Mr. King's expenses, plus $395.04 in fares and $168.75 in New York hotels. At the bottom was a note, signed by the Doctor, "Expenses to Bermuda, Hon. W.L.Mackenzie King & self," then a stamp: "Paid by Beauharnois, June 30, 1930."

"The Beauharnois power project was approved about this time, just before the election?" Bill asked, trying to sound casual.

"Yes. At least that was the understanding. It was approved, but the order-in-council never went through."

"Why not?"

"Well, you know what a cocktease Willie is. He'll dangle the bait, then snatch it away. He's a hard lay. The more the Doctor was willing to pay for Beauharnois, the longer Willie stalled. Willie can't be bought, you see. *Nobody* has enough money for that. But he likes people to try. He did promise to put Beauharnois through *after* the election. Then he lost. Anyway, that's old news. What does it matter now?"

"Sure, I suppose his *affaire* with my mother is old news too? Nice Uncle Will who used to hang around the cottage every summer when we were kids, his Bible in one hand, his pecker in the other."

"She was in love with him."

"He broke her heart."

"Men are fickle, aren't they."

"He ruined her life."

"He's ruined a lot of lives."

"She wasn't even cold when he was on the phone to my dad, wanting to buy the cottage. Right next door, such warm memories, fond associations blah blah blah. My old man hated the place so much he damn near gave it to him."

"And now Willie's ruined Kingsmere too."

"You should have seen him at my wedding. He gathered up roses from the vases, a great fistful, and then insisted on kissing the bride. Millie damn near threw up!"

Well, good for you, Willie. What does Bill want? Revenge? Blackmail? The leadership of the Liberal Party?

I suppose I'm supposed to pass along the news about the expense voucher, hippety-hop, so the Tories can watch Willie sweat. I would too, except Willie doesn't phone any more either. If the sky is going to fall, he'll have to hold it up himself.

TWO WEEKS LATER, THE FIRST CRACK APPEARS:

Laurier House, May 19, 1931:

This afternoon Gardiner of the United Farmers of Alberta introduced a motion re Beauharnois as a matter of urgent public importance. I knew nothing of it 'til that hour. His speech was contemptible. He spoke of what Dr. McDougald held in Beauharnois shares & then went on to say he was a near friend of mine, insinuating that the government had been profitting by the deal. Bennett granted a committee of inquiry. I welcomed the committee.

AND GROWS WIDER...

July 10, 1931:

The committee inquiring into the Beauharnois development seems to be anxious to make a sacrifice of Dr. McDougald, & if possible reflect on me through our friendship. I confess I am amazed at some of the things that are being disclosed of which I knew nothing. I did not like the company being made up of stenographers in Haydon's office & Haydon the one to form the company. It looked suspicious. It would seem that McDougald tried to leave the impression that his friendship with me gave him an influence in Ottawa he did not possess. I did not know of Henry's association with McDougald when I appointed him deputy minister. Also Moyer, a previous secretary of mine, being retained by McDougald has, to an evil mind, the appearance of design.

I gave the committee to understand that I have nothing to hide & have no reason to shield McDougald in any way, beyond his having been a friend to the party in 1921. The extent to which he has misled others in relation to myself he himself will have to answer for. It would look as tho' he has deliberately 'used' me to further his ends. The truth is that Beauharnois meant nothing to me in any way.

July 13. 1931:

Mackenzie (Lib.-Vancouver) came with me to Laurier House this afternoon. He showed me a copy of a voucher McDougald had turned into the Beauharnois Co. in which there was the statement — "Travelling expenses to Bermuda, Mackenzie King & self, $800" (in round figures), also some expenses for a trip to Europe in 1928. I was amazed at this document and gave the facts at once to Mackenzie. Haydon & I had gone alone and returned alone from Bermuda. McDougald joined us there and paid part of the hotel bill. This voucher is being passed around among the Tories. It upset me somewhat to have anything of the kind started. I felt incensed at McDougald. It looked as tho' he were trying to have the company feel he had influence with me, etc. etc.

At six p.m. I sent Bennett a note to speak to him in his room, which I did. He had a copy of the voucher in his pocket. I explained the facts to him. He said he would tell Gordon (chairman of the committee) that this must not be used. It would be most unfair to me & the high office of PM. He then told me my recent remark re 'dictator' had hurt him greatly. I explained that he had been rude etc. It ended by his putting forth his hand to shake hands. Later tonight I saw Cahan in his office and spoke of the voucher. He spoke in the nicest manner possible, of his faith in my integrity, etc., then went on to tell me what the Conservative members knew of funds from Beauharnois to Liberals. I was amazed when he gave me the figures. The sittings of the committee bring out very much concerning fees to lawyers for all sorts and kinds of purposes.

July 15, 1931:

This morning I had a dream in which I saw dear Mother and once more had my arms around her. It seemed to me I was travelling somewhere, and was at an underground station. I had come on to the platform, but left behind in the car my valise, a brown bag, in which was the key to the valise itself. The conductor seemed to know of it and said he would get it. Then I went back to meet dear Mother who was coming off another train. She came down a stair, having also left behind the luggage she had. I was so glad to see her. She looked very frail, had a shawl around her, but her mind was quite intent. I put my arms around her and felt her love, my love for her so great that it seemed as if my heart would burst. I said to her that we would not bother about anything else, luggage or the like, but would now have a chance to read quietly together and to think about all the beautiful spiritual things. We were just about to walk along the platform together when I woke up.

It seemed that dear Mother was making it plain she was near me in this time of anxiety, guiding and helping me. I felt I could be happy with nothing, a long as I had her love and a good name. I felt the besmirching influence of politics. There was comfort in the dream.

While I was at the House tonight, my former student, Peter Gerry and his wife, arrived from New York. It seemed too terrible that they should be on my hands at this of all times. I went over to the Château to see them & arranged for dinner at the Country Club tomorrow night. Later I saw Mackenzie re McDougald. McDougald's refusal to go before the committee & Bennett's threat of a Royal Commission or further legislation has created a sensation. I feel very anxious of McDougald's appearance. He has so little sense & is so devoid of the ethical side of things that one dreads the outcome of any testimony he may give. This is a real Gethsemane thro' which one is being called to pass at this time.

To bed about midnight — the one peace in my heart, the thought that dear Mother is near. It is very lonely, all alone at this time, on this solitary journey of life.

July 16, 1931:

I took Peter & Mrs. Gerry out for a drive, returning to lunch at Laurier House. I showed them over the house, and at three p.m. took them to the office. I took them both over the buildings, library, restaurant, Senate etc. In the Senate, Hardy was proposing to have McDougald appear before the Senators. Dinner was a very hurried-up affair, and I had much trouble getting the guests together, tried several in vain. The dinner cost quite a sum & I confess to wishing I did not have to have association with the rich, but could spend my time and money among the poor.

July 17, 1931:

I came into my office a few minutes to eight p.m. Lapointe said "The lid is off." At the morning session of the committee, there had been complete disclosure of the funds given for campaign purposes to Liberals and Conservatives. The revelation was appalling, especially the $50,000 given directly to Haydon. I felt particularly concerned about Haydon, who is in no condition to suffer shock and strain of this kind & who has been chivalry personified in his actions with the party. The experience was humiliating one, and I felt ashamed at it occuring when Peter and Mrs. G were here, but thankful they were not arriving just at that moment.

The atmosphere around the lobbies was one of sensation & suspicion. Bright, a press man, came to tell me that despite all rumours etc. he still believed in me! I hardly knew how to accept his words, which were meant in a kindly way I know. I can see that the Tory party intend to do their worst to destroy me. Fortunately I have been careful with McDougald right along, but the thing that distresses me greatly is the interpretation they will try to place on our association — on the voucher — but most of all any contribution he may have made to the Laurier House

Fund, which they know of, I'm sure, and which will be completely misrepresented. The association with Haydon will also be magnified into one relating to Beauharnois. All this makes me very depressed & sick at heart. But I have the knowledge that my course was straight, & nothing that McDougald has done has influenced me in the slightest particular.

July 18, 1931:

This has been one of the hardest days of my life. I felt sick at heart & mortified at the revelations, reflecting as they do on the administration which bears my name & on those who have been close political friends & associates. For years to come there will be repercussions. One does not know yet to what further lengths matters may go. I have worried over every possession I have, wondering if poverty would not be better than the wealth that has become, if anything, too great. All I have may be misunderstood, misinterpreted, or, what is worse, may lead to my separation from the poor & simple & humble & honest folk of the world. It was very trying to go about with wealthy friends on such a day, to be arranging a dinner party with wines etc. when I really should be in prayer, in sackcloth & ashes. Phoned Haydon. His voice sounded sad, but he seemed to be philosophical & cheerful.

July 19, 1931:

I did not sleep too well last night. It was hot & my heart was sick, but while I was dressing in the bathroom, almost like an inspiration from beyond came the thought that if McDougald should be questioned as to any of his contributions to me personally, and the Laurier House Fund, I would be given a chance to review the whole matter of what Larkin & others have done for me, to make perfectly clear how my possessions came to be what they are, how the fund was raised, etc. etc. People may believe I am being helped by party funds & it would give me a chance to explain everything. When this thought came my whole feeling changed. I pray to God that I might rise to greater heights of greatness before my fellow men & in His sight.

July 20, 1931:

I am immensely relieved tonight. To the surprise of everyone, Dr.

McDougald made the best witness the committee has had before it. He was calm & collected & did not hesitate in his replies. McDougald made it plain that he had been away during the election campaign, had not had to do with the funds, had not sought to influence the ministers & mentioned in particular myself. It took an immense load off my mind & heart. Everything has been like a pall over me in the last few days, the ignominy of the whole business in the eyes of those who don't understand.

July 21, 1931:

This has been a day of great trial and anguish. During the afternoon, Mackenzie sent word in to me that the Beauharnois committee was taking up the matter of the voucher with McDougald, and I had better speak to Bennett. I crossed over & spoke to Bennett. He said it was not any of their boys who had brought the matter out, it was Gardiner of the UFA. I got Mackenzie, Power & Jacobs in my office to talk over matters. They said McDougald had covered, or rather uncovered everything satisfactorily, the only point was that he said *I* had invited him to Bermuda. This upset me very much for I had no recollection of it. I called on Haydon. He had no recollection of any invitation. I had Henry come up to Laurier House with me & we looked over files but could find nothing. I felt still more annoyed when I read McDougald's evidence later & saw an affidavit he had prepared. It was all to make much of his friendship with me, of other trips to New York at Easter, etc. etc., and his outlays on my behalf. The man is either a knave or a fool. I am inclined to regard him as both.

July 22, 1931:

I slept very little last night. This morning I spent trying to straighten out the invitation to Bermuda. Finally Pickering remembered a Bermuda file & there we found a telegram I had sent McDougald inviting him, making mention of the Easter plans for the trip. It is clear that the inspiration was from McDougald himself, who was trying to get alongside me & be seen with me. He has been doing that right along, turning up in Charlestown, S. Carolina, in London, Eng., always in Montreal, etc. and publishing from the housetops every visit of mine to his house there, or in the Adirondacks. It makes one's heart sick, for if ever there is a man living I have been careful to keep at arm's length, it is McDougald.

July 28, 1931:

The Beauharnois report was tabled at eight-thirty p.m. The clerk read it aloud. There was not a line in it which reflects on the government, nor a line on myself, save what can be drawn from my friendship with Haydon & McDougald. Certainly I have been deceived in my friends. I go to bed tonight with heart greatly relieved, and believing that God's mercy has been great.

July 29, 1931:

I attended Liberal caucus this morning. I told the members that we were in the 'Valley of Humiliation' & should do some searching of heart. The men, tho' clearly concerned, were in good fettle & sympathetic. The position is most difficult as respects Haydon. I cannot endorse what he has done in accepting the $50,000 from Beauharnois. It has left an unpleasant taste. On the other hand, Haydon has been loyalty itself to me & I do not intend to have him sacrificed to a lot of canting hypocrites and wolves. I feel thro' all of this that it just has to be endured, that it is a penalty for having permitted myself to become the friends I did with McDougald & Haydon.

Bennett is taking the right course on Beauharnois. The only sinister part of it all is the transfer of power from a financial group which was friendly to the Liberals, to a Tory group, from one predatory interest to one even more predatory — the Royal Bank group. That has been the battle from the beginning.

Kingsmere, August 4, 1931:

Vincent Massey rang up about noon. He wants to see me about something he must soon make a decision on. From now on he will have to make his own decisions & will get his rewards in accordance with his service to the party & nothing else. This idea of helping *me* is all nonsense. I am the one being used by everyone else. Massey is not less selfish that McDougald. I intend to get my house in order, from basement to garret.

I went out on the lawn and lay on my back gazing at the splendour of the Heavens to seek to gain some of their calmness & to become like them, 'untroubled and impassionate.' I changed my phone number today to Sherwood 876 — to avoid Massey.

August 14, 1931:

This has been a day of commotion, beginning with the Masseys getting my long-distance number but failing to get through. I complained to head office, and found that it was Vincent's persistence. However, I did not answer. They sent a message they were coming today. The matter 'would not brook delay.' They arrived by motor from Port Hope at six o'clock.

Thomas, Secretary of State for the Colonies, has offered Vincent the post of Governor of Australia. Vincent wanted my advice. I told him had it been governor of a dominion, I would have felt the offer fitting, but I could not feel so about a state. Vincent is in a desperate frame of mind. He feels like getting out of Canada altogether. Both he & Alice feel terribly the days & months passing with nothing to do. She came around to Vincent beginning a study group on Liberalism & he said 'if he could help me' etc. I opened out straight from the shoulder, said I was tired of others speaking of helping *me*, that it was the party that needed help, Liberalism that needed help, that I had been doing all in my power but had been left very much alone, that I had made up my mind that unless there were more division of labour, the party would have to find itself a new leader. I would not & could not do the work of organization & publicity. I said I had been appointing men senators, judges etc. but had been doing all the work as well. I would do my best in Parliament etc. but would not be the one around whom others were to hang their weight. Alice said I was right in this & Vincent later agreed.

Vincent asked if I thought if he were away, eg. in Australia, for three years, it would affect his chances of getting London. I said most decidedly so, that those who left the party in its time of need would get no recognition later on. I said that if I had been treated by Bennett the way he had, I would not die until I got that man out of power. I did not say what was equally true, that if I had been done for by another as I have done for Massey, making him Privy Councillor, a member of Cabinet, a Minister to the U.S. and High Commissioner to London, I would help my friend in time of need. They are purely selfish. They are always thinking of the social set in London, the Duchess of Devonshire,

Dawson of the *Times* etc. etc. They seem concerned about the party's chances to win. I told them I felt certain Bennett would not win the next election, would not even last out two years. I believe he might be shot, or the victim of a bloody revolution, before his term is up.

The Masseys had come for the night, but Dora, the country cook, had left with bag & baggage, not even prepared tea. They saw the situation and left about ten p.m. To bed about eleven-thirty p.m. very tired and overwrought.

23

Vivian has a job! Not just any old job either, but a government job. They're the best, her dad says — you never get fired. Just as well too, because she flunked out of college. She felt sick about it, and figured she'd *never* get a job, but then she went to a UFA dance with the Brownlees and met Mr. Smale, who hires everybody for the government, and he said that a girl had quit *that very morning* and could she start on Monday. Could she! Oh wow!

So now she's in the Attorney-General's office, very classy, just down the hall from Mr. Brownlee's office. The work's not hard, filing mostly, and she's already learned how to go real slow so she doesn't end up sitting around with nothing to do. Vivian sometimes reads the files. They're a lot better than *True Story* magazine, although the murders are really horrible. Who could imagine all those things happening in Alberta! The other girls are okay. She's already made one friend, Myrna, who's from Medicine Hat. At first Vivian was embarrassed that they might think she had "pull," but it turned out they'd all been hired pretty much the same way, through knowing somebody in the government. It's just the way it's done, Myrna said. Of course if the government gets defeated, they'll lose their jobs, but there's not too much chance of that since just about everybody in Alberta's a farmer, though Myrna says with the drought so bad in the south a lot of people are leaving the land and going on Relief. It makes work for secretaries, though, with forms and stuff to be filled out, so it's an ill wind, isn't it?

Vivian hardly ever sees John at work. He's in meetings, mostly, or away in Ottawa trying to get more Relief out of Mr. Bennett, without much luck. Actually, Vivian sees more of Mrs. Brownlee and the boys than she does of him. She doesn't really mind helping out with the cooking and housekeeping. It's only good manners, they've done so much for her, and the maid's gone home for the harvest, and Mrs. Brownlee isn't strong. It's just that Vivian's so tired sometimes, being on her feet all day, and it's so late when John drives her home, and she has to be at work by eight the next morning. She's lost nearly ten pounds. It's okay with her, but Mama would have a fit. Her own cooking's not so bad, and the rooming house is better than the Y. She doesn't feel sick, except when she takes the awful black pills John gives her when her monthlies are due. The pills give her cramps. Mostly she just isn't very hungry.

She's trying to save money too. Twelve dollars a week seemed a fortune at first, but with carfare and room and board and winter clothes, Vivian can't save a cent. Her dad sure was right — she'd starve to death playing the piano! They've shut down the Edmonton Symphony, and Jasper Park Lodge will close this winter. Vivian hasn't played the piano in a year. She doesn't really miss it, except she felt a little jealous last spring when the musical festival was on, and the test piano piece was one she used to know by heart, back home.

She phones home a lot. There's not much to say. Her dad might get laid off. It scares Vivian to death. What if he gets deported? John says all the eastern bums will be sent back where they came from. Her dad's from Nova Scotia. She knows John means foreigners mostly, people from Poland and places like that, but the *Bulletin* had a story a while ago about some Reds from the coalfields being sent back to Scotland. Her dad was born in Glasgow, and he *is* a Labour man. Vivian knows she's being silly, her dad's been in Canada forever, but John's so terribly strict about things. Like, he doesn't want her going to the movies. He says they're "trash." Well, they're not *all* trash, so sometimes she goes anyway, with Myrna — she's nuts about Gary Cooper — but Vivian always feels guilty afterwards. Trouble is, she never knows when John's going to phone. It's usually late, after a meeting, and there's only one phone in the rooming house, outside the landlady's door. Mrs. Carruthers goes to bed early and doesn't like to be woken up, so Vivian has to run and grab the phone as fast as she can, then wait for Mrs. Carruthers to go back to sleep before slipping out the back door. She hates it, but what can she do? If she's not home, John is furious. Where was she? Who was she with? What was she doing? And sometimes he doesn't phone at all. Those times are the worst. Like now. How can it be so lonely, being in love?

24

Christina Coolican is tired of trees. It's not that she has anything against trees, as long as they stand still in one place, the way they're supposed to, and don't run past her window backwards for two days and a night, all the way from Toronto. What will happen when the trees reach Toronto? She imagines them marching down Yonge Street, running in along Bloor, crowding into Queen's Park, filling the ravines, the yards, the streets, tramping along until they stop suddenly at the lake shore, dig in, put down roots, the newcomers backing up behind, crushing against the buildings, the banks, the churches, until the stone walls crack and crumble, great roots running through the fissures, and the city is nothing more than a heap of rubble covered with trees waving their arms in the wind, triumphant.

She smiles and closes her eyes, soothed by the rocking of the coach and the chatter of the track, *clickety-clack clickety-clack*. The train reminds her of the asylum: the bustle, the noise, the excitement, the strange cries the conductors make when they come to a station, and the way everyone sways drunkenly down the aisles. The darky doctors treat her very well. They call her Ma'am, and make up her cell at night with their own hands, and don't even lock her in. She is pleased when people get off, quite cured, and tries to be especially friendly to the new ones who take their places, assuring them that it won't be long until they get off too, but the worst simply shake their heads and sigh "Vancouver."

She does miss room service. She'd gotten into the habit of eating alone, at all hours of the day and night, and had so impressed the chef at the Château with her prophecies that he sent squads of boys into the country to catch grasshoppers so the Mahdi could feast on locusts and honey. The grasshoppers were good deep fried too, or sautéed in garlic butter, and she had suffered a deep disappointment when the Mahdi disappeared as strangely as he had come, the day Willie King lost the election. Willie was upset and blamed the Mahdi for his defeat, saying that he had promised a great victory, and had lied, and must be an agent of the Devil.

"I thought he meant a victory over sin, not the Conservative Party," said Christina Coolican, shocked that Willie had interpreted his struggle for salvation in a purely worldly way.

"It's all the same to him," Lily said. "You're wasting your time, Mum. Willie has no soul."

"No. He's just lost it. No, he's sold it. That's what he's done. It's not a very good soul. I can see it quite clearly. It's a poor, Presbyterian thing, all puffed up with pride and spotted with self-righteousness, a small, pale, frightened little soul. He can't have gotten much for it. We'll have to get it back."

"The Doctor drives a hard bargain."

"So do I."

Willie never came to see her again. No one else did either. Word went around that *she* had caused the great cataclysm that turned money to dust and cast a pall of despair over the land. That was nonsense, of course. It was the Lord who smote the golden calf and broke it into a thousand pieces, so its worshippers would humble their hearts and follow Him. She was only His messenger. Hadn't she said that money was the root of all evil, and counselled her followers to get rid of it as quickly as possible? Some had taken her advice and sold their stocks at the peak of the market and become millionaires, but Mr. Morrison the baker threatened to sue when he cast an entire day's output of Morrison's Bakery Ltd. into the Ottawa River, and watched it float away towards Montreal.

Christina Coolican is relieved to be rid of the Mahdi's single patchwork garment. It was miserably cold in winter, and the Mahdi complained that her woollies itched. It kept her indoors, so she couldn't speak to people in the market, or sit in Union Station listening to the Lord's voice boom beneath the great glass dome OOOMMM MAAAR-ROOOOOOMMM KAAARROOOOOMMM BOOOMMMM. She wrote to Dr. Livingstone in the asylum, asking him to please return the plain black dress she had arrived in, saying she could hear the Lord better in it, and received it by return post with a nice note telling her to keep up the good work.

She did her best in Ottawa. She was puzzzled that no one else seemed
to hear the booming voice in Union Station. People wandered about, or
sat dumbly, staring into space, or ate sandwiches. One day when the
OOOMMMBAAARROOOOMMMM was particularly loud, she stood up on
a bench beneath the dome and cried out:
"Listen to the Lord!"
She found that the words came effortlessly to her tongue,
"I AM the resurrection and the life!"
Her voice carried quite easily to the farthest walls, so that people
everywhere stopped and looked at her, and fell silent, and listened.
Christina Coolican had scarcely begun her message when she felt herself
being lifted into the air, and believed for a wild, ecstatic moment that she
might whirl right up through the dome, like Ezekiel, but then her feet
touched ground again, and a rough voice said: "This here's a public
place, lady. It ain't no place for the Lord." The policeman saw her back
to the Château.

After the Crash, all the necromancers, soothsayers, palm readers,
trumpet blowers, astrologists, phrenologists, table rappers and alchem-
ists crept out of the Château, one by one. Christina Coolican was the last
to leave. The manager was very nice about it. He said he needed her
room to make a suite for the new Prime Minister, Mr. Bennett, but it
was really because she was bad for business, and they wouldn't let her
stay for free anymore, and she couldn't afford to pay. In Ottawa, the
Lord's word isn't worth a plugged nickel.

They are going west, to Edmonton. A nice boom to it, ED-
MMMONNNNTONNNNNNN OOOMMMMMMMM. In the asylum, when
somebody died, the soldiers said he'd "gone west." Is she dying? At least
she'll be closer to Heaven, in Edmonton, when the time comes. Perhaps
she'll be born again, in EDMMMONNNNNTONNNNNNN.

The trees stop. The train is crossing a broad, flat plain. The ground is
gold. The sky is blue. And far ahead, at the earth's edge, a shining dome
grows larger and larger, until Christina Coolican can see a golden figure
glittering on top. Beneath the dome the building is white. In fact,
beneath its canopy of trees, the whole city is white — tiny white houses,
tall white buildings, a wide white street pointing to Paradise. The sun is
so bright the city seems to shine with an inner light, city of light, city of
God.

"Jerusalem," says Christina Coolican.

"Winnipeg," sighs Lily.

"I'll get off here, I think."

Christina Coolican hops up and darts down the aisle before Lily can gather her wits. She's the first off the train. The station rotunda is right where she'd imagined it, smaller than Ottawa, but with a nice BAAAAOOOOOOMMMMMMM nonetheless, and a huge throng of people waiting to hear the Word. She finds a bench directly beneath the sky-blue dome.

"I AM the light of the world," she says from the bench, hardly raising her voice. The thunder of the Lord's words caroms off the walls and the people fall silent. "I AM the ressurection and the life! He that believeth in me, though he were dead, yet shall he live!"

Lazarus is just emerging from his grave, still swaddled in his shroud, when Lily catches up to her and persuades the policeman that the Bible is not sedition. The policeman gives Christina Coolican time to get Lazarus safely on his way before ushering them into the street.

It's the same policeman who carries Christina Coolican out of the Bank of Montreal the next day. She'd seen the huge, white sarcophagus from the train, its bronze doors flanked by two great pillars, a graven soldier standing in front, Moloch before the Temple of Mammon. Inside, the altars are marble, and the ceiling is carved with swastikas in gold leaf. The black-coated priests move silently, bent obsequiously in prayer. The worshippers wait patiently in line with looks of anxious anticipation.

Bang! Bang! Bang! She overturns three of the little oak tables in quick succession. Leaves of pink and green and white flutter through the air, and the blue blood of broken inkwells stains the marble floor. The worshippers don't cry out, or raise their hands, but only shrink back against the iron cages. The priests begin to wail and dance about. The Lord sweeps all before Him, tables, chairs, coat racks, pens and blotters, counter cheques and deposit slips, whosh, until Christina Coolican herself rises into the air and flies, feet flailing, out the door into the light.

"Look here, Granny," the policeman says, setting her down. "You trying to start a revolution?"

That's it, isn't it? That's exactly it!

The policeman's name is Donald and he's from Skye, like herself, and a Presbyterian too, as she had been years ago, before she found God. Donald doesn't like banks any more than she does, and when Christina

Coolican asks: "If the Bank of Montreal isn't a heathen temple, then why does it *look* like a heathen temple?" Donald scratches his head and lets her off with a warning that the Lord would be safer in church.

The story of the raid on the bank is in all the newspapers. The *Free Press* says it was the work of agitators, led by the notorious Bolshevik, Tim Buck, disguised as a woman. The story creates a sensation among the unemployed, who swarm into Market Square, give three loud cheers for Tim Buck and the International, then march to City Hall where they throw stones at the windows and slash the tires on the aldermen's cars, until the city council agrees to raise a single man's Relief from $4 to $5 a week. The Communist Party takes all the credit. It sends a cable to Comintern.

"Where's Winnipeg?" says the Comintern.

The next afternoon, when Christina Coolican finally reaches the great temple in the centre of the city, the one with the naked man in gold leaf on top, Donald is waiting for her, and whisks her out before the Lord has a chance to open his mouth, although He can hear the devils buzzing like bees beneath the dome. She can't see a thing from the paddy-wagon, and when Donald finally opens the doors, she's surprised to find herself in a market square, where a great throng is rejoicing. Donald clears a path for her past the stalls of cabbages and carrots, and leads her towards a wagon where a woman with fiery hair is leading the congregation in a beautiful hymn. Christina Coolican has never heard it before, and doesn't understand the words, but everyone else seems to know it by heart, and they sing with radiant faces.

When the hymn is finished, the young woman jumps down. Donald lifts Christina Coolican up onto the wagon.

"Go to it, Granny," he says. "Let's see if the Lord can give Red Annie a run for her money."

The straw beneath her feet is clean and sweet, and the newly-dug potatoes at the back of the wagon smell of cool, fresh earth. Somewhere a lamb is being roasted. The fragrant smoke drifts over the square. She looks out over the sea of faces, men's faces mostly, boys, her own boy's age and younger, boy's faces browned by the summer sun, earth-coloured, their clothes mud- and dung-coloured, grey and brown and khaki, like the boys in the asylum huddled in their old greatcoats against the cold stone walls, her own son too in jail now, in EDMMMONNNNN-TONNNNNN. A few drops of rain spatter against her face. Someone hands up an umbrella. BAAARRROOOOOMMMMMMM. Thunder rumbles across the square. I AM. I AM that I AAMMMMMMMM.

"I AM the God of thy Fathers,
And I have seen the affliction of my people,
Which are in Egypt,
And have heard their cry,
For I know their sorrows,
And I am come down to deliver them out of
The hand of the Egyptians,
And to bring them up out of that land to
A land flowing with milk and honey.
Let my people go!
LET MY PEOPLE GO"

Mum preaches in the market every day. Lily watches her standing beneath her umbrella, the centre of a rapt crowd who don't seem to mind the wind and the dust. Mum's voice is strong for such a small person, and she knows the Bible almost by heart, having read nothing else as long as Lily can remember. She recites it in a strange, melodic cadence that has a hypnotic effect, calling down plagues on the head of the Pharaoh, who everybody knows is the Prime Minister, Mr. Bennett. When Mum extends her arm to part the Red Sea, half the crowd sways one way, half the other, so a path opens across the market square right at her feet, and nobody would be surprised at all to see the chariots of the Pharaoh galloping in from the Rupert Street police station.

The Red River is so low you can almost walk across it. The city is full of frogs. The hobos camped on the riverbanks swear that the legs, fried up with onions and a little salt, are just as good as everyone says, but frogs only remind Winnipeg of the grasshopper plague last June, and nobody has much appetite for slimy things, with legs. The first day Mum preached, a terrific thunderstorm tore through the city. The sewers backed up, and lightning set fire to a lumber yard. The fire burned for a day and a night. A pall of black smoke hung over the city, and red-hot cinders flew through the air. After the smoke cleared, a wind from the west brought a fine, brown dust that darkened the sun at noon. Marx doesn't have magic like that.

God knows, he tries. The streets are full of kids selling *The Worker*

and shouting about capitalist-fascist-imperialist-opportunism. Poor
kids, they might as well be jugglers, Lily thinks, or dancing bears. They
take an awful lot of shit. Some of them don't look any more than
sixteen, skinny kids with glasses, nice Jewish boys who wouldn't know-
ingly step on an ant. What is Communism, a children's crusade? Why
don't they occupy Eaton's? Surround city hall? Set up a Soviet? Bake
bread, for God's sake?

Lily is thinking about Esselwein when she bumps into Red Annie at a
fish stall.

"Don't tell me you've bought all this God shit," says Annie, nodding
towards Mum on her wagon.

"You could call me a fellow-traveller." Lily laughs at her own joke.
Annie doesn't. One of Annie's most endearing qualities is her total lack
of humour, especially about the party.

"How's the revolution?" Lily asks, to make amends.

"No bad. Eight comrades are in jail. That's a good sign."

"Jack's in jail too, just for a month."

"He should get life."

"For what? The Crash? He should get the Order of Lenin."

"Well, I may be next. For jail I mean." Annie sounds as if the Order of
Lenin is a distinct alternative. Maybe it is. She seems pleased.

"What have you done?"

"Nothing, yet. You don't have a truck, do you?"

"No." Annie always makes you feel so useless.

Annie sighs.

"Look at all this stuff," she says. "There's enough food in this city to
feed us all until we're stuffed, *forever*. Yet you go around the corner and
what do you see? A soup kitchen. A cup of dishwater and a slice of bread
a day. That's it. And up at the woodyard? Grown men, married men,
with kids, lining up to beg a bag of beans. *Feh*. Filthy fascists."

It's true. The market stalls are heaped high with vegetables and crates
of eggs and chickens and baskets of apples, and the square is full of
people; but hardly anyone seems to buy anything, and the mounds of
produce never diminish. Water into wine, in Winnipeg. Breadbasket of
the World, that's what the Chamber of Commerce says. It's true too.
Grain in the granaries, money in banks, fish in the sea. It was true in
Ireland too, in the famine. *Plus ça change*. Lily looks down. She catches
the eye of a lake trout. It's still slippery and smells of weeds. What if she
picks it up and hands it to somebody in the crowd? Then another? And

another? Would there be a riot? Riots remind her of Esselwein. Where is
he now?

"He's probably cleaning out the Mounties' horse barns," Annie says.
"That's where he hid out after his little revolution, when he was supposed to be in jail."

So. No wonder Esselwein hates barns. A cop's life isn't all a bed of
roses. Maybe they even sent him to the Interior. He always dreaded that.
Lily smiles. She feels no fear now. When you've got nothing left to lose,
no fame, no fortune, no name, no love, life can be a lot simpler.

"Maybe I could borrow a truck," Lily says. "There's a cartage
company that lends them out to charities to collect old clothes."

"Risky. We might lose it."

"How do you lose a truck?"

"Easy. Ever heard of Beanfate, Saskatchewan?"

"Bienfait? Sure, it's one of my favourite places. I always thought it
was French."

Annie looks sceptical.

"I'm not kidding," Lily insists. "Beanfate made my fortune."

"Coal?"

"No, the ... um ... export business."

"You Irish and your *goyische* drink!"

"Mr. Bronfman of the Bienfait Import-Export Company is a Jew, I
think. Nice man. He wants to be a senator, too."

"Mr. Bronfman ain't in Beanfate now, I can tell you. There's nobody
in Beanfate except a bunch of poor bastards digging coal. The place is
dried out. Not a cow, or a chicken, or a dog, or a grain of wheat, or even
a blade of grass. The wells have run dry. It's like that all through the
west. Difference is, in the other places, the nice, God-fearing *goyische*
places, the churches bring in Relief. But because Beanfate's a mining
camp, and full of Commies and Wobblies, and bohunks and aliens and
degenerates, the churches won't touch it with a ten-foot pole. The coal
companies want to starve 'em out and close the mines. The government
says they're all foreigners, and won't give Relief. So when the people
come to the Party, and we try to send in a truckload of food, the truck is
stopped on the outskirts of town and everything's confiscated. We've
lost two trucks this month. Fascists."

"How do they know it's a Red truck?"

"*All* trucks are stopped, except ... except ...." Annie's face lights up.
"Can you drive?"

25

"An' where youse ladies headin'?"

"Beanfate, officer." Lily smiles. "As you see, we represent the Canadian Red Cross."

Lily's heart misses a beat as the Mountie squints at the big, cloth cross tied to the side of the truck. The cross, tattered after two days driving, is dusty, disreputable, more like a red rag, or, as Annie has pointed out with satisfaction, a Red Flag. The Mountie ponders the cross for a long time. The colour Lily notices, exactly matches his scarlet tunic, dust and all.

"Annie," she whispers, "where did you get . . . ."

"Hershfield's Men's Wear," Annie hisses. "Remnants."

Lily watches the Mountie in the rear-view mirror. He circles the truck like a dog sniffing a post. A kick at a tire, tug on a rope, poke at the the tarp, scratch of the head, a thoughtful gob of spit into the dirt, brown boot on the running board, black notebook in hand, raw, red farmboy face in the window.

"Names?"

"Mrs. King. This is Mrs. Mason. She's a nurse."

Annie, in her borrowed spectacles, blue suit and hideous hat, glowers in a matronly way. The Mountie labouriously prints their names in his little black book. He prints every "s" backwards.

"Purpose of visit?"

"To bring succour to the suffering," Lily says, curious to see what he will make of that, but he just prints "Help."

"Youse ladies'd be better off doin' your suckerin' somewheres else," he says squinting down the road towards town. "Them bums don't deserve nothin'. Nothin' but Commies 'n crinimals."

The Mountie's eyes shift uneasily from side to side. He glances repeatedly over his shoulder, as if a bunch of bohunks might leap out of the ditch at any moment and surround the truck. Lily glances up and down the road. There's nothing but blowing dust and tumbleweed caught in the fences. The Mountie leans into the window and says in a low, conspiratorial voice: "My advice to youse is to dump the stuff on Main Street an' get out quick. There's gonna be trouble."

"How do you know?" asks Annie, leaning towards him.

The Mountie looks around carefully, then leans further into the window.

"The Reds is here," he says softly. "Buck an' the boys, from Tronna. I seen 'em." He pauses. His shining eyes shift from face to face. Lily pats his arm.

"I thought they were all in jail," Annie says. Her face is white.

"Don't you worry, Ma'am. They will be, soon as they start somethin'. Sedition, incitin', disturbin' the peace, it's all there in the Crinimal Code."

"We'll be careful, Officer," Lily says, turning the key in the ignition. "We've both been through the war. Mrs. Mason was decorated for bravery at Vimy."

"VC?" asks the Mountie, his face lighting up.

"VD," says Annie. "*Valeur Distinguée*. It's French."

"Jeez, you got a real talent there for languages. The sergeant says I'm gifted that way myself. That's how I picks out the Reds, see. The Reds is Yids, right? An' Yids talk funny. Pretty simple, eh?"

The Mountie plods back to his Packard. It's a big, black V-8, a rum-runner's car, Lily thinks. Where the hell's his horse? And what's he doing on the backroads, dressed to kill?

"Annie, there *will* be trouble."

"Of course," Annie says. "That's why I'm here."

The Packard wheels around and disappears in a cloud of dust. Sahara, Saskatchewan.

"God, I hate the redcoats, Annie."

"That's because you're Irish. It's like the Jews and the Cossacks. Ever see a Jew on a horse?"

So here they are, the red-haired Jew and the black Irish *shiksa* (How she hates that word!), riding together into the western sun. Lily could use a gin, a stiff one, with lemon and lots of ice.

Before long, the road curves and narrows into a street of stark little shacks. Not a leaf or a living soul in sight. Bienfait is bleached out, dried up, a picked bone. The Bienfait Export Co. is only a big white shed with iron bars on the windows.

They turn off on a sideroad that winds across the top of a windswept bluff. The ground is covered with coarse brown grass except to the east, where bald, barren humps loom against the sky, the moonscape of a strip mine. They stop at a high, barbed-wire fence. Behind it, weathered white houses in three straggling rows, a bunkhouse, the company store.

"Where's the mine?"

"In the coulee." Annie points to where the bluff drops off into a deep, narrow valley. "Most of the miners live there too. Dig a little cave in the side of the hill, put in a window, a door. Snug as a bug. Beats this company shit up here."

"But Annie, they're not animals."

"Yeah? Tell that to the company."

"Why don't they quit?"

"Where can they go? They're all immigrants, Poles, Ruthenians, Ukrainains. They can't go home. Nobody wants them here."

Unpeople. Prehistoric burrowing beasts. Lily pictures the whole bluff honeycombed with tunnels, black tunnels filled with dark, mole-like creatures furiously digging, then BOOM a mine explodes, and everyone blows up. Nomen. Nomensland. She remembers how, after the war, soldiers went down the mines because they said they were used to being underground, in the dark, and felt happier there. What is happening to us?

"Do you think it was worse for them in the Ukraine?"

"In the Ukraine they lived in mud houses. Above the ground."

The barbed-wire fence has a gate and a sentry box, but the gate is open and the box is empty. Lily drives through. Not a soul in sight. The company store seems to be closed. It's been boycotted since the strike began. Annie is pleased. A lot of the miners are in debt to the store, and if the store is closed, it can't collect.

Behind one of the houses a line of washing flaps in the wind. Lily stops in front of the house, but nobody comes to the door. The house had once been painted white, with green trim, just like the company houses in Kirkland, but only faint traces of paint remain. The steps are broken, and boards are nailed over most of the windows. Lily would think it deserted if it weren't for the wash and two children scrabbling in the dirt by the door.

Annie goes around to the back. Lily watches the kids in the dirt. They stare back, fingers in mouths. God, they're dirty! She must have looked like that herself once. How long, thirty years ago? Shanty Irish.

"Everyone's in the union hall," Annie says. She returns without her spectacles and hideous hat. "I scared the poor woman half to death. She thought I was from the Children's Aid, come to take her kids away."

The union hall is only a shed on the outskirts of town with "Mine Workers Local 2" crudely painted over the door. Local 2 is less than three weeks old, and not recognized by the companies. That's what the strike is about, not to mention money. As Lily pulls up, the door opens, and a dark suspicious face peers out.

"Go 'way! Go 'way!" A gaunt young man with a shock of straw-coloured hair comes out waving his arms.

"No stuff!" he shouts. "Don't want! Go 'way!"

"This is a hell of a welcome." Annie clambers down and scowls at the boy.

"Замкнися, дурню. Де Михайло? "

The boy looks startled. He disappears inside. Another face appears at the door, older, swarthy, Tartar cheekbones and pale-green eyes. The hair is grey now, but Lily would know that face anywhere.

Big Peter runs towards Annie and gives her a big bear hug.

"Annie! *Towarzysz! Dobry! Dobry!* Lily! Lily! *Towarzysz! Towarzysz!*"

He hugs them both at once.

"Peter! I thought you were dead, or deported!"

"I run away. Guard, he go out for a smoke, so me, I take a powder, hey?" He laughs uproariously. "I am Mike now. New name, same me." He laughs again. "Nick here, he say you more church ladies with stinky stuff!"

The stinky stuff is inside. It was delivered by a carload of women in white gloves who dumped the gunny sacks in front of the hall and fled. The stinky stuff is now piled up in the centre of the union hall floor. Women in *babushkas* squat around it, passing pieces from hand to hand, shaking their heads.

"I think to eat," Mike says. "I take little bite. Bleh!"

The stinky stuff looks like broken concrete. The slabs are flat, irregular in shape and hard as rock. Annie throws one against the wall. It chips the wood and falls to the floor intact. The stuff is the colour of porridge, tastes like salt and smells ... it smells like Gramp's old sweater, the sweater he came to Canada in, years and years ago, from Ireland. It was a fisherman's sweater, and it smelled of the sea. As a little girl Lily loved to sniff it and dream of ships.

"Cod," she says. "It's dry, salt cod. It's supposed to be, um, very good for you."

"But how we cook, hey?"

Let them eat fish, the English said when the potato failed. And the skeletons came and sat by the shore of the western sea. But they had no boats, or lines, or nets, or money to buy them, or fuel to cook their catch, and when they ate fish raw, it made them sick. And they starved. Sometimes the fishermen rowed them out to the sailing ships in the harbour and stowed them in the hold, like wood, and one day Gramp stayed on board. When the skeletons died at sea, he threw them overboard, food for the fish. Here, on this Saskatchewan sea, there are no ships.

"Trucks," Annie is saying. "We'll need at least a dozen, plus our own, as many as we can get, twenty people to a truck, more with the kids. The more women and kids, the safer we'll be."

They are driving west again. The sun is in Lily's eyes, and it's hard to see the road. The road isn't much more than two ruts in the dirt anyway. The shifting weight of the men in the back keeps throwing the truck off balance. The ground is frozen a little now, and the wind is still. Behind, a great cloud of yellow dust hangs in the air. The procession must be strung out more than a mile. Where have all the trucks come from? This morning they appeared as if by magic, rumbling into town simply crammed with people. Lily was embarrassed. Their pathetic little load of groceries couldn't possibly feed all those people, but most of them brought sandwiches and cold tea in glass jars. There are a lot of women, thanks to Annie. She knows the men won't chicken out in front of them.

Lily can see the grain elevators on the horizon straight ahead. A three-elevator town, Estevan. Bienfait is a no-elevator town. It isn't even a town at all. Unorganized territory. That's why they're driving to Estevan: to see the mayor, hold a meeting, have a picnic.

The mayor has forbidden a parade. The telegram arrived at the union hall this morning. "So, it's Saturday," Annie said. "Tell him we're going shopping. How can the greedy buggers complain about that?" In the back, the men are singing. Lily can't make out the words. They sound cheerful.

The road ahead is clear, not a soul in sight. Lily keeps her eye out for a Packard V-8. What would their multilingual Mountie make of them now? The red crosses have been cut into two-foot letters spelling FAIR WAGES, FAIR PRICES, stitched to bedsheets draped along both sides of the truck. The hood is covered with a Union Jack, thanks to the Bienfait Legion, and the slats of the truck box have been painted red, white and blue. Would he uncover the formidable Mrs. Mason in the gap-toothed *babushka* huddled in a shapeless coat on the front seat? Or Mrs. King beneath Lily's shabby smock of Robin Hood flour sacks? Whenever Lily looks at Annie, she can't help laughing.

The road narrows. A few houses appear.

"Coast is clear," Annie says. "They'd stop us here if they were going to."

More houses arranged into streets. A flat, plain, dusty little town. They are driving along the railway tracks now, in front of the grain elevators.

"Turn here," Annie says, pointing to the right. "Town hall's about half a mile down, corner of Queen Street."

They round the corner. Annie stiffens and straightens in her seat. A shout comes from the back. Far ahead, a row of small red figures is strung across the street. Lily takes her foot off the gas.

"Keep going!" Annie says.

Lily swallows hard. The figures grow larger. The Mounties are on foot. They are standing about ten feet apart, legs astride, hands behind their backs, two rows of ten men each, and in the centre of the front row, a stout figure in blue.

"That's McCutcheon, the town cop," Annie says.

"What do I do now?" Lily would like to turn around, fast.

"Don't stop. That's what they want. Keep going. We can go right through."

The street looks very wide. It has been cleared of cars. There is no barricade. Lily can see the town hall's flag flying right over Chief McCutcheon's head. The flag looks pretty against the blue sky. The whole scene is still and silent, very beautiful. The figures come closer, grow larger, red coats, blue sky, white faces in the windows, on the sidewalks, staring at her. Well, it *is* a parade. Lily feels as if she too is watching, from very far away.

"I'd feel better if Gary Cooper was here," she says.

"This isn't Hollywood."

"If this was Hollywood, we'd be up against the Klan."

"McCutcheon's a Kleagle. How did you know?"

They are less than a block away from the Mounties now. Lily is scared to death. She drives slowly, her foot steady on the gas. She heads straight for McCutcheon. The Chief doesn't flinch, but his mouth is a perfect O, and a fat hand in a clean, white glove is placed over his heart. The Mounties shift uneasily in line. Lily prays they'll break ranks.

"Look!" Annie is pointing to the right. They are coming to an intersection. McCutcheon has placed his men on the far side: the sidestreet is perfectly empty.

"We can detour right around them!" Annie calls out to the men in the back: "Hang on! Here we go!"

Lily puts the pedal to the floor. The truck lurches forward. It picks up speed. They are going very fast. At the intersection, Lily slams on the brake. The truck skids into a hairpin turn and roars up the sidestreet. She makes a left turn at the next corner, then another left and the truck screeches to a stop in front of the town hall. A cheer goes up from the back.

"*Ben Hur*," Lily says. "I saw it six times."

But Annie has already jumped down and disappeared into the throng of men pouring off the truck. Lily watches McCutcheon and the Mounties running towards them. Two other trucks have followed her route, the rest are pursuing the Mounties up Main Street. Suddenly the street is packed with people. Some of the Mounties have lost their hats. The miners have the police surrounded, outnumbered ten-to-one. What will they do now?

"We're wantin' the mayor, not you McCutcheon!" The voice comes from the back of the truck. It must be Martin Day, president of the union local. Another cheer goes up. Waving his nightstick, McCutcheon shoulders his way through the crowd towards the truck. Lily realizes she is still clutching the steering wheel.

"You're under arrest, Day!" McCutcheon bellows. "The rest of youse got five minutes to clear the hell outta town! Ya hear me!"

"BOOOOOOOOOOOOOOOOOOOOOOOO!"

"You scared of women and kids, McCutcheon?"

"Here I am, honey! You come 'n git me!" Ma Davis, the big cook from the Blue Goose boarding house, waves from the middle of the street. She lifts her skirt, bends over and shows McCutcheon a withered, waning moon.

"WooWoo!"

"I want you buggers outta here! You got no business in this town!"

"We got our rights, McCutcheon. You ain't orderin' us around!"

McCutcheon is beside the truck now, his stick raised. Lily rolls up the window and locks the door. In the back, the men are jumping up and down and screaming at McCutcheon. McCutcheon flails at them with his stick. Someone grabs his stick. McCutcheon is swallowed up by the crowd.

Pok. A starburst appears in the windshield. In the centre of the starburst is a tiny, round hole. There is another hole in the upholstery, right where Annie would have been sitting. Jesus! Straight ahead, a Mountie is pointing a pistol at the truck. Lily crouches down behind the dashboard.

"Look out!" a voice cries. "Get down, Day!"

The truck rocks. The men are jumping off the back.

Lily peeks through the windshield. The Mountie is pointing his gun at the crowd now. His hat is askew and there seems to be ketchup on his cheek. It runs down his neck. He wipes it with his fingers, looks at them, licks them. He points his gun at the ground. *Poof! Poof! Poof!* Little puffs of dirt fly up in front of the truck. *Ping!* Something hits the fender. God, Lily thinks, all I need is a flat.

Stones are raining on the roof of the truck and glancing off the hood. The crowd had drawn back to the sidewalk and the men are hurling chunks of dirt and bits of broken concrete at the Mounties huddled together on the steps of the town hall, their backs to the wall. Lily seems to be all alone in the middle of the street. The Mounties try to shield their faces with their arms. They fire randomly at the ground or into the air. From time to time a window shatters, or someone falls down, as if by magic. A hat blows down the street like a tumbleweed.

Lily hunches on the seat. The truck is very hot and stuffy and the sounds from outside seem strangely muffled. She hears a siren and looks up. A fire engine comes around the corner from behind the town hall. Men in black slickers are clinging to it like flies. The engine stops in the middle of the street. The men jump down and unwind the hose. They point it at the mob. Nothing happens. The hose is limp and dry. The firemen swarm over the engine, pumping handles and twisting valves. No good. Not a drop. The crowd boos, laughs. The firemen hover around the engine, irresolute.

A boy runs across the street towards them. His chest is bare. In one hand he waves his shirt, in the other a knife. He utters a high, piercing war cry. Others start running after him. The firemen crouch on the engine, holding the hose, then, all at once, they jump down and flap away between the buildings.

The running boy leaps onto the engine and scrambles to the top.

"Here I am!" Nick shouts. "Shoot me!"

He laughs and waves his shirt over his head.

A tiny, black hole appears in Nick's pale chest. He steps back, sways, slips and slides off the engine into the dirt.

Screams, then silence. The crowd shrinks back. Everyone is running now, running every which way, running to the trucks, the trucks turning around, turning back. Where the hell is Day? Annie? Lily can't just leave them, can she? And how the hell does she get out of here? She turns the key in the ignition.

A bloody face appears in the window. Mike climbs in.

"Hospital, quick!" he gasps. He rubs his hands distractedly over his face. His hands are wet with blood.

"Where are you hurt?"

"Not me. Up there." Mike points to a Texaco station down the street.

Behind the service station, another kid is lying in a pool of blood. Annie is wiping his face with a towel. His eyes are glazed. He howls when Mike lifts him and carries him gently to the back of the truck.

"Shoot in gut," Mike spits. "Pigs!"

The Estevan hospital is a low, white building behind a wire fence. The door is open. Lily finds herself in a long, narrow hall filled with people sitting against the walls or lying on the floor. She wonders if she looks as bloody as they do.

"Please, I need a doctor," she says to no one in particular. "Someone's been shot."

Nobody moves. They stare at her in silence or look away.

"Please," she says again. "I must find a doctor. Is there a doctor here?"

Some eyes shift towards the end of the hall. A sign says "ADMITTING"

above a wicket. Lily's rubber boots make an awful squishing noise on
the waxed linoleum. Behind the wicket a nurse is filling out a form. She
glances up, then looks down.

"Take a seat, please."

"Excuse me, it's not me," Lily says. "There's a boy outside. He's been
shot."

"Take a seat, please. Doctor Millions will see him when he's free."

"I'm sorry, you don't understand. He's been shot in the stomach. It's
an emergency."

The nurse gives Lily a cold, malevolent stare.

"Take a seat, please, Madam. The doctor is very busy."

"Another doctor, then...."

"Doctor Millions is our only doctor. Now, if you will please...."

"May I borrow a stretcher, then?"

The nurse looks down the hall.

"Our stretchers are all in use at the moment. You'll have to wait."

"Look here, Miss...."

Lily knows what she wants to say: Look here, Miss, I am *Miss* Lily
Coolican from Ottawa and I know the Prime Minister and my brother's
a Senator and *you will do what I want*. But none of that is true any more.
She's just a hunkie from the Beancan.

"Miss...?"

"Miss Taylor. Now, if you don't mind...."

"How many kids have you murdered recently, Miss Taylor?"

"Hey, just you wait a minute!"

"You enjoy watching people die, don't you?"

"Look here, you got no right..."

"It'll be something to see a boy bleeding to death right here on your
shiny floor, won't it?"

"Listen, you just stop that! Stop it! You can get the hell out of here!
Get out! *Get out!*"

"What the hell is going on here?" A door flies open and an old man in
a soiled white coat comes out.

"She said the most awful things to me!" Miss Taylor is shaking like a
leaf.

"I'm sorry, Doctor. It's an emergency, outside, he's in the truck...."

The doctor follows Lily to the front door. He stops when he sees the
truck. The bedsheets are drooping, the red letters spell AIR AGE FA R ICE.

"That yours?"

"Yes."

"Can't take him, then. Ain't paid up."

"What do you mean, paid up?"

"Hospital privileges are three dollars a month, per man, cash, in advance. Union thinks that's too much, okay by me. Let 'em find someone else to patch 'em up."

Doctor Millions turns to go in.

"I'll pay," Lily says. "How much?"

"Who're you? His mother?"

Mother! God, Lily doesn't even know his name!

"Yes. Yes, I am."

"Might as well take him home, then. We're full up here."

"*But he's dying!*"

Doctor Millions shrugs. He looks at the truck. "You might try Weyburn."

Weyburn is an hour's drive north on a rough gravel road. At least the rattle drowns out the kid's screams. At least he's still alive. The waiting room of the Weyburn hospital is empty. Lily places a five-dollar bill on the receptionist's desk. Mike carries the boy inside in his arms. The boy is unconscious. The nurse takes one look and runs for the doctor.

"Accident," Mike says. "Rabbits." He places the boy onto a white trolley, and the trolley is wheeled away through a swinging door, *thuck, thuck, thuck, thuck*. The door stops swinging and remains closed.

They have supper in a Chinese café. Lily isn't hungry, but she eats a plate of scrambled eggs anyway. She has blood on her hands. She doesn't mind. The Chinaman doesn't bat an eye. Maybe he's used to it. Lily resolves to think more kindly of Chinamen. Mike goes back to the hospital. Lily and Annie strip the flag and bedsheets from the truck and hide them under a fence in a vacant lot. When they get back to the truck, the lights are winking on around the town and the sky is luminous.

"We can drive with the lights off," Annie says. "Moose Jaw's not that far. I know a Comrade there. You can ditch the truck. There's a train going east at eleven o'clock."

"Shouldn't we go back?"

"Back? You want a year in the clink?"

"But we haven't actually *done* anything."

"Haven't you heard about the Crinimal Code?"

"But Annie, we can't run away!"

"I'm a lot more use to the Party out of jail than in."

"But Annie, all those people, we can't just *leave* them!"

"Why not?"

26

After work on Saturday Vivian slips into her old blue coat and jostles with the other girls in front of the mirror. Jeez, another winter in this awful coat. Why doesn't John buy her a new one? It's part of the deal, isn't it? John's got lots of money. He never buys her a thing. Not a single goddamn thing. She pulls at the top button. It snaps off in her hand.

"Damn it!"

"Coming for lunch?" says Myrna.

"Sorry."

"My treat. Dad sent me five bucks."

Vivian hesitates. For five bucks they could eat at the Macdonald Hotel. She's starving.

"My mum's here. We're going shopping."

"Lucky you."

Vivian fiddles with her scarf. The other girls crowd out the door ahead of her. She follows them down the stairs. Their high heels clatter on the stone *clacketyclackety clacketyclacketyclackety*. The sound echoes through the building. Even whispers can be heard three floors away. It's spooky. They say it's the dome.

Vivian is the last to punch out: 1.04 p.m. The other girls are whirling through the revolving door. She slips into the Ladies. She waits, staring at her face in the mirror. If only she could wear make-up! John won't let her. He says he wants her to look just the way she did when they met. She could swear she'd been wearing lipstick. Too bad. The other girls think she's *so* straight-laced. Sometimes Vivian is tempted to tell Myrna everything, just to see the look on her face. She smiles in spite of herself.

Vivian combs her hair, listening. She is alone. The hall outside is quiet. She peeps out the door, then runs back up the steps and darts into the office. If anyone sees her, she's forgotten something. Vivian throws her coat over her chair and sits at her desk. If the janitor comes in, she's working late. But the janitor never comes in. The janitor always starts at the other side of the building, in Agriculture, and works his way through Public Works, Education and Natural Resources before he gets to the Attorney-General. The Premier's office is always last because Mr. Brownlee is known to work late on Saturdays.

The phone rings.

"Viv? Coast clear?"

"Think so."

"See you in five minutes then."

Vivian glances at the clock, then at the rows of empty desks, each with its Underwood and stacks of files. She likes being here by herself, when it's quiet, and there's nobody to nag at her. It's amazing, how stuff's just left lying around. Like she could walk out of here with anything, court records, trial transcripts, secret police reports, anything, and who would know? You'd think the *Bulletin* would love to get its hands on some of the juicy stuff, like the private eye's notes on Mr. McPherson, the Minister of Public Works. Gee, imagine four people having an affair together! And then mousy little Mrs. McPherson runs away with the other woman's husband, and the other woman marries Mr. McPherson! Vivian has seen the second Mrs. McPherson. She's a real knock-out. Nobody can figure out what she sees in dumpy little Oren. The girls call him Oreo, because he's dark, and round, and supposed to be rich.

Vivian peeps out into the hall. The door halfway down is slightly ajar. Vivian tiptoes over and closes the door behind her. She's in Mr. Brownlee's private washroom. His familiar brown coat hangs in its usual place, his hat on top. Mr. Brownlee often uses this door to escape people waiting for him in his front office. From the outside, it looks just like a broom closet. It's their little secret.

John is sitting at his desk, as usual, signing letters. He barely glances up and puts his finger to his lips. Vivian can hear the clatter of Miss Chisholm's typewriter in the outer office. It makes Vivian nervous. John says that Miss Chisholm being there is a perfect alibi, just in case, and the door is locked. Nonetheless, Vivian would prefer to be by themselves. She kicks off her shoes and sits on the sofa.

"Am I the first, Vivian?" John whispers in her ear. "Am I the very first?"

"Yes, Mr. Brownlee."

He pushes her down, shoves up her skirt and forces his way in, just as he did the first time, in the Studebaker. It's a game they play. No matter where they do it, here, or in the car, or in bed, John always wants it the same way, as if she's still a virgin. Vivian tries to please him. He must like it because he wants it all the time. She's tried to like it, and hoped she'd get used to it, but she still finds it sort of dirty, and sometimes it hurts so much she wants to scream. There must be something wrong with her. Myrna says you're supposed to see stars.

Vivian listens to Miss Chisholm shutting drawers. What if she catches them? So what?

Miss Chisholm raps softly on the door.

"I'm off now, Mr. Brownlee."

"Thank you, Miss Chisholm," John calls out, natural as you please. "I won't be long."

Vivian stiffens. John groans softly, shudders, subsides. Vivian listens to the outer door click shut, then Miss Chisholm's shoes click away down the hall. She shivers. John puts on his glasses, then carefully washes his hands. Vivian hates that.

"John, when are we getting married, I mean really married?"

He looks at her, frowns.

"You know Mrs. Brownlee isn't well. I can't simply leave her."

"Mr. McPherson did."

"Mrs. McPherson left *him.*'

"What's the difference? They still got divorced."

"I would have to confess to adultery."

"Yes."

John wipes his hands impatiently.

"I would have to resign."

"But you always say you *want* to resign. You want to start a new life with me. Don't you?"

"I can't, Vivian. Not right now. I'm needed here. The people need me."

"What about me? Aren't I 'people' too?"

"We have each other, Vivian, our love for each other."

"Well, yes."

"Isn't that what really counts?"

John looks at her in the sad, tired way that always makes her feel so badly. How could she be so selfish? Here he is, so burdened with troubles, and she only makes things worse! If only she could always be serene and composed, like Mrs. Brownlee, and not put her foot in it. Vivian feels terrible. She looks at the floor.

"I'm sorry."

"It's late," John says, putting on his coat. "Mrs. Brownlee will be wondering where we are."

27

I joined the Communist Party after Julian died. That was the kid's name. A nice name. He died of peritonitis in the Weyburn hospital the day I got back to Winnipeg. Mike took his body back to Bienfait, and he was buried there with Nick, the kid who jumped onto the fire engine, and another boy I didn't know. The government of Saskatchewan ordered an investigation into conditions in the mines. The miners went back to work. The police ransacked their homes and patrolled Main Street with a machine gun. (Esselwein used to say that the Mounties only had one machine gun; they shipped it back and forth across the country so often it always arrived too late; thank God.)

I joined the Party for Julian. No, that's the kind of sentimental slop you get from Old Commies in their memoirs, the same self-righteous shits who suddenly discovered they didn't like Stalin, after Stalin had died. Who was Julian to me? Another dead kid. Besides, for people like me, the Party wasn't something you joined like the Girl Guides or the Eastern Star. You didn't get a badge and a funny outfit to wear, although we women were expected to dress with a certain proletarian plainness, and when it came to mumbo-jumbo, Marxism had it all over the Masonic Lodge. (Is that why guys like Smythe confused the two, and confused them both with the Jewish cabal, because they couldn't make head or tail of any of it? Well, they weren't alone.)

There were actually very few "card-carrying Communists," to use Senator Joe McCarthy's later, memorable phrase; quite a few good comrades escaped his clutches by saying, perfectly truthfully, that they had never had a party card in their lives. You'd have to be crazy running around with a card in your purse saying, "Hi! I'm a member of the Communist Party, cell 51, Winnipeg branch." All the same, the American comrades should have stood up to McCarthy. It was embarrassing the way they sleazed around and hid behind the Fifth Amendment. Real Communists would have said: "Yeah, sure we're Reds, and the reason we are is jerks like you, Joe." They could have blown McCarthy out of the water. On television. You can never trust the Yanks. They're all *kulaks* at heart. A capitalist isn't afraid to kill, but he *is* afraid to die; a Communist isn't afraid to die, but he isn't afraid to kill, either.

Annie was like that. The police picked her up a month later, in Toronto. She was tried in Saskatchewan for inciting to riot. Annie was defiant. "I was defending the interests of my class," she said. Annie was sentenced to a year in Saskatchewan jail for women. I expected the cops to come for me any day. They didn't.

The story of the Estevan riot made only the early edition of the Winnipeg *Free Press*, then vanished. It was a small story, too. The editor, Mr. Dafoe, was only interested in large questions, like Liberalism, or Dominion-Provincial Relations, or the League of Nations. The *Free Press* was famous for its foreign news.

I dropped by Bobak's Bakery to apologize to Mr. Bobak for losing his truck. He just shrugged. "Is okay," he said, and pointed to a brand-new truck sitting outside. It was my first inkling that the Party might have more money than I'd supposed. I went back to work photographing underwear for the Eaton's catalogue and volunteered to help out at the Red Cross clothing depot, where they were trying to decide what to do with the boxes of rubber boots and broken umbrellas on their way to drought-stricken Saskatchewan from Ontario. It wasn't an entirely futile gift, I suppose, since ten thousand people dancing around in rubber boots waving umbrellas at the sky would produce rain as certainly as the incantations of the politicians would produce prosperity.

One evening towards the end of November, I got a call from Judge Stubbs, "Subversive" Stubbs as he was known in Winnipeg. Judge Stubbs was famous as the friend of the poor and unemployed. He refused to convict a vagrant, saying it was no crime not to have a home, and he let off petty thieves on the grounds that theft was the perfect expression of the capitalist system that the law was pledged to uphold. Judge Stubbs gave the cops fits. He was tremendously popular. Annie said he suffered from "anarchistic negativism," but I liked him, so when he invited me to a meeting of the Civil Liberties Association, I accepted immediately.

It was a big meeting in the basement of Westminster United Church, a lot of fat ladies and tweedy men with pipes, nervous young law students, Miss Hind of the *Free Press*, and Godless Gauvin, the local atheist, who preached against the Lord every Sunday in the Walker Theatre. He was almost as popular as Judge Stubbs. Winnipeg was a very weird place. One of the young lawyers stood up and denounced the Estevan massacre, but he got his facts all mixed up, and Julian's name wrong, and it was all I could do not to jump up and set him straight. A subscription was organized to help defend the miners charged with rioting, and more than a thousand dollars was pledged on the spot. The Communist alderman, Jacob Penner, came up to speak to me at coffee and shook my hand warmly. I felt pretty conspicuous, but Miss Hind said that Alderman Penner attended every meeting in Winnipeg. Alderman Penner was even more popular than Judge Stubbs.

The next week I was invited to a Friends of China meeting, then to a benefit tea for the Saskatchewan Relief Committee, a Women Against War and Fascism rally, and a demonstration at the legislature to prevent Judge Stubbs from being removed from the bench. The same people were at all the meetings. I had a good time. I didn't know many people in Winnipeg, and they were all very friendly. I was invited home for dinner by a woman I'd only met *that very same day!* Imagine! In Ottawa, dinner invitations were engraved and placed on silver trays and accepted, or rejected, in writing, after much cogitation as to the consequences. In Winnipeg, dinner was to eat.

Winnipeg was different in other ways too. The houses were very hot. The colder it got outside, and it got damn cold, the hotter it became inside. Nobody seemed to have a maid, and nobody bothered to tidy up, so you found yourself crammed onto a sofa with three other people, a year's supply of the *National Geographic*, an ashtray, a cushion embroidered with a view of Niagara Falls, and a cat. Maids were a pretention reserved for the rich, and nobody in Winnipeg spoke to the rich, except the other rich: the rich had married each other for so long they were even nuttier than everyone else. Everyone lived on meat-and-potatoes-and-gravy, or a terrible stew-like thing called "mince," but there was lots of it, all washed down with rye-and-ginger, a drink that took some getting used to.

It was after one of these cosy dinners at Judge Stubbs' that I was asked if I would care to remain to join the political study group that was meeting in the Stubbs' living room *that very night*. How could I refuse? I hadn't finished my ginger ale. (Stubbs was Temperance.)

The discussion was led by a skinny, somewhat smelly young student from the University of Manitoba. His name was Ken. It might not have been his real name, since Ken addressed all the others in the room by names I'd never heard before. Obviously it was a code. It seemed rather unnecessary, since I knew them all, and we'd just had dinner together, but I'd learned a long time ago that Communism had nothing to do with common sense. That's why it was so attractive.

Who would I be? Rose, I said. Ken frowned. It did sound banal. Roses are red, violets are . . . . Oh, oh. Violet? I could be Violet. No, I couldn't stand Violet. Red Rose is only tea, after all. I could call myself Orange Pekoe. Earl Grey? Salada? Salada made me think of Peter Larkin, who made me think of Willie and Willie's Mother.

"Call me Isabel," I said.

We discussed the war between China and Japan. Nobody seemed to know exactly what was going on, but Ken made it clear that the correct "line," as he called it, was to be pro-China, anti-Japan. That was okay with me. I'd never met a Jap. I knew quite a few Chinamen, and they did have a rough time. It was especially cruel not to let them bring their wives and families to Canada. When I raised this point, and suggested we discuss the Chinamen (sorry, the *Chinese*) in Canada, Ken said in a contemptuous way that communism concerned itself not with minorities, but with the masses, and referred me to Lenin's *Left-Wing Socialism: An Infantile Disorder?* I didn't tell him I'd read it, and thought Lenin was an arrogant son-of-a-bitch.

I went to Party meetings regularly after that. I still wanted an answer to my question: What do I do now? Marx can get you in the gates of the Winter Palace, but then he goes all wishy-washy. What does he mean by "abolition of classes?" If you abolish classes, don't you abolish the proletariat too? And if you abolish the proletariat, how can you have a "dictatorship of the proletariat?" The proletariat must turn into something else. What? Is Stalin what Marx had in mind? Stalin isn't exactly withering away.

I didn't ask any of these questions at the meetings. I would have been denounced as a counter-revolutionary and a Trot. (Lev Davidovich should have stuck with his original name, Bronstein, then his followers wouldn't have sounded like diarrhoea.) Trotsky represented everything from "the right danger" to "bourgeois depravity" to "left extremism," depending on Ken the *aparatchik*'s mood. I had no idea what *aparatchik* meant, but it described the boy with B.O. to a T.

I did talk about the riot. It was a relief to get it off my chest. I don't like to run away, and I felt guilty as hell. God is guilt, and I was suffering from a bout of puritan negativism. Lenin never suffered from puritan negativism. Lenin spent his life on the run. Hell, he never even turned up at the Finland Station until the revolution had been won. I tried to imagine travelling in a sealed train from Moose Jaw to Ottawa, and failed. I still felt I'd been right about not running away, and made up my mind to see it through.

I was absorbed into the underground, or G section, of the Party, although that makes it sound more formal and organized than it actually was. I don't know where the myth originated that Communism is efficient, but it was a masterpiece of deception. In Canada, at least, the Party was in a state of chronic disorder. It was always so busy organizing that nobody had time for revolution. That was a hazard of trying to run everything from the top, especially when the guys at the top were usually in the clink.

The Party was more afraid of social democracy than fascism. It combined the two bogeymen into "social fascism," whatever that meant, but then language had pretty much lost all meaning. It was so common to call almost everyone a "communist" or a "fascist," whatever his opinions, that words no longer had the power to harm: by becoming associated with the Conservative Prime Minister, Buggerall Bennett, fascism became completely discredited.

I became the seventh member of my cell. The maximum was ten. We had no idea who belonged to other cells, or if there were other cells, although Ken encouraged us to think they were springing up like dragon's teeth. Communism was a state of mind, and the Party was an act of faith that somewhere out there, someone was doing something. It was a lot like Methodism, only the meetings were more interesting. We discussed politics, economics, Germany, the "woman question" (I wasn't quite sure exactly what that was, either), history, dialectics and the vices of the rich. Jack's name came up frequently. I kept my mouth shut about Jack, but was able to make a contribution on the question of the Masseys, including an imitation of Vincent that had everyone in stitches. Perhaps it made Ken forgive me for raising the thorny question of the famine in Russia, where Stalin himself couldn't make the rain fall any better than Buggerall Bennett.

G section was quite separate from the rest of the Party. We were all respectable *bourgeoisie*: a judge, a doctor, a university professor, two churchwomen, a businessman and me. We were not required to take part in demonstrations, or sell *The Worker* on the street, or scuffle with the police. Exactly the reverse. Our invisibility was our strength. We were required only to contribute money (hard enough!) pass along information, and influence public opinion against the government. This wasn't hard, since the public already hated the government. We shared an interest in Marxism, and a commitment to the Party platform: more jobs, fair wages, decent Relief and free speech. Who but a politician could disagree with that? (It wasn't that the politicians didn't care about the unemployed, no, no, it was just that too much Relief would plunge them into an abyss of moral depravity, so going without, you see, was only for their own good.) The Party did not ask us to become atheists, or soldiers, or even proletarians. We had the best of both worlds: the *frisson* of revolution, and supper dances at the Manitoba Club.

Ken resented us, I think. I couldn't blame him. Who wanted to sell *The Worker?* What a rag.

"It reads as if it's written in Russian," I complained one day.

"It is," Ken said. "I mean, it was. A lot of it has been translated."

"Why can't it be written in plain English?"

"Russian is the language of the revolution."

"This isn't Russian, it's gibberish."

"You just don't understand it."

"Who does? No wonder we don't sell many papers."

"We aren't in the newspaper business."

"Why do we publish a newspaper then?"

"To educate the masses."

"But the masses can't read it!"

This was pretty typical of my discussions with Ken. He was perfectly right, of course. *The Worker* wasn't meant to be read. It was only published because it had been banned, and selling it on the street caused a ruckus with the police. The ruckus attracted a crowd and with any luck a fight would break out. Next day, the fight would be written up in the *Free Press* or *Tribune*, where the masses could read, in plain English, how free speech was suppressed, and feel guilty about the kids who were sent to jail. Jail was getting to be chic. All the best people were going there — stockbrokers, bankers, lawyers, grain merchants, even the general secretary of the Archdiocese of Rupertsland, Mr. McRae, who impoverished the widows of deceased clergymen and bilked the Anglican Church out of a million dollars. As usual, Jack was ahead of his time.

The Communist Party was not chic. Ken disapproved of my make-up, my high heels and my silk stockings. What was I supposed to do, go to the Manitoba Club in a *babushka?* Trouble was, we in G weren't *real* revolutionaries. Real revolutionaries were the masses, and from what I could make out, the masses were guys who worked in factories, with their hands. I worked with my hands, but I didn't count; Ken didn't work with his hands, but he did count.

Still, being a Communist was a lot better than being a Liberal. At least I didn't have to sit through those endless arguments about who-gets-what, and whether Vincent and Alice should go to Washington, or London, or tour China, and should the trim on Laurier House be painted dark or light green?

Agit-prop was really very easy. All I had to do was mention the word "Communism." People immediately talked of nothing else. What was it that produced such intense paranoia? Lenin's cheekbones? Stalin's piggy eyes? You'd have thought Genghis Khan and the heathen hordes were camped across the Red River. I found that denouncing Communism had a bigger effect than praising it, so I gained a reputation for being rather right-wing. (In a later age, this would be known as "product recognition," and the dialectic would involve Pepsi and Coke, but I'll always give Stalin the credit.) The trick was to imply that Communism is inevitable, like it or lump it, and the smart people will be on the winning side.

The biggest fish my "line" caught was Victor Sifton, publisher of the *Free Press.* Victor was so alarmed by the Red Menace that he assigned a reporter to do a six-part, front page *exposé* of Communist activities in Winnipeg. All the *aparatchiks* went into a tizzy. The reporter was scared out of his wits. He earned only $20 a week, so he tended to be sympathetic, although reporters believe they write the truth, and the truth is what the publisher wants to read. The *exposé* created a big row between

Victor and his editor, Mr. Dafoe, who didn't like the publisher meddling in his paper, and who believed, sensibly enough, that the more publicity Bolshevism received, the more popular it would become. Victor, however, liked to be one jump ahead of his employees. That way he could make them feel even more inferior.

Victor also wanted to do a front-page *exposé* of Dr. Hamilton's seances. Dr. Hamilton's seances were all the rage in Winnipeg, and very exclusive. I'd been avoiding him. Mum no longer needed intermediaries, and as for me, the hereafter could stay right where it is. Willie had apparently had a "sitting" with the Hamilton circle and had written to Victor about the amazing results. Victor asked me to arrange an invitation for him.

The seance was held in the attic of the Hamiltons' home. The windows had been boarded up and it was terribly hot and stuffy. Mrs. Marshall, a homely little Scottish woman, sat on a chair in front of a cupboard big enough to hold Harry Houdini. The cupboard, it was explained, attracted the spirits. It appeared to be empty. Opposite, Dr. Hamilton had his camera set up, a huge, old-fashioned thing with glass plates, and his daughter sat at a table taking a shorthand transcript of the conversation.

Once Victor and I had taken our seats around the table, the lights were turned out. It was pitch-black. We began with a lot of hymn singing, very loud, then we heard shouting, followed by terrific rappings and bangings from the direction of the cupboard. It was quite frightening because it was impossible to see who, or what, was making the noise. Mrs. Marshall began to speak in the voice of someone called "Walter." "Walter" seemed to be a jolly fellow. He told music-hall jokes, pulled Dr. Hamilton's leg, and kibitzed around with several people at the table. Soon we were all laughing and bantering with "Walter" as if he were really in the room. Dr. Hamilton took several photos with a blinding flash. However, when I saw them later, they showed only dishevelled people with our eyes shut and our mouths open. Dr. Hamilton explained that an "alien spirit" had been present. Victor?

"Walter" was followed by a spirit believed to be Robert Louis Stevenson, who dictated long passages from a book. It was a disappointment, I'd never found Robert Louis Stevenson boring before. Unfortunately, the alien spirit prevented Mrs. Marshall from coughing up any ectoplasm. I was just as glad.

Afterwards, Dr. Hamilton showed us some photos he'd taken on previous occasions. They showed Mrs. Marshall with stringy white stuff, like bread dough, hanging from her lips. One of the photos clearly showed a black thread running from Mrs. Marshall's chair to the cupboard. Dr. Hamilton explained that the thread must be ectoplasm.

Coming home, Victor asked me if I thought Stalin was the Anti-Christ. Hitler, rather, I said. He seemed shocked. But Hitler is right about the Jews, he said. They should all be rounded up and deported to Palestine. He had written a letter to Mr. King, advocating such a policy, and had received a most cordial reply.

Victor must have written about me too, because two weeks later I received a Christmas card from Willie. It was gold-embossed, with an angel on it. Inside was a letter saying that he'd dreamed of me on his birthday. I had appeared as he'd first known me, very young and beautiful, and he'd felt a return of the old affection for me, an overwhelming happiness. Had I by any chance been thinking of him at the time? I had, actually, because it was his birthday, and I hadn't sent him anything, and was feeling guilty, and thinking perhaps I should phone. I was angry, too, at being once more sucked into the vortex of Willie's insatiable expectations. I hadn't phoned.

I sent him a Christmas card, although I had resolved to give up Christmas. In the past year, Willie has peopled the Valley of Humiliation so thickly with men I despise that I couldn't help feeling some affection for him. After forcing Jack to resign from the Senate ("moral turpitude," I think was the reason), Willie had offered the seat to Harry Oakes in exchange for a $70,000 contribution to the Liberal Party. However, Willie refused to make the appointment until after the election. When Willie lost the election, Harry Oakes lost both his Senate seat *and* the $70,000. I heard Harry had suffered an attack of apoplexy that nearly cost him his life. Then the Abominable Bennett slapped a tax on gold mines. Now Harry Oakes was Canada's biggest taxpayer. Harry was feeding the unemployed.

On Christmas Day, 1931, Willie sent a bouquet of white roses from Broadway Florists. It felt like Christmas, 1914, when Willie had fallen in love with the idea of being in love with me. I felt old. A telegram followed on New Year's Day, then the letters began, one or two a week, full of trivia about Pat (sore paw), gossip about who was sick (Haydon), and dead (Fielding), and a stream of astonishing vituperation about Bloated Bennett (a boar, a pig, a bully, a brute, a miserable cur, a tyrant, a hypocrite, a skunk, a viper etc. etc.) The letters also contained, as usual, requests for help: "I am certain that a note from you would persuade Dr. McDougald to resign. This clinging to a seat in the Senate which *I* bestowed in return for *services to the Party* is pure selfishness in view of all the trouble he has caused, etc. etc."

How many women did Willie write to? One? Ten? A hundred? I could see him in the attic at Laurier House, bent over the rosewood table that once belonged to Matthew Arnold (he claimed), Mother's portrait to his left, her wedding ring in a silver casket on his right, writing, writing, writing, a blizzard of notepaper flying out the window and whirling away into the Ottawa night. Love, at long distance. I didn't write to the Doctor.

At the next party meeting, as I watched Ken the *aparatchik* bent over *Capital*, his eyeglasses slowly slipping down his nose, I remembered how Papa used to sit that way over a book, squinting behind his spectacles, and how Willie's *pince-nez* always fell off, and once broke, until he tied it to his vest with a string, and how Talbot had pretended to lose his glasses, to find me, and I saw how irrevocably my life had been shaped by men who looked at life obliquely, through a lens, in the pool of the printed page: too careful, or afraid, to look it in the eye.

"Where's Esselwein?" I asked suddenly.

Ken looked up. He dropped Marx, and shoved his glasses up the bridge of his nose. He looked pale. Traitors are never mentioned in the Party. Traitors have ceased to exist. They have never existed.

"Why do you want to know?"

"We should be on the alert, shouldn't we?"

Ken picked up *Capital* and smoothed the pages.

"Out west, somewhere, I think." Ken submerged himself again in Marx.

"Where?"

"Edmonton, I think."

EDMONNNNTONNNNNNNNNN.

28

Vivian lies very still listening to the house creak. Everything in the Brownlees' house creaks, the walls, the floors, the beds, especially this one. It's only the maid's room, after all. What a dump. No wonder the maid quit. Well, never look a gift horse, as Mama says. Vivian would just as soon be back home in Edson in her own bed (it's *soooo* comfortable!), but with her dad laid off, that's out of the question, and Mama is *so* proud that Vivian's living with the Brownlees now. Vivian hasn't breathed a word to Mama about John. She hasn't breathed a word to anyone. That's the worst part. The other girls talk about their boyfriends and she doesn't dare say a thing. She can hardly stand it, Myrna and the rest of them bragging and giggling and showing off their two-bit engagement rings from Woolworth's when she's twice as pretty as any of them, with a catch that would make their eyes pop out, but has to pretend that nobody likes her enough to ask her out. Boy, does she feel like a drip! Sometimes the girls offer to fix her up. They've introduced her to some nice guys, ones she's really liked, but she made excuses and invented a boyfriend back in Edson, even though she is sitting alone every night in her rotten boarding house waiting for the phone to ring.

Vivian doesn't like to lie, particularly to her mother. She's had to invent stupid excuses for changing her boarding house twice this year. Landladies never sleep. It's bad enough, the Premier's car delivering her to the door at midnight or one a.m., but when she goes out at nine p.m. or even later, landladies get suspicious. The last one, Mrs. Nelligan, phoned the office to make sure she really worked there, and said, hanging up, "I only thought she might be keeping bad company, if you know what I mean." Vivian does feel awkward, standing on street corners waiting for John to pick her up, and on top of that, he drives the only Studebaker V-8 in Edmonton. One night they drove right past Myrna standing at a bus stop on Stony Plain Road. Vivian is sure Myrna suspects. Myrna looks at everything in a dirty way. Well, if John doesn't care who knows, neither does she.

Does Mrs. Brownlee know? Sometimes Vivian is tempted to ask, but how do you raise the subject? Excuse me, Mrs. Brownlee, but . . . . Mrs. Brownlee doesn't seem to be dying after all. When she was sent away to the sanitorium after her little girl died, everyone thought it was TB, but she only went off her head. What will she do after the divorce? It worries Vivian a little. What if Mrs. Brownlee goes nuts again, and kills herself? Vivian couldn't face that. She really likes Mrs. Brownlee. Yesterday Myrna said that Mrs. McPherson, the *first* Mrs. McPherson, was drinking herself to death on skid row. It gave Vivian a scare. Mrs. Brownlee doesn't drink, but she does take a lot of pills.

Vivian peers into the darkness, listening for the creak of footsteps on the other side of the wall. Her bedroom is next to John's. The bathroom is on the other side, then Mrs. Brownlee's bedroom at the back of the house. Allan, the older boy, sleeps in his mother's room, little John with his father. It must be embarrassing for Allan, but he's so shy it's hard to know if he minds or not. At least Vivian knows John wasn't lying. Not that she suspected him of it, but Myrna said once, "A man will say *anything* to get into a girl's pants," and the phrase stuck in her mind.

She hears John's door open and the floorboards creak in the hall. A dark shape looms in the doorway.

"Viv?"

"Okay."

The shape moves on. Vivian listens to the creak of the bathroom door, the hiss of piss, the sudden whoosh as the toilet flushes. What a racket! Enough to wake the dead. Vivian slips out of bed, praying that the toilet's thunder will hide the singing of the springs, and tiptoes to the door. John is waiting in the hall, a solid shadow in the dark. He envelops her in his warm, woolly bathrobe, and together, in lockstep, just the way they practiced, they quick-march into his bedroom and close the door. Vivian's heart is pounding. She can't see a thing.

John guides her hand to the end of the bed, and she gropes her way around the far side next to the window. The bed is very narrow. John has to lie pretty much on top of her. Vivian is shocked to feel his skin. She has never seen John naked, or even touched his bare flesh, except for his hand. His body feels soft and loose, flabby, an old man's flesh, creepy. Vivian draws away. John is breathing so hard she's afraid he'll wake up the boy in the next bed. Little John isn't three feet away, on the other side of the night table. Vivian can hear him mutter in his sleep. She shivers. What if the kid wakes up? What if Mrs. Brownlee throws open the door and turns on the light? Vivian listens, listens, hearing only the beating of her heart. John groans. In the next bed, little John sighs and turns over.

Afterwards, Vivian is surprised to find the room still silent and dark. She giggles with relief. She feels like she's just gone over Niagara Falls in a barrel. Vivian lies very still, catching her breath, listening to the wind rattle the windows, thinking it would be nicer in a double bed, with a *négligé* instead of her flannel nightie, and Clark Gable. This just the sort of thing Clark Gable would do. Who would ever suspect it of Mr. Brownlee? In Edmonton? Vivian giggles again.

"Shhh," says Mr. Brownlee.

"I love you," whispers Vivian.

"Gomorrah," says Mum, peering out the train window at Edmonton's squat, square skyline.

"Why not Sodom?" I ask.

Mum stares at the dirty, pockmarked ice of the river as the train creaks carefully across the trestle bridge. To the west, an ominous brown dome is silouetted against the sky.

"This is definitely Gomorrah," Mum says. "Sodom is the other place, to the south. There is a difference, you know."

29

Lily stands with her back to the wind. Edmonton's main drag, Jasper Avenue, runs due west, towards the Rocky Mountains, and even when the sun is hot, the wind is cold. Edmonton is the coldest city of its size in the world. Did she know that? No, she didn't when she arrived, but she does now, having been told at least once a day since she got here. Edmonton is very proud of being the coldest city of its size in the world. It was built specifically with coldness in mind, perched high on a bluff to catch the full force of the Arctic winds, the streets being made especially wide to give the wind lots of scope. The only warm people in Edmonton are the bums who live near the garbage dump in the gully by the river.

Lily is standing in her usual spot at the corner of 100th Street, her Leica on a tripod and a little sign out front: " The *Bulletin*'s Mystery Citizen Contest." It had been her idea to publish a "candid" of some local personality in every Saturday paper. The first person to phone in with the correct identification wins a thirty-minute joyride with the famous local aviator, Wop May, courtesy of Interior Airways, and the mystery citizen gets two free tickets to the Capitol Theatre. It sure as hell sells papers. Good thing too, because the Liberal *Bulletin* (circ. 25,000) is a lot smaller than the Conservative *Journal* (circ. 65,000). The *Journal* says the *Bulletin* will do anything to sell papers. It does.

Lily's grey, herringbone slacks caused an uproar at first. All kinds of little old ladies of both sexes cancelled their subscriptions, aghast that a woman should appear on Edmonton's main street in *pants*, but once word got around that Mrs. King was a poor widow whose husband had leaped from a tall building after the Crash, her Sapphic tendencies were welcomed as another manifestation of Edmonton's frontier spirit.

Edmonton's frontier spirit is as famous, in Edmonton, as its frigidity. Lily has never met a city which made so much of so little.

The street is always busy here. Shoppers stream towards her, smile shyly, glance away, dart sideways, peek back, a little wistful, curious to see who gets caught with his fly undone. As soon as people see the sign they glance up, *click*. But not just anybody can be a Mystery Citizen. It has to be someone a little unusual, someone whose face grabs the eye, but not too well known. Last week Lily was thrilled to get a swarthy little man in a fur hat and red leather riding boots. He bowed, clicked his heels and handed her his calling card. But Ernie, the editor, just tossed it aside and said: "Shit, *everyone* knows Prince Galitzene." Edmonton, apparently, is also famous for its *emigré* aristocrats. Like their ranches, they tend to be small, seedy and poor. However, in Edmonton a ranch is a half-acre of cow pasture with a horse in it. Lily does not like horses or men who smell like them. Edmonton has plenty of both.

Lily sees the girl first, tall, slim, smiling, her fair hair tousled by the wind. The girl is looking up at the man beside her, a big, slope-shouldered man, older, elephantine. The man looks up as Lily clicks the shutter, scowls, and pulls his hat over his eyes, as if shielding them against the sun. Lily holds out the movie tickets and asks their names. The girl stops. "Will I be in the paper?" She reaches for the tickets but the man pulls her roughly away. The light changes and they disappear into the crowd.

Lily has forgotten the incident when their faces swim up at her in the darkroom. She tosses the photo aside, then retrieves it. She washes it carefully and hangs it to dry. She hadn't thought the girl was all that pretty, her nose was too long, but the camera thinks differently.

"Isn't she a knockout?" Lily says, laying the photo on Ernie's desk. "It's too bad...."

"Jesus Christ!"

Ernie's swivel chair crashes to attention.

"Do you know her?"

"Jesus, where did you get this?"

"On Jasper. You know, the Mystery...."

"Do you know who this is?"

"No, that's the problem. She...."

"She! For Chrissakes! Him! *Him!*"

"Her father?"

"Brownlee hasn't got a daughter."

"Brownlee? *That's* . . . ."

"It's her. It's gotta be."

"*Who?*"

"*Her.* The girl. *His* girl. His *girl.*"

"But *who is she?*"

"Oh boy, we're gonna find out!"

The photo runs as the Mystery Citizen on the first Saturday in May. The very first caller is Mrs. Brownlee, who identifies her husband, the Premier of Alberta, and Miss Vivian Macmillan, a friend of the family. "Vivian's almost like a daughter to us," says Mrs. Brownlee.

"Shit," says Ernie.

Lily put the photo away. She would have forgotten about it in all the fuss over the poor Lindbergh baby being found, except people kept telephoning, or dropping by, and asking for the negative. Mrs. Brownlee was the first, saying she wanted it for her husband's collection of political memorabilia. She seemed quite crestfallen when Lily explained that the negative was the property of the *Bulletin*, and offered to make a print instead, when she had time. The next day, coming out of the darkroom, Lily was startled to find Vivian herself standing by her desk looking through a stack of Hollywood cheesecake pictures.

"You're so lucky," Vivian sighed, stroking Jean Harlow's hair. "Imagine working here, surrounded by the stars."

"Would you like to be a movie star?"

Vivian blushed.

"Wouldn't *everyone?*"

Vivian wanted the photo for her scrapbook and seemed quite happy to settle for a print.

"I only make $12 a week," she said, brushing at her faded dress.

"That's okay. No charge."

"Oh, thank you!"

Vivian was shy, and rather awkward, but she seemed confident and cheerful about life. Lily liked her. Lily wondered if she herself had seemed that strong at twenty, before the war, and felt afraid.

The President of the United Farmers of Alberta came in to see the publisher the next day, followed by the Attorney-General of Alberta,

Mr. Reid, who claimed the photo was faked. Mr. Reid was accompanied by the Minister of Public Works, O.L. McPherson, who tried to sweet talk the negative out of Lily, and when that failed, swore at her. Baron Wittgenstein was the last straw. Wittgenstein was a Kraut and the Imperial Klizard or whatever of the Edmonton branch of the Ku Klux Klan. He sent Lily a $100 bill in an envelope with instructions to enclose the negative in the same envelope and give it to Ralph, the elevator boy at the Corona Hotel, by ten o'clock that night. Lily kept the $100 and the negative, but damned if the Corona Hotel didn't burn down that night.

About four a.m., just as the Extra was coming off press, Lily heard a deep, melodious voice at the city desk.

"Ver iss, plese, Missuss Kink?"

She peeked around the corner. Shaven head, broad back, riding breeches, sash, sword, *sword?* Ben, the city editor, was pointing in her direction. She ducked back and closed the door.

A sharp rap. "Ja, Missuss Kink?"

Lily opened the door for Baron Wittgenstein and closed it quickly behind him. He wheeled around, hand on sword, eyes bright with alarm.

"Esselwein — " Lily smiled — "don't you ever give up?"

The baron blinked twice. He looked at her, then at the door, then at her again with an expression so blank, she thought for a moment she'd made a mistake.

"*Lilichen*," the Baron whispered, finger to his lips. " '*Meine jungfräuliche Lilichen.*' Does that, how do you say, ring the bell?"

"Look, Esselwein, can't we drop this Boris Karloff stuff?"

"Well, okay. It's hard to get out of it, you know, once you're started. Insidious language, German."

"Have you joined a circus?"

"More or less. I'm a Nazi, for the time being."

"Do they know you're Jewish?"

"I am *not* Jewish."

"You *sound* like a Nazi."

"And you?"

"Me?"

"Count von Ribbentrop wishes to be remembered to his '*jungfräuliche Lilichen.*' Such happy times together in Ottawa, before the war."

"*Joachim?* Jesus."

"You were so young, so tender, so naive, so *sympatico*...."

"He took me to the movies once."

"...so beautiful, like an opening flower...."

"He caused a scene in the theatre. It was very embarrassing."

"...so exotic, irresistible, so passionate...."

"He was *so* vain. The girls were nuts about him. He was sexy, in a creepy sort of a way."

"...had it not been for the terrible tragedy of the war...."

"I gave him $10 to get back to Germany. That was a mistake, wasn't it?"

"...your love would have bloomed...."

"Our *love?* Oh, come off it, Esselwein. What sort of crap is this?"

"You weren't in love?"

"With *Ribbentrop?*"

"He suggests...."

"Joachim was 'in love' with half the girls in the May Court club! His speciality was an intimate picnic *à deux* with plenty of chilled champagne."

Esselwein reached into the folds of his trenchcoat and placed a big, green bottle of Henckel Trocken on Lily's desk.

"He knew you'd remember."

"He married the Henckel heiress, didn't he? Trust Joachim. How crude he is, underneath."

"Shall we celebrate?"

"What does he want, Joachim?"

"He misses Canada."

"You mean he's coming *here?*"

"He misses all his dear Canadian friends, good old Dickie Bennett, the present Prime Minister, Eddy, his buddy at the CPR, the boys at the Bank of Montreal, he seems to know everyone."

"Everyone thought he was a spy, after he left."

"It's a living."

Esselwein poured the wine into two chipped cups.

"To love?"

"To war."

"Mud in your eye."

"*Heil Hitler.*"

Esselwein sighed. "It's not my idea, this Baron von Krap-Korruption business."

"You don't like it?"

"I butter my bread, I lie in it."

As soon as Esselwein's skull splits open, his stomach will erupt. *Bleh.* Is this a Nazi plot to poison the world with Henckel Trocken? He must alert Smythe. Forget it, Smythe drinks scotch. The Baron is going home to bed. The Baron is unwell. The Baron may die. Damn! A year it's taken him to build up this disguise, and now it's blown to hell. *Kaput.* Will Lily tell? Of course she will. Hell.

And he doesn't even have the negative. He'll have to steal it. How? Break-and-enter is not something Esselwein enjoys. It makes him feel cheap, skulking around at night, and he's no good with locks. Now a good entrapment, that's different. Last February, the Baron enticed J.J. Maloney, Edmonton's Imperial Wizard of the Ku Klux Klan, to drive out to the Mayfair Golf Club in a blizzard. Maloney's car got stuck in the snow, so Maloney broke into the club's toolshed to get a shovel and some sand. Later, the Baron's testimony got Maloney two months in jail for petty theft and damage to private property. The new Imperial Wizard is Baron Wittgenstein. It's fun wearing a sheet.

The Baron is so disconsolate as he trudges back to his rooming house that he doesn't even rattle his sword at the Reds who heckle him from the sidewalk. On most days, he can get them hotter than hornets in a couple of minutes and they'll buzz around harmlessly for hours. Lenin knew that talk did not make a revolution. Poor Trotsky didn't know that, and now Trotsky blows around the world like a tumbleweed in a high wind. The Baron sighs. Talk has been his undoing too. Living a lie, he does not expect to be believed. When he suggested to Smythe that Premier Brownlee has "socialistic inclinations," he was amazed that Smythe took this as definivite proof Brownlee was a Communist. All of Premier Brownlee's actions are now interpreted in light of this information: if Brownlee raises the dole a dollar a week, he is being "soft" on the Reds, if Brownlee refuses to meet a delegation of the unemployed, he is "inciting unrest." Premier Brownlee is the most dangerous man in Alberta. The Baron's job is to destroy him.

Trouble is, John Brownlee is also the most powerful man in Alberta, and, inadvertently, the Baron's big mouth has helped make him that way. It is part of the Baron's *persona*, as a leading fascist, to see Bolshies under every bush. He assumed his extremism would be taken for what it was, a script in a melodrama, but at RCMP headquarters, his paranoia is not only taken seriously, it is exaggerated. Thus, when Esselwein estimates privately that there are no more than one thousand Communists in Alberta, including Ukrainians and transients, and the Baron reports ten thousand to Ottawa, the RCMP puts the figure at fifty thousand, including every member of the United Farmers of Alberta. The RCMP, on the other hand, numbers fewer than three hundred officers and men, and the Canadian militia, while brim full of beer, is unarmed. Any fool can see that the cavalary is completely surrounded by the Indians.

Fortunately Edmonton has a number of veteran Indian fighters, grizzled old sods who trekked west to Fort Edmonton with the police in 1874, or who fought Riel in the rebellion of '85. Now, with the wisdom of victory, they advise that when the enemy is in possession of the ground, and has a taste for blood, the best strategy is to bluff, bargain, bribe and blackmail.

Bluffing only takes you so far, and with Brownlee there isn't much room to bargain. Brownlee holds all the cards. In spite of drought and the debt crisis, or perhaps because of them, Albertans still prefer their homely, handmade government to any fancy Eastern import, and the less the government does, the better they like it. Personally, Brownlee is not popular — "stick" and "fish" are the words commonly used to describe him — but he inspires almost fanatical respect. John Brownlee is an oddball, and Alberta is a province of oddballs. They have all bowled happily across the flatlands of Saskatchewan, only to come up with a thunk against the Rockies, and here they've stayed, seven hundred thousand rolling stones caroming around a snooker table that seems to be blowing away.

Brownlee is unusually incorruptible, for a politician. In an attempt to break the UFA stranglehold on Alberta, Bennett has offered Brownlee the Supreme Court, the chairmanship of the CNR, the Treasury Board and the High Commissioner's post in London. Brownlee turned them all down. ("He must be mad!" said Vincent Massey.) Rumours of these offers have made Brownlee suspect among the farmers as a closet Conservative, yet Brownlee's determination to remain in Alberta "to see it through" has only convinced the Conservatives that he has some secret scheme to nationalize the banks.

So it comes down to blackmail. Even that looks like a blind alley.

Unlike the Minister of Public Works, O.L. McPherson, John Brownlee
doesn't drink, gamble or screw his best friend's wife. He works sixteen
hours a day, attends political meetings and spends the rest of the time at
home with his invalid wife and two sons. He goes to church on Sundays,
plays a little golf in the summer, and occasionally drives Miss Macmillan home in the evenings. Until the photograph appeared in the *Bulletin*,
nobody took any notice of Miss Macmillan, and the photo itself aroused
only casual interest ("nice legs") at RCMP headquarters. It seemed
reasonable that Miss Macmillan would stay with the Brownlees sometimes to help out. Her dad was a big UFA man, and Brownlee's got her a
job with the government. Besides, she was just a kid, a cute kid.

It wasn't until McPherson and the Attorney-General, Reid, phoned
the Inspector to suggest Mrs. King be prevented from taking photographs on the street that Esselwein took a good look at the picture.
Brownlee was striding along, briefcase in hand, his usual dour self, but
there was something about the way Vivian was leaning against him,
looking up, that suggested, suggested . . . oh, shit, and now he's completely buggered it up. How could he *not* know Lily was here? Ribbentrop
knew. Mrs. King. Of course! What a joke! Why didn't she assassinate
the little bugger when she had the chance? Now he'll have to kill the
Baron off, lay him to rest, with Nazis coming out of the woodwork like
cockroaches. Half the Luftewaffe seems to be here, Froelich, Himmel,
von Braun, Richtofen's kid brother. Back in Berlin, they just pop into
their Fokkers and hop, skip, jump, here they are. *Guten Tag, mein Herr,*
lots of nice *Lebensraum* here, *nicht war?* A bunch of them are flying for
Interior Air, hopping, skipping and jumping all over the north, nice
guys, friendly, polite, a little bit wild, Dietrich in leather. What do they
do with the ugly ones? Chop them into wurst?

Esselwein spent the last war (the first?) in New York City, then in an
internment camp in Amherst, Nova Scotia, then in the RCMP barracks in
Regina, where he came to respect the fierce hatred the Mounties bore
towards the Hun. It was the only thing they had in common. His
admiration was shot to hell this spring, when the new Commissioner of
the RCMP General MacBrien, held a mess dinner in honour of *Reichmar-
schal* Schmidt. MacBrien proposed a toast to *Freiheit,* Then spent the
rest of the evening drunkenly embracing Schmidt as they refought the
Battle of the Somme, from both sides. Esselwein was more deeply
shocked by the Canadian and German pilots, most of whom had met in

the skies over France, and now met again on the ground, chummily comparing kills.

"I am getting sentimental." Esselwein sighs. "I must develop a more modern outlook."

Esselwein's spirits rise as he sheds the Baron's trappings. He stuffs the Tyrolean hat, the *lederhosen,* sword, sash, and Klan regalia into a padlocked dunnage bag. In a day or two, the bag will transform itself into the Baron's bloated body bobbing down the river, a tragic victim of accidental drowning. After all, Baron Wittgenstein's *coup* in the Klan has not been much appreciated by his superiors in the RCMP. Once the Baron got his hands on the Klan membership list, he discovered that it included every leading businessman in Edmonton, several prominent politicians, the mayor and the chief of police. The Baron was told to cut down on the burning crosses "so as not to embarrass our friends." It took some of the *élan* out of life. Without the Baron the Klan will pretty much fall apart. Just as well. It was draining members from the Masons, and General MacBrien is a Grand Master of the Scottish Rite. He may perform human sacrifices, for all Esselwein knows.

Naked now, Esselwein hacks away at his handlebar mustache with the nail scissors, then shaves it clean off. With his shaven head he looks like a pickled egg. "I'm just another oddball." Esselwein grins at the mirror. His hair will grow the regulation one inch soon enough, certainly before Ribbentrop arrives, if he arrives at all. His scarlet tunic is much too small. All those dumplings! He can't even button his breeches. A Royal Canadian Mounted bologna won't exactly impress Ribbentrop, but come to think of it, that's exactly what the Brown Shirts look like on the Movietone news. The Black Shirts are thin, except for Hitler, who looks like Charlie Chaplin.

Esselwein has about four weeks to become the lean, muscular, steely-eyed Great Red Hunter the Nazis have all heard about, Sergeant Leopold of the Royal Mounted, just the chap to introduce Count von Ribbentrop to his long-lost love, Lily King, *née* Coolican, of Ottawa, Kirkland Lake and Edmonton.

Will Ribbentrop talk? Will Lily tell? Of course she will!

LATER THE SAME DAY:

"Jack, Baron Wittgenstein is Esselwein. Did you know?"

"Yeah, sure. He's not very good at it, is he?"

"Ribbentrop is coming, he says."

"Yeah. Ribbentrop wants me to fly him up to Great Bear Lake."

"What does he want?"

Jack rummages in his desk drawer. He takes out a tobacco tin, pries off the lid and dumps out a chunk of ugly black rock.

"I picked this up on the east side of Great Bear, the winter we staked Eldorado. Stuck it in my parka pocket. When I got home I hung the parka in the closet and forgot about it. Couple of months later, the parka's still hanging there, but the rock is on the floor. It burned a hole right through the pocket lining. Look, I'll show you."

He turns the tin upside down and shakes out some pieces of cigarette paper. The paper is brown, as if it had been scorched.

"You mean it's a *hot* rock?"

"Uranium. Radium, you know, the cobalt bomb, cancer."

Lily pokes the rock with her finger, then picks it up. It lies still and stoney in her hand. She looks at it for a long time.

"It doesn't seem like Ribbentrop, somehow, curing the sick."

"It doesn't, does it."

"Is there something else?"

"I wish I knew."

A burning stone. A living rock! Wait 'til Mum hears about this!

30

"What else do you expect?" said Christina Coolican.

Do grasshoppers not blacken the fields, and obscure the sun in their swarms?

Has the great river not shrunk to a foul stream, and does the stench not hang over the city like a cloud?

Do whirlwinds of dust not race across the sky by day, and to the south, near Sodom, does not the sky redden at night with the fires of retribution?

Do not thunderclouds roll out of the west, black with rain, yet no rain falls?

And today, at noon, did the sun not turn to a lump of coal, and did the Dark Angel's wing not shadow the earth, causing the air to chill, and the birds to fall silent?

To the east, in Saskatchewan, women tear off their clothes and walk naked, singing, in the roads, their homes aflame behind them. To the north, at the Edmonton Flying Field, airplanes fall like meteors, and corpses fly through the air. In the south, where the soil has turned to sand, mothers slit their childrens' throats to stop their suffering, and decent men disembowel themselves, from grief.

What else do you expect? It's only a matter of time.

The People are gathering now. By thousands upon thousands they come, young men on the freights, families from their farms, landless, homeless, everything left behind. Even their clothes are cast-off. The churches are full, the Labour Temple can hold no more. Even Edmonton's market square is crowded. The People sleep under newspapers, in the stalls, crouched in doorways. Those who have wagons, or cows, camp in the stables at the Exhibition Grounds. The soldiers, who like to stick together and fend for themselves, are bivouacked on the flats by the river. Christina Coolican can see their campfires at night. She listens to their melancholy songs drift from fire to fire until the river itself seems to be singing.

Christina Coolican can hear better at night. During the day, the wind is full of wings. Sometimes the wings touch her face, or lift her hair. She is nearly swept away as they brush by her. Such a racket! She must listen. When the Word comes, they will go west, into the mountains. Up, up, up! In the mountains, at sunrise, she will see the pearly gates gleaming, row on row, against the golden sky, and she will feel God's grace in the cool, west wind.

It won't be long now. The Beast is in the city. She smells him in the stink from the river, and sees his mark on the faces of the people. She has even seen him prowling in his big, black limousine, licence number SA-666.

"John?"

"Umff."

"Are you awake?"

"Ummmffumuh."

"John, aren't we going to Ottawa after all?"

"I don't know."

"But the *Bulletin* says...."

"For God's sake, Vivian, do you believe everything you read in that rag?"

Vivian did, actually. What were newspapers for, if you didn't believe them? And if you didn't believe the newspapers, then what did you believe?

"But you said..."

"I haven't made up my mind."

"But that's not what you...."

"Look, Vivian, don't you trust me?"

"But I do, I do! It's just...."

"It's just that I want to do the right thing, the right thing for *every*body. What's wrong with that?"

Vivian bites her lip. Why does she always say the wrong thing? *He's* the one that talks all the time about quitting politics. Even at work everyone's talking about who's going to take over from Mr. Brownlee after he quits. Why should she be the last to know?

"Are you going without me?"

"Vivian, I am going to sleep, if you'll let me."

"Sorry."

Vivian stares into the darkness. She has her heart set on Ottawa. John will have an important job, and she'll be his private secretary. She'll have an office with a rug, like Miss Chisholm, and everyone will wonder who the beautiful girl is John Brownlee brought with him from Alberta. All the big men in Ottawa have girlfriends. That's what Myrna says. She says that's why politicians are so anxious to get elected, so they can screw around on their wives. Everyone does it, in Ottawa.

Vivian still feels a little strange, lying here in Mrs. Brownlee's bed. It even smells like Mrs. Brownlee, sort of sickly sweet. It was funny, Mrs. Brownlee going off to Victoria all of a sudden, by herself, for no particular reason, when she never goes *anywhere*. It was almost as if she was giving them a chance to be together. At first it was pretty scary, like playing hide-and-seek, doing it right here in Mrs. Brownlee's own bed. Vivian was sure Mrs. Brownlee would sneak home one night, fling open the door and cry "Gotcha!" But John always bolts the door from the inside, and she hasn't.

John is out most evenings, so after the housework is done, Vivian plays games with the boys and writes to Mrs. Brownlee. Dear Mrs. Brownlee.... It's hard to think what to say, so Vivian fills up the space with stupid things like the cake she made that sagged in the middle, and the contest the *Bulletin* is running to find a "Panther Woman" to star in a Hollywood movie. Vivian doesn't tell Mrs. Brownlee that she's entering the contest herself. She hasn't told *anyone*. Actually, the idea never crossed her mind until Mrs. King phoned and asked her. She said it wouldn't cost anything, and Vivian might learn something.

Well, she's learned that posing for pictures is no fun, and trying to look like a panther is very hard work. She has to contort her body a dozen different ways, then look up under her eyelids until she's nearly crosseyed, then open her eyes wide, wide, wide and stare into a strong light until she's half-blind. Making faces makes Vivian feel silly, and she gets flustered being looked at by that cold, black eye. Think of the camera as a man, said Mrs. King, a very sexy, dark, handsome man. Valentino. Robert Taylor. You are crazy about him. You're alone, in the jungle. He can't take his eyes off you. You are going to pounce on him, sink your teeth in his neck, devour him. Show some teeth now, just a little, good, now lick your lips, tip of the tongue, *ymmmmmmmmmm*, good, good, a little smile.... Vivian thought of the camera as John, but Mrs. King yelled, "For God's sake, Vivian, stop looking like a scared rabbit!"

Vivian is not optimistic. Mrs. King has the makeup all wrong. She puts white stuff on Vivian's eyelids where the blue shadow's supposed to go, and rouge *under* her cheekbones instead of *on* them, the way the girl at Eaton's said to do it. She even puts rouge on the end of Vivian's nose! But then, Mrs. King is getting kind of old, and is probably a little out-of-date, although her own face is done okay. Vivian is planning to pluck her eyebrows. Her eyes will look more like Bette Davis' then. Her eyes are her best feature. They make up for being flat-chested. No, nothing makes up for being flat-chested. Mrs. King is not flat-chested, and she has beautiful clothes. Her evening gowns are covered with sequins and tiny beads that shimmer when you walk. She let Vivian wear one as the panther woman. Mrs. Brownlee wears tweeds. Mrs. Brownlee has taken all her clothes with her... hey... hey! Is that it? Maybe *Mrs.* Brownlee's getting the divorce!

"John, have you told Mrs. Brownlee?"

"Told her what?"

"About... us?"

"Mrs. Brownlee is not well. It would kill her."

"But isn't that why we...."

Vivian feels very mixed up. John always makes her feel so dumb. Back home, everybody said how smart she was. That just goes to show you, doesn't it? She should have known her place, like her dad said, and married Carl when she had the chance. Now she might never get married at all!

"Maybe I should go back to Edson."

"And quit your job?"

"I hate my job!"

"I hate my job too, but I do it. Would you rather not have a job at all?"

"I could get married."

Vivian feels John tense. Well, he's awake *now*. His voice is cold, cautious.

"Do you have a boyfriend?"

"Lots of boys like me."

"Do you like them?"

"Sure, a couple of them."

"Are they nice boys? Decent, honest, clean-living?"

"Yes, I think so."

"And do you really think, Vivian, that a nice, honest, Christian boy, an innocent boy, would want to marry a girl like you?"

"No," Vivian cries. "No. Oh no no no!"

"You must wisit Germany, Lili."

Ribbentrop's lips linger on the back of my hand. He is fatter now, *von* Ribbentrop (where did he get *that?*), and his sleek hair more silver than gold, but the style is still sly, insolent. His uniform twinkles with stars like the sky at sunset. *Der Rhinestonekavalier.*

"And what would I do there, darling?"

"You would make a film! In Germany, we have everything the best, you know, the best cinemas, the best studios, the best film stars, the best scenery, the Klieg lights, moving picture cameras. The camera was inwented in Germany, did you know?"

"But what would I film?"

"You would film history! You would film the birth of the greatest civilization in the world, the rise of the Thousand Year Reich!"

"It sounds a little ambitious, for me. I have been thinking of something simpler, a western . . . ."

"Western! Ah, excellent. They are the favourite with the *Führer*. Tom Mix. The Crisco Kid . . . ."

"Cisco, Joachim. *Seeeeesco* Kid."

"Stick 'em up, eh? Bam! Bam! The cowboy film is the true people's art. *Volkwerke*." Joachim lowers his voice, his lips against my ear. "The *Führer* is, how you say, a *fan*."

"He must like Dietrich, she's . . . ."

"Dietrich! Dietrich iss *dreck*! Shit! Dietrich iss a Jew!

"Marlene?"

"It is her mother who is a Jew. That is why Dietrich is in Hollywood. The Jews run everything there."

Ribbentrop stares stonily across the room. A sea of blue eyes stares back. Every Kraut in Alberta must be here. The place is jammed. Ribbentrop rubs his hands together in a smug, proprietary way, as if to say, Aha, you are all mine, *mine!* It's a gesture he must have copied from the Prince of Wales. It is said that the Prince himself will attend the reception. The Prince is vacationing on his ranch, south of Sodom. The silence between Joachim and me lengthens. I feel I have been dismissed, yet no one else is approaching, and I can't just walk away, leaving him all alone. What to do? What *do* you do with a Nazi?

"Do you still play the violin?"

Ribbentrop relents, smiles.

"You remember, yes? The *Führer* is kind enough to praise my poor efforts. Of course, we Germans are a musical people. All the greatest composers are German, the most brilliant performers. Music is in our blood. We cannot help but express it. It is not like Canada, where there is no *kultur*. It is a beautiful country, Canada, but primitive."

"We haven't been around too long."

"That is it, precisely. Canada is a country of immigrants, mongrels, Semites, Slavs, gypsies, Orientals. There is too much intermarriage, the dilution of the pure blood by poisonous strains. We too have this problem. Until we purge these poisons.... Who is that?"

It's Vivian. She's standing just inside the door. She is wearing a blue dress with puffed sleeves and a round, white collar. Her hair is a golden halo. She looks lovely and rather lost. What on earth is she doing at this *Bundfest?*

"Would you like to meet her?"

Joachim doesn't take his eyes off Vivian. With a flick of his gloves he motions to a young sun god in a black shirt standing by the window. The boy follows Joachim's gaze, nods, clicks his heels and makes his way swiftly across the room. He stops in front of Vivian, bows, clicks his heels again, and raises her hand to his lips. Vivian looks startled. The sun god speaks a few words. She looks up, sees us, and smiles. The sun god is taking her elbow when a scowling shadow looms behind them and pulls Vivian brusquely out the door.

"Her father?" Ribbentrop frowns.

"Have you not met Mr. Brownlee, the Premier of the province? He's a social fascist. Isn't that rather like a National Socialist?"

"Yes? I had heard the opposite."

"Mr. Brownlee is not terribly popular at the moment...."

"It is the fate of we fascists to suffer...."

We are interrupted by a terrific ruckus from outside. Everyone rushes to the windows. A crowd of men has surrounded the Premier's limousine. They are shouting and booing as Mr. Brownlee pushes his way through towards the car. I can see Vivian's blond head bobbing in his wake. On the hood of the car, a tall man in a crumpled top hat and dirty cutaway coat is capering about, waving a walking stick. It's "Balls-to-you" Bennett, Edmonton's version of the Prime Minister. His songs are a riot. One of the best is a version of the Twenty-third Psalm:

"Bennett is my shepherd, I am in want.

He maketh me to lie down on park benches,

He leadeth me beside still factories...."

I can't quite make out what Balls-to-you is singing. It seems to be something about Brownlee and brown-nose.

"What iss this?" cries Ribbentrop. "Who are these hooligans?"

"It's only the unemployed."

"But why are they here? Why doesn't someone drive them away?"

"They'll just turn up somewhere else. They have nowhere to go."

"Put them in jail, then. In work camps. In the army."

"They haven't done anything. They're just kids, really. What can you do?"

Ribbentrop turns away, disgusted. He offers me a cigarette from an onyx case, touches my hand as he lights it, then lights his own from mine.

"In Germany," he says, blowing smoke through his nose, "this scum iss not permitted to exist."

MEANWHILE, IN OTTAWA,
WILLIAM LYON MACKENZIE KING EXAMINES HIS CONSCIENCE:

Laurier House, Tuesday, Sept. 6, 1932:

At eleven a.m. I was interviewed by Mrs. Freiman and two other women from the Jewish League about the question of Jewish Refugees. The Germans have apparently given assurances that Jews who wish to do so will be encouraged to leave Germany as long as there is a country willing to recive them. Mrs. Freiman claims that as many as 25,000 or more of them could be brought to Canada to live with relatives etc. I reminded her that the Liberal record on immigration is an excellent one, and that we would always champion the cause of the poor and down-trodden, but since we no longer form the government, our hands are virtually tied in this matter. With unemployment where it is, at nearly twenty-five per cent, there would be little chance that Premier Bennett would wish to bring in more mouths to feed, and it could cause even greater physical hardship and possibly social disruption than is presently being experienced in Germany.

Mrs. Freiman quite appreciated my arguments. She said there is great fear among the Jews, that they were being beaten and robbed, and forced to shut their businesses, all for no apparent reason. It seems to me that these people have brought trouble on their own heads by accumulating great wealth, influence, etc. etc. and by keeping to themselves. The Jews don't mix well. There is something suspicious, shifty about them. The Freimans themselves have been none too loyal, a big donation to the Tories last election, hardly anything for the Liberal Party, yet now the worm has turned, asking for favours, always pushing for preferment in a way that's quite sickening. If Germany no longer wants the Jews, there is probably a good reason for it.

This afternoon a letter arrived from Charlie Fleury's solicitor offering me his remaining 100 acres at Kingsmere for $2,000. To purchase the property is to be free of all doubt and uncertainty, and the possibility of vindictive or other acts & possible injury to scenic effects. It means too to be freed of others having rights of way over my property, and acquiring the finest site around for a view. I decided to accept the offer, and wrote a cheque on the Bank of Montreal for half the amount. I might have got Fleury down to $1,800, but I doubt I would have done better. It is hard to know what it is best to do with unemployment etc. and need and suffering on the part of many. To increase one's possessions seems unwise. On the other hand, it may mean doing more for others in the end, as I believe it will. It is the long run one has to keep in view.

Tonight at nine I went to see Haydon. He is again dependent on dope to sleep, eats nothing, hands and feet swollen and blue. I am afraid he cannot last long. He has been the sacrificial Lamb for the Liberal Party.

Wednesday, Sept. 7, 1932:

The papers today are full of the 'Château' affair. It is very damaging to Bennett. His suite there cost $125,000 to decorate, nothing paid for his rooms, enormous entertainment expenses, all picked up by the CNR at public expense, waste and extravagance on all sides. Bennett has countered with insinuations that I grafted by using the Experimental Farm and Dept. of Public Works, and is putting it out if we raise the Château issue in the House, he will have something to say about Kingsmere. There are incidentals here & there which every PM has in the way of perquisites, but there is nothing which, if disclosed, could do injury to the party or to myself. There are a few things I would refrain from doing, had it to be done over again, but I can honestly say that there is nothing that cost the government anything to speak of. Flowers, etc. from the Farm is what the Lauriers, Borden & others got, and the same is true for the few things here & there.

I feel a real sympathy for Bennett in what he has been thro' today. He looks wrought up, hardly able to speak. The revelation of what he is receiving from the railways, a multi-millionaire profiting in that fashion, is damning in the extreme. I feel sorry for him.

Thursday, Sept. 8, 1932:

The mental anxiety I am experiencing at the thought of any discussion of Kingsmere or Laurier House is very great. I have perhaps accepted more in the past than I should, and have not been strict enough in watching everything to see that no suspicions could be aroused. Anything that touches the personal side I cannot bear to have discussed in public, and much of the joy of Kingsmere is already gone, knowing that it is talked about by the Tories in a suspicious way. It is the one bit of sanctuary I have left and a violation of it would be terrible.

I have a feeling that Grisdale, the present director of the Farm, who was then the veterinary, has been talking to the Tories about the sheep, and saying that the Farm men had been consulted about the sheep, when as a matter of fact it was Grisdale who offered, as a matter of interest, to have a look at them. What was done I know very little of. Some washing tub was loaned and returned, but in no way did I press any request. I always felt that the director — a little Tory — was an enemy. Without doubt the Tories have been spying in all quarters, but have found so little all they have left is insinuation. Still, the mere possibility of the latter fills me with pain & dread & I cannot feel too grateful to God who has permitted dear Mother to be at hand to comfort me.

Today I counselled the men not to bring up the Château matter for discussion in the House. Bennett would at once assume the role of martyr. He would pay the hotel a sum and move out. Meanwhile, the Tories would launch a campaign of vilification, slander, etc. in the House. We would get the worst from their methods.

Brockville, Ont. Friday, Sept. 9:

Left at ten-thirty a.m. and travelled to Brockville. Went to Fulford Place. Mrs. Fulford and I had a short talk. She then had Miss Hitchcock come in with the Ouija board. She recited what she said others in the Beyond were saying to her.

Sir Wilfrid was the first to speak, addressed me as his very dear friend, wanted to speak very personally, said what a pleasure it was to him and Lady Laurier to see me in their old home, that he wanted me to get out as much as possible among the people, let them see my personality, have any number come to Laurier House, entertain as much as possible, that I had gone back into my shell, too much a recluse. He was much concerned about present conditions in Ottawa and said I was needed at this time in the country's affairs. In two years time the election would come.

Lady Laurier came. She spoke of how happy they all were, had a very happy home over there. Mrs. Fulford asked if she played bridge. She said she did everything. The music was wonderful. She would be near me in my efforts to entertain etc. Father was just coming but Miss Hitchcock was tired so we stopped. After dinner, we had another sitting. I took down practically all that was said in pencil:

Mother: 'I am anxious to come as you know I always am. Between us there is a special bond. The only regret I had in coming over was leaving you. I go often to the little house in Kingsmere and sit there, where we were together. I will be with you often there. When the time comes for you to come over, I will be the first to greet you. The veil between our worlds is a very thin one. I am in your home every day in Ottawa. Take the advice Sir Wilfrid gave you. You don't mix enough with people. It is the one thing necessary to win the next election.

'Your father sends his love tonight. Remember, love is all that is eternal. We are both pleased, proud, gratified and satisfied with you. Every day I am beside you. Don't go to any new mediums. I don't want you to. We don't want any little gossip about this before the elections.

We don't want them to talk. It is a mother's love speaking. Goodnight, my beloved son.'

Laurier House, Monday, Sept. 12:

Last night I wrote very frankly to C in regard to some of the mysterious forces of life. I shall await with interest the answer that will come. I believe it will reveal a real understanding of invisible things, a willingness to explore and a trust equal to my own. I feel certain that she would not have sent the telegram at Easter, in reply to my own, were she not experiencing the same 'awareness,' deep answering unto deep. She is a person of great character & responsibility and together we may help each other rise to greater heights of knowledge.

I stayed in the House all evening. Would like to have gone to see Ethel Barrymore in *The School for Scandal*, but so few members in the House, I felt I should stick to duty and did.

Tuesday, Sept. 13:

This morning I overslept, or rather, slept in a half-awake, half-asleep sleep, the worst kind of rest. I wakened with a sort of fire thro' the veins. It may be that what I am experiencing in writing to C is a passion. I fear I have aroused part of my nature which should be subdued. It may be the fire that shuts out paradise. It may, on the other hand, be part of a divine fire. On this as on all else, I pray for guidance. Unless it leads nearer to God, I want no more of it.

At two o'clock I went out to Kingsmere with Joan, Godfroy and the two little dogs. Climbed one of the high spots on the land I brought from Fleury. Pretty poor quality, rock and scrub, with very few views.

Thursday, Sept. 15:

Last night I was conscious as never before of magnetic forces sweeping thro' me, some attractive power which it was impossible to resist, and which seemed to gain an almost infinite strength. It was about midnight when I became conscious of this reaction. I began to feel it as I was saying my prayers. It became absorbing and overwhelming later in the night I am wondering if what I experienced was self-intoxication, as it were, my own thoughts, or influences of spirits round about, brought near by my own thoughts, or nature's urge to be free after being dammed. This I have to learn. I am almost certain it was the thoughts of C, to whom I had written, and who in all probability had received my letter. It will be interesting to hear when my letter was received.

This morning I was none too keen on my work & suffered a nerve reaction, a sort of tension, which discloses that last night's experience was not right.

Kingsmere, Sunday, Sept. 18:

During the past week I have been troubled much with constipation. My system has been poisoned with toxic poisons, head ached, depressed & eyes bothering me a good deal. Was shocked tonight to discover that even my long-distance sight not as good as it was. I ate too much at dinner & was not in a happy frame of mind. Still feel the injury done to brain, perceptions, visions etc. in the early part of the week. Was quite lonely tonight.

Warm & sultry. Promise of rain.

31

Willie is sending the weirdest letters! They're all about "magnetic forces" and "electrical impulses" and "outside influences." What strange, subterranean seas are you sailing now, Willie Winken? And why do you want to drown me too?

Willie sounds as mad as he was that summer at Kingsmere, during the war, when he thought he had syphilis. Oh God, maybe he does have syphilis! Doesn't it rot your brain, at the end? He wants me to send him telepathic messages at certain times of the day and night, then keep a record of each message, and the hour transmitted, so we can see if he receives my vibrations.

"I believe that before long the Loved Ones in the Great Beyond will be speaking directly to us via radio," he says. Can you imagine? I can hear it now: "Dial CKM for *Mother*, coming to you *live* from the beautiful Bluesky Ballroom in the Heavenly Hotel! Swing to the sound of St. Peter and the Angels, the sweetest music on the *other* side!"

"That'll be the end of Lombardo," said Jack.

"What am I going to do?"

"Sounds like he's jerking off. Send him the message 'Let's fuck,' full strength. He'll blow up."

"But I don't want to encourage him!"

"Send him a picture of Panther Woman, then. He'll go nuts."

"I can't even send Panther Woman to Hollywood. Vivian won't let me. She's changed her mind, she says."

"She's crazy. She's a shoo-in."

"That's what's so maddening. All she said was that there'd be trouble if she didn't win and 'people found out.' Now I can't even find her. I called her rooming house yesterday and the landlady said she'd moved out, no forwarding address."

"She's shacked up with Brownlee."

"What!"

"Sure. She's been living there for a while. Mrs. Brownlee's in Victoria."

"How do you know?"

"No big secret. They drive to work together every morning. Vivian's supposed to be the 'mother's helper.'"

"Maybe she is."

"Yeah? Brownlee's oldest boy is nearly as old as Vivian. What does she do? Change his diaper? No sir, it's the old man who's getting his oil changed."

"That's impossible! She's much too young!"

"She's twenty."

"But he's, he's nearly fifty!"

"So? How old were you, kiddo, when you took up with...."

"Oh, damn."

"Horny bunch, you dames."

"But Jack, it's *impossible.* He'll have to quit."

"Nope. McPherson's still there, and you should see what the cops have got on *him.* The farmers are shitting bricks. You know the farmers, eh, simon pure, holier 'n thou. Well, seems they've been electing a nest of fornicators all these years. What to do, eh? Blow the lid off, and bring down your own government? Keep the lid on, and watch your support melt away like a snowball in spring? Word gets around. The UFA is losing a thousand members a month."

"But it's just gossip."

"So far."

"But he'll be ruined."

"We can hope."

The next Sunday, Lily was lying in bed transmitting dirty thoughts to Willie as hard as she could, knowing he'd be in church, when there was a timid knock at the door.

"I should be in church," Vivian said, looking over her shoulder.

"So should I. Come in."

"I sort of thought I'd like to see the pictures, if I can."

"Sure."

Lily took the Panther Woman portfolio from her drawer and spread the photos out on the table.

"Oh, wow! Is that *me*?"

"Sure, pretty much. I had to return the tigerskin. Too bad. It goes well with your hair."

"My hair looks almost white!"

"Klieg light."

"And I've got eyelashes!"

"Maybelline."

"And no freckles!"

"Movie stars never have freckles. No, Hepburn has freckles. But Hepburn is not the Panther Woman. Thank God."

"I don't look too pantherish."

"You look sexy. That's what counts."

"Imagine wearing a fur coat with nothing on underneath. My dad would kill me."

"I think fur coats should always be worn with nothing on, but then I no longer have a fur coat."

"I'd have one, wouldn't I, if I won?"

"Thousands. Mink, sable, chinchilla, and millions of shoes, and hundreds of slinky dresses, with trains, and dozens of movie stars falling in love with you."

Vivian sighed. "That's why I can't do it, the contest."

"Why not?"

"I may be going . . . away."

"Ottawa?"

"No, farther than that."

"Farther? London?"

"Oh, no. Promise you won't tell?"

"Of course not."

"I may be going to Germany!"

"Good God."

"It's not certain yet. I haven't really told anyone."

Vivian flushed and fiddled with her bracelet. "I may be getting married."

"*Married!* Vivian, you told me two weeks ago you didn't even have a boyfriend!"

"Well, I didn't then. And he's not really a boyfriend. I mean, I haven't seen that much of him, he's been up north a lot, but he says he's in love with me and wants me to marry him."

"And you?"

"Oh, I think he's very nice. It's just that . . . my mum and dad . . . ."

". . . will be shocked?"

". . . him being a Fascist and all. Dad's very left, you know."

"Maybe he's just Conservative . . . ."

"Oh, no! He's very proud of being a Fascist! He's told me all about it. He says I'm the perfect Aryan type. I told him I was Scotch, mostly, but he said that was okay, it was pretty much the same thing."

Lily sat down. "Have you thought about the consequences?" she said carefully.

"I know it sounds crazy. It *is* crazy, but . . . ."

"You're crazy about him."

"Oh, yes! Like, I mean, it was love at first sight, kapow, you know. He was standing there in front of the window, in his uniform, and the sun shining on his hair turned it into a sort of a halo, like an angel's, and I had this strange echo in my head, *baaaooooommmmmm*, and that was it. I was a goner."

"He was holding a glass of wine in his hand, against the sun, and it splintered into a rainbow of rubies."

"How did you know?"

"I was there."

"Oh, right. Anyway, his name is Wolfgang, like in Mozart. Isn't that nice? Mozart is really German, you know. Austrians are pretty much the same thing."

"All the great composers are German."

"How did you know that?"

"I get around."

"The Germans are a very musical people. Wolf plays the oboe."

"What is the SS? A philharmonic?"

"Wolf says I can have a concert career in Germany. At the moment, all the best engagements go to the Jews, like they do here, but when his party takes over they'll fix it so everybody gets a chance. He says the *Führer* adores piano concertos, and blondes."

"So you're not going to Hollywood, then."

"Wolf says I wouldn't have a chance, the Jews have everything 'fixed' for their own people. I'd be better off in Berlin."

"Do they have panther women in Berlin?"

"Oh, no, nothing like that! The Germans are very moral people. Wolf says that German movies, I mean German *films*, are very cultural. Rhinemaidens and stuff like that."

"Well, let's celebrate. Want a Coke?"

"Thanks, but I can't stay. I'm supposed to be in church. Mr. Brownlee is picking me up. We're meeting Mrs. Brownlee at the station."

"Is he happy about your engagement, Mr. Brownlee?"

"He doesn't know, yet. I mean, I haven't exactly said yes."

Vivian looked down at her shoes. "Can I ask you something?"

"May. Sure."

"Should a girl get married if she isn't, you know, pure?"

"Why not?"

"Isn't it sort of, cheating?"

"What are you? Soapflakes?"

"But don't men sort of *expect* . . . ."

"Vivian, think of the girls you know. Why did they get married?"

"They were . . . . I see what you mean. But what if you're *not* pregnant?"

"Lucky for him."

"But what if he *thinks* . . . ."

"Let him think."

"What if he *asks*?"

"Tell him to buzz off. Any man who asks is a creep. Do you want to marry a creep?"

"I hadn't thought of it that way." Vivian looked relieved.

"Don't rush into anything, Vivian. Divorce is difficult."

"Yes," she said. "I know."

As I was putting the photos away after Vivian left, I came across the snapshot of Vivian and Mr. Brownlee on the sidewalk. Why had I taken *this* picture? Why not someone else? I taped it to the fridge door and looked at it as I made breakfast. It wasn't a very good shot. Vivian's face was turned away from the camera, towards Brownlee, and he was looking at the ground. Why had it caused a fuss? You could hardly see their faces. No, it was something about the way they were walking together, in step, Vivian looking up, laughing, leaning slightly towards him, pressed against his arm. Something about them seemed very familiar.

It was late afternoon, as I was rummaging for an ice-cube, when it hit me. They were holding hands.

A FEW DAYS LATER,
WILLIE KING VISITS THE UNDERWORLD,
AND LOSES HIS LUGGAGE:

Ottawa, Laurier House, Sat. Oct. 22, 1932:

After luncheon, I became conscious of a very direct communication from the west. I was thinking of it when a telegram from C was placed in my hand. I am perfectly certain she was seeking to influence my thoughts at that time, and was able to do so to a remarkable degree, so much so I had to give up dictation for awhile.

I called at Haydon's at two-thirty p.m. Andrew has been resting better, is conscious, but very weak, has had an egg-nog and a little cocoa today. May linger on awhile, but no hope, I fear. It is a surprise that he lasted this long.

For dinner had some oysters on the half shell, wild duck and russet pears, all gifts from friends.

Monday, Oct. 24:

During the day I felt a good deal of strain from what seemed to be an outside influence but did my utmost to ward it off by an effort of will. A letter received from the west made it clear what has to be faced. I reflected upon Salome & Delilah and made clear to myself my determination that nothing of this kind should be permitted in my life. I prayed God for strength to overcome all temptation to evil, however subtle it might be.

Sunday, Nov. 6:

While I was reading before going to sleep, I felt another influence sweep over me, and felt perfectly sure it was C trying to communicate with me. The impression was overwhelming after I had turned off the lights. At five o'clock, I woke dreaming of dear Mother. It seemed to me we were together in old Berlin, and going on a road towards the station. I had a train to catch. I was in time for the train, but I was arguing with Mother, resenting her efforts to hold me by pleading for me to love her, to be absorbed in her love. It was a selfish love, I felt, the kind I have experienced with others, but never with her.

When I awoke I said at once 'Dear Mother is here guiding me.' What I experienced of resentment was not towards her, but towards a selfish love that seeks to claim & hold & bind me. It was never the love she disclosed to me on earth, for that was the most unselfish and spiritual. She was making clear that carnal love was wrong, and if I felt resentment towards her for any kind of love, that love must be wrong. The number five seemed to come into the dream — it was exactly five as I looked at the clock.

I then saw a painting of Mother, and her picture by my bed & said "There are five pictures of Mother, that is the meaning of the five." Just then I saw another on my little writing table and I thought "There must be yet another for seven is the mystical number." I went to the dresser and took out the little picture of dear Mother in my purse, which made the seven.

Later I saw the significance of the five and seven in the Book of Judges, in the story of Gideon, which was so reminiscent of the struggle I have had all my political days ever since, in 1921, I saw the Holy Grail burning at the end of my journey. Surely this is a parable, and at the end of it all, having kept the tryst, having overcome, I shall yet see the Holy Grail.

Friday, Nov. 11:

I had a remarkable vision before waking this morning. I was travelling in a pullman car. Mother was with me. I thought I had lost her & in looking for her went thro' a series of compartments in the car which opened one into the other. In each compartment there were ladies sleeping, or about to sleep. It seemed that I had gotten into the women's section of the car. When I crossed the aisle, I found Mother resting lengthwise on a side seat. She seemed to be put out a little & said that someone else had given her $100, but I had given her nothing. I sought to explain the position I was in, re funds, feeling that perhaps I should have given more. The vision vanished before I had finished the conversation.

To me it is quite clear. Reading the letter from C before I went to sleep aroused feelings in my nature which I should not have permitted. I did not encourage them. I was confirmed in this as I read the chapter for today in Judges, where the story is told of the wife of Manoah who, in consequence of a heavenly visitation, gave birth to a son who was to deliver Israel from the Philistines. Clearly the vision was a warning to beware of Delilah. Because I am the son of good, honest, God-fearing, non-wine drinking people, God's mission for me, being moved at times by the spirit of the Lord, is to help deliver the people.

This afternoon I wrote a letter to C.

After dinner, called at the Haydons' & saw dear Haydon lying in his coffin, his face very noble, a fine, scholarly head, so peaceful, not a look of scorn or disappointment but just as one who had come thro' great tribulation and won perfect peace.

Saturday, Nov. 12:

After lunch, I drove to Haydon's house on the Driveway to be present at the funeral as a pall bearer. Dr. McDougald was inside in the dining room with a few of the friends. It seemed like seeing Mephisto coming out of a church to see him leave the room. Haydon's whole life would have been different but for McDougald's selfishness. It was pleasing to me to see the little picture of dear Mother on the mantlepiece above the spot where Haydon lay, surrounded by flowers in abundance. I just missed seeing the lid of the coffin close over his remains. I was looking out the open door at the moment.

The funeral was a large one, the church well filled, many prominent Conservatives present. A great many came to the cemetery as well. The scene there was one of triumph. The church buried Haydon as one of their saints. He merited all.

At six o'clock I went for a walk and had one of the most wonderful experiences, or revelations, I have yet had. I was feeling regret at not having said what I meant to say about Haydon when I spoke in Parliament about the Beauharnois affair. I should have said that no one could make me believe Haydon was capable of a dishonourable act. I would have said this, but for Bennett's intimation that he had evidence which would convict Haydon, and would bring it out if I spoke of him, or tried to protect Haydon's name. That was the only reason I refrained. Haydon now knows I did this for him, & he knows my every act was to protect him & the Party, and that there was no lack of chivalry on my part.

As I was walking around the Driveway, communing with Haydon aloud, saying 'Well, Haydon, you now know all,' I felt, as it were, someone pressing my right shoulder. I said 'Yes, Andrew, I know it is you, continue to press,' and I could feel the pressure, as of a bag of air, a spiritual body, against my shoulder. When I crossed the Laurier Ave. bridge, I was struck with the reflection of the moon in the water, the symbol of love in Heaven & its wavering image here.

Sunday, Dec. 25:

At breakfast, I turned on the radio & heard most of the world-embracing British Empire broadcast. It was truly inspiring. The mention of Bethlehem and the Star nearly 2,000 years ago was too much for me. I felt that the little babe would yet conquer the world. We have now heard a voice speak on Xmas day from the Holy Land & proclaim peace on earth. The day will yet come, and I *may* live to see it, when we will have a radio broadcast from some of the spirits proclaiming God's message to the world. That may be the 'second coming.' It may come in that form, the voice of Christ himself speaking to the whole world, as the King of England did this morning from London.

I enjoyed the King's speech very much. He has been a great king & has the hearts of his people. His reference to the blind, poor etc. was all quite beautiful. I had all the servants come in & listen & we stood together as the National Anthem was played. Later, I went and saw them all in their diningroom. Their little Xmas tree & humble gifts greatly touched my heart. I am helping the poor by keeping these people around me. I distributed $20 to McLeod, $20 to Mary, $15 Kate, $15 Lay, $10 Nancy, $10 Armstrong and will give Nicol $25 or $30.

Thursday, Jan. 12, 1933:

Last night I dreamt I crossed the Ottawa River in a car like a freight baggage, with small windows to look out of. I saw a most beautiful view. It must be as the soul sees it in the Beyond. When I got out, I walked along a road with two women who were very poor & much distressed at their poverty. When I got back to the car, it seemed to me my valise was gone, or I had gone without it, or a hat. This means I have to beware of forgetting anything, one's principles in particular.

I walked back thro' Hull. At a corner store, I saw a woman dressed in tights singing 'Come, come, oh come.' in a very wistful, wailing voice. I assumed she was some siren.

Sunday, Jan. 15:

After the banquet last night, I joined a number of those present in rooms upstairs where there was more in the way of refreshments. On top of the champagne I had taken after speaking, I took some scotch & ginger ale. It was after two-thirty a.m. when I got to bed. I woke up at three or four, dreaming that I had been in some beautiful room, but had made a mess of what I had in hand. I was responsible for having done in public what should have been an act of privacy, relieving a demand of nature quite proper in itself, at the right time & place, but wholly out of place as it was. I felt a terrible humiliation & sense of shame. Very remorseful and unhappy.

Wed. Jan. 18:

Last night I dreamt I was going somewhere on a long journey. I was alone. I went into a building like a hotel, into a room like a bar room (but had nothing to drink), then to a room upstairs. While there, it seemed that the car I was to take was about to leave. I felt I could catch it all right, but when I came down, the one I wanted had gone. I could not remember the name of the place I was going to. My memory seemed completely gone. I asked the conductor of the car I got on whether it went to the spot I could not remember. He told me it only went a certain distance. I got out and began to walk back. I came to a long, dark tunnel which I went to walk thro'. I found numbers of people coming in the opposite direction. I found that my money was stolen, and later my clothes, except for the shirt on my back. I felt the cold & pain. I wakened finding I was cold, some bed clothing off, but feeling the dream was a warning. I have been distressed in mind and soul.

Saturday, Jan. 21:

Mr. Bracken, the Premier of Manitoba, called on behalf of Brownlee to see what my attitude would be were Brownlee to go on the Tariff Board.

Bennett has evidently given the British the assurance that Brownlee would be one of the commissioners. The Governor-General has even spoken to Brownlee, saying 'the Empire' required his services. I feel it might be just as well to get him out of Alberta. It might give our party a better show there.

Bennett looks like a man who has been on a drunk, very tired, nervous, eyes pinched & face drawn, like an animal caught at bay, his colour very red & skin almost blotchy. It would take very little to bring on a collapse. Anything may happen. I believe he has entangled himself with a Mrs. Colville. Whatever he does so far as she is concerned will end his career.

32

At first the cop on duty at the Single Womens' Relief Office doesn't pay too much attention to the lady in the fur coat. He's seen plenty like her: scared. They'll come to the door, then back away as if they'd got the wrong address, circle the block once or twice, stand on the sidewalk as if they're waiting for somebody, then, zip, they'll scoot in and close the door behind them, not looking back, afraid they've been seen. Why do they care? Hell, half of Edmonton's on Relief. No shame to it. "Everybody's doin' it," as the song goes. The cop hums to himself as he rubs his mitt on the window to make a hole in the frost.

There she is, across the street, sheltering in the doorway of a boarded-up jewellery store. Must have been pretty well fixed, at one time. You don't see many single gals in fur coats. Hooker? Nope, too old. Mind you, some of the stuff you see walking the streets these days. Coat could be secondhand. You can pick up a lot of good stuff dirt cheap, real sealskin too, not your dyed rabbit. Stealin's way down. No point, these days. Just go down to the Sally Ann. Well, good luck to her. It's forty-three below zero out there. The air's as hard and blue as the inside of an ice-cube. The lady's breath hangs in a still, white cloud above her head. Well, lady, the cop mutters, freezin's quicker than starvin', if that's what you've got in mind. There's plenty of them too, frozen stiffs. Popsicles, they call them at the cop shop, except most of them are curled up into a ball. Ever seen a guy buried in a round grave?

The cop wishes the lady would freeze somewhere else. He can see the headline now: STARVING WOMAN DIES STEPS FROM SAFETY: INQUIRY ORDERED. She may be one of them Red provokers. They're always up to funny things, gettin' people into trouble. The next time the lady drifts past the door, the cop jumps out and grabs her by the arm. "Might as well make up your mind where its' warm," he says, and pull her inside.

She sits on a chair by the wall until she stops shivering, then takes her place at the end of a long, shuffling line, She is of no particular age, or size, or colouring — nondescript, except for a bright slash of orange lipstick smeared across her mouth. She stands very straight and looks neither right nor left.

"Name?" the clerk says at last.

"McPherson."

The clerk flips through a sheaf of papers.

"I don't see a McPherson on our list."

"I haven't been here before."

"Oh, you're in the wrong line then. You'll have to go to 'New Applications,' over there."

"I'm sorry. Thank you."

She takes her place at the end of another line.

"Name?"

"McPherson."

"First name?"

"Cora."

"Occupation?"

"None."

"You are unemployed?"

"I have never had a job."

"I see." The clerk looks askance at Cora McPherson's sealskin coat and bright lipstick.

"Age?"

"Fifty-two."

"Place of birth?"

"Illinois."

"Oh, you're an American. I'm sorry, but...."

"No. I've lived here for years. I'm a Canadian citizen."

"Do you have proof of citizenship?"

"Proof? My husband....."

"Husband? Madam, this office is for *single women only*. Married couples may apply down the street...."

"My husband...left me."

"I see. You're divorced."

"Yes."

"When?"

"Two years ago."

"Is your former husband destitute?"

"Oh, no! He's very well off."

"You must receive some support, do you not?"

"I received $30 a month until last August. Since August I have not received a cent."

"Has he given any reason?"

"He doesn't answer my letters."

"I'd advise you to consult a lawyer, Mrs. McPherson...."

"How can I pay a lawyer? I have no money. Miss, I have nothing to eat. That's why I'm here."

"I see."

"You see, I don't need *Relief.* All I need is something to tide me over for a few days. Perhaps I can persuade...."

"Your former husband lives here?"

"Yes, in the winters. We...he has a farm as well, near Vulcan."

"His name?"

"Oren. Oren Lloyd McPherson."

The clerk writes the name down then puts her pencil down very slowly. She cracks her chewing gum between her teeth.

"Madam," she says, "Oren McPherson is the Minister of Public Works. Mr. McPherson runs this Relief program."

"Yes. That is correct."

The clerk chews vigorously and blows a small, Spearmint bubble.

"Just a minute." The clerk clickety-clacks across the room and disappears behind a partition. Cora can hear voices, and a phone being dialed. The clerk is gone so long the women behind Cora are shuffling and muttering by the time she comes back.

"We have information, Mrs. McPherson, that you recently received a cheque for $1,000 from your former husband." The clerk purses her lips.

"Yes. That was an old insurance policy I had. Oren cashed it in."

"But you *do* have money."

"I haven't cashed the cheque."

"Why *not?*"

"I can't. You see, Oren says the thousand dollars is instead of alimony. If I cash it, he'll never pay me anything more."

"But you do have the cheque?"

"Yes."

"I'm sorry then. Next, please."

LATER THAT MORNING:

Miss Chisholm looks askance at the woman in the shabby sealskin coat. Dyed rabbit, she'll bet her bottom dollar. The woman is getting on Miss Chisholm's nerves. She's been sitting there for an hour, bolt upright, looking neither to right nor left. She refuses to give her name. "Just tell Mr. Brownlee an old friend is here," she said. Miss Chisholm did nothing of the kind. She's learned a thing or two in her years on this job. One of them is to protect the Premier from the loonies. Mr. Brownlee has the misfortune to represent the rural constituency of Ponoka, site of the provincial lunatic asylum, and hardly a week goes by without some former inmate, or some soon-to-be-inmate, shuffling in to affirm his sanity and complain about all the people who are having him followed.

Miss Chisholm can usually get rid of them with the gift of an official Province of Alberta wild rose lapel pin, but her supply has run out, and no more are being made, to save money, so today she is feeling rather at a loss. There seem to be so many more nut cases than there used to. They say it's hard times, driving people off their heads. Well, who can wonder? Just look at poor Mr. Brownlee, working day and night, weekends too, and things just going from bad to worse, Mrs. Brownlee at death's door too, the poor man, such patience, a true Christian martyr and no thanks for it either. Everybody in the province seems to have an opinion about what's wrong with Alberta, and they all expect Mr. Brownlee to do exactly what they tell him, spend more, spend less, take over the land, give the land away, print money, abolish money, money, money, money, that's all people talk about any more. The less people have, the more they want. That's what Miss Whitton the social worker says, never had it so good, a lot of them, and she should know, her doing an unemployment study for the government.

Just look at all those horrid hoboes making the Premier's life miserable with their hunger marches, then when the police raid the Labour Temple, what do they find? Why, they find these poor starving souls sitting down to roast turkey, with the trimmings! Doesn't that just show you! If the bums don't like it here, they can always go back East where they came from, good riddance too. Farmers are just as bad, sending their money to that Prophetic Bible man in Calgary, what'shisname, the fat slug with the blubbery lips and googly eyes. He's on the radio every Sunday, preaching the end of the world and asking for money, money, money. The farmers, the fools, send in their dollar bills then write to Mr. Brownlee demanding another dollar in Relief! The gall! Can you imagine? A racket, that's all it is, scaring people half out of their wits with four-headed horses like that old lady who preaches in the market square downtown. Armageddon my eye! Throw the prophets in jail, if you ask...."

Miss Chisholm is pounding so apocalyptically on her typewriter that she jumps half out of her skin when the phone rings. It's Ida in Public Works.

"There's a looney on the loose," Ida says. "She's trying to blackmail the Minister. She's already been causing trouble at the Relief Office. The story's all over town. Listen if you...."

Miss Chisholm quickly puts the receiver down. Mr. Brownlee has come out of his inner office. Miss Chisholm jumps up to warn him, but it's too late.

"Cora?" he says, taking the strange woman's hand. "What on earth are you doing here?"

After they've gone inside, Miss Chisholm has difficulty concentrating. Her confidence is shaken. She looks out the window. It's so dark the street lights are on. The cold has everyone spooked. Only last week, Betty, in Public Works, jumped from the third floor railing, underneath the dome. Everyone was watching. It was coffee break. It was the third suicide in the building in the past year. It's all been hushed up. Miss Chisholm thinks she would prefer the river, herself, most people do, even the Mayor. It's amazing, all the important people killing themselves. You half expect to see the funerals on the society page, the latest craze.

"Everybody's doing it," Miss Chisholm says absently to herself. She hums happily as she does a little soft-shoe back to her desk.

"It must be Mrs. Mattern, now?" John Brownlee speaks carefully, hiding his fear.

"No, I ... he changed his mind."

"Oh. I'm sorry to hear that."

"I am on my own now. I can't even see my children, you know. Oren says I will corrupt them. He says he will have me arrested for vagrancy if

I 'pester' him. I am wicked, you know."

"You left him, Cora. It was your idea."

"It was his idea, Oren's idea. We were both...guilty. He said if I divorced him, it would ruin his political career. So I agreed to take the rap, you know, provide the evidence, to protect his 'reputation.' What a joke! The four of us had pretty much been living together for years."

"Four?"

"Yes, the Matterns, Roy and Helen, and Oren and me. We met, we liked each other, went to parties together, bridge, Jasper, you know, one thing led to another. They were younger, very attractive, sophisticated. You know how Oren likes women, and Roy, well, I thought Roy was the most wonderful man I'd ever met. Once you start this sort of thing...."

"I thought the rumours...."

"Rumours!" Cora's laugh is loud and hard. John Brownlee remembers how much he dislikes her. He's always avoided the McPhersons. They represented the vulgar, popular side of politics that he loathes. He fumbles in his pocket for a cigarette.

"The rumours were only half of it!" Cora laughs. "You know, I think that's what Oren liked the most, the game. What would his pious constituents think if they could see all four of us in bed...."

"Why have you come here, Cora?"

"I've shocked you, haven't I? I'm sorry. I should have realized...."

"What do you want."

"Well, I thought, John, I thought you might...you might...help me."

"How much do you want?"

"Want? Oh, it's not that. It depends on Oren, you see. It's really up to him. I thought you might speak...."

"Cora, how much *do you want*?"

"Money? Do you mean money? Well, I really only want what Oren owes me...."

"You, Cora? What Oren owes *you*?"

"Why...."

"Shouldn't you give some thought, Cora, to what you owe *him*?"

Cora sits very still. She opens her mouth to speak but says nothing. She picks up her purse and pulls her coat around her. She stands up very straight. She sways slightly as she walks to the door. John Brownlee shuts it sharply behind her.

Vivian looks up, startled. A spooky-looking woman is peering in the office door. The woman hesitates, as if she's looking for someone. Vivian is about to get up and ask her what she wants when the woman disappears down the hallway.

"That was Cora," Myrna hisses from the next desk. "She got dumped by her boyfriend and now she wants old Oreo back. Fat chance, eh? Just goes to show you, gotta get that ring on the finger before you put out."

Myrna waggles her ring finger with the so-called diamond from People's Credit Jewellers on it. Myrna's boyfriend has pimples. He used to be a garage mechanic, but now that everybody's going back to horses he works in a stable. Big deal. All Myrna does is brag about nothing.

"So, when are you gettin' your ring?" Myrna says.

"None of your beeswax." Vivian turns her back and scowls at her typewriter.

"Sorrreeee."

Vivian fights back tears. She cries a lot these days. What's the matter with her? Is she pregnant? She's taken the awful pills John gives her every month, but so far this month nothing's happened. Well, if she is pregnant, he'll have to marry her. Or she'll jump over the railing like Betty in Public Works. Poor Betty. She told *everyone* what she did with the Minister. At least John didn't ask her to do anything awful like that. She should be thankful.

Vivian has tried to tell John about Wolf. She can't. The words won't come out. She hasn't told Wolf about Mr. Brownlee, either, although they met, by accident, at the station when Vivian was coming back from Edson after Christmas. They both turned up to meet her. She hadn't expected either, and it was pretty embarrassing. Mr. Brownlee refused to shake Wolf's hand. He just turned on his heel and walked away. Wolf was mortified. He has such beautiful manners. He pestered Vivian about it for weeks. It drove her nearly crazy.

Wolf is difficult that way. He gets a bee in his bonnet about something and goes on and on about it. Does she have other boyfriends? How many? Who? How often does she see them? What do they do together? Has she ever let a man undress her? Make love to her? At first Vivian was flattered but Wolf's possessiveness is beginning to wear on her nerves. The Germans are so *moral*. Wolf insists that his wife must be a "wirgin." It makes her laugh, like the way he says "Wiwian." Wolf is very charming. The trouble is, he won't keep his hands off her. He's always trying to unbutton her dress, touch her thighs, so she has to fight him off all the time. Vivian knows that if she gives in she'll never see him again. She's lost a lot of weight. She's too nervous to eat. It feels like there's a big, cold lump where her stomach's supposed to be. Vivian quite likes herself skinny. It makes her eyes look larger, but Wolf complains that her breasts are too small, and her mother says she'll get TB. "Dad and I don't approve of you associating with foreigners," her mother said. "You never know what's wrong with them." Her dad has been impossible since he got laid off, not really laid off, made redundant, whatever that means, but it seems to mean the same thing. Her dad is very bitter towards Mr. Bennett, the Prime Minister, and he blames Mr. Brownlee for sucking up to Bennett. "Brownlee looks like a banker," her dad says. That's about the worst thing her dad can say about anybody. It's funny, because Mr. Brownlee hates banks. And the banks hate him. Just about everybody seems to hate John these days. Sometimes Vivian thinks she's the only friend he has in the whole wide world.

Vivian blows her nose and looks at the clock. Five minutes to coffee break, oops, *tea* break. *Yech.* She shouldn't gripe. Coffee costs so much these days it might as well be . . . .

"Myrna, have you ever had champagne?"

"Me? You kiddin'?"

"I have."

"Yeah? What'dya do, pass out?"

"I don't remember."

They are trying to stifle their giggles when Miss Chisholm appears in front of Vivian's desk.

"The Premier would like to see you for a few moments, at your break, Miss Macmillan."

"Heyyy," says Myrna, sticking her tongue in her cheek. "You two are getting pretty thick, eh?" Myrna winks and rubs her index fingers together like an Indian making fire.

"It's just something he wants me to do, for Mrs. Brownlee," says Vivian, trying to look *blasé*.

"Sure, I'll bet!"

Miss Chisholm does not approve of Miss Macmillan's sweater. It is much too tight. However it is old, and darned at the elbows, and Miss Macmillan doesn't have much to speak of up front. One can't be too critical in times like these. One can't be too picky, either, about the people the Premier chooses to see, or ask too many questions, but Miss Chisholm can't help asking herself why the Premier locks his door after Miss Macmillan goes in. When Miss Macmillan comes out, looking a little flushed, Miss Chisholm notices that her skirt is hitched up at the back.

"Miss Macmillan!" she calls out after her, "your slip is showing!"

LATER THAT NIGHT:

"HELLO *CANADA*! AND HOCKEY FANS IN NEW*FOUND*LAND AND THE YEWNITED STATES! WELCOME TO *HOCKEY NIGHT IN CANADA*, COMING TO YOU DIRECT FROM *MAAAYPUUULLIEEEEF* GARDENS IN...."

"Who the hell is it?" Lily shouts, furious at the insistent banging on the darkroom door.

"It's Kate."

"Just a sec. The game's just starting."

"There's a woman in the washroom."

"Kate, there's always a woman in the washroom. Look, the game's just...."

"But I think she's dead!"

"Oh, good God. Why do people have to die at the *Bulletin?* What is this place, an elephants' graveyard?"

"Should I call the police?"

Lily turns off the radio.

"Let's go see. It's only the Red Wings."

The woman is curled up in a corner of the washroom floor. She is still warm. When Lily tries to lift her, she shudders and pulls her fur coat tighter around her. They splash her face with cold water. She opens her eyes and sits up, leaning heavily against the wall.

"I'm so sorry," she says, trying to smile. "It's just that...I haven't eaten much today. I'll be all right."

Lily scrounges a sandwich and half a thermos of coffee/rum (whew) from the sports editor. He's too absorbed in the game AND IT'S CLANCY IN OVER THE BLUE LINE O! A TERRIFIC SHOT! HE *SCORES!* to pay much attention. When she gets back, Kate has the woman settled on the sofa in Society. Kate bends over her with the anxious attentiveness of a reporter sniffing a story. The woman certainly smells. But just about everyone does, these days.

"She says she hasn't eaten in two days," Kate whispers. "She was evicted from her room this morning. Couldn't pay the rent. She says Relief turned her down. Her husband 'fixed' it, to make her go away. She says I should call Mr. McPherson, the Minister of Public Works, to get the 'real' story. Mr. McPherson 'fixed' their divorce too, she says, to get rid of her, and now he's got the police after her. Lily, it sounds absolutely incredible. I don't know, she could be a phoney. People will do *anything*...."

"Let's check the morgue."

The paper's only photo of Cora McPherson is an old one, about 1925, but the pale, heart-shaped face and sad eyes are unmistakable. She looks like Lillian Gish, in deep trouble.

Kate's eyes are shining. "Oh, boy!" she says. "Here we go!"

We took Cora to Nellie's. In a flash, Nellie had Cora ladled full of broth, popped into the tub, and tucked into bed.

"I never did like that man, McPherson," Nellie said, setting her jaw.

Nellie McClung is my best friend in Edmonton. No, it's the other way around. When Nellie decides that you are her friend, you don't say no. I'm a little frightened of Nellie. Everyone is. Nellie is famous. She's a famous writer, a famous suffragette, a famous person. Nellie is also fierce, the way only the Irish, and the Indians, can be fierce. She wears reputations dangling from her belt, like scalps. Her victims deserve their fates. They're all Conservatives, or crooks, wife-beaters, assholes. Nellie has an unerring aim for an asshole. It's just that you never quite know who will be next. Nellie is a good Liberal, but she bears a terrific grudge against Willie, for passing her over for the Senate in favour of *that* Mrs. Wilson, and another terrific grudge against the United Farmers for winning the election in 1921, the year Nellie ran as a Liberal, expecting to be the first woman cabinet minister in the British Empire. She found herself instead on the farthest row of Opposition backbenches, and she was beaten by the UFA in the next election.

Nellie's trouble is Temperance. For all Nellie's efforts, and Nellie is a Napoleon of political strategy, Temperance is as popular in Canada as bubonic plague. She won't budge. Temperance has turned her into something of a crank. She keeps asking me why I work at "that filthy newspaper." Nellie sees Canada as a large house, with many rooms, and the purpose of politics is to keep there rooms well-aired and dusted, the floors scrubbed, the walls washed, the larder full, with plenty of nourishing food on the table, the house plants watered, the family warmly dressed and well-mannered, and no booze in the basement. Since women are obviously superior to men at these tasks, why shouldn't we run the country? An admirable ambition, except Nellie never thinks about where the money will come from to support this household, or who will provide it. Somewhere in Nellie's political universe, a Husband brings home the bacon. God help him if he drinks, or gambles, or cheats on his wife.

"Perhaps we should call McPherson," I said. "He may have an explanation."

"He may have a cock-and-bull story," Nellie snapped.

"But what if Cora's story isn't true?" said Kate.

"True? Of course it's true! Who could make up a story like that?"

Cora's story was also libellous.

"I can't print *that*!" Ernie said when he saw it. "So she says they cooked up a deal. Okay, where's the proof? She's got to put her money where her mouth is. Hire a lawyer. I know just the guy. Good Grit. Hates Brownlee's guts. Get Cora to take the bugger to court, then we'll have a story. Woooeeee!"

TWO DAYS LATER:

"I understand Cora is back, Oren."

"Yeah. She been to see you?"

"Yes."

"Well, you don't pay Cora no mind, John. She ain't well, you know. Change of life. Makes 'em funny in the head. Don't give her no dough. She's rollin' in it. Gave her a thousand bucks a while back. Once she sees the situation, she'll take off."

"I hear Cora is staying with Mrs. McClung."

"Yeah? Well, they deserve each other."

"Mrs. McClung, as you know, is a Liberal."

"She's a cunt."

"Let me ask you something, Oren. Have you ever heard of Sir Rodmund Roblin? He was premier of Manitoba, at one time."

"Nope, can't say I have. Before my time, I guess."

"During the last war, Sir Rodmund opposed the vote for women. Mrs. McClung, as you know, favoured it. One evening Mrs. McClung dressed up as Sir Rodmund Roblin and mimicked him before a crowd of two thousand people in Winnipeg's Walker Theatre. The resemblance, I am told, was uncanny. Mrs. McClung brought the house down. Overnight, Sir Rodmund Roblin became a household joke."

"Yeah, well Cora ain't . . . ."

"Shortly after, Sir Rodmund was implicated in a serious scandal involving graft. The department responsible was Public Works. His government was defeated, and Sir Rodmund was forced to retire from politics . . . ."

"Lookit here, Mr. Brownlee, let me handle this, eh? It's personal. Cora ain't gonna get up on no stage, I can tell you. Cora's a lady. She ain't gonna tell how she and Roy Mattern got it off in the music room with Helen and me not ten feet away! Damn right I threw her out!"

"I think you should see her."

"Not a hope! Jeez, she'll bleed me dry. She's Mattern's problem, the bugger. She gives me any trouble, I'll prosecute."

"That, Oren, is precisely what I wish to avoid."

MEANWHILE, ON JASPER AVENUE,
IN THE OFFICE OF NEIL D. MACLEAN, K.C.:

"No, Mr. MacLean, I did not have a lawyer for the divorce. Oren said it wasn't necessary."

"Why not, Mrs. McPherson?"

"Oren said he would arrange everything. I . . . Roy and I would provide the, the evidence, and Oren would look after the rest of it. It seemed perfectly straightforward."

"There was no argument over the children?"

"Not really, no. We agreed that the older ones would be better off where they were. I would have liked to take Kenny, the youngest, but Oren said it would be a bad influence, me living in sin."

"But he was living 'in sin' with Helen Mattern, was he not?"

"Yes, but no one else knew. He didn't take the blame, you see."

"But he didn't forbid you to see your children?"

"Oh, no! I simply assumed . . . it was all very friendly."

"You simply agreed to switch partners."

"Yes."

"Mrs. McPherson, have you ever heard about collusion?"

"No."

"When you went to court, didn't you swear...."

"Court? I was never in court."

"But you must have been. Divorce actions are always heard in open court. It's the law."

"No, I was in Winnipeg. I believe Oren arranged it with the judge, to be heard in private. Mr. Lymburn, the Attorney-General, set it up, I think. He was Oren's lawyer. They wanted to keep it quiet."

"But you did receive your decree?"

"Oh, yes."

"And Mr. McPherson agreed to pay you $30 a month until you remarried."

"Yes. He assumed that Roy and I would marry immediately."

"But you didn't."

"No. Roy...married someone else. A younger woman."

"Roy Mattern is a handsome man, isn't he, attractive to women?"

"Oh, yes! I must admit, I fell pretty hard."

"He paid a lot of attention to you."

"He swept me off my feet. I thought he was in love with me. I felt so lucky."

"Roy had quite a few women on the string, didn't he?"

"Oh, *everyone* had a crush on Roy. He has such beautiful manners."

"He was a sort of a gigolo."

"Oh, well, *now* I can see how he...."

"He didn't care much for his wife?"

"They had disagreements."

"He didn't mind, about his wife and your husband?"

"He didn't seem to. But we were so crazy about...well, he *seemed* to be wildly in love...."

"Roy would just as soon get rid of Helen."

"Yes, I suppose. That's what happened, wasn't it?"

"You might say he deliberately seduced you."

"It didn't seem...but looking back...."

"Roy Mattern deliberately alienated your affections from your husband and destroyed your marriage."

"Now that you put it that way...."

"You became upset and confused."

"I was very emotional, yes."

"You didn't really want to leave your husband."

"Oh, I wouldn't have, had I known then...."

"You were pushed into it, weren't you."

"Well, they all seemed decided. I didn't have much choice."

"It was a kind of conspiracy."

"But the Matterns were *friends*...."

"Once Roy got his divorce, he lost interest in you."

"Yes. We went to Winnipeg together. Then he seemed to be away a lot. After a while, I heard that he was seeing another woman. I took it pretty hard, I'm afraid. There wasn't anywhere I could turn. You know, Mr. MacLean, you have certainly opened my eyes. I was used, wasn't I? *They* all have what they want, and I have nothing."

"You were prepared to go to court to obtain a divorce, Mrs. McPherson. Are you prepared to go to court to have it revoked?"

"But that's not possible! Oren's married again...."

"I'm sure you don't want to ruin your former husband's life, Mrs. McPherson. I think you'd settle for fair and reasonable compensation?"

"I want my trunk, my piano, Kenny, and...."

"It will be very unpleasant, I must warn you. You will have to tell everything, Mrs. McPherson. There will be some very intimate questions."

"I don't mind. For a long time, Mr. MacLean, I felt that I deserved all the punishment I got. I don't feel that way now. I've hit bottom. What have I possibly got to lose?"

"Oh, boy! We'll bring down the government!" cried Nellie McClung. She gave Lily a big hug. "Isn't this wonderful? I haven't had such fun since the war!"

On March 16, 1933, Cora McPherson files a petition in court asking to have her divorce revoked. That same morning, in the Alberta legislature, the leader of the Liberal Party, William Howson, brings a charge of graft in the awarding of gravel contracts against the minister responsible, the Hon. O.L. McPherson. As Mr. Howson is speaking, copies of the infamous Toronto scandal sheet, *Hush*, appear in every public washroom in Edmonton. Each copy of *Hush* is open to the page containing a hot tip that the Hon. O.L. McPherson is a bigamist. By noon, Edmonton newsstands are sold out of *Hush* and the city is stunned. Hardly anyone knew Mr. McPherson was supposed to be divorced.

On March 18, Mr. McPherson brings a libel suit against *Hush*, its distributors and all the newsstand vendors. Everyone now knows that Mr. McPherson has something to hide. The McPherson scandal creates such profound shock that when the Reichstag burns down in Berlin, it only makes page seven, and when Hitler becomes Dictator of Germany on March 23, nobody complains except Jack Coolican.

"Look at this!" he shouts at Lily, waving the newspaper. "Hitler says he wants the death penalty for all speculators! That's me, eh? Speculators, he says, are worse than the Jews! *Me*, I'm worse than the *Jews!* Can you believe it? He wants to kill me, the bugger. And I thought Ribbentrop was my friend!"

"That's Ribbentrop for you."

"Shit, politicians are all the same. A guy can't make a decent living any more. What's everybody got against money?"

"They don't have any."

"Well, I do. I can buy and sell this pisspot province."

"Why don't you?"

"It's not worth a plugged nickel."

"The mountains are nice."

"Yeah, scenery sells."

"You could make it into a sort of ranch, you know, a resort for speculators, and Jews of course, Princes of Wales, photographers, prophets, airline pilots, ex-wives, people who don't fit in...."

"Raise our own beef...".

"...a Promisory Land...Mum might like that."

"God's Country, Inc. J.R. Coolican, Esq., Proprietor. No assholes admitted."

"Alberta is full of assholes."

"Yeah, you're right. Okay, I've got it. We'll trade 'em, eh? Assholes for Jews. Hell, we'll be rich, and the Reich'll be kaput in six months. Such turds, the Krauts. Who the hell won the war, anyway?"

"I think we're only in the second reel."

"Well, they gotta lose in the end. No guy in a black hat ever had a chance."

The Hon. O.L. McPherson was supposed to resign. He didn't. The Hon. O.L. McPherson was supposed to settle out of court. He didn't. Cora was supposed to chicken out, but on May 3, Cora turned up at the courthouse right on time. She looked frail ("Why, she's just a wisp of a thing!") but composed. In the witness box, Cora sat very straight and answered every question in a clear, strong voice. ("She looks perfectly normal, doesn't she?")

The lineup for seats in the courtroom began at noon the day before. People brought air mattresses and sandwiches and slept on the courthouse steps. Every seat in the court was taken two hours before the case opened, but a large crowd remained camped on the steps and on the lawn beneath the windows. As the case progressed, the heat in the courtroom became so intense the judge ordered the windows opened, and the mob on the lawn was entertained by the shrieks and gasps of the spectators in the gallery. Inside, a woman fainted, and an ambulance was called, but she came to and refused to give up her seat.

The newspaper reporters handed their shorthand notes to copy boys page by page as they were finished, and the copy boys ran the pages to the *Bulletin* and *Journal*. By the time the court recessed for lunch, cries of EXTRA! EXTRA! were heard on the streets of Edmonton. Popcorn and ice-cream vendors gathered in front of the courthouse, and refreshments were passed through the windows to those still clinging to their seats inside. In front of the *Bulletin*, the best tidbits were chalked up on a board, like baseball scores: THREE IN A BED ON CAMPAIGN TRAIL: COZY THREESOME SHARE MINISTER'S COMPARTMENT. HUBBY'S PYJAMA PARAMOUR DEMANDS DIVORCE. WIFE DISTRAUGHT. ADMITS INFATUATION WITH OTHER MAN. FORCED TO SIGN AWAY HOME, CHILDREN.

Cora's testimony lasted three days. At the end of the first day, Cora left quietly by the back door, while the Hon. O.L. McPherson and his present wife, the former paramour, smiled and waved on the front steps. At the end of the second day, Hubby and his Pyjama Paramour were hissed as they left the courthouse. The third day, they left secretly by the back door, and Cora was escorted down the front steps by an honour guard of the unemployed, to the sympathetic applause of the patient housewives who had waited outside every day. The news that sex could possibly involve more than two people at once had so shaken Edmonton that, by comparison, Cora's little fling with Roy seemed perfectly staid. ("Who can blame her, married to a man like that McPherson?")

"Do you think she's telling the truth?" I asked Esselwein, who was guarding the back door.

"Does it matter?" he said.

Willie must be terrified. Just the word "divorce" makes him shake. No wonder he keeps losing his luggage. He seems to think that the luggage represents me. Isn't that what Freud says, that women are valises? Screw you, Siggy.

The next day, the judge dismissed the case for lack of evidence.

Nellie announced her intention to take Cora's case to the Privy Council, if necessary. (The Privy Council makes me think of a ten-holer, all these guys in wigs and gowns, sitting in a row, solemnly shitting.) At the *Bulletin*, we organized a public subscription to pay Cora's legal fees. Hundreds of dollars in dimes and quarters began to pour in. Cora was entertained to tea by respectable married women who, in other circumstances, refused to have divorced persons under their roofs. Important people, who had never paid any attention to Cora as Oren's wife, now asked her to speak to meetings about "A Married Woman's Legal Rights." ("It's a short speech," Nellie said. "She has none.") Cora's face became so familiar that strangers stopped her on the street to wish her luck, saying they hoped the old s.o.b. would get *his* at the next election. Cora said she hoped so too. The Liberals invited Cora to be a candidate.

"I believe a woman's place is in the home." Cora said.

"Some women define themselves through sex," Esselwein says, "unlike you."

"Me! You used to say I was too *bourgeois* . . . ."

"Shhh."

Esselwein twiddles the knob. The static slowly solidifies into a screech.

Lily leans closer, listening.

"What's he saying?"

"The usual. The Jews. *Die Juden.* Listen for it."

"It sounds so ugly. How can he scream like that for hours?"

"He's an animal... wait a minute, what's that?"

A new voice is superimposing itself on *Führer*'s broadcast from Berlin. The voice is faint at first, barely audible, cutting in, interrupting, causing static. The *Führer* fades. The new voice is sweet, symphonic. It is speaking English:

"GO TO NOW, YE RICH MEN, WEEP AND *HOWL*

FOR THE MISERIES THAT *SHALL* COME UPON *YOU*.

YOUR RICHES *ARE* CORRUPTED,

AND YOUR GARMENTS ARE *MOTH-EATEN* ...."

"Oh, God," says Lily, jumping up. "It's Mum!"

33

The microphone is like an old friend, although it's not as nice as the round one with the halo she had in Kirkland Lake. This microphone is square and severe, like Edmonton, and like McDougall Church where Christina Coolican has been preaching, and living, since last winter.

She had been reluctant to enter the church. Can the Lord be put in a box? Her tent in the market square was perfectly cosy, but so many of the People had no tents, no shelter at all, and the Bible said nothing about fifty below, so one day several hundred of the People simply walked into McDougall Church and sat down. There they stayed. Every pew was filled. The chairman of the board of stewards came and yelled at them to Get Out! Get Out! but they rose as one and sang *Jerusalem* so beautifully that the pastor burst into prayer and said they could stay, no smoking, no swearing, no drinking, no cards.

A lovely big kitchen was discovered in the basement, and once the Ladies' Aid got into the swing of things, and the Red Cross came up with old army blankets, the little ark became quite comfortable. Every morning, after clean-up, the drinkers, smokers, swearers and card players wander off into the streets, and those remaining devote themselves to the history and geography of the Holy Land. It was a small group at first, but everyday it grows as the word spreads that Tom Mix is no patch on King David, and a Bible story doesn't cost a quarter. The church produced a map of the Holy Land, and some wonderful coloured pictures of Babylon, and Jerusalem, and all the Hebrew kings in their handsome curly beards. The pastor became alarmed when beards sprouted everywhere among the People, but he calmed down once he understood the saving in hot water and razor blades.

Brown paper from the meat market has been taped to the wall, and now the progress of the Children of Israel in their wars is plotted in coloured pins: white for the Children, red for the Philistines, black for the Egyptians, blue for the Gideonites, and so on. The soldiers among the People spend hours arguing the tactics of each campaign, and bring books from the library to show the weapons and armour of the time. A former sapper with the Royal Engineers explained that the walls of Jericho had obviously been undermined, and all that horn-blowing and marching around was just a feint, to distract the enemy's attention from all the digging and boring that was going on, and to keep him awake all night. A few of the drinkers put this theory to the test by marching around city hall for several hours. Sure enough, nothing happened, and they were driven away by police on motorcycles.

By pooling their Relief rations, in addition to the money won from the heathen by the card players and crap shooters, the People live very well. Among them is a music teacher. He is so small his legs barely reach the pedals of McDougall Church's organ, but he loves to play, and now the People awake in the morning to the mighty thunder of the organ's voice. The floors tremble as the People go about their chores, and the walls reverberate with the Lord's praise. Hallelujah!

A choir has been formed, and an orchestra — five harmonicas, a squeeze-box, two tin flutes, several spoons, three washtubs (when not in use) and four unemployed fiddles from the now defunct Edmonton Symphony Orchestra. Every evening, when the dishes are done, and the pews are filled, a joyful noise is made to the Lord. Some among the People are lifted out of their seats by the great swell of sound and come forward to testify.

"I am Joe. I'm from Red Deer. I AM. And I am unemployed. But I am a man, still, with a God-given soul, and I'm not beat yet."

Sometimes the singing can be heard outside, through the walls, and the whole church seems to shake with the organ's roar. When spring came, and the doors could be opened, more People would gather in the lobby or on the steps. A loudspeaker was installed outside, and the police kept watch to see that traffic wasn't blocked. When Christina Coolican preaches, and the Lord's voice is heard in the street, they say you can hear a pin drop all the way to Jasper Avenue.

Radio station CJCA is right across the street. One night, seeing the great crowd on the church steps, the station manager rushed over with a microphone and a cable and told Christina Coolican she was going to be a star.

"You're better'n Bible Bill on CFCN," the manager said, "And Bible Bill's the hottest thing on the air!"

"Does he have a chariot of fire?" Christina Coolican asked, alarmed. It was not time, yet.

"Him? Aberhart? You kiddin'? Christ — sorry, heck — the guy's a blimp!"

A blimp! Of course! A zeppelin! That's how it will be done! Blimps! The People will climb in and float away to the Promised Land. They will fly!

"And when is he coming, this blimp?"

"Aberhart? Oh, he'll be here before too long, I figure. He's got a heck of a following. He's got it all figured out, you know, the end of the world. Could happen any day, he says. That would be something, eh? KAABOOOOOOMMMMMMMM!"

BAAAARRRRROOOOOOOMMMMMMMMMMMMM

"Wow, that's some organ, eh? Great stuff. That's what the folks really go for, these days, music, you know, simple stuff, singalong. Not much else to do. Can't complain, keeps me working. We'll put you on right after the Ajax Hour, okay? Good audience. Great commercials. You heard 'em? 'Ajax, the foaming cleanser, foams the dirt . . . BUBBABUBBABUBBABOOOOMMMMMMMM.' "

"I like that. I haven't heard it before."

"No? You got a radio?"

"I am a radio." I AM.

"Yeah, I guess you are. Okay, let's give 'em hell."

"I thought I'd begin with Judges, 16:4. Do you know it? 'And it came to pass, afterward, that he loved a woman in the valley of Sorek, whose name *was* . . . .' "

MEANWHILE, THE BEAST MEETS HIS BACKBENCHERS:

Backbenchers:	(all at once, loudly, with much emotion): McPherson's gotta go He's killin' us dead Rats leavin' the sinkin' ship What is this place, a hoorhouse Orgies in the halls I got the Klan on my tail
Mr. Brownlee:	Gentlemen, the suit against Mr. McPherson has been dismissed. Mr. McPherson is not a criminal.

Backbenchers: Cora's goin' to the Privy Drag on for years Election's comin Shit'll hit the fan Bible-thumpers givin' us hell Three in a bed Whoever heard of that stuff You want a burnin' cross on your lawn

Mr. Brownlee: This province is governed by law, gentlemen, not by slander. I intend to uphold the law. Mr. McPherson has not offered his resignation, nor have I requested it. The matter is closed. A politician's private life is not a matter for public speculation.

A Backbencher: Oh, yeah? Tell that to my wife!

34

Things seem to be falling apart, don't they? Rosa Luxemburg was right, revolution does just happen. People can only take so much, then somebody stands up and says: Hey, guys, why are we sitting around like a bunch of bums? Let's take over! Then off they go to storm the Winter Palace, or occupy the post office, or whatever. Storming is hardly necessary, here. The government is collapsing all by itself, Edmonton is already occupied by an army of unemployed. A couple of thousand men could simply walk into the banks, the legislature and the radio stations, sit down, and that would be that. I doubt the police would give them much trouble. The police don't earn much more than the guys on Relief.

So, what's the matter with the Party? I can't believe it. The Communist platform is an exact copy of the new socialist manifesto put out by the CCF. Bread and roses. Whatever happened to armed insurrection, or good old violent overthrow? Not a peep. You can only organize so many Hunger Marches. People get tired of them, especially when they're not all that hungry. Most of the time the Reds seem to sit around on the street corners, tossing coins. I guess Stalin still thinks that capitalism is on the upswing. Maybe it is, in Russia. At least Stalin is rounding up all the *kulaks* and sending them to communal farms. Alberta is a province of *kulaks*, according to the Party. The farmers are all terrified. Who wants to be shot, or sent to Siberia? Besides, most of the farmers don't have a pot to pee in. When they explain that they're poor, the Party says okay, then, you're a peasant. The farmers find this very insulting. It makes it hard to win popular support, doesn't it?

I have tried to explain this problem in my reports to the Party. I have no idea if my analysis has made any impression, or if my reports are even read, or, if they are read, by whom. On the last Thursday of every month, I leave the typed pages in the bag of the Hoover for Maria, my Communist cleaning lady. There is never anything in the bag for me, and Maria speaks only Ukrainian. It's very frustrating. Can anyone else in G section have such good gossip?

The Party obviously wants Brownlee beaten, but who will replace him? The *kulaks*? Fascists? The army? Charlie Whitton says the Department of National Defence is going to build concentration camps for the unemployed this winter. They'll be built miles and miles away, in the bush, where the men can't cause trouble. Charlie thinks the unemployed are all deadbeats. "They're living on easy street," she says. "Most of them used to be unemployed *without* Relief." Charlie is trying to persuade Bennett to hire social workers to screen Relief cases. Good God, as if the busybodies weren't busy enough already!

You'd never know from the way Charlie talks that she used to be dirt poor. Her old man was unemployed most of the time. Maybe she thought he was a deadbeat too. It seems too bad to take it out on the country. Charlie's determined to whip us all into shape. She's death on drink, and unpasteurized milk, and all the other things we grew up with as kids. She wants to run in Renfrew South as a Conservative in the next election. I said I'd run against her, for the Liberals. Charlie got quite huffy. She's lost her sense of humour, now that she's a social worker.

The Doctor is in town, a bird of ill omen. He insisted I meet him at the Macdonald Hotel. It was urgent, he said. He showed me an envelope. In it were letters from Willie to the Doctor, written in the 'twenties when Willie was Prime Minister, before Beauharnois blew up.

"I have enough here to destroy Mr. King's political career, as he destroyed mine," the Doctor said. "I want these letters published in the press. Money is no object."

The first letter was dated August 10, 1922:

My dear Doctor,

I wish I could tell you how very much I enjoyed the weekend visit in your Adirondack Mountain home. I cannot begin to speak of your own many thoughtful kindnesses. I must, however, not fail to mention the travelling clock and golf shoes with which Mr. Lapointe and myself were presented.... With sincerest thanks for all your many, many kindnesses....

There were several more, some quite long, all written on Willie's heavy ivory notepaper in Willie's tiny blue scrawl. They were essentially the same:

November 20, 1927

My Dear Doctor — Your kindness and courtesies of the past few days have been so many and so great that I am at a loss to know how to begin to express the depth of my feeling. It was more than good of you to give the dinner in my honour . . . .

August 23, 1928

My Dear Doctor — You will be very much in my thoughts when I see Paris again. I shall always remember with delight our visit together there . . . .With kindest remembrances, believe me, as always, yours very sincerely. W.L. McK. King.

Dec. 30, 1928

My Dear Doctor — On this quiet Sunday afternoon, I have been giving myself the joy of looking at some of the gifts and greetings which have come to me at this Christmas season. I wish I could tell you the delight which your gift inspires. It is so exquisite, so generous, you have given its selection and engraving so much personal thought, time and attention, I am very proud indeed to be in possession of anything so beautiful and valuable, doubly so when it comes to me from friends as dear to me as you . . . .

June 1, 1930

My Dear Doctor — This is the first piece of gold plate I have ever possessed. It was characteristic of you to have thought of something so precious and so beautiful . . . with my affectionate good wishes to you all . . . .

I felt a little sick. It was like reading someone else's love letters. Their obsequiousness was obscene. The Doctor put them back in the envelope. When he spoke, his voice was shaking.

"These letters were written to me, over a period of eight years, by my most intimate friend, a man I trusted, confided in, advised. Mr. King and I spoke on the phone almost daily. Yet when, as a result of our friendship, I came under investigation by Parliament, my friend, my dear Mr. King, stood up in the House of Commons and *denied that he knew me.* Dr. McDougald? Ah, yes, I know him slightly. A 'friend to the party in 1921.'"

"Willie lied, of course."

"He lied to *Parliament.*"

"Why didn't you reveal the letters then? It would have ruined him."

The Doctor cracked his knuckles and stared at me.

"My dear young woman, to have revealed the extent of Mr. King's indebtedness to myself, and others, would have ruined *me*, and the Liberal Party."

The Doctor produced another letter from his breast pocket. It was dated April 29, 1930:

Dear Doctor — This is just a line again to thank you for your great kindness to Haydon and myself both at Bermuda and New York. Your generosity is a constant surprise as well as a delight, but was never more so than in connection with this latest expression of it. We were the ones who should have done the entertaining, and, indeed, such was the expectation when I wired from Ottawa. The trip was a very happy one . . . .

"So you did pay the Bermuda bill."

"He tried to deny it. He even denied that he had invited me."

"Why dredge all this up now? It's blood under the bridge."

"Mr. King is demanding my immediate resignation from the Senate. I have refused. I have been convicted of no crime. I have committed no crime. Mr. King is now saying that if I do not resign my seat, he will support a motion of censure to have me removed. I have decided that if I am forced to resign, I will force Mr. King to resign as leader of the Liberal Party."

I told the Doctor that the *Bulletin*, while a muckraking paper, was also a Liberal paper. He hasn't got a hope. I don't think he really wants to publish the letters. It's just an excuse to go around the country talking

to Willie's enemies in the Liberal Party and start a dump-King movement. Trouble is, the Liberal Party is so full of dimwits and dodos that
only Willie's hysteria keeps it going. Who's the heir apparent? The
Doctor? Massey? I hear that Bill Herridge has fallen out with Bennett.
Things *are* falling apart, aren't they?

THE NEXT DAY:

The Panther Woman has been chosen. Her picture came over the wire
today. Her name's Kathleen, and she's from Chicago. She's Irish, at
least. Vivian came in after supper to have a look.

"I wouldn't have won anyway," she said. "She has black hair. Pan-
thers are black. I looked it up in the encyclopedia."

Vivian can be perfectly exasperating at times. Was I like that at her
age? Probably. God knows, we both have terrible taste in men.

"Where's Mozart?"

"Up north. Great Bear."

"Have you two split up?"

"Not exactly. It's just that . . . Mr. Brownlee doesn't want me to see
him."

"What's Mr. Brownlee got to do with it? You're twenty-one, aren't
you?"

"Not 'til next week."

I was tempted to ask Vivian about Brownlee straight out, but there is
something about Vivian's manner that doesn't invite questions, certainly not embarrassing questions. I don't like to be rude. What if I'm
wrong? And why would she tell the truth? Confidences are always used
against you. I like Vivian. I don't want to wreck her life.

"Here, why don't you pick the pictures for Saturday's photo page?
Just go through the stack and pick who you like. Anybody but Joan
Crawford."

"Is she a Jew too?"

"Look, Vivian, the editor thinks Joan Crawford is ugly. Isn't that
enough?"

Vivian sifted abstractedly through the photos: Barbara Hutton, Roosevelt, a giant watermelon, Lindbergh, Barbara Hutton, Mussolini,
Gary Cooper, Princess Elizabeth, Barbara Hutton. She divided them
into a large and a small pile. At exactly nine p.m. she put down the piles
and said, "I have to go now."

I watched her go out through the revolving door. She lingered on the sidewalk for a moment, looking around. She didn't seem in a terrific hurry. Surely Vivian couldn't be a hooker? It didn't seem possible, yet the streets are full of farm girls with nothing but their sad little selves to sell. The thought made me smile. It was about this time of night, nearly twenty years ago, that I met Willie on a bridge, in Ottawa. He tried to pick me up. Too bad. If he'd succeeded, things would probably have turned out much better.

Vivian stood on the corner for awhile, watching the traffic. Then she glanced over her shoulder and walked quickly away towards 100th Street. I was about to turn away, when I saw a shadow in a slouch hat separate itself from the newsstand across the street. The shadow had a rolled newspaper under its arm, and it followed Vivian with the short, determined steps of a man who knows exactly where he's going.

The Studebaker is idling at the corner of 106th Street and 99 Avenue. When the girl opens the door, the shadow in the slouch-hat can see Brownlee's face in the light from the dash. He watches the girl get in. The Studebaker heads north on 106th Street, then turns west on Jasper Avenue. Good, same route as last time. The shadow crosses his fingers.

Several miles to the west, beside a deserted country road on the outskirts of town, a man in hip-waders hunkers down in a water-filled ditch, listening to the frogs sing.

"You're late, Viv."

"I was busy."

"Doing what?"

"Just busy."

John frowns. The car picks up speed.

"I think I'd like to go home, please."

"What's wrong with you?"

"I don't think we should see each other any more, John."

"We'll have to see each other less often, for awhile, until things settle down...."

"Ottawa's off, isn't it?"

"I can't leave here. Without me, everything will fall apart."

"*What about me?*" Vivian screams. "Maybe *I'm* falling apart! Don't you care about that? Maybe I'm sick of these stupid drives, and sneaking around, and lying, and standing on street corners at night like a, a *prostitute*, and sleeping in your stupid servant's bed, and sitting around waiting until you *might* have a spare moment or two. Vivian come here, Vivian go there, Vivian make dinner, Vivian be nice, do this for Mrs. Brownlee. Well, I'm fed up. I'm nearly an *old maid.* I want to get married."

"We can't get married. Cora's fixed that, hasn't she?"

Vivian looks out the window into the darkness. The gravel pings against the running boards. The car is going very fast now. She has an impulse to open the door and jump out. She hangs on to the door handle very tight.

"I don't believe that," she says. "I think that's just an excuse. I think the truth is that you don't love me any more. I think the truth is that you *never* loved me. I think you've lied about *everything.*"

"Don't be stupid, Vivian."

"I'll marry somebody else."

"You can't."

"Why not?"

"I won't let you."

Vivian is frightened. The car is swaying from side to side in the ruts.

"Stop! Please!" she cries. "I want to go home!"

John brakes violently. The car lunges. Vivian is thrown against the dashboard. The Studebaker spins around in a hail of dirt and speeds back towards the city. Vivian still clutches the door handle very tight. Her forehead hurts where she hit it. She touches it gingerly. Only a bump.

"I'm sorry," she says. "I didn't mean . . . it's just, just that . . . I'm so *lonely.*"

They drive back without speaking. In the faint light from the speedometer, John's face is a green mask of fury. He stops in front of Vivian's rooming house.

"You needn't come in to work tomorrow."

"But . . . ."

"Since you're so busy in the evenings, Miss Macmillan, it's hardly worth the money, is it, typing?"

The door handle feels very cold in Vivian's hand. Her hand feels a long way away, disconnected, as if it belonged to someone else. She opens the door carefully and gets out. She slams the door behind her. I'll remember that sound for the rest of my life, she says to herself. She watches from the steps as the black Studebaker turns the corner. She watches until the red tail-lights vanish behind a fence.

The landlady, Mrs. McKay, hovers outside Vivian's room for the rest of the night, alarmed by her crying. You never know what the young people are up to these days. No good, usually. It's them moving pictures. Puts ideas in their heads. It won't do. Miss Macmillan seemed like a good girl too, but here she is, out to all hours, now bawling fit to wake the dead. It won't do to have a suicide in the house. Word gets out. Only this morning, a girl was found in a house two blocks over, hole in her chest you could put your fist in. Ugh. It's the death of a decent establishment. It just won't do. Too bad, but tomorrow Miss Macmillan will have to find another place to stay.

Not long after midnight, a man in hip-waders crawls out of a water-filled ditch beside a country road on the western outskirts of town.

"Damn Esselwein," he says. "He must have got the wrong road."

LATER THAT AFTERNOON:

Vivian arrived at the *Bulletin* just after four o'clock. She wore rouge and mascara and a lot of very red lipstick. Lily was startled.

"Do you have the day off?"

"I quit." Vivian shrugged and rummaged in her handbag for a cigarette. "I just couldn't stand it any more."

Lily didn't pay much attention. She was in no mood for Vivian's vicissitudes. Lily was ready to quit herself.

"No more Jews," Ernie the editor had said when Lily came into work. "People are upset."

"They're *supposed* to be."

"Not so upset they cancel ads. I don't want to be unemployed, do you?"

The Jews were Lily's triumph. Mrs. Freiman had sent her several snapshots smuggled out of Germany by a Jewish refugee. The pictures had been taken surreptitiously, because the stormtroopers all have their backs turned to the camera. The pictures show groups of Jews with shaven heads, wearing prison-looking rags and armbands with the Star of David. The Jews are on their hands and knees, washing the pavement, while soldiers prod them with their boots. The Jews are running down a city street, chased by a mob throwing stones. The Jews are being whipped and clubbed by police while a crowd looks on. The Jews are being herded into trucks at rifle-point. The Jews are thin, almost skeletal, and their expressionless faces are ghostly white. The pictures are the most horrifying Lily has ever seen.

She published six of them, over three days, placing them discreetly on the foreign affairs page. The *Bulletin* is very anti-Hitler (Lily always chooses the ugliest photo of the *Führer*) and runs a lot of stories about Germany. The photos, as far as Lily knew, were the first published in North America to *prove* that what the Jews *say* is going on *is true*. She was very proud of them. Public response was immediate and overwhelming. Either the photos were faked, and the *Bulletin* was printing Zionist propaganda, or they were obscene, and unfit for a family newspaper.

Blood, on the other hand, is not obscene. Edmontonians adore gore, and the more macabre the murder, the better they like it. Today they've got a beaut, an eighteen-year-old girl from the country spattered all over her boyfriend's bedroom wall. Even better, her boyfriend happens to be one of Edmonton's leading businessmen, a member of the Chamber of Commerce, and a married man. Lily's present job is to go through the police photographer's pictures and choose one that's suitably sickening, but not *too* sickening.

As Lily lays them out on the table, she's surprised to find Vivian hovering over her shoulder. Vivian hates blood.

"Do you think it's really true, that Mr. Kelly did it?" Vivian asks.

"Oh, sure. The cops found him with the gun in his hand, pissed to the eyeballs."

"But Mr. Kelly's an important person! I mean, I didn't think respectable people ... did that sort of thing."

"He's just an insurance salesman. I guess he got a little possessive."

"Do you really think she was his ... girlfriend?"

"Well, there she is, stark naked, sprawled on his bed. Kelly was naked too, when the cops got there, and screaming blue murder. I gather the girl told him she was going to marry somebody else. He shot her with his service revolver. I have one. Would you like to see it?"

Lily hasn't fired her old .45 in years, but it sure scares the hell out of drunks off the street who think they're going to party it up in the newsroom. No bums in the *Bulletin*, bam, bam.

"It's heavy, isn't it?" Vivian picks it up delicately.

"I was supposed to kill Germans with it during the war, to defend my chastity, such as it was. But I didn't meet any. Come to think of it . . . ."

"Is it loaded?"

"Sure. No point in a gun that isn't."

Vivian puts it down quickly. She looks for a long time at the photograph of the dead girl's bloody, shattered body.

"She's younger than I am," Vivian says.

Vivian's face looks very white under the garish make-up. Lily is struck by how thin she's become.

"I'd better go now," Vivian says. "I'm going to look for a new place. I can't stand that Mrs. McKay. She's a real snoop."

After dinner, Kate comes in with another picture of the murdered girl. It's a high school graduation photo, a pretty girl with wavy hair, a white dress, flowers, a garden.

"Can't run it," Ernie said. "She's a hooker. This is a family newspaper."

Lily left early. She went home and drank half a bottle of scotch, straight. Cursed Ernie. Passed out. Bad dreams. Phone ringing. Kate.

"Get here quick!" Kate said. "There's a girl asleep in Society with a gun in her lap!"

35

"I'm sorry," Vivian said. "I wasn't really going to use it. It was just in case...."

I retrieved Vivian's suitcase from behind the wastebasket, where she'd hidden it, and took her home. How could she possibly be so proud, not to ask for help? And how could she get into so much trouble?

"But Vivian, *why* did you get fired? What *happened?*"

She wouldn't tell me. She just broke into sobs.

"It's just that I'm *no good*," she cried. "Everybody *hates* me!"

I gave her a hot scotch-and-water and made up a bed for her in the studio. Vivian was still asleep the next afternoon when Mr. Brownlee phoned. Word certainly gets around.

"We haven't seen much of Miss Macmillan recently," he said. "I have been a little worried that she might have fallen into bad company."

Thanks a lot, buster.

"Please tell Miss Macmillan that her job is still open. I'm afraid there was a misunderstanding. Vivian is a very emotional girl."

"We women are, aren't we, Mr. Brownlee, especially when we're young and in love."

"I...I didn't know...did she say...who?"

"Oh, I thought you knew. Vivian said you...never mind. It doesn't matter. Things are still, how shall we say, up in the air. Thank you for calling, Mr. Brownlee. It's very kind."

On Sunday, Mr. and Mrs. Brownlee came to take Vivian home for dinner. Brownlee was very dour, disapproving. He wore a black suit. I half expected him to spread his great buzzard's wings and carry Vivian away in his talons. Mrs. Brownlee, on the other hand, was a robust, sunburned woman with a pleasant, toothy smile.

"I've just come from the Glenora Club," she said. "Do you golf, Mrs. King?"

"No, I don't . . . ."

"Splendid exercise. I'd be happy to put your name forward . . . ."

"Thank you, but I have very little time, I'm afraid. Perhaps Vivian would like to play . . . ."

Mrs. Brownlee looked over at Vivian and gave a high, incredulous laugh.

The three of them walked to the car together. Between them, Vivian looked very small and vulnerable.

When Mr. Brownlee brought her back at ten-thirty p.m., Vivian was happy and excited.

"The Brownlees have invited me to spend July with them, at the lake," she said. "Wow, I've never stayed at a real cottage before!"

"What about Wolf?"

"Oh, I think I should wait awhile."

God, was I ever such a goof? How did I ever survive?

Vivian goes back to work. Myrna and the other girls thought she'd left to have an abortion. Vivian can't be bothered thinking up a different story. What does it matter? It's just another rumour. That's the trouble with bad times, people have nothing to do but talk. Pretty soon you don't know what to believe. Everyone is saying the end of the world is coming. One girl in Agriculture says it's going to happen on August 25. She has it all figured out from the Bible.

Vivian has a hard time concentrating. Things that used to be familiar — her typewriter, the filing cabinets — seem strange and far away. Sometimes when people speak to her, she doesn't hear. Vivian can see the sun shining outside the window, but everything seems gray, and when she sits on the lawn at lunchtime, she feels cold.

I am in eclipse, she says to herself, but can't even smile at her own joke. She's being stupid again. She should feel happy. John still likes her, after all. She'd feel better if she could talk to Mama. Mama always said that women are born to suffer, and the only thing to do is to make the best of it.

On Friday afternoon, Vivian goes to see Mr. Smale, the civil service director, to arrange for her holiday in July. Mr. Smale looks puzzled and scratches his head.

"But Miss Macmillan, you've just had some time off."

"I was... sick."

"Yes, I see that you have used up all your sick leave. I can't possibly allow you more time, Miss Macmillan. I can't make exceptions."

"But I do have some holidays coming."

"Let me see. Yes, here we are, August 14th to 21st, inclusive."

"I'd like to change that to July, you see I've been invited..."

"Oh, you're much too late, Miss Macmillan! Everyone had made their vacation arrangements. Why, it's almost July now. Change must be requested months in advance. It's in the regulations."

LATER THAT NIGHT:

"John, I thought you were going to arrange...."

"If Smale says those are the rules, I don't see what can be done."

"But you *said* I could come...."

"Vivian, I can't meddle. It's unethical."

"But you *did*, I mean you got me the job...."

"As it happens, I won't be spending much time at the lake this year. I'll be travelling. I've been appointed to the Banking Commission."

"Well, I could go with you. I could be your niece. Mrs. King says a lot of politicians take their nieces with them on trips."

"Those girls aren't nieces, Vivian."

"I know."

Lily had never seen Vivian angry before.

"Do you know what *I* think?" Vivian shouted, stamping around the kitchen. "*I* think the Brownlees only invited me to the cottage because they knew I couldn't go!"

"It does seem suspicious."

"Well, I've *had* it with the Brownlees! Up to *here*. They can *have* their crummy lake!"

"It probably has leeches in it, anyway."

"Ooooo...."

"Slugs, toads, snails, frogs, worms...."

"Ooooooooo, *ick*!" Vivian shrieked, laughing. "You make it sound *disgusting*!"

Lily's feet felt ticklish. They must be down in the reeds now. They'll hit bottom soon.

36

We threw a big bash at the Mac for Vivian's twenty-first birthday. I felt we should, by now she was almost my daughter. Wolf flew in from Great Bear. It was a surprise. Vivian was thrilled. We hired the whole band, and danced on the patio under an opal sky, drunk on a springtime cocktail of lilacs and sweet clover. Vivian looked sensational in green silk. Wolf wore a dinner jacket as white as his teeth. His face was sunburned, his hair bleached platinum. Siegfried arriving on a swan. Do you suppose the Nazis could be right, about being superior?

We drank countless toasts, and Wolf made a speech. His English is much better. You can understand what's he's saying. He was very charming and gracious. He told "Wiwian" how "vonderful" she was, and presented her with a diamond ring. Then he kissed her, and we all clapped, then we all kissed each other and cried.

"You getting sentimental?" Jack said, handing me his handkerchief.

"I'm a sucker for love."

"Fat lot of good it's done you."

"Are they really going to Germany?"

"Don't know. All that *volkische* stuff, you know, you got to be related to Attila the Hun or zip, it's the *wurst* for you."

"Yech, Jack, for God's sake."

"Sorry. Esselwein's joke. Made you laugh, anyway."

The band struck up "Good Night, Ladies." A waiter drifted from table to table, snuffing candles. The sky faded from emerald to indigo. At the far end of the patio, leaning against the balustrade, two pale shadows gazed out over the river, one a glimmer of gold, the other a shimmer of silk, ephemeral as moths.

"Time to go," Jack said, slapping his neck. "Skeeters are out."

"Good night, ladies."

Good night.
Good night.
Good night.

ONE WEEK LATER:

"Good morning, Mrs. King?"

"Mmmumnph."

"This is Neil MacLean. I'm sorry to wake you. I know you work nights. However, I have a young lady in my office who says she knows you. Do you think you could come in? It's rather urgent."

"Mmmumnphokay."

Vivian was huddled in one of Neil McLean's enormous leather armchairs. Her eyes were red and puffy. Wolf was pacing the room, pounding the air with his fist. Neither appeared to have slept all night. Neil MacLean, K.C., was seated at his desk, holding a pen in trembling fingers. Hangover, or anticipation?

"From what you know of Miss Macmillan," he said to me, "would you say she is of good character?"

"Yes."

"Have you ever known her to lie, perhaps invent stories, exaggerate things?"

"I don't think so. Vivian strikes me as very down-to-earth. She is rather suggestible, but that's only because she's young, and anxious to please. There's a lot of nonsense going around these days, Mr. MacLean. Vivian doesn't make it up."

"Ha she shown signs of emotional instability? Obsession, fantasies?"

"She has her ups and downs. She has been upset and highstrung recently. I suspect there is good reason for it."

"Mrs. King, if Vivian Macmillan were to tell you that she is the mistress of the Premier of Alberta, and has been kept by him, for nearly three years, as a slave to his sexual appetites, would you believe her?"

Vivian sobbed. Tears were streaming down her cheeks.

"Yes, I would believe her."

"Please take a seat, Mrs. King. This may take some time."

What is to be done?

The engagement is off. Wolf is all swords and thunderbolts, Wotan

on the warpath. His righteousness is awesome. Vivian is *dreck*, dama-
ged goods, return to sender. Wolf wants to charge Brownlee with rape.
"But it wasn't rape," Vivian says. "I agreed." Neil MacLean wants to
charge Brownlee with anything, just to see the fur fly, but Vivian refuses.

"It's my fault," she says. "I shouldn't have let people think I was
something I wasn't. It was dishonest. Mr. Brownlee was right. He told
me that nobody else would want me."

Vivian has not told her parents.

"My dad is a lot like Wolf," she says, and shivers.

Come to think of it, Vivian may be the only girl in the world who
really needs a stormtrooper.

SIX DAYS LATER:

Wolf has gone. Jack says he turned up at the airfield one morning at
sunrise, hopped in his plane and took off. He hasn't shown up at Great
Bear, or anywhere else up north. Poor Vivian, trust her to get stuck with
a chickenshit stormtrooper. Wolf was probably landing in Berlin when
Esselwein arrived at my door, in uniform. He looks nice in red, it goes
with his beady black eyes.

"I see you have an attractive young boarder," he said.

"Lay off, she's a guest."

"Too bad about Mozart."

"Friend of yours? What do you play, Esselwein, the piccolo?"

"He didn't really want to go back to Germany."

"Oh, sure."

"It took some 'encouragement.'" Esselwein rubbed his thumb and
forefinger together. "One thing you can count on with the Fascists:
money. Funny, that's what *they* say about the Jews, isn't it?"

"I thought you guys would be happy to see Brownlee beaten up."

"On the contrary. The Commissioner, General MacBrien, has developed a warm personal regard for Mr. Brownlee. Mr. Brownlee, as
you know, has become a strong champion of law and order. He gives
the police a completely free hand. Mr. Brownlee is so highly regarded at
headquarters that there is talk of restructuring things in Ottawa, with
Brownlee at the head of a National Government."

"It's blackmail, isn't it? Blackmail seems to be the 'thing' these days."

"It's common sense, kiddo. Miss Macmillan has nothing to gain from going to court, and everything to lose. I can assure you, her loyalty and discretion will be amply rewarded."

"How much?"

"Five thousand dollars."

"That's peanuts, Esselwein. Stuff it."

Was I wrong? With five thousand, Vivian could move away, start a new life. Doing what? All she does is lie around all day, reading *True Story* and crying. Every time I close my eyes, I picture Vivian's dead body floating downriver on an ice floe, her hair streaming out behind her. Thank God it's July.

THREE DAYS LATER:

"You know, Lily, I've been wondering. Who do you think told Wolf about me?"

"I thought you did."

"No. I mean, I *did*, but he already knew. He brought it up."

"There've been rumours."

"But he was so *certain* there was someone else. It was as if . . . I was wondering if Mr. Brownlee might have told, himself."

"It's possible. Men tend to do those things."

"But it's so *cruel*."

"Magistrate Murphy says it happens all the time, and she should know. Respectable married man seduces young girl, keeps her until he's tired of her, then throws her out on the street and says she's a whore. Nobody will believe her story because she has a 'bad' character. Neat, eh? Mrs. Murphy sees these girls in court every day, up for prostitution. There's nothing she can do."

"But I thought it was only *me*."

"Vivian, it's been around forever. In my day, it was called 'white slavery.' Exotic, eh? Girls weren't supposed to ride on streetcars in case somebody stuck you with a pin and dragged you off to a life of sin."

"A pin?"

"A needle, you know, drugs. It gave streetcars a very bad reputation."

"And did it really happen?"

"Oh, sure. It happened to me once, in Ottawa. I was walking on a little footbridge at night, smoking a cigarette — cigarettes in those days were ranked down there with streetcars — and a man came up to me. He seemed nice enough, well-dressed, good manners. I thought at first he was a banker, or a clergyman, but he turned out to be a politician."

"Did he stick you with a *pin?*"

"An imaginary pin. An arrow of desire, Cupid's arrow, zing. It's all imaginary, isn't it, love, hate? Trouble is, some people can't tell the difference. I'm a pretty good hater, myself. Mind you, I'm Irish, and it's expected of us. A good hate can be tremendously satisfying."

Vivian thought about that for awhile. "Do you think Mr. Brownlee hates me?" she said at last.

"What do you think?"

When I came home from work at midnight, Vivian was packing her suitcase.

"I'm going home to Edson," she said. "There's a train at six a.m." I made us some bacon and eggs. Vivian downed a whole plateful, smothered in ketchup, erk, then she drank two Cokes and finished off a bag of Oreos. I guess she'll be okay.

Allan Macmillan is big and bald and thickset. He has a prize fighter's large, square, knobby head and two clenched fists the size of boxing gloves. Allan Macmillan has the expression of a bulldog with its teeth in somebody's leg. Allan Macmillan is an angry man, an aggrieved man, a man to gladden a criminal lawyer's heart. Neil MacLean, K.C., smiles and gingerly inserts his fragile fingers into Macmillan's right mitt.

"I can appreciate your feelings as a father, Mr. Macmillan," he says. "But as a lawyer, I must advise you that murder tends to be a self-destructive form of redress. However, I can suggest an alternative, if you'll permit me. Would you care to join me in a wee drop?"

"MUCHOBLIGED," roars Allan Macmillan, and bursts into tears.

On August 5, 1933, as John Brownlee is leaving a meeting of the Banking Commission in Ottawa, he is served with a writ. The writ states that "by false statements, wiles, flattery and expert love-making," he seduced eighteen-year-old Vivian Macmillan, and maintained her in a state of sexual servitude for two-and-one-half years. The charge is brought by Vivian's father, Allan Macmillan, who is claiming $10,000 in damages for loss of his daughter's services, and by Vivian herself, who claims nothing because, in Canadian law, her virginity and reputation are deemed of no value.

John Brownlee says the charge is false and motivated by political malice.

The following week, he and Mrs. Brownlee drive to Edson and knock on the front door of the Macmillan home. Mrs. Macmillan refuses to let them in. "I told them there was nothing to talk about," she said triumphantly. "If they wanted to see my husband, he was at the shop. They slunk away like a couple of beaten dogs."

All of Vivian's friends, boyfriends, fellow workers, relatives, teachers, doctors, and casual acquaintances are visited by a provincial government detective. The detective, Harry Boyce, carries a big wad of bills and wants to know what Miss Macmillan was really "up to," wink, wink, over the last three years. One night, Vivian finds Harry Boyce waiting in her room. He offers her $10,000 to drop the charge. "I'm not doing it for the money," Vivian says.

"She's doin' it for the dough," Harry Boyce reports to his superior, the Attorney-General.

"So is Cora McPherson," the Attorney-General says tartly.

Of course, once the news came out, everyone in Edmonton had known all along/guessed/figured something was up/smelled a rat. Everyone knew that John Brownlee was a queer bird/strange one/pervert/nut case/Communist.

"You see, I *was* telling the truth!" says Cora McPherson.

The wives of several cabinet ministers refuse to allow their husbands to go to Edmonton.

John Brownlee doesn't resign. He carries on as if nothing has happened.

Rumours run on the wind. Pornography is news. Edmonton enters an ecstasy of prurience. Opinion is divided:

Vivian is a hoor/good-time girl/gold-digger/martyr/innocent child/simple country girl.

Allan Macmillan has been put up to it by the Liberals/Conservatives/CCF/Moscow/Mussolini/Bible Bill Aberhart. He has been paid $10,000/$100,000/$1,000,000 by Moscow/Social Credit/Vincent Massey/Jack Coolican/Hitler.

Leon Trotsky is seen on the streets of Edmonton.

Vincent Massey is seen on the streets of Edmonton. ("*Edmonton?*" cried Vincent. "Where *is* Edmonton?")

Mrs. Brownlee is known to be dying/crazy/a shrew/filing for divorce.

The Liberals have promised Neil MacLean/Nellie McClung the Senate/Supreme Court/High Commissioner/knighthoods. "It's about time," say Neil MacLean/Nellie McClung.

John Brownlee will kill himself/Vivian/divorce/leave the country/ get a share of the money/go to the Senate.

The Russians/Germans/Socialists/Prophetic Bible Institute/banks/ Big Interests/Jack Coolican/Ottawa will take over Alberta.

The whole thing is a tempest in a teapot/a terrible scandal/a tragedy/a shame/crime/time to clean house/good lesson/plot/revolution/ beginning of the end/end of the world.

Half the UFA goes CCF. The other half goes Social Credit. J.R. "Rudy" Coolican goes Social Credit. "I'll be in charge of the credit part," he says, "since I'm the only guy in Alberta who knows how to make money."

Golddiggers of 1933 opens at the Capitol. It's a smash. Everyone is humming the hit tune, "We're in the money, we're in the money...."

A meteor falls on southern Alberta. The sky turns purple.

Grasshoppers eat the gardens.

The wheat dries up. It's not worth anything anyway.

John Brownlee charges Vivian with attempted extortion. He files a counter-suit for $10,000.

The *Bulletin*'s circulation soars.

Lily gets a raise. She gets a letter of commendation from Tim Buck.

The McDougall Church Revival Hour passes one hundred thousand listeners.

Kathleen, the Panther Woman, gets married and divorced.

Amos 'n Andy are discovered to be white.

The unemployed realize that unemployment isn't so bad after all. They have a lot of time to think, and talk, and read the papers, and listen to the radio. Lily's RCA shares go up in value dramatically.

Edmonton cheers up. It *is* good to be alive, as long as you're not John Brownlee. Everyone agrees on one thing: politically speaking, John Brownlee is a dead duck.

37

Macmillan vs. Brownlee didn't come to trial for nearly a year. Lily didn't see much of Vivian. Vivian spent most of her time in Edson, or in Neil MacLean's office preparing the case. She seemed cheerful. Edson had rallied behind her, and she was something of a local celebrity. Everywhere else, people talked of nothing but Social Credit. It was supposed to have something to do with an A plus B therorem, but nobody could figure out what A and B were, so Bible Bill simply said it meant we'd all be rich. That was good news. The basic idea of Social Credit, that money belonged to the people, not to the banks, was socialist, but Social Credit's assumption that the people's money would be managed best by a single-party state bureaucracy appealed to the fascists. The only people who didn't like Social Credit were the capitalists, so it became enormously popular.

The Communist Party became popular too. It was rather embarrassing. But it was obvious that the only people who'd stood up for the unemployed were the Reds, and now the unemployed formed twenty-five per cent of the population. They were organized, outspoken and angry. Working people weren't in any better temper. Strikes spread and became violent, thousands turned out for May Day and Labour Day parades, marches and demonstrations were almost constant. Every time a Red was sent to jail, there was a public outcry, and every time a Red was released, there was dancing in the streets.

The politicians became panicky. Elections were coming, and they didn't like to make enemies, but they didn't have any money to buy votes. Alberta alone was $12 million in debt. In Ottawa, Buzzoff Bennett called out the RCMP to drive away a delegation of unemployed. The RCMP surrounded Parliament Hill with tanks. Even Conservatives were appalled. In the *Bulletin*, J.R. "Rudy" Coolican pointed out that the Royal Canadian Mint was sitting on some $6 billion in gold reserves. "Why not spend it?" said Mr. Coolican. "There's lots more where it came from." Roosevelt brought in the New Deal. It seemed that Roosevelt, too, was a Communist.

Lily was invited several times to join the Communist Party by comrades who didn't know she already belonged. It was awkward because, in declining, she had to profess a passionate loyalty to Liberalism, and to policies which, in private, she considered disgusting. She also hated being condescended to as a "social reactionary" or "dupe of the Big Interests," and it was difficult to deceive her friends. However, she was, by temperament, an "underground" person. She continued to write her reports, and leave them in the Hoover, and she was not at all unhappy with her success as a subversive, so far.

Dr. Bethune was Lily's severest test. He turned up in the winter, on his way to Vancouver for a medical convention.

"You're supposed to be dead," Lily said.

"I chickened out. So I invented a cure for TB. Tried it on myself. I was out of the san in three months. I deserve the Nobel Prize."

That's Beth. He probably *will* get the Nobel Prize. He's a genius. You can tell because he does such weird things. The first night, as he was waiting for Lily, he stood on his head in front of the *Bulletin* for an hour. Attracted quite a crowd. The next afternoon, walking back from the groceteria (Beth loves groceterias — they look like hospitals), he was barked at by a stray dog. Beth got down on his hands and knees and barked back. Beth and the dog barked at each other for a good twenty minutes. Attracted another crowd. The dog nearly had a fit.

"I'm turning Red," Beth announced when they were into the wine. "Communism's the only thing that makes sense."

Beth, it turned out, was also a member of G Section, Montreal division. He told Lily all about it, about the other members of his study group, about Stan the *aparatchik*, the books they were reading, Party tactics, the current line, his ideas on socialized medicine. His excitement was contagious. Lily had to bite her tongue. It was all she could do not to kick him in the shins and tell him for God's sake to shut his big yap. As Dr. Bethune, the famous surgeon, Beth would be a priceless asset to the Party, but as Dr. Bethune, the Commie quack, he'd be useless.

"You'll make a terrible Red," Lily said. "You have too much taste for the good life, wine, women, the Cotton Club. Does Stalin like jazz?"

"God, no! You're right, the Party's pretty stiff. Inspirational showers. Dialectical callisthenics. I have to indulge my decadence with *petites bourgeoises* like you. But the Party's wrong, isn't it? Jazz is the music of an oppressed people. It's honest, it's beautiful, progressive, proletarian. Communists *should* like jazz. I'll say so at the next meeting."

Lily was relieved, at least, that Section G contained another individualist as unregenerate as herself. She suspected that in the long run, Dr. Bethune would cause the party more headaches than she would. "They'll have to take me as I am, warts and all," he said. "They can't afford to be too choosy."

As for Lily's own politics, Beth was quite content to view her as a crypto-fascist feminist.

"The only place for women is in bed," he said.

"With you?"

"What a good idea!"

Beth suggested that Lily read Lenin's pamphlet, "What is to be Done?" He promised to send her a copy. She figured he'd wrap it in red paper, with a note on it: WARNING: SUBVERSIVE MATERIAL INSIDE. *Oi.* Lily reported Dr. Bethune's visit to the Hoover, and hoped for the best.

In April, it rained. It rained, and rained, and rained. It rained so much the river rose, and the bums were flooded out of the flats, causing a housing crisis. On May 23, 1934, Bonnie Parker and Clyde Barrow were gunned down in Oklahoma. Bonnie and Clyde had been fighting everybody's war with the banks. They were great favourites with *Bulletin* readers. Lily had seen their pictures so many times she almost felt she knew them personally. When she saw Bonnie's bullet-riddled body, Lily hit bottom, bump. There was nowhere to go but up.

The next day, a mysterious American, a Mr. Charles Bedaux, checked into the Macdonald Hotel. Lily was dispatched to photograph Mrs. Bedaux and her companion, the Contessa Chiesa. Both women were tall, extremely thin, and dressed in the height of drop-dead Paris *couture*. Lily thought Dior and Chanel a little *de trop* for a wilderness expedition across the Canadian Rockies, which was what Mr. Bedaux was proposing. Charles Bedaux had an accent like Maurice Chevalier, and wore his hair slicked back like the Prince of Wales, who was, Bedaux said, a close friend. Mr. Bedaux also declared himself on intimate terms with von Ribbentrop, the Aga Khan, Henry Ford II and

Stalin. He had invented something called the "Bedaux system" for speeding up workers on assembly lines, and spent his time travelling around with world selling his plan. Mr. Bedaux was a very rich man. Lily pegged him right away as a dope smuggler.

Mr. Bedaux had arrived in Edmonton with five gleaming white *Citroën* tractor-trucks, half-touring car, half-tank. He proposed to drive the *Citroëns* across the Rockies, through trackless wilderness, towards the Pacific Ocean. Exactly *why* Mr. Bedaux was doing this was not clear. On various occasions, he explained that he was on a hunting trip/prospecting expedition/geological survey/vacation. None of it made sense.

"Why doesn't he fly?" Jack said. "You can even hunt from the air."

Nobody asked too many questions, because Mr. Bedaux was spending a great deal of money in Edmonton. He bought horses and packsacks, tents, stoves, camp cots, rifles, ammunition, gasoline, radio batteries, boots, bush jackets, fishing tackle and tons of tinned food. When it was discovered that Bedaux had also outfitted his party with cases of vintage wines, a library of French novels and a gramophone, he was written off as a screwball. By the time the *Citroëns* were packed and the expedition ready to leave, it included, as well as Bedaux, his wife and his mistress, the Contessa, a dozen cowboys, several guides, a mechanic, a radio operator, a big-game hunter, a geographer, a surveyor, a gamekeeper, a cook, a lady's maid and a famous Hollywood cinematographer, Floyd Crosby, who was to film the expedition. Hollywood had come to Edmonton, after all. It was too late. Vivian already had a role most stars would kill for, and she was writing her own script.

MACMILLAN VS. BROWNLEE:

The trial opened in the Edmonton courthouse on June 25, 1934. The crowd was so great the police had to be called to keep people from breaking down the courthouse doors. Very few people had any idea what Vivian looked like, but they must have pictured her as some sort of floozie with big boobs and bleached hair, because when Vivian arrived, walking beside Neil MacLean, a gasp of astonishment went up. Vivian was wearing a brown-and-white check dress, white pumps and a loose white coat. Her hair was brushed behind her ears. She didn't look a day over seventeen. The crowd fell back to make way for her. Vivian walked slowly, slightly apart from MacLean, smiling shyly. Lily half-expected her to raise her hand in a little wave.

The courthouse was built of stone, in the Classic style. Lily was seated behind the prosecution bench, next to the Macmillans. As she watched Vivian climb into the witness box, head bowed, Lily was struck by a strong sense of *déjà vu*. Vivian raised her hand to place it on the Bible, and turned towards the judge, her profile silhouetted against the stone. As the judge rose to recite the oath, hovering over Vivian in a menacing way, Lily remembered that she'd seen this scene a thousand times. It was Willie's beloved etching, "Death of Iphigenia," which he had hung over his desk, in the place of honour, during their courtship. Sure enough, here was Agamemnon sitting beside her, grinding his teeth, and behind them, in the gallery, the Furies. The Fates were sitting out front, six good men and true from rural Alberta, an undertaker, a druggist, a teacher, two farmers and a mechanic, all sound, moral men and, Lily prayed, fathers. She wondered vaguely if Vivian had read the *Iliad*, and hoped to hell she hadn't.

Vivian told her story simply, in a clear, calm voice. She began with the first meeting in the back seat of the Macmillan's car, and went on to describe the seduction in the Studebaker, sharing John's bed, Mrs. Brownlee's bed, the sofa in the Premier's office, the black pills, her visits to the Brownlee home, Brownlee's temper, his threats, her fear, her broken engagement, her panic and despair. No detail was spared. Every scene was recreated, every conversation repeated. Neil MacLean's questions were often brutal; Vivian's replies were blunt.

"Did he force his way into you?"

"Yes."

"Was it painful?"

"Yes, it hurt. It hurt a lot."

"What did he say, afterwards?"

"He asked me if he had been the first."

"What did you say?"

"Yes."

A terrible stillness descended on the courtroom. People shifted uneasily in their seats, several women wept. The jury sat with bowed heads. It was as if a rape *were taking place*, before us all. There was no respite. Hour after hour, the two voices asked and answered, MacLean's questions soft, relentless, Vivian's replies cold and implacable. The effect was hypnotic. The courtroom went into shock.

Vivian never looked at Mr. Brownlee, although the defense table was directly in front of her. Mr. Brownlee sat hunched over a notepad.

Occasionally he scribbled something and handed it to his lawyer. By the end of the first day, all eyes had shifted from Vivian to the man she accused, and the verdict in the eyes was: Guilty.

"We've won the first round," said Neil MacLean. "The sofa did it, I think. Imagine fornicating at taxpayers' expense!"

As it turned out, even Brownlee's lawyer, Mr. Smith, believed Vivian's story. Instead of trying to discredit her incredible evidence as the sexual fantasies of a mentally deranged young woman, he tried to challenge Vivian on the facts, admitting, by doing so, that they *were* facts.

"What was the colour of the rug in Mr. Brownlee's office, Miss Macmillan?"

"Blue."

"And what colour was Mr. Brownlee's dressing gown?"

"I'm not sure. You see, it was always very dark. It felt woolly, sort of fuzzy."

"Weather office records show that there was a snowstorm the night of your alleged seduction, Miss Macmillan. Doesn't it seem strange, going for a drive in a blizzard?"

"The Studebaker has a good heater."

"It must have been very cramped in the back seat of a car, Miss Macmillan, and Mr. Brownlee is a big man."

"The Studebaker is a big car."

Once or twice, when Mr. Smith got very nasty, Vivian broke down and cried, but she composed herself quickly and remained unshaken. After a full day of cross-examination, Mr. Smith failed to catch Vivian in a single lie, or uncover any ulterior motive. Vivian left the witness stand as composed as she had entered it.

The defense collapsed completely when Brownlee testified on his own behalf. He denied everything, but he did so in a voice so low it could barely be heard. He looked gaunt and exhausted. He produced no proof that he had not been in Edmonton on the nights in question, and he admitted that he had taken Vivian for drives, kissed her, and passed her notes at the supper table. John Brownlee suggested no motive Vivian might have for bringing the suit, other than the obvious one, and refused to criticize her, saying over and over that Vivian was a wonderful, warm-hearted girl of whom he was very fond.

"Why does he say that?" whispered Neil MacLean. "You don't kiss your executioner!"

"Because he knows it's the truth," Vivian said.

Then, during cross-examination, John Brownlee stepped into one of the traps that had made Neil MacLean's reputation as the best criminal lawyer in Alberta. MacLean started out on a positive, even jocular note.

"You're a respectable, upstanding citizen, Mr. Brownlee?"

"Yes."

"Premier of the province?"

"Yes."

"A devoted family man?"

"Yes."

"You don't play cards, run around?"

"No."

"You go to church on Sunday?"

"Yes."

"You don't smoke or drink?"

"No."

Brownlee's reply was so soft that few people in the courtroom heard it, but the reporters did, and Mr. Brownlee's sworn testimony was printed verbatim in the *Bulletin* the next day, alongside a front-page photo showing him coming down the court house steps, holding a lighted cigarette in his left hand.

Not a single witness was produced to testify that Vivian Macmillan was of loose morals, or dishonest, or emotionally unstable, or avaricious, or psychotic. Carl, her first boyfriend, was brought all the way from Nova Scotia, for the prosecution, but he never took the stand. Wolf was supposed to be flying in from Germany. He didn't. On the last day, John Brownlee withdrew his countersuit for extortion. No evidence had been found to suggest that Vivian had ever asked him for money, or received any.

"Darned right!" she said. "The skinflint!"

The case went to the jury on June 30. The jury asked to see the Studebaker. The jury asked to see the country road where Vivian said the seduction had taken place. The following morning, a solemn procession of cars made its way out Stony Plain Road. Sure enough, there it was, a deep ditch on one side, a screen of trees beside it, just as Vivian had described. The jury asked to inspect the Brownlee home. The next day a solemn procession of cars made its way across the High Level Bridge to 88th Street. The jury took note of the arrangement of the upstairs bedrooms, the bolt on the inside of Mrs. Brownlee's door, and Mr. Brownlee's fuzzy bathrobe.

On July 2, the jury brought down a verdict of guilty, and awarded $10,000 to the Macmillans.

On July 3, Mr. Brownlee resigned as Premier of Alberta.

On July 4, the presiding judge, Mr. Justice Ives, announced that he disagreed with the jury's decision. Mr. Justice Ives dismissed the Macmillans' suit, with costs against the Macmillans.

The Macmillans were stunned. The jury was offended. Who was this guy Ives? How could he suggest they were liars? Idiots? What had they been there for, anyway? The Civil Liberties Association screamed "Star Chamber!" The UFA was jubilant. The Communists called Ives a "czar" and a "fascist." The feminists were fighting mad.

"We'll go to the Privy Council," said Nellie McClung. "Again."

"We'll appeal," said Neil MacLean.

The *Bulletin* launched a subscription fund for Vivian's appeal. Two hundred dollars came in the first day, most of it from men. Actually, the fund was just a publicity gimmick. There was no lack of money, and nobody asked where it came from.

"I am acting without fee, in the interests of British justice," said Neil MacLean, K.C.

"Do you think I should go to Hollywood, after all?" said Vivian.

HEARING THE NEWS, THE LIBERAL LEADER, MR. KING, CHEERS UP:

Laurier House, Aug. 30, 1934:

Last night I had a very clear vision of being with Sir Alan Aylesworth, who is ninety years of age. We were laughing very heartily together, really rejoicing, in a way almost playing together. We were in some large public building, a sort of palace. I was to have a painting made, but before that I was to go out in front of the building dressed in full uniform and mounted on a horse. When I came in front of the building, I was able to get a good look at it. It was set back from the street, an iron fence in front, and shrubs, then grass, then this truly fine building, not high, or massive, or pretentious, but dignified and of true proportions, three stories, and in three divisions, each adjoining, with verandahs, suitable towers etc. It was the seat of government.

It seemed to me that I was at the head of a great army of people, a great throng. I was dressed in a gold uniform, my head uncovered, but hair quite strong and thick. I saw and felt that I was the leader of the people, a general in uniform — civil, not military uniform — and that all were rejoicing and happy and there was great peace and gladness, no sense of pride of position, or of power for the love of power.

It seemed to me that the occasion was in my honour, and that my place was at the head table, seemingly at its very centre. I woke before it came to the banquet stage. I had a feeling of strength and contentment and of triumph. It was exactly seven when I got up. The sun was shining thro' the windows brightly, gloriously.

As I walked along the hall to the bathroom, I threw out my body like a man on horseback, like one who was riding, and then walked like a man at the head of an army, feeling I was a true general — I thought of Ulysses S. Grant. After shaving, I came back to my room and went through my exercises, feeling I wanted to get new strength and could enjoy the feeling of it. I had a bath and dressed.

When I came back to put on my pearl tie-pin, I saw myself clearly in the surface of the pearl, a bright light on either side of me, and a bright spot above my head. I saw myself literally surrounded by light. It was the reflection of the window, and its reflection in the mirror, but I was as one seated with pillars of light to the left and right, and light above and beneath my body.

While shaving, I made a tiny nick in my throat, just enough to make a spot of blood in the middle of the neck. I wiped it off with the towel, feeling it meant nothing serious, but possibly something significant — the red was the colour of the Holy Grail. It was like a blossom. 'Baptized with the blood' came to my mind.

Saturday, Sept. 1:

This morning I had a clear vision of being in some expensively and extravagantly furnished house. It was filled with the best of everything, expensive woods, staircases, heavy rugs, a collection of magnificent vases under glass, ferns etc. I was talking with Burton of the Robert Simpson Co. He was explaining about the company's affairs. A little white dog I had was playing about. It picked up a still smaller dog and swallowed him. I felt very badly, but soon after someone else's dog, also white, swallowed him with the other inside him.

I saw three women in heavy mourning, black crepe from head to foot.

Their grief seemed to be for the animal. I was coming down a staircase and found the stairs beginning to narrow. They seemed to close together here and there. I had to hurry to avoid being in difficulties. I encountered numbers of society women coming up. They were holding onto the bannisters. I tried to get out of their way & was a little ashamed at seeming to be impolite.

When I wakened, I said at once 'This related to the department stores and riches accumulated in that way.' It is a case of 'dog eat dog.' The women and the staircase clearly meant social climbers. There comes to mind the Masseys, the Marlers, the Wilsons, all the people who have occasioned me the most worry and concern in my leadership of the party. Every blessed one comes into this category. The interest of all in politics is social position.

I have been not a little annoyed at the number of reports that have come to me lately about my health. I am very ill, etc. etc. It's amazing the stories that are going the rounds. Today a telegram came from the *Border Cities Star* asking if it was true I was very sick, etc. etc. It is of course mostly Tory propaganda, a desire to weaken my hand and that of the party. I am coming to the conclusion that the tapping table and these mental conflicts re spiritualism have been sapping my strength, and that I have been undernourished, not eating enough solid foods. Weight 164 this morning. I was 172 last week. My face looks rather gaunt.

Saturday, Jan. 5, 1935:

This morning while still asleep I had the most distinct vision of dear Mother. I saw her first in a room where there were others, a rather dark and crowded room. I gave her a garment, a pretty little gown I had secured for her while abroad. I saw her get up and go out of the dark room along an open way. She had put on the garment, but it was still open above the waist behind. I went to see where she was. It was through a sort of ladies' dressing room. I looked into the room where she was. She was lying on a bed, her head on a pillow, and she had on the garment I had given her. Her hair was the most celestial silvery quality I have ever seen, her features most celestially pure and refined, very delicate, her eyes clear & limpid & sparkling.

Notwithstanding there were others in the room, women, I walked round the foot of the bed where she lay and took her in my arms. She seemed very frail, so spiritual was she, but she put her lips to mine as I lifted her up, and kissed me in a manner that breath seemed to come from her to me. It could not have been a more affectionate or firm embrace. I seemed to be in my underclothing, but did not feel embarrassment with the little group of other women who were also resting, feeling they were admiring my love for my mother and understanding it. What impressed me was the spiritual loveliness, as if the real life were spirit and there was just enough of flesh & bone to give form to the features. The hair, the curls, with their silvery beauty, were full of the vitality of heaven itself.

Earlier, I had a curious experience. I appeared to be taken to a great height. I was lying flat on a board which was to be fastened to another for some structure being raised. It was very high. I felt that if I turned, I would fall to infinite depths. I held on. Then I had a feeling of being seized all over by a sort of blackness, black waves seizing me like some monster. I said, 'This is no vision, this is nightmare. I must throw it off.' I did, using the word 'Go!' in my determination to wrench myself free from the numbness in which I seemed bound and held.

I may have wakened when my soul was still away from my body & not yet fully returned to it. Or it may have been the pheasant I ate for dinner. There is always danger in cold storage game.

A New Year's Message from the Tapping Table:
  Lorenzo de Medici speaks:
  "You will be Prime Minister this year.
  You will have a great name in history.
  You will be a peacemeaker.
  You will make people happy.
  You will have a long life."

38

Can Willie be dying? Vincent arrived this morning with the news. It was a terrific shock. I can hardly believe it. Vincent says the diagnosis isn't certain, but it seems to be cancer. Apparently Willie doesn't know. He's wasted away to a shadow, hardly ever goes out, sees no one, spends the day in bed, complains of fatigue, pain in the joints, headaches, blindness. He is receiving some sort of electrotherapy treatment but it's having no effect. Vincent suspects a brain tumour.

"Last week Mr. King received me in his *pyjamas*," Vincent whispered. "He seemed not to notice. He told me that he had 'spoken to' Armand Lavergne the night before. Lavergne died six weeks ago. He then accused me of trying to 'control' him through 'evil spirits,' and that if I didn't cease pestering and harrassing him and leave him in peace and quiet, he would not be able to carry on. He asked me if I believed in the Anti-Christ, and what shape Christ would take if he came again, angel or human. He then showed me drawings of a 'shrine' he is planning to build at Kingsmere, a 'combination of the Parthenon and Westminster Abbey,' he said, and asked me if I thought the Jacobean furniture he'd picked up second-hand at Shenkman's would be suitable."

Willie's butler, McLeod, says there's a room in Laurier House that's kept locked at all times, and in the evenings Willie and Mrs. Patteson are in there for hours on end, hooting and hollering and thumping on the floor enough to wake the dead. "It ain't decent," McLeod says, "and her a married woman." Willie moans and cries out so much at night the servants can't get a moment's sleep. "He must be dyin'," McLeod says, "He keeps yellin' for his ma."

I haven't heard from Willie for awhile, it's true. But that's not like him, is it? If he were sick, or in pain, I *would* hear from him. Willie isn't one to suffer in silence. Has the photo of the Panther Woman been too much for him? I can see the headline now:

"LIBERAL LEADER SUCCUMBS TO SELF-ABUSE:
EXPLODES IN FLAMES!"

Vincent is going across the country rallying support for a leadership convention. Bennett has to call an election this summer. With Willie dying, and Bennett abominated, Vincent says it will be a sure victory for Socialism. He says the Jews already have Willie in their clutches. Apparently he's promised Archie Freiman a Senate seat. Vincent is furious. "One Jew in the Senate is one too many," he said.

I phoned Laurier House as soon as Vincent left. Willie was having a nap, said his secretary, Miss Sawyer. "He's been under a great deal of strain lately," she said carefully. "You know how Mr. King takes the plight of the poor so much to heart. It's almost as if he wants to share their suffering. I'm afraid Mr. King might starve himself to death."

Willie?

"He eats nothing but mashed vegetables, tea and toast. He says that meat makes him ill. We half-expect to see him in a loincloth any day now, although Mr. King is sensitive to cold. Canada isn't India, after all. You can't have the leader of the Liberal Party wandering about barefoot and begging in the streets. Vincent is distraught."

"But he's not... Mr. King hasn't got...."

"Pooh, that stupid rumour. Where do these things start? Somebody goes on a diet and he's good as buried. Cancer, heart attack, paralysis, TB, it's the same thing with Mr. Bennett. Everyone is saying he hasn't got six weeks to live. The poor man's just tired out, like Mr. King. You can blame that Dr. Bradley, if you ask me. It's his stupid diet, a few tablespoons of mush, not enough to keep a bird alive."

"You mean that Mr. Bennett is *thin*?"

"Not thin, but thin*er*. To tell the truth, I haven't seen him for weeks. He hardly ever leaves his room at the Château, never appears in the House. He seems to have given up. Bill Herridge is running the country now, they say, and *he's* drunk most of the time. The Speaker has gone off his head. We're really in quite good spirits here. It's just that Mr. King *looks* so awful. You know how the skin sags and his clothes simply *hang* on him. It makes him look old and wizened, as if he were simply withering away. Do you know a good tailor?"

The State is withering away! The revelation struck Lily like a thunderbolt. The revolution has already happened! The masses *have* seized power, they just don't know it yet. All that remains is to build the stateless society!

For once, Lily got a response from the Hoover. Her message didn't strike the Party with the same self-evident clarity, but it did bring Red Annie up from Blairmore in the coal fields, where the Communist city council was renaming Main Street "Tim Buck Boulevard."

"That's exactly what I'm saying," Lily said. "Communism is *in*. It's *popular*. Isn't that what you want? Look, Tim Buck *filled* Maple Leaf Gardens for his rally last December. The Leafs can't do that. Tim Buck is the most popular politician in Canada right now!"

"Yes, Comrade Buck is aware of the dangers inherent in the cult of personality."

"Nobody gives a fig for Tim Buck's personality, Annie! People want someone to run the country in a fair and sensible way. They want to know where their next meal is coming from. They want to *have* a next meal. How it's done I don't think they much care."

"The ignorance of the masses is our greatest obstacle."

"Oh, come on, Annie! The masses *aren't* ignorant. Whatever the Party may think, Canadians are not serfs. *This is not Russia.* People here are educated. They read, they think, they argue politics. And they've made up their minds. You don't have to memorize *Capital* to understand how the world works. Annie, why don't you trust the people?"

"Canada is a capitalist state. The majority of the people are reactionaries, counter ..."

"But how can we be capitalist without any capital? You can count the capitalists in this country on the fingers of one hand, and most of them are broke. The banks are broke. The railways are broke. Governments are broke. There *is* no government, because there's nothing for a government to do except dole out Relief. The Ladies' Aid of McDougall Church could run Alberta and take the afternoons off."

"*Christians?*"

"Here, let me read you something. I found it last week in a book. Here goes, it's short:

" 'If a situation (war, agricultural crisis) develops in which the proleta-riat, a minority of the population, is able to group around itself the immense majority of the working masses, *why should it not seize power then?* "

Annie looked suspicious.

"Do you know who wrote that, Annie? Lenin, that's who."

"But the question is, how . . . ."

"You just *do* it, that's all. Lenin did it. How many Bolsheviks took St. Petersburg? A few hundred? Out of how many Russians, a hundred million? Everybody else just jumped on the bandwagon. Well, here they're already *on* the bandwagon."

"What about the army?"

"Willie got rid of it. Guns make him nervous. The militia's a joke. The Army of the Unemployed, on the other hand, is five hundred thousand strong, sixty thousand in the work camps alone, a million-and-a-half people on Relief, counting women and kids. Annie, that's not an army, that's a *horde*, and it's a *socialist* horde!"

"Social democratic deviationism is a ruse fostered by the capitalist-imperialist . . . ."

"Oh, bugger that Comintern crap! A Communist is a Socialist with balls, right? Well, I don't see many comrades out there with balls. Oh, they talk a good fight, but someone gives them a little knock on the head and they come whining into the *Bulletin* bleating about fascist oppres-sion. Do you know what I think Communists are? I think they're chickenshits."

"Our Canadian comrades have been instructed to take a defensive posture. The Comintern has advised us that in a pre-industrial, colonial economy such as ours, revolution is impossible."

"What does the Comintern know? Has anyone from the Comintern ever been to Canada? Does the Comintern even know where Canada is? Does the Comintern *care*? And who the hell cares about the Comintern? The Comintern will be handing out leaflets at Armageddon. Annie, we are at the Finland Station. *Where is the train?*"

39

It's raining. It's always raining in Vancouver. Not a warm, gentle Ontario rain, or a sweeping, stormy prairie rain, but a hard, wet, West Coast rain as cold as the sea itself. Esselwein can't see the sea, it's too dark, but he can smell it, a sharp, somewhat greasy smell, like the train. He can smell the train too, steam and axle grease, wet wood, cinders, a whiff of cattle, steel, empty space. The numbers on the boxcars stand out ghostly white in the dark.

Comrade Sands shines his flashlight along the top of the car. Esselwein bangs on the door and throws back the bolt.

"Outa there, you bums, if you know what's good for you!" Sands yells, banging his baseball bat against the side of the car. Sands' flashlight sweeps the corners of the car. Empty. Esselwein bangs the door shut and the little group of men squelches on down the track.

Esselwein's relieved. He can live with being a spook, but he hates being a goon. It's degrading, beating up defenceless kids. Who'd have thought the Party would terrorize its own men, just to keep them in line? Only proves the Relief strike's on its ass. Everyone's sneaking away. Vancouver's bummed out.

Novelty's worn off. What's next? Damned if the Party knows. The *aparatchiks*' idea of an "action" is to march a hundred men through the Hudson's Bay Company store. Zowee! That's going to bring capitalism crashing right down! No wonder this little Red army is melting away like a snowball in hell. There aren't nine hundred men left of the two thousand who came out of the camps in April. In a week, there won't be fifty. Maybe he'll get to come in out of the rain.

Suddenly the freight shudders, lurches, begins to roll forward. Its bell clangs forlornly in the night. Shadowy figures scamper across the

cinders and clamber up the boxcars like monkeys. Esselwein pretends
not to see. Poor buggers if they think they'll find a warmer welcome on
the other side of the mountain! He pulls the collar of his mackinaw up
around his ears and forms up with the others.

"Hep, one, two!" calls Sands. "Left right left right left." They march
in perfect order to the union hall.

The secret meeting's been called for midnight. Some secret. There are
at least two hundred men in the hall and dozens more milling around
trying to get in. They stand back to make way for the picket patrol and
Esselwein shoulders his way to a corner at the back. Slim Evans, the
leader of the Relief Camp Workers' Union, is speaking from the
platform.

"Are we beaten, boys?"

"NOOOOUUUMMMMGRRRRRUUUHHHHHUUUMMMMMMM?"

"Comrades, we must get militant!"

"GRROAAAANNNNNNNNNNNN."

"What the hell do you think we've been doin' for two months?" yells
a voice from the floor.

"Then we've got to get *more* militant, or admit defeat."

"Let's have a Hunger March!" cries another voice.

"GRROAAAANNNNNNNNNNNN."

"I'll tell you about hunger marches," shouts a voice, "hunger marches
make you *hungry!*"

"YAAAAAAYYYYYDAMNRITE!"

"Are we going to call off the strike, then?"

"NOOOOOOOOOOO."

The meeting becomes a babble of proposals and counter-proposals,
motions and amendments and amendments to the amendments, a
rehash of stale gimmicks and impossible schemes, an ear-splitting,
mind-numbing illustration of the total futility of the democratic process.
Esselwein is bored stiff. His beard is wet, and water keeps dripping
down his neck. His steel-rimmed spectacles from the Sally Ann keep
fogging up in the heat. How can there be a dictatorship of the
proletariat, Esselwein wonders, when the proletariat can't make up its
mind?

"Comrades," Esselwein says quietly, climbing on his chair. A hush
falls. The Professor is much respected. During the winter, he was
expelled from two slave camps for subversive activities, and when the

strike began in April, the Professor was one of the first to walk out of camp. Also, he is older than most of the men. His frizzy mane of hair is quite grizzled, and his beard is streaked with gray. The Professor is an eloquent speaker. He can recite Marx by heart. But most important of all, the Professor is Russian.

"Comrades, here we are in Siberia, eh? I have been in Siberia. It is the same. In fact, here we are closer to Siberia than we are to the rest of Canada, are we not?"

"YEHHUUMMMMMUMBLE."

"Let me ask you, did the Russian revolution take place in Siberia? No, of course not. Troublemakers like me were sent to Siberia because, believe me, nothing could happen there, or, if it did, no one paid any attention. If you were sent to Siberia, you died there, or you escaped."

The hall is absolutely silent.

"We have escaped, comrades. We have escaped the *gulag*, the prisons in the bush where we could starve, or have our throats slit, and no one would be the wiser. We have come far. We are no longer slaves. We are free men. We are organized. We are an army, and we are a powerful army because *we have the people with us.* Why stop here? Where is the Czar? Is the Czar in the Hudson's Bay Company store? Is he in Vancouver city hall? In the Relief Office? No, the Czar is in Ottawa, in his Château, counting out his money. Is the Czar going to come here to visit us? No, of course not. Why, then, don't we visit him? It's not far, and we can take the train."

"OTTAWA? OTTAWA!" *OTTAWA!* ON TO OTTAWA! ON TO OTTA-WWWWAAAAA!"

Half the men are ready to jump on the next freight. It takes Evans a while to calm them down and persuade them to draw up a plan. By the time the details are thrashed out, everyone has forgotten the Professor, and when someone thinks to ask, the Professor is nowhere to be found.

ODDAWAODDAWA ODD...A...WA ... ODD...A...WA...ODD...AAA ... WAAAA....

The Professor listens to the freight labour up the grade. Where are they? Who knows? At least it's not raining in the mountains. The boxcar is stuffy, but warm enough, and the steady rocking of the train has a soothing effect. Did the poor buggers in the Trojan Horse have this sense of spacelessness? Or did they flip coins, sing "Hold the fort, we're coming," and reminisce about the last war? What if the Trojans hadn't dragged them in, and they'd been left out there to fry in the desert sun?

What if the freight stops in the next tunnel? They could be gassed to death "accidentally" in a few moments. The Mounties won't miss him. One wop informer more or less isn't going to make that much difference. As for the other eight hundred guys on board, they wouldn't be here if anybody gave a damn. Quick cure for unemployment: a hundred guys in a boxcar, a whiff of cyanide, poof.

Is he getting paranoid? Yes. Take the train, for instance. Sure, it's the good old Ten-Ten, the freight that leaves Vancouver every night at ten-ten p.m., more or less, but the Ten-Ten is usually loaded, and locked up tight, and patrolled by bulls with nightsticks. Any bum lucky enough to grab a handhold lives to regret it the next morning when he's clinging to the top for dear life and peering down at a boiling mountain stream a thousand feet below. But this Ten-Ten was empty, and the doors were open, and there wasn't a bull in sight. First class, all the way. To where?

Why were his instructions changed? They had been perfectly simple: get the strikers to Vancouver and keep them there. It wasn't that easy. It had been the Professor's idea to occupy the Vancouver City Museum. Who but the Professor would think of that? It had been a coup. The city fathers couldn't bring themselves to storm the stuffed seals, so the Professor and his company had camped out quite comfortably for days, ordering their rations sent up in baskets, through the window. Once the Relief ran out and the weather warmed up, Smythe predicted the strike would collapse, and that's exactly what happened, until yesterday.

Going to Ottawa suits Esselwein okay. Once he gets there, maybe he'll land a desk job and a promotion to inspector. O joy! But with an election coming, why does the Prime Minister want ten thousand angry 'bos on his front lawn? Unless that's exactly why he *does* want them. What better reason to declare a state of insurrection, proclaim the War Measures Act and form a National Government? Quick cure for elections, poof. When Esselwein closes his eyes, he can see the bright green grass of Parliament Hill, and a lot of dead bodies lying around. One of them is his.

The Professor keeps to the far corner of the car, away from the lantern where some men are playing rummy. He gets up to piss out the door only when most of the men are asleep. He opens the door as the freight is crossing a chasm on a trestle bridge, and he feels a sudden impulse to leap into the void, just for the hell of it, but someone yells "Shut the goddamn door!" and he does, anxious not to be noticed. Most of the men in the car are strangers, and its just possible that someone might see, beneath the hair, the infamous Leopold. Fortunately, all the Reds he used to know have been purged from the Party. Only Annie is left, and it's not likely she'll turn up here, although with Annie you never know. The present Party bosses are all chickenshits. Nevertheless, when the Professor curls up to sleep, he turns his face to the wall.

The Bum Express lumbers into Kamloops late the next afternoon. It's dry here, almost desert. The Professor's lips are parched. He peers anxiously out the boxcar door. No cops, anyway. Nobody at all, as a matter of fact. Where is the promised crowd of comrades with their delicious socialist stew? It seems that the Party has forgotten that even an army of bums marches on its stomach, and the Professor's stomach is complaining bitterly.

The men climb down and form up sullenly on the cinders. A pump is located behind the station. A long line forms behind it as one by one they drink the brackish water out of cupped hands. The last cigarettes are passed carefully from hand to hand. Patiently, the men sit in the hot sun. There is no shade. Scouts return to report that Kamloops has never heard of the On to Ottawa trek. They are as welcome as a plague of grasshoppers. Kamloops has no soup kitchen, the mayor is not home, the Relief Office is closed and there are only two cafés in town, each one seating twenty-five. The United Church minister, however, will see what he can do, and the union of unemployed married men is making coffee.

It's nearly midnight when the last man has finished his mug of coffee, his slab of bread and cheese and two stale doughnuts. There's a lot of bitching and grumbling. Some of the boys are for calling the whole damn thing off right then and there, but the hard truth is that there's only one way out of Kamloops, and that's the way they came in.

"You and your big mouth," Slim Evans tells the Professor. "They've cut us off at the pass. We'll be ambushed."

"You have been watching too many westerns, Comrade Evans," sighs the Professor. "It is a weakness I myself share. But do the good guys not win in the end? And are we not the good guys?"

"Yeah, but this ain't...."

"You are tired, comrade. Your unflagging dedication to the cause of the oppressed masses has opened your mind to negative thinking. We must lead, Comrade Evans. The Party must be in the vanguard of the spontaneous revolutionary impulse of the proletariat. We must seize history by the throat!"

"Yeah, but hell shit damn Professor, it's not supposed to happen *here!*"

"We shall see then, eh?"

Such a *bourgeois,* Evans. A weathercock in the wind. 'Revolution if necessary, comrades, but not necessarily revolution.' *Oi.* And this is the Red Menace that has Canada shaking in its shoes! The Professor crunches along the cinders to the end of the train, stepping carefully over the bodies sleeping in the shelter of the boxcars. He glances back over his shoulder. Was Evans testing him? Is the Party on to him? The last informer was buried in the coal car and sucked down the turnscrew into the firebox. The fireman screamed blue murder. Fellows disappear all the time. You don't know where or why. They just aren't there anymore, and nobody mentions their names. Nobody knows their real names anyway, so there's not much point.

The Professor sits alone in the grass at the edge of the embankment. The grass smells green, and the soft night wind carries the smell of apple blossoms. There was an apple tree in the yard of his house in Tzaritsyn, a big one, and in the spring he sat under it, reading, until he was covered in a blanket of blossoms. It was the closest thing to perfect happiness he could imagine. It will be midday in Stalingrad now. Stalin's city, the new Tzar. Will someone be sitting under the tree? The tree will be there, he has no doubt. A serviceable, proletarian tree, the apple. But who will be living in his house? Many people, for certain, the rooms all divided up into cubbies with washing on the line everywhere. Perhaps the house was destroyed in the civil war, like his family, and his friends. Esselwein doesn't really care. He's done without a house for a long time now, although he remembers with affection his little shack in Kirkland Lake. He has become used to camping out in other people's clothes and other people's names and other people's lives. He wouldn't have it any other way.

The Professor removes his glasses and tucks them in his pocket. He wipes his eyes on his sleeve and blows his nose.

"Ah, Trotsky, *tovarich,*" he sighs, "has it all come to nothing?"

When the train reaches the divisional point at Golden the next day, a cheerful crowd is waiting at the station, and bathtubs of savoury stew are simmering over fires in the park. There is fresh bread too and homemade pies, all provided by the Golden branch of the Communist Party of Canada, which is just about the entire population of Golden. After the meal there is a singsong, with rousing choruses of the *International*, and rumours that four thousand men will join the trek in Calgary, ten thousand more in Winnipeg, twenty thousand in Toronto. There is so much excitement that no one notices the Professor is missing until the train reaches Calgary the next day. The Professor is immediately denounced as a police spy/agent provocateur/journalist/*bourgeois* intellectual/chickenshit/who has gone back to Vancouver/gone ahead to Winnipeg/Ottawa/Moscow/been murdered/killed himself. There is some disappointment when it's discovered that the Professor has simply gone to Edmonton with the rest of Comrade Sands' picket to bring down more recruits for the trek.

"Bugger off, Moses, soup kitchen's downtown."

Rudy Coolican scowls impatiently at the ragged, grey-bearded 'bo who has suddenly materialized in the waiting room of Interior Air. The bum doesn't move. Instead, he smiles and makes odd winking motions with his eyebrows.

"Oh, shit, Esselwein, when are you going to get a decent job?"

"Shhh. I'm undercover."

"You're under a lot more than that, from what I can see. Jesus Christ, Esselwein, you *stink*."

"Part of the job. Whoever coined the phrase 'the great unwashed' sure hit the nail on the head. You know, I think most revolutionaries could be bought off with a bath."

"Have you passed that on to Smythe?"

"Oh, sure. He says Commies like to smell. It's something to do with cleanliness and Godliness. Communism is sort of like B.O. Smythe would rather be dead than dirty. Come to think of it, so would I."

"So you give them a nice bloodbath, right?"

Esselwein winces and looks at the floor. "So it seems. I'd just as soon not be there. I can't very well wear a sign saying 'Don't shoot, I'm a spy,' can I? But I can't bail out now. You haven't heard anything, have you?"

"Hell, I was going to ask you the same thing. Your boss, MacBrien, flew through here yesterday. He says it's Us or Them. He's talking some sort of *putsch*, military takeover, himself at the head, of course. It's the same old crowd, Herridge, Meighen, the CPR, the banks, the army, Byng's Boys. Bungo is in California right now, lurking in the weeds."

"But Bungo balled it up the last time!"

"MacBrien offered to make me Minister of the West. Neat, eh? No more provinces. Give me a free hand. Soon as I said I was Social Credit, MacBrien took off out of here like a scared rabbit. Too bad. Guess he thought I said Socialist."

"What about Bennett? Is he in on it?"

"Nope. MacBrien thinks Bennett's a Red, you know, bringing in the Bank of Canada, public radio, that sort of stuff. So Bennett doesn't know. Besides, he's at sea, somewhere in the Atlantic. Tell you the truth, the timing's perfect. Willie King's about to croak, I hear, King George too, and you know how the Prince of Wales feels about the 'king crap.' The Governor-General's in Quebec, on his way home, and the new one ain't got here yet, so who's left? It's all set up for July first. I figured you'd know all about it, seeing as you got to get the Reds there on time, and in a suitable warlike mood. Listen, Esselwein, there's just one thing I want to know. Who's going to win?"

Esselwein scratches his beard, thoughtfully removes a louse and crunches it beneath his thumbnail.

"Who won last time, in '26?"

"We did. I mean, the Liberals, King did. Hell, Willie won!"

Esselwein leaves quickly, his pockets stuffed with enough Havana cigars to convince his comrades that the Professor has been on a successful mooch. He walks rapidly in the direction of the Labour Temple. As he gets closer to downtown, he becomes aware of shouting and singing and the incessant blare of car horns. Shopkeepers are standing on the sidewalks, peering anxiously at the source of the racket, and cars are backed up for blocks on the streets.

As Esselwein turns the corner opposite city hall, he is swallowed by a surging sea of Relief strikers chanting WORK AND WAGES WE WANT CASH WORK AND WAGES WE WANT CASH. He struggles to push his way through, but he is swept along for more than a block as the mob circles the building, placards bobbing along above their heads like ice floes at spring breakup. A few cars try to inch their way through, drivers leaning on their horns, but the people simply eddy around the cars and drum on

their hoods BOOMBOOM DADA WHUMP WHUMP WORK WORK WORK!
BOOM BOOM DADA WHUMP WHUMP CASH CASH CASH!

"Work and wages!" the Professor cries out, raising a clenched fist. He keeps the fingers of the other hand crossed. A false move and he could be torn limb from limb in this crowd. It's the women you have to watch for. Revolutions are always started by women. Bread and roses, baby, or watch out!

The Professor extricates himself at the next corner, only to run into a picket line of angry women in front of the Adelphi Café. The waitresses are on strike. The Professor detours around the block, and finds himself in front of the *Bulletin*, where a small knot of men is staring silently at the Extra posted in the window. One of the men turns away, dabbing at his eyes with a Kleenex. The Professor shoulders his way in, standing on tiptoe to peer over the heads.

> **"LORD BYNG DIES SUDDENLY**
> Heart Attack Fells Vimy Hero"

"Oh, God, Bungo," the Professor says aloud, "You've buggered it up again."

It's hot in the ark, and the People are restless. In and out, up and down, here and there, round and round they go, chattering constantly. It started this morning when a wild-looking bearded man appeared on the steps. Christina Coolican thought at first he might be the Blimp, but the man was too small and dirty, and no one showed him much respect. He whispered in ears, and waved his arms, and pulled people by their sleeves until they all started doing the same thing and the ark began to hum like a hornets' nest. Now some of the People are packing their gunny sacks and rolling up their blankets and stuffing their pockets with bread and sausages and sticking cigarettes in their hatbands like cartridges and shaking hands good-bye, good-bye, good-bye.

Christina Coolican has listened to the People singing outside, and has heard the same strange hymn she first heard in Winnipeg. She has heard the horns honking too. The Bible is very specific about trumpets. She has asked the Lord about it, but the Lord is silent. When Christina Coolican opens her mouth to speak, no sound comes out. Even the organ's voice is stilled. Paul, the music teacher, is standing in front of it, his hat on his head and a Woodward's shopping bag in his hand.

"It's time to go, Granny," he says, taking her hand. "Why don't you come with us?"

Christina Coolican looks down the nave of the church. The front door is open, and a shaft of sunlight makes a golden river to her feet. Beyond, she can see the mountain peaks turning gold, then amber, then ruby, and high above, a flaming host of angels rides the wind. Perhaps she'll hear the trumpets when she gets a little closer.

The crowd carries her into a part of the city where she's never been before. Overhead, tiny silver airplanes drift out of the sky, slipping lower and lower until they seem to be swallowed by the earth. Christina Coolican pushes eagerly ahead. They come to railway yards. The People stop. Some sit down. Someone offers her a bedroll to sit on. Impatient as she is to reach the airplanes, she's glad of the rest. Perhaps not everyone is here yet. There are no women or children. Is the Lord going to begin again from the beginning? A clean slate? She waits.

It grows dark. The People are quiet. Some curl up on the cinders and sleep. Someone wraps a blanket around her. The night smells of fresh-cut grass. She'll miss that. Somewhere nearby a chorus of frogs rejoices in the Lord brrrrrrrrrrrrrillllllllllllllllllllllll. She'll miss them too. The world is really quite a nice place, at times. Too bad they've botched it up. She closes her eyes.

She hears a silver trumpet, no, a brass trumpet: no, iron, an iron trumpet, not a trumpet an engine, a fiery furnace spewing smoke and noise, walke up, WAKE UP! It's here! It's here! Someone is shaking her shoulder. Christina Coolican looks around, confused. The People are scrambling to their feet, rolling up their blankets. There is thunder. In the west, a bright white light grows larger and larger. A bell clangs, and the iron trumpet shrieks LOOK OUT! LOOK OUT! LOOK OOUUUUUUT! Christina Coolican is pulled to her feet and dragged towards the railway tracks. She looks to right and left, puzzled.

"But we're going the wrong way!" she says, tugging at a sleeve. No one hears. Christina Coolican darts out onto the tracks. She runs towards the blinding light, waving her arms wildly to make it stop.

40

At least Mum's arms and legs weren't cut off, as usually happens. She was thrown into the air and flew over the heads of the crowd, blown, as Paul the music teacher put it, to Kingdom Come. There wasn't much left of Mum anyway. She couldn't have weighed more than eighty pounds. It must have been Mum who inspired Willie to wither away, although Lily could find no trace of correspondence between them. But then Mum never relied on anything as banal as the mail. Now Mum is a handful of ashes in a tea tin. Tomorrow she will be scattered to the wind over the Rockies. Poof. The next day, a note of sympathy will arrive from Willie, written in his own hand, explaining how Mum's death will help him become Prime Minister again. Perhaps he will include a fragment of conversation from the Beyond.

Lily feels elated, lightheaded, her brain a helium balloon ready to float away on the slightest breeze. Nothing is important. Everything is irrelevant. She feels detached, a drifter, a vagrant, a Displaced Person, WithOut Passport. Destination: unknown. She is unreasonably, blissfully, happy. She knows catastrophe is coming, she doesn't doubt that for a moment, yet the world seems fresh, newborn, amazing, as if she is seeing it for the first time, and she finds it beautiful. Nothing has really changed. Life goes on as before, and Edmonton is Edmonton, but now Lily's spine tingles, and Edmonton shimmers in brilliant Tintoretto sunshine.

The gift of grace had often been described to her. She had struggled for it as a child, and given up in disgust, yet here it is, effortless and unbidden, just like Mum said. Amazing. Don't ask questions. Rejoice! Lily knows the feeling will fade, but the memory will always remain. In the meantime, she says little and walks cautiously, afraid to break the spell.

"I'm saved!" she wants to write to Willie, or tell him by phone, but he'll only be jealous, and spoil everything.

Granny Coolican's funeral delayed the Edmonton trekkers for two days. Smythe was upset. Hurry up, hurry up, he told the Professor on the phone. The Professor explained there was nothing he could do, it was an Act of God. Lord Byng would be buried in England, but a memorial service was arranged in Ottawa, and Prime Minister Bennett rushed back to attend. He had barely stepped off the train when Miss Whitton, O.B.E., informed him of several anonymous tips she'd received warning of armed insurrection/coalition government/*coup d'état*, and Mr. Bennett's own imminent demise/departure for the House of Lords. Mr. Bennett immediately called an election for October 14. He told General MacBrien that he was a nincompoop/incompetent/traitor and ordered the On to Ottawa trek stopped in Saskatchewan, now.

In Saskatchewan, the Bum Express mysteriously slowed down. It ran out of coal and water. The engine developed complaints that couldn't be fixed. The men on board didn't really mind. They sunbathed on the roof, swam in the creeks and saw the sights of Gull Lake, Swift Current and Moose Jaw. It was nearly the end of June before the freight reached Regina. Slim Evans and several others from the strikers' executive went on to Ottawa alone to meet with the Prime Minister. Mr. Bennett called them Commies and crooks and kicked them out the door. They came back with their tails between their legs.

The Bum Express was forbidden to leave Regina. The RCMP constructed internment camps for the trekkers on the outskirts of town. The men were offered free passage to a camp or back home. Many began to drift away. Some went north, where work could be found on farms or in the bush. Going to Ottawa seemed like a pretty dumb idea. Slim Evans tried to organize truck convoys to Winnipeg, but the RCMP blocked the highway. Relief rations ran low.

On July 1, 1935, the army of the unemployed was still in Regina. In a desperate attempt to rally public support, Evans organized a mass meeting in the market square. A lot of people came out of sympathy for the trek — they'd rather have the men in Ottawa than in Regina. As Evans was speaking to the crowd, furniture vans backed into the streets leading out of the square, blocking the exits. The van doors opened and squads of policemen swarmed into the square, swinging clubs. Tear-gas canisters were fired at random. In a moment the square was enveloped in a pall of stinking, blinding smoke. Slim Evans was dragged from the platform. Trekkers fought the police with their fists, then with stones and knives. The fight spread out of the square into the surrounding streets. It went on far into the night before it finally blew itself out in showers of shattered glass. One man was beaten to death. He was a plainclothes detective with the Regina City Police.

The Professor read about the riot the next morning in an Edmonton barber shop. After he finished the story, he sighed, and tossed the paper on the floor.

"Buncha thugs, the lot of 'em, if you ask me," the barber said.

"A little more off the sides, if you would," the Professor said, and closed his eyes.

MEANWHILE, IN OTTAWA:

Laurier House, June 26, 1935:

Caucus this morning was spent in a general discussion on what should be said to those who were protesting against the camps for the single unemployed. Bradette is very fearful of Communist developments. The other men were concerned with what the Liberal policy should be. I told them to point out that the Liberal Party was not the government, we were not in office. I pointed out that during the coming election campaign, I did not intend to propose any plan or 'ism' as a cure-all, and that these various plans are only possible by means of a dictatorship. I said I thought we should make our fight for the liberty for which the Liberal Party stands, and that all these plans were mere expedients to meet conditions that had their causes elsewhere, namely in the restriction of trade. A Liberal government would foster trade. I stressed the importance of the Liberal Party not making itself a target for its enemies to fire at. The main thing from now on is to realize that people vote against, rather than for something, and to keep their minds focussed on Bennett and his mismanagement of things.

At the conclusion of caucus, Lapointe moved a vote of thanks to myself for my leadership during the year, and expressed the faith of the members in my leadership during the coming campaign. The motion was carried with applause.

Kingsmere, Tues., July 2, 1935:

The morning paper carried an account of the unemployed riots yesterday in Regina, with the death of one city policeman and possible fatal injury to members of the Royal Canadian Mounted Police, with casualties among the unemployed. It was expected that this would give rise to a debate in the House. In conference with Lapointe, I found he was very fearful that the impression might be fostered that we were sympathetic to Communism. I pointed out that the riots in Regina were the outgrowth of labour problems which had been brewing for months, all due to the failure of Bennett's policies. It was clear he was seeking to draw attention away from that fact, and to get an issue — the suppression of Communism — which might serve for the formation of a National Government. I stated that only a few of the men were Communists.

On the whole, it seemed preferable to let Woodsworth of the CCF introduce the subject. He did so. Later, I was able, without getting into a debate on the issue, to secure from the government a promise to produce all telegrams between themselves and the government of Saskatchewan, an important step. The debate on the Regina riot lasted part of the afternoon and most of the evening. There is a sort of Nemesis about the fact that it was in Regina, where Bennett sought to stir up prejudice and incite the unemployed, that this tragedy should have taken place. The trek eastward of unemployed, homeless men discloses the complete failure of the government to provide work, which was the ground on which they obtained office. The whole five years is summed up in the police helmets of 1935 — a record of incompetence and tragedy all along the way.

Batterwood, Port Hope, July 19, 1935:

I reached Port Hope at nine last night, Vincent was at the station. At Batterwood, Alice gave me a cordial welcome. I enjoyed a glass or two of scotch before going to bed, being very tired. The *Star* reporters turned up & we had a short interview in Vincent's library, which I regarded as the beginning of the election campaign. We were photographed together.

A very restless morning, aches & pains in the body — I believe rheumatic pain caused by damp & wet. Thunder showers at dawn. I had a restless hour or two afterwards, with snaps of a vision here & there. I recall thinking I was going into a large arena to run a race. I recall starting off in my bare feet, and having to return to put on my slippers. In another glimpse, I was with members of a press party. It was a campaign. There was a carpet which I was showing to those present. I told them it had been bought by Mr. Larkin in London, but it has become mine. It had a beautiful embroidered pattern, a red, or rose, on a light golden-yellow background. Later, McLeod brought to me the pearl tie-pin Mr. Larkin had presented to me, saying it had nearly been swept up with the carpet sweeper in the living room.

Larkin & the carpet — does it mean Mr. Larkin is letting me know he is watching proceedings? Does it mean the London Office, the post that will be mine to offer Massey very shortly? It would seem as if Mr. Larkin is saying to me: 'You gave me London, I gave you the pin & all else in gratitude. The pearl is symbol of our affection & love.' As to the shoes, it would seem to be Mother warning me of my health, so as to be in shape for the race ahead.

Before the day was out, this vision was fulfilled in a more remarkable way than I had believed possible. As I was taking a bath, I suddenly saw on the chair & the curtains in the bathroom the pattern I had seen in the vision of the roses. I said, 'There is the carpet & its association with the Masseys and the London office." But more remarkable still, Vincent and I had just spent an hour with the press men, one with his flashlight camera, and we held our interview on the carpet in Vincent's library. This was the meaning of the press we were showing and telling things to. I was in the bathroom, having put on my slippers to go to & from, and was preparing for a massage for my health. Could anything be clearer?

It all means God is near. He is beside me. Mother, Mr. Larkin, all the heavenly host are at hand and ready to help. I believe they will give me the needed aid & inspiration.

Vivian was married in August. Her husband, Henry, was a druggist in Edson. He seemed a nice enough guy, and he had to have guts. Henry had a soda fountain on the side, so at worst Vivian would have a lifetime supply of Cokes. He couldn't have done it for the money, because the Macmillans had lost their appeal and the case was still before the Supreme Court. Vivian looked very happy. Just a small-town girl, after all. It seemed too bad, in a way, but when you've brought down a government, what do you do next?

As it turned out, Vivian had more sense than poor David, who thought he could live in a shack in Canada, be King of England, and marry another man's wife. Lily thought he should have dumped the rest, and kept the shack. He was always happy on the ranch. The ranch house was hardly a shack, but it was spartan, sparsely furnished, with no amenities. David loved it. Needless to say, Mrs. Simpson loathed it.

The Alberta provincial election was called for August 22. The Liberals were very confident. The provincial leader, Mr. Howson, spoke of "*when* the Liberal Party is returned to power." Nellie McClung ordered a spiffy new wardrobe, befitting the first woman lieutenant-governor in the British Empire. Neil MacLean, K.C., switched from Seagram's Five Star to Chivas Regal in anticipation of the Senate. Within the past year, the Liberals had won three provincial elections, so it seemed simple enough to beat a bunch of sex perverts, Commies and Bible thumpers.

Everyone expected John Brownlee to resign his seat and leave politics. He didn't. To everyone's astonishment, he accepted the UFA nomination for Ponoka, believing it his duty, he said, to expose the evils of Social Credit. There were only seven people at his nomination meeting. It was said that the hostess in charge of the dainties, who had baked twenty-five pies, broke down and wept. By amazing coincidence, the Privy Council in London chose the period of the election campaign to ponder the case of McPherson *vs.* McPherson. The *Bulletin* devoted five full issues to a thorough rehash of the McPherson scandal, not neglecting to mention at every opportunity the case of Macmillan *vs.* Brownlee. Oren McPherson punched the publisher of the *Bulletin* in the nose in the hall of the Alberta legislature, but John Brownlee did nothing. Hundreds of people attended his meetings. They sat in awful silence, then slunk away, eyes averted.

Lily left the *Bulletin* the first week of August. Jack needed her to run the office at Interior Air while he and Bible Bill stumped the province in "The Spirit of Social Credit," a gleaming white twin-engine Fokker that wafted out of the sky like a feather from an angel's wing. Bible Bill's weekly itinerary was announced every Sunday morning on CFCN's Prophetic Bible Hour, and sure enough, right at the appointed time, the Spirit would descend into a farmer's pasture, or a schoolyard, or a road allowance, and Brother Rudy would hand out pamphlets explaining The Meaning of Social Credit, each with a crisp one-dollar bill inside, and Bible Bill explained that there was a lot more where that came from after August 22, $25 a month for every man, woman and child, no Relief, no lineups, no vouchers, no snoopy social workers, no means test, no O.L. McPherson, no sin, no sex, just honest government and cold, hard cash, praise the Lord!

Lily's friends thought she must be crazy to be suckered by "funny money," but she saw nothing wrong in giving money to people who had none, especially when it gave them hope, and it wasn't any more radical than what the Liberals did. On her last day at the *Bulletin*, Ernie the editor gave her a bouquet of roses and $50, cash.

"What is this, serious money?" she joked.

It was certainly Liberal money. Everybody in the *Bulletin* editorial department got $50. Kate bought a train ticket to Toronto, where she got a better job at the *Star* for twice the wage.

Lily gave her $50 to the Civil Liberties Association. To tell the truth, she didn't need the money. In the back of Mum's Bible, she'd found one hundred thousand shares of Lakeshore Mines stock. The stock was old and dogeared. It had apparently been acquired ages ago, in Kirkland, as payment for Mr. Legion's "conversations," at a time when the stock was cheap and people had nothing else in the way of cash. It was now worth $64 a share, plus the accumulated dividends, which Mum had never bothered to collect. What to do? Buy Famous Players? Break the Bank of Commerce? Mum was right. The train was a delusion. From now on, the revolution will fly, first class.

In Edmonton, no one paid attention to Social Credit. The *Bulletin* published the speeches of the Liberal candidates, the *Journal* published the speeches of the Conservative candidates. No one listened to CFCN, or to the Prophetic Bible Hour, or to Brother Rudy, who told of finding, in areas believed to be totally unpopulated, crowds of people so eager to touch the Spirit he nearly decapitated them with his propellers.

On election day, one hundred thousand unexpected voters turned up at the polls. Many had never voted before. Some weren't on the lists. Many polling stations had only a single ballot box. The lineups stretched for blocks, and the police had to be called when fist fights broke out. Not a single voter went home without casting a ballot. When the ballots were counted, it was discovered that every one of those one hundred thousand new voters had voted Social Credit. It was a landslide.

The UFA failed to elect a single candidate. In Ponoka, John Brownlee ran last. The Liberals, with seven seats, formed the only opposition. The Communists, however, were jubilant. Out of more than 150,000 ballots cast, they had polled 5,903, to only 4,507 for the CCF.

The next morning, several dozen people turned up at the Alberta legislature looking for their $25. They were sent away disappointed. Three detachments of RCMP arrived from Regina expecting to quell riots. There were no riots. The banks did business as usual, the phones rang, trains ran (late), the sun shone and the ripening wheat rusted on the stem. God was up to her usual tricks. Heaven looked exactly the same as Hell had looked the day before. There was only one difference: the people were happy.

Lily was triumphant. So much for social fascism. Whatever it was, it was done for. The Hoover, however, was silent. She received no message in code, cipher, Russian or plain English. It was a puzzle. As the days went by, Lily noticed too that the hunger marches had stopped, and the Red agitators had vanished from the streets. This was particularly strange, since the federal election campaign was in full swing. The mystery continued until a Saturday in September when Lily encountered a small boy selling *The Worker* in the market square. The headline caught her eye:

> "COMINTERN DECLARES POPULAR FRONT
> Left-Democrat Alliance Against Fascism"

She read the story through carefully, then handed the paper back with the dollar bill.

"That's for you, not the Party," she said. "Okay?"

The boy looked at it dubiously.

"My dad says the money's no good now."

"Does he have a lot of it?"

"My *dad?*"

"Why don't you try it and see?"

The boy stuffed the dollar in his pocket and dashed off towards the Rite Spot. Lily was so furious she phoned Ken the *aparatchik* in Winnipeg, collect.

"A left-democrat sounds a lot like a social fascist to me, or is my objective analysis failing me?"

"Regarded from a progessive perspective...."

"Last month we were fighting social fascism."

"Today's struggle is against *true* fascism...."

"And now we're supposed to make friends with all the socialist reactionaries...."

"Expediency demands...."

"And all the leftliberaltraitors and the farmerfascists and co-operativecommonwealthcollaborators and all the sons-of-bitches *we've just destroyed?*"

"To the masses! As Lenin said...."

"Oh, bugger Lenin. I quit!"

Even Annie couldn't persuade Lily to change her mind. "I'd rather go to Ethiopia," Lily said. She gave her furniture away, put the house up for rent and packed her trunk, not sorry at all to see the end of Edmonton. She was all alone, the house stripped bare, when Joe, alias Mike, alias Big Peter, turned up at the back door, a pedlar's pack on his back.

"I don't need anything, Peter. I'm going away."

He set the pack down resolutely and rummaged inside.

"Look, Peter, I really don't have room."

"Shhhh." He held up a packet of needles.

"Inside," he hissed. He touched his cap and lumbered down the steps.

Inside was a folded piece of paper with a brief typed message: "Tea for two, tomorrow, 3 p.m. Red Rose." There followed a hand-drawn map marked "Gardiner Estate," with an X at the western end of the balustrade facing the river. The paper was a fly-leaf from *The Secret of Heroism*, by W.L. Mackenzie King. On the other side was an inscription, in Willie's hand, "To Miss Coolican, with kindest wishes, August, 1914, W.L. McK. King."

Lily was indignant. Who the hell would rip up her book? It had been missing for years, lost, she assumed, in one of her moves. Who had it now? Not Willie, surely. Doesn't Red Rose know she's quit?

"I quit," she said to the empty house. "*I quit!*"

41

Lily has been to the Gardiner Estate a number of times. It's a popular picnic spot in summer, but now it's a cold and windswept point of land jutting into the river. The Gardiner Estate had been part of a housing development during Edmonton's Great Boom, and from the streetcar it's still possible to see the scars on the prairie where streets had been laid out, and lights installed, and here and there a house built. The boom had bust before more than a dozen lots had been sold, so now the streetcar rattles along through a wasteland of buffalo grass.

During the boom, John Gardiner had built himself the most magnificent house in Alberta, an Italianate villa of limestone and marble, surrounded by a formal garden with fountains and reflecting pools and enormous beds of prize peonies. Gardiner and his wife tended the peonies. When all his lots were reclaimed for taxes, and his money disappeared, he replaced the peonies with cabbages, and now John Gardiner sells cabbages from a wagon in the back alleys of Edmonton.

The villa burned down in the twenties. The Gardiners moved into a cottage by the gate. As the years passed, the ruined villa and shattered statues became overgrown with weeds, an Edmontonian simulation of the decline and fall of Rome. The city council could have expelled the Gardiners, and closed the Estate, but that would have made the streetcar unnecessary, and as long as the streetcar runs, Edmonton can claim to be twice as big as Calgary.

Lily looks around cautiously as she gets off. The Gardiners are in the cabbages as usual. Lily picks her way along the broken flagstones towards the river. Around her, the garden's crumbling arches look very cold and white in the hard light, and the empty pools are full of withered leaves. There are no shadows. She sees no one.

A Greek gazebo stands at the end of the path. There, behind a pillar, seated on the balustrade, is a man in a gray suit. He is reading a book. Lily stops. She turns to run, but he has heard her and jumps up. His glasses fall on the stones with a tiny clinking sound.

"Okay, let's get it over with," Lily sighs. "Are you going to turn me in?"

"I might ask you the same thing." Esselwein retrieves his glasses and stuffs them in his pocket.

"You're the cop."

"And you?"

"Me? I'm a dope."

Esselwein looks at her closely. His eyes are narrowed, expressionless, his lips tight. Lily looks away.

"Maybe you should give me your gun," he says quietly.

Lily pulls it out of her pocket, not sorry to be rid of it, and puts it on the balustrade.

"I'm a pretty crummy terrorist, aren't I?"

Esselwein reaches into his pocket and puts an identical pistol beside it. "We've forgotten something," he says, opening the book.

Lily takes the folded fly-leaf from her pocket and flattens it out. The tear fits perfectly. "You stole my book."

"No. It was given to me yesterday, with the page missing. I've enjoyed your reports, Isabel. Hopelessly revisionist, of course, pure Trotskyism. Too bad the Party didn't pay attention. But then, the Party listens to only one voice."

"Anyway, I've quit."

"You can't do that. I need you."

"You need *me*! That's a laugh. If you think I'm going to turn informer, Esselwein . . . ."

"You'd rather be shot!"

"Yes."

"Good."

Esselwein picks up his revolver, raises it, cocks it, and throws it in a long arc towards the river. It makes a little "plop." Her own gun follows. Plop.

"Friends, okay?" He holds out his hand.

"Isn't that a bit much?"

"We were friends once."

"Times have changed."

"They have, haven't they? Years ago, when I was a Red, the Party had only a few hundred members. Now, it has thousands, and hundreds of thousands of supporters, maybe a million. Communism is the most powerful political force in the country right now, at least my superiors think so."

"You cops have done all right out of the Red Menace."

"And the Reds?"

"It hasn't hurt. You guys are about the best friends . . . ." Lily stops short. She glances slowly sideways at Esselwein.

He smiles. "Do you think it's been easy, eh? I can tell you! Mind you, with guys like Smythe around, revolution sort of comes naturally."

Esselwein says nothing more for a while. He sits very still, shoulders stooped, looking at the flagstones. He seems cool, almost detached, a different Esselwein from the others Lily knows. This one's no fool. His voice is calm.

"During the war, when Trotsky and I were in that hole in Nova Scotia, Smythe offered us a deal. He would release us on condition that we stayed in Canada and fed him information about the 'foreign element.' Trotsky turned it down, of course. Smythe was quite offended, but then Smythe had no idea exactly who Trotsky was. He was just a noisy, troublesome Jew. So when Kerensky requested Trotsky's release, at Lenin's insistence, Smythe happily put him on a boat for Murmansk. Even Trotsky was astonished."

Esselwein smiles at the recollection.

"I remained in Canada. It was decided between us, Trotsky and me, that I should accept Smythe's offer, on condition that I become a member of the Mounted Police in full standing, with the same rank I once had in the Russian army, even though I would be 'undercover.' This would prevent my being deported, or bumped off, when the police had finished with me. We also hoped it would give me access to British military information, since Trotsky had already anticipated the invasion of Russia by the Allies when the war ended. Therefore, I became the shortest man in the Mounted Police, the only Jew, and, a far as I know, the first Bolshevik."

"And you've been working for the Party all along."

"For the revolution! There is a difference, as you know. I work for the revolution, for Trotsky, as long as he lives. When Trotsky was in

Moscow, I worked for Moscow. Since Trotsky was expelled from the Soviet Union, I have been pretty much on my own, as he is. We keep in touch. It was at the time of Trotsky's betrayal that I allowed myself to be 'exposed' as a police spy. I was getting bored anyway. I have been much more effective working within the police than without."

"Why should I believe this story any more than all your other crazy stories?"

"No reason. I just thought it might be nice to spend some time together again, in Ottawa."

"Ottawa!"

"I've been promoted, a reward for thumping the Reds in Regina. General MacBrien is now pretending that the Regina riot was his plan all along. Poor buggers. If only they *had* been Reds. Just a bunch of bums, after all. It takes time, revolution. We won't live to see it. Just as well. Then what would we do, eh? In the meantime, the Red Menace gets a desk at HQ and roast beef in the officers' mess."

"Congratulations."

"I'm in charge of subverting the Popular Front."

"I don't see where I . . . ."

"Who could be more popular, at the moment, than that great Liberal, Mr. King . . . Mrs. King?"

"It's a common name."

"I went to the Holiness Movement Church, to check the register. The church had burned down."

"A Pentecostal flame, no doubt."

"Willie destroys everything, doesn't he? Even the language: 'Etc. etc. etc.' "

"Willie will win."

"It's 'King or Chaos,' isn't it?"

"King *is* chaos."

"And you shall be Queen."

"Dilly, dilly."

"Willynilly."

42

Laurier House, Election Day, 1935:

I was up after eight this morning, having had a good night's rest but feeling pretty tired. As I looked out the window of my bathroom, I saw blue sky and white clouds reflected in the background. I said to myself 'A new heaven & a new earth, God's will be done on earth as it is in heaven.' That was the prayer I prayed most earnestly this morning, also that I might be an instrument to do *His holy will.*

After breakfast, I went out to vote. When I opened the front door, the sun shone in a straight path from across the street to the door. The sun itself was visible in the water on the stone near the steps. I saw it as a symbol of God himself.

As I walked along Laurier Avenue, the sun was shining through the leaves of the trees, the golden leaves. I said, 'This is the vision of the leaves, symbolical of votes, leaves everywhere.' Little Pat was walking joyously at my heels. As we walked along Charlotte Street and neared the polling booth, I saw a station car which I thought looked like mine. Two ladies and a little boy were walking on the sidewalk. The fatigue of my eyes was such that I could not distinguish them. They spoke, & it was Mary, the cook, and Mrs. Lay & her little boy. They had just voted. I shook hands with them all. As I came to the door of the booth, McLeod & Lay walked out. Here was the whole household putting me in my place. I could not help saying to myself, 'I could never have dreamed of being thus situated in life.' I thought much of Mr. Larkin's kindness.

Pat followed me into the polling booth. The scrutineers & others spoke to him and seemed pleased that he was along. I shook hands with them all. They said they knew how I would vote. I said they were quite right. I said that Pat seemed to think he had a right to vote — like everyone else, he's had a dog's life for the past five years. I marked my ballot and went back rejoicing in the beauty of the day.

I came in and got to work on the interview for the Canadian Press to be given out after the returns tonight. At six-thirty p.m. I went down to a little dinner of soup and fish in the dining room. It was lovely sitting there with the paintings of Father, Mother, Sir Wilfrid and Lady Laurier & Mr. Larkin all around me. When I came up, I learned we had carried several seats in Nova Scotia. It was clear we were winning. The radio was giving returns in the sun room. It sat on the round table which I had covered with mother's paisley shawl. It was on this shawl that we got word of victory.

C arrived at seven. I got her to come & sit in the chair in which Mother had been photographed and listen to me revise the interview for the press. I went over it line by line. C was most helpful in her critical attitude towards thoughts and expressions. Later in the evening, when I saw we had won all along the line, I added a great deal giving the true significance of the victory & giving Bennett the broadside he deserved. I waited five years to do that. It was in the hands of the press by eleven p.m. In Saskatchewan, it was clear we were sweeping all before us. Alberta will have to go unrepresented for a while, and work out her own salvation.

When it was clear we had won, Norman & Senator Cairine Wilson came to call. I felt a moment's annoyance, which C helped me control. *That woman* is always intruding. She & the Masseys have been my 'bait noir' for years. I went downstairs & shook hands but did not ask them to be seated. I said I was working on a statement for the press. They understood & went away. Many callers came to the door. There was a task keeping them out. I intend to maintain the tradition that my home is my castle. At midnight, the national radio offered me its use for a statement. I declined. I listened to the others, Bennett as egotistical as ever, not at all gracious, not a good loser, Woodsworth even less gracious. After listening to these speeches, we all went downstairs & had coffee & sandwiches. I was desperately hungry & almost faint for something to eat.

C and I returned to the library. I showed her Grandfather's Bible. Then I read aloud from the Bible and the little books with their messages for today. I spoke to C of our victory. At last the Holy Grail has been found. We have seen the vision face to face.

C and all the secretaries left in my car. I got off the last messages, cables, etc. & then Pat and I went for a walk. The moon was shining thro' the white clouds. I thought of the white that filled the room in our seances & of the symbol of the Holy Ghost. It was a new heaven and a new earth. When I came back, wires came from Prince Albert telling of my sweeping victory there.

I knelt in prayer after all had gone, thanking God for his mercy & goodness & remembering all the loved ones. Grandfather's Bible I placed on the little table, our altar, beside the gold case with Mother's hair and wedding ring. I kissed the photos of all the loved ones. It is their victory. To their training, their sacrifices, I owe all there is of triumph tonight. I went to my bedroom & knelt by my bed & thanked God. The last I saw before turning out the light at a quarter to four was a glimpse of the picture of Oliver Cromwell's mother by the side of my bed, with the words written there, 'My dear son, good night. I leave my heart with you.'

SOME MONTHS LATER:

May, Willie's upstairs maid, is pregnant. Willie blames McLeod, the butler. Willie insists that McLeod marry May. If he does not, May will be dismissed. "But I din'na!" cries McLeod, "I *din'na!*"

Willie talks of nothing but May. He is obsessed. The secretaries are alarmed. They have never known Mr. King to show an interest in sex before. May refuses to say who.

Ah Willie, did you really do it at last? I feel responsible. What can I do? He should marry May. It's what Willie's always wanted in a wife, a pretty, young, upstairs maid. Too late, too bad.

May will be sent back to Scotland. Willie and I are going to Berlin. Willie and I and two senators, a deputy minister, four secretaries and a reporter from the *Star*. His harem, we are called. Esselwein isn't coming. Sergeant Leopold of the Royal Mounted has been posted to Aklavik, in the Interior. Apparently a Russian aircraft landed there some weeks ago. The pilot claimed he was blown off course and ran out of fuel. Smythe, of course, suspects a plot. Esselwein says he has already flown to Siberia twice and is in regular radio contact with Yakutsk and Kolynskaya. "All my old friends are there!" he says. "Hooray for Stalin!" He sent me a picture of himself dressed up in caribou skins. He looks just like an Eskimo. He says raw fish isn't so bad when it's frozen, and the Eskimos invented Communism about four millennia before Marx. He's happy as a lark.

Everyone is going to Berlin these days. It's the 'in' thing to visit Hitler, like visiting the Matterhorn. Willie's date comes after Lord Redesdale, but before the Duke of Windsor. In every photo I see of the *Führer*, he has his mouth open, a black hole in the middle of his face. The Cyclops. Will any of us come out alive?